The
Zimbabwean
Psychiatrist's Hat

Circumnavigation route around South America

The Zimbabwean Psychiatrist's Hat

SPENCER JAMES CONWAY

'Spencer is a masterful storyteller.'

John Allsopp, editor, *Moto Gusto Magazine*

'Spencer Conway is the real deal - exploring by motorcycle on his own terms without flash or pomp, he lives the life of a true modern day adventurer.'

Jim Martin, Adventure Rider Radio

'Spencer James Conway is one of those rare authors who surprises you on every page. His off-the-wall sense of humour, and his big-hearted attitude towards the world, shine through with his acute, multi-layered observations. Spencer emerges from his travels, challenged, exposed to full-on adventure, and he learns much. His travel style and adventures come across as filled with confidence, but the man is never arrogant; he is quick to make fun of himself. For a person of his achievements, Spencer is humble, and that makes his writing even more enjoyable.'

Sam Manicom, adventurer and author

Copyright © Spencer James Conway, 2022

No part of this publication may be reproduced, stored in a retrieval system, or transmitted in any form, or by any means electronic, mechanical, photocopying, recording or otherwise without the prior written permission of the copyright owner and the above publisher.
The right of Spencer James Conway to be identified as the author of this work has been asserted in accordance with the Copyright, Designs and Patents Act 1988.

ISBN 978-0-9956290-7-3

Set in Times New Roman 11pt

Photos by Cathy Nel and Spencer James Conway
Additional photos are in the public domain
p9 Photo of Spencer Conway and Cathy Nel, by Radko

Editor
Michael Conway

Cover graphics
delipps

Typesetting
YouByYou Books
www.youbyyou.co.uk

Printing
Scan-Tech, Hastings, UK

Contents

Foreword		7
1.	Barrio of No Return	9
2.	El Tapon del Darien: The Darien Gap	28
3.	The Naked Peruvian Customs Officer	46
4.	Gigolo Off a Cliff	54
5.	Hiawatha - Jumping into the Fire	71
6.	Surviving the Salar	85
7.	Butch, Sundance, Tequila and Tupiza	101
8.	The Bi-Polar Pole and a Joey	115
9.	Condor Man and the Smoked Trout	131
10.	Chucky and the Triceratops	144
11.	The Cave of Dodgery	156
12.	The 'No You Cannot' Ischigualasto/Talampaya National Park	163
13.	Amazonas and the Ghost Road	175
14.	Tarantulas, Cane Toads and Hell Town	190
15.	Love Motels	205
16.	Butterflies and Colonialism	213
17.	Suicidal Tendencies	227
18.	I Am an Accident Waiting For a Place to Happen	245
19.	My Mother is Drifting Away… and it Hurts	279
20.	The Jewel and the Clown	287
21.	The One-Legged Tyre Smuggler	307
22.	Pablo Putin: the Cartel Cocaine Dealer	316
23.	The Golden Aztec King	328
Acknowledgements		348

Dedicated to my parents, Michael and Wendy.
Thank you always and forever.

Foreword

Spencer Conway is one of those enviable people who made a decision to 'chase his dreams, or for ever regret'. He gave up teaching in the UK to follow a *small* ambition: to circumnavigate Africa, through 34 countries, solo and unsupported on a motorcycle. I wrote about his progress for *The Times* in 2011 – he'd escaped by the skin of his teeth after being shot at by rebels near the border between Ethiopia and Kenya, just one little adventure in a trip full of scrapes, challenges, courage and luck, both good and bad. It also raised useful funds for Save The Children.

He returned exhausted and set his goal higher: to circumnavigate every continent. Now, with his partner Cathy Nel, he has completed the next challenge, a circumnavigation of South and Central America. This is the story of the South American part of that journey. Although the chapters are in chronological order, this is not a travelogue or route map. There are geographical gaps that will be covered in another book. These are 23 episodes that stuck hard in Spencer's consciousness as he explored another magical continent. Enjoy the journey…

Alan Copps
Freelance writer and Editor of *The Times* motoring section, 1994-1999

Chapter One
Barrio of No Return

It is a very strange scene when you are standing at a bus stop in Bogota, Colombia, talking to a completely naked prostitute, about the best market to get fresh fruit and vegetables. This was the position I found myself in, on only my third day in South America, and would eventually lead to a violent street mugging for Cathy and me. Not an ideal start. I absolutely love Bogota. I still do. We have all heard the saying, "Well, at least he's not boring," when talking about a friend; who we like, but who is a bit unpredictable, off the wall, or tends to get into trouble a bit too often. Dodgy as hell, but lovable; so we tend to make excuses for them or give a bit more leeway for their eccentricities. That friend is Bogota.

Formerly known as Santa Fe de Bogota it is the largest city, the capital and administrative centre of the wonderful jewel that is Colombia. This country gets my heart racing with excitement even writing its name down. It is insanely interesting if you veer away from the four standard streets that tourists flock to. There is no denying that away from these sanitised, foreigner-friendly areas, it has an edge to it and that's putting it mildly. The clichés are true, so let's get that part over with. Colombia, like Brazil, has a serious problem with crystal meth, crack cocaine and cocaine. Many of the problems stem directly from these addictions and it is a noticeable black cloud in many areas. Addicts are on many street corners, parks and underpasses. But Bogota is so much more than that.

To say Bogota is lively and colourful is an understatement. It is not just the vibrant locals, the constant street bands and performers, the pedestrian outdoor café areas, the designated cycling lanes for the weekend family groups and the beautiful architecture, museums and parks. This is not the only source of colour. The whole city, including the motorway retaining walls leading out of it, are filled with giant murals and artwork. We are not talking low-level graffiti here, or tagging your signature on a dirty wall with a spray can, or on the side of a train or underpass. That is vandalism in my eyes. For vandalism to change to art, it takes one ingredient; talent. The artists in Bogota have it in bucketloads. We are talking about immense paintings, often six or seven storeys high, unapologetically dominating a whole block of the city. It is beautiful, expertly and carefully executed, vibrant artwork. It varies from detailed seascapes, to huge traditional Indian portraits of hard-working, wizened old countrymen and women, to vast revolutionary scenes, the detail staggering throughout. Some are more stencil-like, in the tradition of Banksy, the famous elusive English fellow, who I don't rate too much. These are a level above.

On the very first morning after we arrived, I was in adrenaline overdrive and left Cathy sleeping, our first experience of South America; how amazing, and I wandered out before sunrise. As the sun rose, burning the early morning mountain mist, the buildings revealed themselves, emerging from bland, black, concrete silhouettes. The night lights were turned off around the city as I walked, and the new sunrise bathed the buildings in a glow, revealing the myriad examples of stunning artworks and murals, that reflected the city's culture and history.

The Colombian capital really is one big canvas, with much of the work exploring the country's tumultuous history, and the devastation caused by drug trafficking; from corruption and kidnapping, to murder and controversial US intervention. Some of the murals hold back no punches.

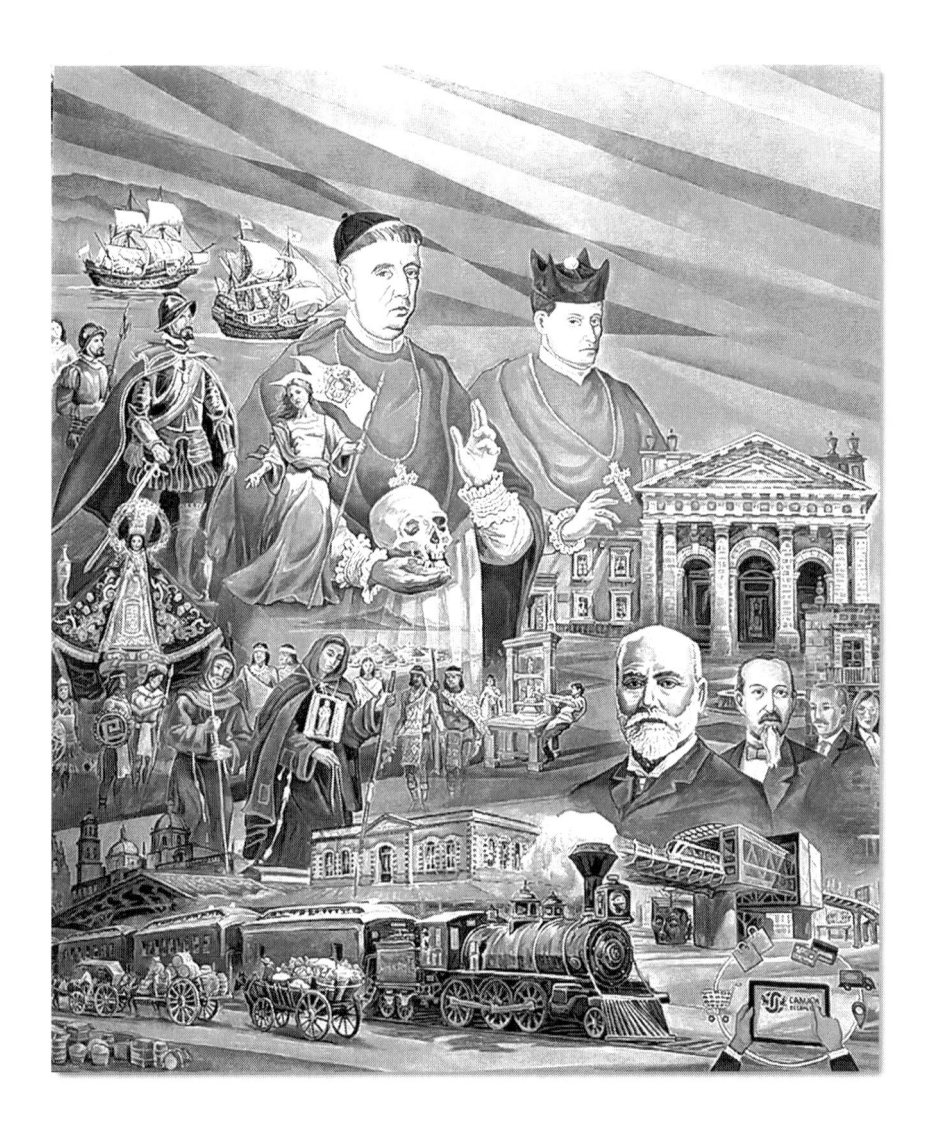

Bogota was not always an outdoor Art museum; its transformation was born out of a tragedy. Today, instead of hunting down and arresting street artists, authorities in the Colombian capital are now hiring them. It was the death of a young artist by a policeman in 2011 which sparked a new tolerance of street art that has now exploded into a colourful, controlled hub for the artistic expression of the talented. Diego Felipe Becerra was painting his signature, wide-eyed Felix the Cat, that is now famous worldwide, when he was killed, with no more than a spray can and some brushes on him. The outcry over the incident was fuelled greatly by the police attempt to portray Becerra as a suspected armed robber who had tried to hold up a bus. This was totally fabricated. It led to protests across the city and the arrest of two police officers on murder charges. They were convicted.

"This was a turning point of massive proportions for street art in the city," said DJ Lu, a semi-famous street artist I met, who had spent most of his career painting under the cover of nightfall before the change in attitude. In response to the outrage over Becerra's death, the city government took a 'if you can't beat them, join them' stance.

In February 2012, the Mayor of Bogota, Gustavo Petro, issued a decree to promote the practice of street art as a form of cultural expression. At the same time, they defined surfaces that were off limits, including monuments and public buildings. I totally agree with this compromise and it is so sad it took the death of a young guy to instill sense.

With governmental blessing and sizeable city grants, selected artists (and I must say, well selected), were given two, three and up to seven storey walls, along main Bogota streets, as their canvasses. What a thrill for them, and what a success they made of their opportunity. An otherwise bland carpark wall suddenly becomes an explosion of tropical birds, swooping down from a majestic seven storey, fantasy tree, full of intricately hidden animals. A carpark wall that becomes an attraction for locals and tourists alike. What is there to criticise. This is just one example of many scattered around one of my favourite cities.

Another depicts two homeless people locked in a kiss, a strong image of love, trying to conquer the despair of homelessness, a real issue in Bogota. Recognition of street art as a legitimate artistic expression, in my eyes is wonderful, but there is always a flip side to giving licence for freedom of expression. Inevitably, this new relaxed view has led to an unforeseen spread in common everyday, what I can politely call, 'scrawlings' on a wall, precisely where the agreement prohibits them. They are exactly what the anti-street-art people are complaining about, and I must agree. Now, near the stunning government-sponsored murals, walls and underpasses are covered with tags and bubble letters and stencilling, that only a moron could produce. Maybe they should have a new law that if you are found guilty of having no artistic talent, you get a quick strong electric shock, to dissuade you from continuing on your chosen path. Many Bogotanos, and two Adventure Motorcyclists would recommend this therapy. We certainly got some comments from passersby while photographing the artwork.

"Pablo Abril, an industrial designer," was his 'handshake comment'.

Pablo was your standard enthusiastic Colombian, with a red shirt with white lapels, intricate and embroidered designs, displayed across his chest, a bit like my mum's knitted doilies. He had tight blue jeans, and pointed, cream cowboy boots. He swung his belly towards a particularly bad scribbling, verbalising my earlier comments.

"This is vandalism," he pointed.

"This is art," he said, swinging his belly in the other direction to point it at an amazing painting of a Sunbird.

"There are streets now where there isn't a single storefront that isn't defaced. It is very ugly," he stated, pointing his stomach down the road and heading off with a flamboyant wave and thumbs up.

A 'defaced' building if it's bad: 'art' if it's good. It's that simple.

Still, Bogota's liberal attitudes have attracted some of the world's top street artists. An Australian artist called Crisp, who offered us a guided tour in the Candelaria district, which we turned down to avoid tourists, said, "Bogota is undoubtedly a trendy Mecca for street artists now, and more each year," pointing out a beautiful flower mural that had sprung up overnight. "Even Justin Bieber got in on the act."

I apologise for mentioning Bieber in the first chapter. I promise the class of this book will improve. After a concert in Bogota in 2017, the pop star set out with his police escort to 'scrawl' (note my choice of word) on city walls that were, in theory, off limits, but strangely police did not act. Some police have gone a step further. In 2018 two street artists were caught by police on the beat, spray painting Christmas themed art on the breezeblock walls of a Bogota police station. However, there were no arrests. Indeed, the Commissioner of Police was so impressed that he hired the two to undertake Christmas decorating throughout the city.

Now that you've had a brief history of Colombian street art, let's get back to a subject more interesting than Bieber; the naked prostitutes at bus stops and why I was talking to them. With a population of approximately seven and a half million, densely packed in, with houses clinging to mountain sides, like many cities it is difficult to find campsites, or too dangerous to camp wild. So our introduction to Bogota was to find the cheapest room possible, and this ended up being the Hotel San Francisco. The hotel was actually fine, it was the location that made it dirt cheap. It was in Dodge Street, Dodgeville. The girl at reception, with the hairiest forearms I have ever seen, which she could have easily plaited and put beads in, made it abundantly clear that we should only use the front entrance and not go out at night. The hotel backed onto the very first pedestrian street of the area, known as the 'Barrio of No Return'. No return is pretty self explanatory and Barrio means District. The word does tend to refer to low-income areas, generally called favelas, ghettos, shanty towns, slums, reservations or locations, depending on which country you are in. But many of them have the same ingredients; poverty, alcoholism, drug addiction, prostitution, filth, violence and crime. A staggering one in five people in Bogota live in slums and we picked a rough one.

Inevitably, shortly after checking into our one-dollar hotel, a good price, I was intrigued to see out of the rear entrance. It was not too encouraging as it seemed to be the site of a recent crime! I ignored the warnings and popped out for a cigarette: my horrible addiction.

The street was fairly quiet, strewn with litter throughout, except at the crime scene entrance. There was a strong smell of urine and alcohol. I sat on a cracked concrete bollard and lit a ciggie. Opposite me in the doorway of a derelict building was a man in filthy tracksuit bottoms, sitting on a hessian potato sack. He had no shirt or shoes. He had long black hair, matted at the back into one huge dreadlock of filth, and a beard caked in dry blood from a recent mishap. He had sores all over his arms and around the corners of his mouth, that he picked at incessantly and had a livid boil on his ankle, which was an open wound. It had become infected, swollen and was weeping pus. It was splitting his skin open, almost up to his knee, like a horrific zip. It looked life-threatening to me it was so bad. He had stuck a plastic bag on the injury, but it seemed to have somehow grown into his skin, and embedded itself in the gaping wound. Horrific. He was lying in the foetal position, desperately trying to stop shaking, so that he could light his crack pipe, which was just the broken neck of a miniature spirits bottle, with a cardboard filter stuffed into the thin end, and a silver foil covering with holes in it, at the wider end. He lit individual matches and it took three or four attempts each time he wanted a 'hit', so the ground around him was littered with hundreds of spent matches. A thread of dribble ran from his mouth to the pavement. He looked ill and feral and wild-eyed and lost. His friend was in a slightly better condition. He was squatting on the road, his mouth contorted from the drug effect, his eyes rolling upwards in his head as he tried to clean his pipe. Other addicts were strewn around the pavement, all focused on one thing, the next fix. Normal life had ended. The drug had won.

It was a sight I would never get used to. The casualties of drugs. Saying they behave like animals, is an insult to animals. Animals don't have addictions that take over every minute of their walking lives. They have stooped much lower, to the depths of hell. As I was pondering this point, a severely anorexic woman in a torn dress, her ribs sticking out of her back, was staggering down the road, bent almost double. Some twenty metres past us, she lifted her dress, squatted down and defecated on the pavement, in a wave of sickly yellow diarrhea. It was rough. This was going to be a learning experience, and sometimes not a pleasant one.

Many South Americans, and Colombians in particular, get sick of people focusing on the drug problems of their country, and here I am going on about the issue almost immediately. I cannot apologise for that. No, actually I do, but I am just writing down my experiences, what I see, and when I see it; simple as that. Believe me, when someone is dying in the street from gangrene and another is defecating in public, it is difficult to focus on the cultural aspect of things. Hard drugs really are the scourge of our world. Drugs have been an everyday topic in Colombia for more than 40 years. The marijuana market emerged in the 1960s, the cocaine market took off in the '70s and '80s, and heroin came along later. Colombia is the world's biggest producer of psychoactive drugs, and the USA is the biggest consumer. The truth is that drug and the drug trade permeate all levels of Colombian society, from the poorest rural farmers through the middle class to the highest ranks of the political and military establishment. More than 900 police officers were arrested last year because of links to the drug trade. That is nearly three arrests a day. Colombia produces two of the world's major stimulants: coffee and cocaine.

Where there are addicts, there have to be dealers and it was the very next morning that I met a very clichéd one. I woke up at 5am and headed down to the strong coffee sellers, the mobile canteens, that are pushed around the city, with much struggle. They have small paper or plastic cups, which they fill with aromatic, strong, black coffee. The best coffee ever. I sat on my concrete bollard and within two minutes was approached by a guy of about twenty five. He was in the uniform of the wannabee rapper/drug dealer; loose, and I mean, hanging-round-the-ankles loose, tracksuit bottoms, glaringly obvious Armani boxer shorts, expensive Nike Air trainers, a Los Angeles Lakers basketball vest, and a Dodgers baseball cap. The look was completed with a single diamond earring and enough gold chains round his neck to buy me a house in Kent, England. He had the twitchy, street-wise demeanour they all seem to cultivate, constantly checking his phone and glancing around, looking as suspicious as any human being possibly could.

His introductory line was, "Hey man. What's up. My name is Johnny Dollar and I am the best dealer in Colombia," offering me a fist pump.

Not just the best dealer in this street, or district, or Bogota. He was the best dealer in the whole of Colombia. How amazingly lucky would that have been, if I was a drug consumer; within hours of arrival, meeting the best dealer in Colombia.

"Where you from brother?" he quizzed, all the time moving from one foot to the other, his eyes darting all over the show.

His face was mahogany dark and he was sweating profusely, even though it was a nippy eighteen degrees. (Bogota is situated at 2640 metres, so is always mild.)

"You need anything my friend?" he continued, without waiting to hear where I was from.

"Yes. Another coffee and a doughnut would be good, and a million pesos," I replied.

He laughed briefly and continued, twiddling his designer sunglasses between his fingers, "What is your name bro?"

It was a pretty good bet that his traditional Colombian birth certificate did not say Johnny Dollar on it, so I answered, "Cedric."

"Cedric, Johnny Dollar has everything you need," he said, glancing at me sideways, conspiratorially.

"Oh, I thought you were Johnny Euro?" I cheekily said.

He ignored my weak comment and continued, even though I didn't really want him to give me more patter. This conversation looked dodgy from four hundred metres away, and I didn't want the squad on my case on the second day.

"I have yerba, weed, marijuana, blow, you know. I have cocaine, crack, crystal meth, ecstasy, heroin, mushrooms, 2CB, MDMA, LSD, PCP, and lots of other initials," he stated.

He was like an encyclopedia of drugs. I almost expected him to bring out a menu from one side of his jacket, and samples on the other side, like some dodgy East End of London, stolen-watch seller.

"Do you have any Wine Gums or some Werther's Original Buttermilk?"

I didn't say that, but I made it pretty clear I had absolutely no interest whatsoever, and wished him well in all future illegal endeavours.

As I was persuading him of my religious sobriety, I was thinking; he must have very big pockets to carry all the drugs he offered. It then became clear where he kept the merchandise.

"OK. No problem. If you need haircut, you come to my salon, two blocks along here and one right, on the corner," he said, pointing down the road with his sunglasses.

The salon was called 'Cut Me Up'. No, I am joking. It was called 'Johnny's'. I went there a couple of days later. I was intrigued. There were another ten Johnny Dollars in the salon and not a pair of scissors in sight. One Johnny Dollar had his feet up on the barber's chair and was asleep, and another Johnny Dollar was having a heated discussion on a mobile phone. Obviously a 'customer' cancelling a cut and blow dry. Various other Johnny Dollars sat around doing very little, but checking their phones and looking suspicious.

I didn't hang around too long, but long enough for the original Johnny Dollar (I think) to give me a piece of advice.

"Don't go to this district behind your hotel. It's called the Barrio of No Return, because you go there, you don't come out."

This sowed a seed in my head. I wanted to film there, but hopefully with a return ticket. All I had to do was persuade Cathy. I knew that would not be difficult. Cathy is tough and street-smart, like no one I know. And interested in the world. This was going to turn into the most incredible week of learning experiences, sadly one of them life-threatening.

My introduction to the Barrio occurred, by default, the very next morning when I wandered a couple of blocks to catch a bus into the centre. I got quite a shock when I turned the corner and was confronted by a vagina and a pair of boobs, connected to an incredibly tall, good-looking 'Lady of the Night'; well, 'Lady of the Day' in this case. How did I know that she was a 'Sausage Servicer', or whatever the politically correct word is? Because she told me and offered me some services. I politely declined, and somehow the conversation turned to the best fruit and vegetable market in the city. I have no idea how the conversation turned, because I was too busy staring into the sky, like some avid ornithologist, trying my best not to look at her private parts while we chatted. It didn't feel right. (They should really be called 'public parts' in this instance, methinks.) The conversation flowed, as well as a conversation with a naked Bogota prozzie and a Swazi motorcyclist can, which was pretty good, but then my bus arrived. Evidently, Valentina was not there to catch buses, and hopefully not to catch anything nastier, and I wished her luck too, with her prostitution that day. She wouldn't have much of a career as a stripper, as she wore no clothes. Valentina was not unusual, in this regard. (To quote Tom Jones, incorrectly.)

The Barrio, I was to discover was full of naked, and semi-naked women and men, and a mix of the two genders. I suppose it leaves you with no doubt about what you are paying for; you see what you get. Despite spending nearly ten days in the Barrio, I never got used to the nakedness, next to someone in a suit and with a briefcase. I don't think that you would get away with it at a Tunbridge Wells bus stop, and anyway, it would be way too cold. All the vital parts would freeze.

My next problem was how to film in the Barrio. Many of the people were dodgy shop owners, drug dealers or pimps and prostitutes. I was not going to be welcomed with open arms, especially if a camera was brought out. Arms maybe, but the metal, shooting, kind. Unsurprisingly Cathy insisted that she wanted to go and film, but suggested a taxi. The bike was too high profile, and difficult to film from surreptitiously, or even 'titiously'. We decided that Cathy would sit in the back and put the camera at the very bottom of the window, to try and get a few shots. The first time we went, it was totally successful, and we got a few interesting biological and gynecological shots, but the second time we were stopped by a single man, standing in the middle of the road, arms outstretched.

Our taxi driver, Alejandro, was about twenty two and looked like Roland Rat of cartoon fame. He had an extremely thin face, as if it had been in a vice, and his teeth stuck over his lower lip, giving the impression he was always looking for a snack. He had dark, Gothic, natural black hair, was skinny as an anorexic rake, white as a Sussex sheet, and was into death metal music. He was pretty laidback, but when the stocky, bald, roadblock fellow leant into the front passenger window, where I was sitting, Alejandro looked worried. The guy ignored me and leant past me, falling into the car, and looked in the back, where Cathy was sitting.

"Where is the camera?" he asked, waving his arm around in the taxi, then pointing in the back.

"I don't have a camera," said Cathy, giving him a beaming smile and the innocent hands-up and palms-spread-out look.

He nearly cracked a smile, but I blurted, "We don't have a camera," regretting it immediately.

He liked Cathy more. I should have kept quiet.

"Don't lie. I saw the lady yesterday," he snapped.

I immediately decided to be semi-honest. As I spoke, he gave us a very clear sighting of his hand gun, in a harness, under his jacket.

"We are tourists and we find it very interesting and we want to see different parts of Bogota, not just Candelaria. We love Bogota."

A bit weak, but it was all that came out. He looked at me, straight in the eyes, about a millimetre from my face and asked, "You are American?"

"No, we are from South Africa and Swaziland," said Cathy.

With that, he extracted himself from the car window, smoothed his jacket over his gun, furrowed his brow, nodded three times, very slowly, and turned on his heels. It was a relief.

We were never bothered after that and spent a month in the area, so we must have got some sort of nod of approval from our gun-toting roadblock fellow. We chatted with all the locals, and with Valentina, of course, and got some more important fruit, vegetable and flower-buying locations. We met her friends and co-workers and it was great. We were never bothered. 'Lean in the car' man, had obviously given us an enthusiastic green light, or he just thought we were mad.

It wasn't to be the filming that was to be our downfall. It was two elements. Firstly, an influx of new faces, and secondly, me making a basic error. I flashed the cash too much. When you are somewhere regularly, you tend to let your guard down a little bit. You start to feel at home. I did that, in a poor area, like a total beginner. I was regularly going to the Barrio of No Return shops, and buying food, essentials and non-essential beers, etc. It was not a lot of money I was spending at all, but to many people there, it was. I didn't follow my own rule of staying low profile, and respectful to all.

I learnt that lesson in Africa during my first continental circumnavigation, when I saw the cameraman Carl take some money out of a cash machine, in a rough Kenyan border town. I was from Africa, so I was horrified. He took the money out and made an open display of counting it.

"Man, you can't do that!" I exclaimed pushing his wallet hand, and money out of sight. "Hey, relax, it's only about $30," was his reply.

"Carl, you may be standing there waving a week's earnings, a month's hard earned salary, to somebody, and you want to stay safe. Don't do it, full stop."

"Fair enough, I get it," he graciously answered.

Eleven years on, and one hundred plus countries experienced, and evidently, I had not learnt my own lesson. I went to the same corner shop each night, in a slum area of Bogota, not exactly flashing my cash, but making it clear I had some. Not very bright behaviour for a seasoned traveller. I let my guard down and felt comfortable because we had been there for two months at this stage and knew all the street people and the shopkeepers by name. But I went to the shop too regularly and was clocked by a gang. Although my visits were not extravagant (difficult in a small convenience shop), it was not the amount I spent, it was the regularity. I am in no way saying that I deserved to be mugged. No one does. But there are desperate people in the world.

You will have noticed I use the singular, regarding the shop visits, because usually I went alone. On this occasion, sod's law, Cathy was with me. I wish it was only me that was mugged. We were attacked by a group of eight 'piranhas', as they are known in Colombia. It was a terrible experience, and when people tell you that after you have been mugged, you constantly look behind you and jumpily react to the merest sound, it is true. Or if someone comes up behind you, too close. It was a feeling neither of us had had before. Those of you who have read my Africa book, *The Japanese-Speaking Curtain Maker*, will know that I was shot at by Boran shifta bandits in Northern Kenya. For some strange reason, this was a lot more personal and direct, and affected me much more. We both agreed, in retrospect, that when we went through Central America, we were jittery, defensive and drove through quickly. It definitely affected us and our interaction with people, for a good six months.

The gangs in Colombia are known as piranhas for obvious reasons; they attack in large numbers, 'bite' very quickly, overwhelming you, physically and mentally, with a flurry of violent activity, steal everything you have, and are gone. This tactic is used in many countries. I saw it in Sudan and even in the centre of Rome, by the Coliseum. A rabble of kids, no older than twelve, surround you, flapping pieces of cardboard boxes in your face, while their compatriots steal your things. It's a shock-and-awe tactic. Overwhelm quickly, and don't give the victim time to react or retaliate. I am sure it works on ninety percent of occasions, but it didn't work on Cathy and me. So, like many muggings, ours was over in seconds; but don't worry, this is where another cliché comes in. When you get mugged, you replay it in your head over and over again. I can confirm that this is true. It is not a pleasant effect. Firstly, it leaves you standing there, incredulous at what just happened. Secondly, if you are as old as me, you think: how young were those bastards? This is a symptom of getting older. Policemen, bank managers, newsreaders, they all look like they should still be at school. I have asked a few officious officials if they shouldn't be in class. It did not go down well. Similarly, when the eight of them rushed up to us, I had my guard down and had no initial fear. They looked like school kids. But before I tell you about the mugging, let me go on a tangent for a second and tell you about the fish these gangs are named after: piranhas.

A piranha is a freshwater fish that inhabits South American rivers, floodplains, lakes and reservoirs, when they are not attacking Adventure Motorcyclists. Various stories exist about piranhas, such as how they can lacerate a human body in the blink of a gill. These legends refer to the red-bellied piranha. None of our attackers had bellies, they were too young to have them, let alone red ones. When President Roosevelt visited Bogota in 1913, he went on a hunting expedition into the Amazon. While standing on the bank of the river, he witnessed a spectacle, created by the local fishermen. After blocking off part of the river, and starving the piranhas for several days (without telling Roosevelt), they pushed a cow into the water. It was quickly torn apart and skeletonised by a shoal of starving piranha. Roosevelt took the story home, and added to the piranha legend. We humans are weird. Our Bogota piranhas were definitely hungry, but not the most coordinated school. The first thing you realise when you are being mugged, is that you have been mugged. It is that quick.

Our local corner shop was directly out the back of the hotel, and left. It is a pedestrian road that leads into the slums. It is, therefore, a perfect road for addicts to inject, smoke whatever, and fall over, because they won't get run over by cars, whilst comatose. We bought a loaf of bread, some fresh orange juice and a packet of Bimbo sweet cakes, all of which were in a plastic bag, wrapped around my wrist. We had nothing else. No passports, no phone, no cameras, no wallets, nothing. Cathy had the room keys in her pocket. This is how we normally travel, when not filming. Take nothing. Four people approached each of us, quick as a flash. (A bit quicker than this story, get on with it.) They circled us, and two grabbed us from behind, aiming to bear hug us and lock our arms to our sides. First mistake. Cathy is slim, but not short, and is very fit and strong. I am six foot four and ninety five kilos. All the muggers, except one, were vertically challenged, so the 'hug mug' failed. That's when it got shitty, for real. They rifled our pockets and ripped the plastic bag out of my hand.

They were frisking Cathy and shouting, "Phone! Phone! Where is phone!"

I heard Cathy shouting, "I have nothing, I don't have a phone!"

"Phone, phone, money!" a short, pock-marked, sixteen-year-old screamed.

I broke free from the two that were holding me from behind. The tallest of the gang was close to my height; a lanky, scared-looking, good-looking guy of about eighteen. He lunged forward and tried to stab me in the head with a knife. Forcefully, believe me. It was bloody awful. I managed to grab his wrist with my right arm and hit him in the centre of the nose, with my left. I would love to be macho and add, 'as hard as I could,' but it wasn't the case. I was too scared and it was more like a swat. (Not that SWAT, sadly.) Also, I am extremely right-handed, so much so that my left hand seems to have a brain of its own. If I try to throw a ball with my left hand, it looks like I have been electrocuted, and the ball generally lands by my foot.

Luckily, my camp, left-hand punch was enough. He fell backwards, still clutching the knife, scrabbled away from me, crab-like, on the pavement, got up and ran. After hitting the piranha, I stepped backwards instinctively, and mistakenly knocked over an old man who was making his way down the pedestrian road, with his walking stick. He fell, hit his head, and blood spread across the road. The rest of the gang followed the guy I had punched, quick sharp. It was over. They were gone. Not quite. As they were about to turn the corner, Cathy shouted down the road, halting the scurrying piranhas,

"Give me my bloody room keys, you don't need my room keys!"

Unbelievably, a mini-Eminem turned around, startled, with a sheepish look on his face. (No surprise there; I put on that expression every time Cathy talks to me.) He stopped, put the keys gently on the pavement and then ran. Cathy is a class act. Best person in the world to travel with. Strong, brave, level-headed, brushes aside bullshit and weakness, the perfect adventurer.

Cathy was obviously okay physically, so we turned our attention to the old man. He was lying still on the ground, eyes closed, with blood soaking through his flat cap, and seeping onto the pavement. By now there were a lot of people watching, including some of the hotel staff.

"Call an ambulance please, call an ambulance, and the Police," I shouted, a bit lamely, I must confess.

We both knew that the Police would not be called: it's Bogota. But we were both a bit shell-shocked. Enter Ali G, to add a bit of comedy to a grim situation. Ali G is a tasteless British comedian, but if you don't know him, don't worry. I will describe. If you do know him, I forgot to mention, our Ali G is a transvestite. He was wearing the latest headgear, a yellow skull cap, so tight, it made him look Oriental. He had black wraparound, framed glasses with a yellow lens tint. The lenses were clear enough that you could see his subtle, bright purple eyeliner. He matched this with a bright yellow tracksuit top and bottom, complemented with platinum-coloured bracelets, rings and necklaces. His beard and moustache were perfectly trimmed into a close crop goatee. The whole look was topped with shiny, white, plastic boots, that looked like mini, emergency, sleeping bags. He looked like a pimped-up banana. Ali was bouncing around, organising an ambulance for the old man, and generally being brilliant. The scenario did involve Ali G very theatrically pulling out a flowery cloth from her, or his, pocket.

With a flurry and a flourish, Ali knelt down and gently dabbed the open wound on the old man's head with some Sprite. It bubbled red and looked sore. He was the highlight of the mugging, and with the old man sorted, and us okay, it was time to look to the day ahead. It took time to sink in, what a violent scene we had endured. Mental defence mechanism, for sure. We decided to find another room. Although the mugging wasn't injurious, it was close, and we needed to distance ourselves from it.

We loved our time in the Barrio of No Return, with the coffee sellers, active and lively at four in the morning, chats with the road sweepers, the various Johnny Dollars, the tiny kiosks, run by friendly, two-hundred-year-old men. Meeting the Valentinas of this world and hearing their stories, Roland Rat who undercharged us and became quite enthusiastic about our clandestine filming. Ali G and the receptionists at the hotel, and a multitude of 'snapshot' encounters, that enrich your life, and understanding of other people's lives. When you nearly get stabbed in the head, it does tend to colour your experiences. Although all the locals we knew said it was 'a new group', 'out of town people', 'Venezuelans', 'Ecuadorians', etc. it made no difference. Foreigners are always blamed, no matter what country you are in. We knew we would meet our attackers on the street, or have to watch them from our room. We didn't call the Police. The muggers were too young. But we didn't want to see them walking around with impunity. Sort of rubs salt in the wound.

On that note Cathy looked on the internet, and found us a room, which was ten minutes from the centre, so pretty ideal. We packed up, thanked the hotel staff, who apologised profusely for the mugging, and waved down the ubiquitous yellow cab, its registration number emblazoned on the side. (Our wonderfully reliable Yamaha XT 660Z Tenere, that was going to shoot round South America, like a healthy bullet, had cleared Customs, but was quite quickly unwell, and, predictably on this day, decided it didn't want to start. Altitude sickness or something. We decided to leave the bike in a locked and guarded car park and would return to solve the problem, once we were settled in a new room; hence the taxi).

We loaded up the boot of the taxi, with the panniers, jumped in the back seat, and gave the driver the full address. He looked at us quizzically in the dusty rear-view mirror, and asked for the address again. I repeated it, wondering if my schoolboy Spanish was as good as

I thought it was, and he raised his caterpillar eyebrows, sighed, and pulled off slowly. He immediately turned right and drove about fifty metres, as slow as a Galapagos tortoise on sleeping pills, turned right again, and stopped.

"Alli," he said, pointing to a dodgy-looking, high-rise building with structural deficiencies.

"This is the place?" I asked, stifling a laugh.

"Si."

Of the thousands and thousands of rooms available, in a city of more than seven million, that stretches for hundreds of kilometres, Cathy had managed to pick a room two hundred metres from our old one. (Yes, we should have checked the location more closely on the net, not the room décor.) We were in hysterics as we lugged our things up the stairs to the fifth floor, as the lift was 'under repair'. From our room we could see our old room, and could see into the whites of the eyes of our muggers, albeit from a slightly different angle and vantage point.

It was a sign to leave the Barrio of No Return, which for us was definitely the Barrio of No Return. You can have too much of a good thing. Luckily, when I returned to fix the bike, it started first time, and the problem never reoccurred. We were off, south. I am not making light of it, I fully realise that we had the privilege of driving off. I wish everyone, including our muggers, the best of luck in life. Bad, bad cards can be dealt.

Chapter Two
El Tapon del Darien
The Darien Gap

I have an elephant in my trousers, or closet, or in my room, or whatever the saying is. Just north of lovely Bogota, and the Barrio of no Return, is the Darien Gap, my nemesis, my mental and physical obstacle. If I am to succeed in circumnavigating every continent, I will have to conquer the Darien Gap, or it is not a real, unbroken circumnavigation. I have obsessed about the Darien for twenty years, and been planning the crossing for more than three, so let's get this topic out, and see if you can understand my fixation and maybe the enthusiasm will rub off on you. Or not.

Obsession (dictionary definition): An idea or thought that continually preoccupies or intrudes on a person's mind.

Obsession (psychiatric definition): A pattern of unwanted or intrusive thoughts, or urges, that recur persistently, often accompanied by symptoms of anxiety. Can lead to compulsive, unreasonable ideas, emotions and behaviour, associated with mental illness.

Not good then.

I have an obsession with crossing the Darien Gap, and luckily it is one shared equally by Cathy, so we must both be suffering from 'unwanted urges and thoughts' and 'mental illnesses'. So be it.

The obsession will not die until we have crossed the Darien Gap, or failed in the process. As well as circumnavigating every continent, this is our next big project which has been put on hold, temporarily. Two years of research, planning, preparation and red tape meant we were on our way to the Darien, from Mexico, when Covid took over the world in early 2020. For those of you who have no idea what the Darien Gap is, hopefully some of the interest and enthusiasm I have for this incredible jungle barrier, will rub off on you. Or not.

So just to be clear; two examples of obsession:

"He was in the grip of an obsession to cross the Darien Gap, an obsession he was powerless to resist," or,

"My wife and kids left me because of my obsession with horse racing. As they were leaving, I shouted, 'Aaaand, they are off!' "

Two different examples, but I hope you are clear about obsession.

When people are nervous about a place they are going to travel to, they tend to Google it. This is the worst thing to do. You will read so much doom and gloom (almost all of it not true), that you will not leave your lounge. According to the internet, everywhere you go you will die, within days, and everyone you meet will kill you, in minutes. The Darien is an exception. Everything that is written about it is true. Or worse. Don't leave your lounge. So what is the Darien Gap?

Many of you will have heard of the Pan American Highway. The concept of an overland route from the tip of North America, at Prudhoe Bay, Alaska, all the way to Ushuaia in Argentina, the southern-most point in South America, was originally proposed as a railroad in 1889. The proposal never got off the ground and was replaced with a proposal for a highway, in 1923, after the automobile began to replace railroads, as passenger and goods transportation. The first conference regarding constructing a highway was in October 1925 and by July 1927, an incredible pact was signed. In an outrageous act of engineering solidarity, in the latter years of the Great Depression, Argentina, Bolivia, Chile, Colombia, Costa Rica, El Salvador, Guatemala, Honduras, Mexico, Nicaragua, Panama, Peru, Canada and the USA signed the convention of the Pan American Highway. They all agreed to achieve speedy construction and, in 1950, Mexico became the first country to complete its portion of the Highway. Well done Mexico. The others remarkably followed suit, and the iconic route was born, a staggering 30,000 kilometres of asphalt highway. The Guinness Book of Records names the Pan American Highway as the 'world's longest motorable road'. This would be true, if it wasn't for the Darien Gap. It is not possible to cross. The only way is to skirt it safely and navigate by sea.

The Pan American Highway, like Route 66, has become iconic with motorcyclists. Without wanting to upset any bikers, these are touring routes, it is not adventure motorcycling. They also happen to be the worst way to see a country. You may as well be on any motorway in the world, cut off from the real country by asphalt, barriers, road signs and speed.

It is no way to see a country. The heart of any country is its off roads. During my circumnavigation of South and Central America and Mexico, we rode over 85,000 kilometres off road, and less than 1,000 kilometres on the Pan American. Anyway, that is beside the point.

The Darien is the place where all bikers come to a rapid halt, no matter what their route, put their bikes on a boat, a famous vessel called the Stahlratte (Steel Rat), and sail around the Darien from Panama to Colombia, or vice versa. This is not for us. We want to go through the centre with the Tenere motorcycle. Anyway, the Stahlratte is no more. Other options are in the pipeline for getting round the Darien but, at present, it is more of a barrier than ever in its history.

The Darien Gap consists of massive mangrove swamps, thick jungle and daunting mountains, located in the northern portion of Colombia's Choco Department and the Panama Darien Province. The Pan American Highway has a corresponding gap of 160 kilometres, beginning at Turbo, Colombia, and ending at Yaviza in Panama. This sounds like a ludicrously short distance, but there is much more to the scenario than that. The Darien is not for small fry. Here, the elements conspire against you. The climate is hot and the air is thick and heavy, making breathing a laborious task. Add altitude to this. Satellite phones and GPS trackers do not work in the Darien. If you don't fall victim to the rebels, the drug runners or the common criminals that inhabit such a lawless place, any number of deadly venomous snakes, spiders, insects and plants are ready to kill you. With my history of allergies and anaphylaxis, I will probably make it a hundred metres into the jungle, before kicking the bucket. Everything alive wants to kill me, or at least, eat a bit of me.

The Darien is not empty, don't get the wrong impression. For centuries, the lawless, 18,000 square kilometre wilderness has attracted explorers, adventurers, scientists, outlaws and the 'different'. Today it is seeing an increasing number of migrants and refugees, from as near as Cuba and as far as the Middle East and the Horn of Africa, who are flying to South America and travelling overland up the Isthmus to reach the USA. They still all believe in the 'American Dream', and are willing to risk their lives to fulfil it. Greater numbers of migrants are risking the dangerous Darien Gap, as traditional paths to the USA get tougher, and Covid complicates issues. As I write this paragraph, there are more 'displaced' people on the move, worldwide, than ever before in our history. The Darien Gap crossing is a crucible, emblematic of this phenomenon. People are dying, without it ever being reported. There is no surprise that the Darien is known as the world's most dangerous journey, and when you Google 'world's most dangerous jungle', the answer is 'The Darien Gap'. The situation is more complex than I have explained, I will get to it.

First, a side comment. I am fully aware of the difference between a refugee, who is fleeing persecution, and is forced through the Darien Gap; and an adventurer, who chooses to put himself in danger. One is a nightmare, the other is a privilege. So, if I die in the Darien, I fully accept that I deserve no sympathy, and nor would I expect it. It is just a place I feel compelled to visit and experience, the dangers and the wonders. Cathy and I have discussed this at length and have decided that if we die, it will only be our children that will suffer. So, we have decided to give them away. Joke.

Evidently, the Darien is not for 'tourists', for want of a better word. Despite that, Swede Philip Braunisch tried his best to walk the Darien in 2013. The 26-year-old disappeared shortly after entering the jungle. In June the following year his body was discovered in a jungle grave.

According to the local news reports, Philip had died from a single gunshot wound to the head. It was reported that guerillas intercepted him on his way to Panama by boat. They found a detailed map of the region and a GPS device (useless in the Gap) on him, and it is speculated that they believed he was a spy. His remains were sent back to his family after seven years. An autopsy report showed graphically how Philip had been killed; his rib cage had been smashed in, his neck vertebrae were crushed, and he had a collapsed cheekbone from a blunt instrument, probably a rifle butt. He was finally killed by a single pistol shot to the side of the head. This was a beating and an execution, which didn't back up the Revolutionary Armed Forces of Columbia (FARC) rebels' claim that he was killed in crossfire with government troops. Philip is not the only one to perish trying to bridge this 'missing link' in the Pan America route, and there will be many more.

Efforts have been made for decades to remedy this missing link in the global transportation system. Planning began in 1971 with the help of American funding, but this was halted in 1974 because of concerns raised by environmentalists. United States support was further blocked by the US Department of Agriculture in 1978, from its desire to stop the spread of hoof and mouth disease. (Much more sensible name than 'foot and mouth' disease in the UK. Never seen a cow with a foot.) Another effort to build the road began in 1992, but by 1994 a United Nations agency reported that the road, and the subsequent development, would cause extensive environmental damage. Yes, road building through the area is expensive, and the environmental cost would be high, but I don't believe this is the reason the project was halted. The fact that it would be an immense and dangerous task of engineering is also of secondary importance. (We have been to the moon.)

I believe, it is a combination of a number of factors, most of them verging on political, rather than humanitarian reasons. It is more to do with the control of the flow of immigrants and illegal drugs. The Darien Gap is a more natural, efficient deterrent to immigrants than Trump and his ridiculous wall could ever be. Another complicating factor is the local tribes of the area. The Embera Wounaan and the Kuna, are among five tribes in the Darien reserve who have expressed concerns that the road would bring about the potential erosion of their health, culture, food sources, and peace and quiet. (I added the last one but know it will be one of the most impactful lifestyle changes.)

Clearly, it is a complicated issue, a lot of it made more murky by the lack of laws in the area. Many people, apart from the indigenous, are opposed to completing the highway.

To sum up, the reasons it will never be completed include; it protects the rainforest, contains the spread of disease, protects the indigenous tribes, prevents drug trafficking and its associated violence, controls illegal immigration and prevents the spread of hoof and mouth and other diseases. Now, we can add Covid 19. Inevitably, alternative options would be a ferry service between Turbo in Colombia and one of several ports in Panama. Another idea is to use a combination of bridges and tunnels to avoid the environmentally sensitive regions. This sounds like a deluded paper-pushing plan, made by someone who has just completed their engineering degree and has never been in the field or, in a field, let alone in a hostile jungle like the Darien.

The geography of the Darien is spectacularly difficult and challenging. On the Colombian side, it is dominated primarily by the delta of the Atrato river, which creates a flat marshland, at least 80 kilometres wide, a nightmare to traverse. The Serrania del Baudo range extends along Colombia's Pacific coast, and into Panama. The Panamanian side, in sharp contrast, is a mountainous rainforest, with SAS-difficult terrain to traverse, varying from 60 metres in the dank, slippery, valley floors, to 1,845 metres at the tallest peak, the Cerro Tacarcuna in the Serrania del Darien.

The Darien is home to the Embera Wounaan and Kuna, of which both tribal leaders I had been in touch with. Travel is often by specialized canoes, known as pirogues. We fully expect that when we go, these canoes will play some part in getting the big lump over the Gap. I am talking about the Yamaha Tenere XT660Z 2009, not Cathy.

The Darien has an estimated population of around 2500, but as you can imagine, this is a total guess. The Cuna or Kuna, were living in what is now northern Colombia and the Darien province of Panare at the time of the Spanish invasion. The Kuna themselves attribute their migrations, deep into the Darien, to conflicts with other chiefdoms, and their migrations to nearby islands, as an escape from the mosquito populations on the mainland. These two elements; mosquitos and the Kuna Indians, will be another vital part of our success or failure. Before Covid struck, we had secured the services of a guide, Isaac Pizarro, and eight porters, all Kuna Indian. Isaac assured me that he had smoothed our route through with the other tribes. There comes a time when you have to trust the assurances of others.

Secondly, the Darien is supposed to be one of the most vicious places on earth, for mosquitoes and malaria, which tend to hang out together. The handful of people I have tracked down who have been in the Darien, all say that there are steroid mosquitoes, who attack in squadrons in the air, and in battalions on the ground. As I have had malaria five times, I fully expect to come out of the jungle, a jibbering, sweating, skinny, hallucinating wreck. And if things stay to form, Cathy will skip out of the jungle, singing, 'We're all going on a summer holiday,' without even a graze or a hint of sunburn. Let's all 'skip' back now, a few hundred years, to give you a laugh.

In 1698, Scotland tried to establish a settlement, through the 'Darien Gap scheme'. This was Scotland's one major attempt at colonisation. This is not the beginning of a joke, by the way. No, it didn't go well. I am not one for racial stereotypes, but lily-white, freckled, red-headed, kilted men, and non-kilted women, who experience a summer in Scotland, that usually comes on a Thursday in August, are not ideal colonists for a sun-baked, mosquito-ridden jungle. (Actually, from my experience of four years in Edinburgh, at least the Scots would be used to the incessant rainfall, and the mosquitoes of the Darien would be child's play, after the Midges of Scotland. Midges with a capital, for a reason. I was nearly stripped to the bone, camping next to the lochs of Scotland. Midges whine at a thousand decibels, bite, and head-butt too).

The aim was for the Scottish colony to have an overland route that connected the Pacific and Atlantic oceans. Claims have been made that the undertaking was beset by poor planning and provisioning, divided leadership, a poor choice of trade goods, escalating epidemics of disease, lack of Nivea sunscreen Factor 1000, lack of wild haggis, and attempts by the East India Company to frustrate it, as well as a failure to anticipate the Spanish Empire's military strength. Apart from that, it was a total failure. In March 1700 after a Spanish siege, everyone died. No wonder Scotland's colonial history is not extensive, with destination choices like the Darien jungle. No 'Hamish's' to be found in the 5790 square kilometre Darien National Park, the largest in Central America. Though never say never.

Wind forward a few hundred years, to add to the gloom of the Darien. On 6th June 1992 Copa Airlines Flight 201, a Boeing 737 jet airliner, from Cali, Colombia crashed in the Darien. Twenty nine minutes into the flight the plane entered a steep dive, disintegrated in mid-air, and crashed over a vast area of the jungle. The conclusion was 'instrument malfunction, leading to spatial disorientation, loss of control, leading to in flight break up'. In English, that means the pilot forgot where he was positioned in the sky, and flew into a Darien mountainside, killing thirty six Colombians, eight Panamanians, two Americans and one Italian, a total of forty seven people. Not all the bodies were recovered. We certainly do not intend to add to the body count of this magnificent wilderness.

The risks of the Darien, plane crashes aside, can be minimised by meticulous planning, building up contacts and vital letters of permission. It is a huge undertaking and not cheap, so the obvious question that is always asked is; "Why?"

George Mallory, when asked,

"Why do you want to climb Everest?" replied, "Because it's there."

Probably the most famous three words ever uttered by a mountaineer, and certainly covers part of the reason for Cathy and I wanting to cross the Gap. But, there is a more practical and logical reason. I am attempting to become the first person to circumnavigate every continent. To that end, I have circumnavigated Africa, solo, through 34 countries and 55,345 kilometres. I have circumnavigated South and Central America, with Cathy, through 20 countries and 108,947 kilometres. During that attempt, the Darien was closed, so we had to fly from Colombia to Panama. That is definitely cheating, so we have no choice to go back and 'fill in the Gap'.

Strangely, when you mention the Darien Gap, it evokes extremely strong reactions from people, and the discussions tend to get very heated, and sometimes, troll-like. People become quite passionate and emotional, and quite frankly, there is a nasty competitive edge, and lots of put-downs and conspiracy theories. I am not interested. I am not hoping to be the first, the fastest, or the one who took the most difficult route. I just want Cathy and I to get our Tenere from A to B, through the Darien. Of course we will not be the first, but we will certainly join an elite handful of people. Many explorers and adventurers have tried to cross the Gap. The success rate is shockingly small, but consequently, doubly interesting. One such person who succeeded is the evangelist, Arthur Owen Blessitt (a very appropriate surname for a religious dude).

Blessitt is a preacher, who said he had a long chat with Jesus, who instructed him to carry a cross to every country in the world. Blessitt started young in the religious business, becoming devoutly religious at seven, can you believe it. In the late '60s he began preaching in Hollywood, California. In March 1968, he opened a coffee house called 'His place', in a rented building next to a topless go-go bar. His first marriage was to Sherry Anne Simmons, who he married within three weeks of meeting. Together, they had eight children; Gina, Arthur, Joel, Joy, Arthur Joseph, Arthur Joshua, Arthur Jerusalem and Arthur Junior (seems to be some subtle Arthur theme going on here). He married Denise Brown in 1990 and they adopted a child called Arthur, (joke); called Sophie. Blessitt traversed the Gap (route not clear), while carrying a 12 foot cross. When he wasn't making new Arthurs, Blessitt started taking short walks,with the cross he made originally to hang on the wall of 'His place'. After his command from Jesus, he headed off to Ireland, to start his walk.

During the Cold War, he carried his cross into the Soviet Union, through Russia, the Baltic States, Ukraine and onwards. He did not shirk from danger and carried his cross through Iraq, North Korea, Iran, Afghanistan, Somalia, Sudan, China, Libya, Israel and the Antarctic, to name just a few of the somewhat 'iffy' spots. On 13th June 2008 Arthur Blessitt walked his 38,102 thousandth mile (61,319 kilometre), in Zanzibar, completing his religiously set task of walking every country and island group in the world. Looks like Jesus added the island groups a bit later on.

He traversed the Darien Gap, travelling with one guide, and with a machete, a backpack crammed with water bottles, a hammock, a Bible, a notebook, lemon drops and the signature stickers, 'Smile - God loves you'. Blessitt popped out the other side, alive and well.

Blessitt has been the subject of numerous documentaries, the most well known, 'The Cross; The Arthur Blessitt Story' (2009), directed by Matthew Crouch. If Blessitt can cross the Darien, with a cross, with the help of Jesus; we should be able to do it with a Yamaha motorcycle, with the help of porters. Blessitt wasn't totally blessed on his journey. He was arrested twenty four times and had his cross stolen twice. That is some sort of lowdown thief. Hopefully the stolen crosses were made into nice cabinets, or chests of drawers, and not used to make a barbecue.

In 1972, renowned explorer and holder of the best explorer name, John Nicholas Blashford Snell, a hero of mine, led a sixty-person crew with two Range Rovers through the Darien Gap. It took three months. The expedition was supported with extra men from the British army, the governments of Panama and Colombia, the Natural History Museum, the Scientific Exploration Society, and numerous scientists, desperate to study the unique flora and fauna, but woefully unprepared for the conditions. The expedition was sponsored by Range Rover, Duckhams Oil, and Marks and Spencer's provided the clothing. Food company Heinz supplied the expedition with no less than three tons of food. No 'wind-assisted' jokes please. Despite plentiful help and sponsorship, Blashford Snell said that the Darien crossing was the toughest challenge of his career.

The seasonal floods came early, and the vehicles and crew were locked in mud. The back axles of the Range Rovers, according to Blashford Snell,

"Exploded like shells, with shrapnel coming through the floor."

Redesigned car parts were parachuted in after a month (can you imagine me and Cathy affording helicopter assistance?). Later, inflatable rafts floated the vehicles across the problem area of the Atrato swamp. Half the team succumbed to trench foot, fevers and other gruesome ailments, but after ninety one days, they succeeded, the team diminished in size and enthusiasm, but victorious.

So, apart from evangelical nutters and madcap adventurers, there are others getting through; refugees, drug mules (including riderless, unaccompanied horses, packed with cocaine, that know the path), criminals, indigenous Indians, and others I will come to. People get through, people don't. The point is that it is a bit of a Russian roulette route. Human skulls, bones and clothes, along the Darien route, attest to this.

Political tensions change all the time and it is difficult to predict the most dangerous time in the Darien, because things can flare up at any point. One chance meeting with the wrong people could spell the end for us. This is the point with remote, lawless places. You can only smooth over so much of your journey with planning. The rest is fate, or luck, or bad lack, brought on by the element of unpredictability.

'Others I will come to,' I said above; these are the FARC rebels, another element of the complex Darien, and a group that we need clearance from, to succeed. The Darien Gap is subject to FARC. Their control of the Darien is disputed, but there is no doubt that they are a powerful rogue group, armed and verging on being bandits. FARC have committed many assassinations, kidnappings and a myriad of human rights violations, during its insurgency against the Colombian government. FARC rebels are at present on both the Colombian and Panamanian sides of the Gap. They force people, upon threat of death, to become drug mules. The upsurge in drug trafficking through the Darien has profoundly altered the indigenous way of life, where families live in wooden houses, built on stilts, to stay safe from jaguars and other animals and insects of the night, and men ferry bananas to market in dugout canoes. Many men now live alone, in riverside huts, having sent their wives and children to live in larger communities, out of fear of rebel raids. Women have largely ceased working in community rice and banana fields, hurting production and the structure of traditional families. It is not only the indigenous that face FARC.

In 2000, two British travellers, Tom Hart Dyke and Paul Winder, went into the Darien National Park to search for exotic orchids. They were kidnapped by FARC rebels and held captive for nine months, threatened with death, before thankfully being released, unharmed and without the ransom paid. Very lucky and very unusual. Hart Dyke and Winder later documented their experience in the brilliant book, 'The Cloud Garden', and they are also featured in 'Locked Up Abroad'. I had to laugh; Hart Dyke is the Patron of the British Cactus and Succulents Society. Brilliant. So English. Nearly as funny as the Kent Lesser Marsh Warblers Society.

Other victims weren't so lucky; three New Tribes Missionaries disappeared on the Panamanian side in 1993. FARC guerrillas snatched the missionaries on 31st January, in the Eastern Panama village of Pucuro, near the border with Colombia. The three wanted to 'plant' a church, among the Kuna Indians. I need to explain the strange context of the word 'plant'. These missionaries believe that they need to infiltrate communities, learn the language, and then translate the teachings of the Lord into the local language. Why? Because they want to indoctrinate their beliefs on people that are perfectly happy, and have had their own belief systems for thousands of years. The arrogance of man never ceases to amaze. As soon as someone has a different outlook on life, they are abnormal, a threat, need to be saved, whatever. I am not saying that the missionaries deserved to be killed. They should have taken their arrogant attitude to… maybe the Congo. Maybe not. That didn't go too well either.

In 2003 Robert Young Pelton and two companions, on assignment for *National Geographic Adventure* magazine, were detained by the United Self Defence Forces of Colombia. (Oh yes, I forgot about them. Another hazard to deal with.) Luckily, they were released after a week. The release, however, came as the leftist Colombian rebels said they had also kidnapped the British reporter Ruth Morris and the US photographer Scott Dobson, who were later released under secret circumstances. Ironically Robert Pelton made his living travelling to dangerous places, providing advice on how to stay safe, for any who wished to follow in his footsteps. In a series of bestselling books, including *The World's Most Dangerous Places*, Pelton gives readers the inside track on how to avoid the perils of civil war, disease, drugs and kidnapping, especially kidnapping. He must have done something right when it came to the real thing. On a serious note, we only hear about victims when they are Westerners or celebrities. The unnamed, often passportless, and documentless victims, are never heard of again.

Rebels are not the only threat in this magical jungle of hazards. The flora and fauna of this area can also be very angry. I die of anaphylactic shock, if I even look at a bee, so the Darien...ideal. The Darien is a green and unforgiving barrier that stands between mankind and his dreams. Past the deforestation and police checkpoints, wild landscape makes the rules. The Darien National Park is a World Heritage Site, whose upland forest and mangrove swamps provide habitat for hundreds of species found nowhere else on earth, some able to kill a motorcyclist with one stare. I have considered wearing a full body condom, and covering myself in Vaseline and insect repellent, but it would be a slippery affair on rainy mountain slopes. What will sting will sting, as the old saying goes.

Pumas stalk through the shaded undergrowth, ready to pounce on unsuspecting gringos. But Cathy and I are obsessed with wildlife, and this is one of the biggest draws of the Gap. The beauty cannot be ignored. Whilst I am being eaten by a puma, giant green macaws will call out from the jungle canopy, a giant anteater will shuffle past my body, in the shadow of a mountain range, the mountain side ready to collapse from heavy rains, and bury my body forever. If that doesn't happen, let's not forget the highly poisonous, fer-de-lance pit viper, cruising through the forest foliage. The pit viper is irritable, fast-moving and large enough to bite above the knee. Like Cathy. Anti-venom usually solves the problem but, if left untreated, can cause local necrosis (death of the body tissue), leading to gangrene or death.

The heavy hissing counterpart to the viper is the silent, heavy boa constrictor, who wants to do his favourite thing; constrict. Leave your boots unchecked - a spider as big as a mop will take a nap in one of them, or perhaps there will be two. These are Brazilian Wandering Spiders (that's a long wander from Brazil), who cruise the jungle floor at night, and hide in logs, motorcycle boots, and banana plants. At best, you need a hospital, at worst, you are dead in two to six hours. If you leave your hammock unchecked, a black scorpion, as accurate as a calm sniper, will hit you. Botflies like to get under your skin, literally. They lay their eggs on mosquitoes. This conveniently deposits the botfly egg under your skin, when the mosquito bites you. The eggs hatch and the larvae have a nice warm place to live. Through a small hole in your skin, the larvae can breathe. Once they grow into bumble bee-sized maggots, they crawl out to lay eggs elsewhere. It is the most gruesome thing. They also lay eggs in your washing, when it is on the line. That is why it is vital to iron clothes in tropical counties. My brother came back from an engineering contract in Liberia and was staying with me. A maggot popped out of a spot, on his shoulder. He freaked out, understandably, and upon closer inspection, he was infested, with hundreds of the bastards, all over his back. Nothing for it but to squeeze them out. It took three hours. When it gets that bad, it's called a myiasis infestation. I call it 'repulsive'.

Fire ants will be on the prowl and wild pigs will be keen on skewering you. The Darien has many species of poisonous frogs: don't stroke them it is not advised. The hippies of this world can't even hug a tree in the Darien. The Chunga Palm, or black palm, is found throughout the Gap. It has hippie retardant, with sharp, bacteria-covered spikes, that can cause serious infection. Beards, beads and braids have been known to fall out within hours. (Joke - no hippies in the Darien.) Blood-sucking bats also try their upmost to ruin your night's sleep. Then the water is against you. A sip of Darien river water can hold a whole host of viruses and parasites that could have you bent over double, and worse. Ticks in the Panama area carry Rocky Mountain Spotted Fever, which sounds more romantic than it is. Add to this the balmy 100 degrees, and 95 percent humidity. Run out of water and you are up the creek. However, if you do successfully negotiate all these problems, you will probably get Trench Foot which was first described during Napoleon's retreat from Russia in the winter of 1812, but the common name references a condition rife in the trenches of World War One. The condition originates with wet skin, that isn't allowed to dry. Wet conditions and limited blood flow cause the tissue to tingle and itch, often turning red or blue, and decaying. Any open wounds quickly develop fungal infections. All of this can happen in under ten hours in the Darien.

There are also man-made oddities in the Darien, only one of them a danger to people crossing the Gap. Some bright spark decided he could drive through the Darien in the '50s. It went as well as expected, and his rusting Cadillac can be seen, to this day. Historical attempts to build a transportation route have been phenomenally unsuccessful, as has colonisation. (Let's not forget the sunburnt Scots.) The British got in on the madness, and tried to build a railroad to allow for gold mining in the area. Another puffing failure. People who brave the Darien are still confronted by abandoned railway equipment, sleepers and tracks. The third manmade article you may encounter in the Darien, to make your stay more peaceful; bombs. During the Cold War, the US military ran training runs, dropping bombs over the jungle. Most of the bombs detonated. Most.

I am sure it is becoming crystal clear to the reader why we want to cross the Darien Gap. Not to me either. But what are the options? Taking a boat is cheating. No option. Of course we have options - don't do it. I am not moaning, I am pointing out the intricacies of the place. We are excited, not just to push ourselves to the limit, and experience amazing animals and plants, but to meet up with the Kuna Indians, and especially Isaac, our main guide, which will be a learning experience without doubt. The indigenous have carved a home in an extremely difficult terrain, drawing on a deep knowledge of the region's plants, animals and a splintered, maze of waterways. Isaac has been in the Darien region for 40 years and has actually guided a foreign team successfully through the Gap. Cathy and I have been talking to Isaac for more than two years, and can't wait to undertake this challenge together. Having the right contacts is the only way to get through the Darien. We already have written permission from the Governor of the Darien, and we are 70 percent there with the Colombian immigration and army. Isaac and our six Kuna porters will be the key factor in our success. I am loathe to even write the words 'Kuna porters', because it sounds so colonial. But it is not. It is the nature of the expedition and if we don't have their help and guidance, we will fail.

We have our pirogue canoe organised, for the impassable mangroves, and we will have ropes, pulleys and winches, plus the porters, to haul the bike over a 2000 metre mountain range. It is not only for the manpower and physical graft that we need the Kuna. They are the only ones who can clear our route with rival groups. To that end, as soon as we arrive, we will be meeting with the Saila (pronounced sigh-lah), the political and religious leaders of the Kuna communities. There are 49 communities in Guna Yala. There is a general council which is led by three Saila Dummagan, or Great Sailas. These dudes will be the final hurdle, but Isaac assures me, he has their blessing to guide us through. All that Cathy and I know about the Kuna is through long Messenger and WhatsApp conversations with Isaac, who is obviously super proud of his people and the jungle. Enthusiasm always rubs off. He is also crazy about animals, so we should get on like a forest hut on fire.

Interestingly, the Kuna are matrilineal and matrilocal, which means when Isaac married his wife he took her surname, Pizzaro, and moved house to become part of his bride's family. Some of you male readers may be wincing now, at the thought of being that close to your mother-in-law, but I think it's pretty cool.

The Kuna economy is based on agriculture and fishing, and despite their fairly remote position, they have a long history of international trade in clothing. The Kuna are famous for their bright Molas, a colourful textile art form made with the technique of applique and reverse applique. Mola patterns are used to make the colourful blouses, worn daily, by the Kuna women. Plantains, coconuts and fish form the core of the Kuna diet, supplemented with a few domestic animals and wild game. That sounds like the perfect diet to me. The Kuna language is an aboriginal language of the Chichan family, and is spoken by 50-70,000 people. Dulemaya is the primary language but Spanish is also widely used, especially in education and written documents.

We were going to spend between 20 and 50 days with seven strangers, in harsh conditions. It was important that we got on, and common ground always helps. Like the Kuna, we love jungles, a fact we confirmed to ourselves by traversing the whole of the Amazon jungle from west to east, a distance of 2,000 kilometres. It was one of the best expeditions we have ever done. We also love animals, insects and plants: the Kuna ooze the same enthusiasm. We love all the food that they eat traditionally, so there is more common ground. And although I cannot promise to learn the Dulemaya language in ten days, I am fluent in Spanish. That is the biggest bonus of all. Luckily, I was honest with Isaac, right from our very first conversation. I wanted everything to be out in the open.

"Isaac, I am 53 years old, I am fat, I drink and smoke and I have a lung problem, do you think we can make it?"

"It is OK, we can make it," he replied positively.

"I also have a bad leg, poor eyesight and I get lost in my own kitchen," I added.

"No problem, we can make it. I can guide," he answered, just as confidently.

"Also, I am not a very good rider," I said, trying to shake his confidence.

"It is OK. We can carry moto," was his quick response.

"Also, if I get stung by an insect, I die within twenty minutes," I added for dramatic effect.

There was silence on the other end.

I am only joking; the above conversation did not happen. Even if we had worries and handicaps and vices, like smoking, pleurisy and accident proneness, strangled testicle issues and fatal allergies, it would be irresponsible, and unprofessional to burden Isaac with our shortcomings. We did, however, tell Isaac that we were exceedingly excited to do this crossing and would not let him, or the team down.

I promised him, "We will both pull our weight, especially Cathy."

The first serious expedition to cross the Darien was undertaken in 1960, with the use of a Land Rover. It was nicknamed the 'Affectionate cockroach.' They failed.

The first completely overland crossing didn't occur until 1970, when Ian Hibell used a bicycle to get through, which was more often used as a machete than a mode of transport. The next fellow attempted it in a steamroller. Joke.

The first completely overland auto crossing took place in 1985, with a modified CJ-5 Jeep. With this vehicle, Loren Upton spent 714 days, journeying 160 kilometres, to accomplish the task. What a legend, and Cathy and I are proud to call him and Patricia, friends. Incredibly interesting pair. Patricia has been a fountain of advice, knowledge and constant encouragement to Cathy and me. It means a lot. She doesn't put obstacles in your way. She is an optimist. Love it.

In December 1960, on a motorcycle odyssey from Alaska to Argentina, adventurer Danny Liska attempted to cross the Gap. He had to abandon his motorcycle shortly after entering the jungle, but completed the journey by boat and on foot. In 1961 a team of three 1961 Chevrolet Corvairs, and several support vehicles, departed from Panama. The group were sponsored by Dick Chevrolet. After 109 days, they reached the Colombian border, on a disputed route, (as is the nature of these expeditions; competition, and the inevitable shouts of foul play), with two Corvairs, one being abandoned in the Darien. (Cathy is going to leave a message and a photo of father on the Corvette. It is in the middle of the jungle, and is a beautiful way of Cathy saying, "Look where I am, Dad."

As discussed, a pair of Range Rovers were used on the British-Iran-

American attempt on the Gap, led by John Blashford Snell. I was brought up on adventurers and I have decided that all explorers and adventurers should, by law, have double-barreled names. It is much more exciting and evocative. If you have to say,

"Hello, Mr. Spencer-James Anthony Christopher Conway Esquire," you will think twice about being rude, and will respect my accomplishments more than if I accept a cursory,

"Alright, Spence?"

Joking. I love all mankind.

On to more serious issues.The first motorcycle crossing was by Robert L. Webb in March 1975, on a Rokon, a journey that took several months. Ed Culberson was the first one to follow the entire Pan America Highway in 1984 (sponsored by Rider Magazine), including the Darien Gap, on a BMW R80GS, shortly after the Uptons. In 1998, another recognisable name, Helge Pederson, nailed it on a 1981 BMW. According to Patricia Upton, by the time Helge reached Yaviza, he was suffering from a broken arm, severe dehydration, cracked ribs and serious disillusionment. Who can blame the man.

Before I continue, it is interesting to note that lunacy and lies and mis-information, are the staple of our lives. Not only do we have access to more information, more fact-checking, and more googling from all, we still have a problem, Houston. It is too easy to fill people's heads with fodder and lies. Let's get light. For example, Danny Liska's guide did not get eaten by tribesmen, garnished with cracked pepper, lime and chili, in the middle of the Darien. Nor did a Swedish Women's Volleyball team try to cross the Darien in skirts, only to be skewered by poisoned darts. Didn't happen. So, let's avoid the hanky-panky stories and get down to the nitty-gritty. (Sorry if my language is too gangster.) How many motorcyclists have successfully crossed the Darien Gap, without getting skewered or eaten? It looks like it is Robert L. Webb, Ed Culberson, Helge Pederson, Loren Upton and a group of ex-US army guys, whose clutches exploded, and whose story is surrounded by controversy, concerning their extravagant spending and route.

I don't want to comment, and I am sure people will come out of the woodwork who have done it. No matter. Spencer Conway and Cathy Nel are going through. But first the small task of circumnavigating South America. Only 100,000 kilometres to go before the Darien. Piece of cake. Onwards, through 26 border crossings.

Chapter Three
The Naked Peruvian Customs Officer

Many adventure travellers find border posts and their inevitable delays one of the worst parts of the process of travelling. I love them. I do understand that most people are on an agenda and a day's delay for paperwork can eat into a ten-day trip. I am privileged that I don't need to worry about delays, as I am always travelling. That said and accepted, I think it is all the mind frame. People tend to get themselves worked up into a mini frenzy of negativity. I have seen it at ports, I have seen it at airports, docks and land borders. People are on the defensive and behave extremely confrontationally, often before a problem has actually arisen. They would never behave like that at home. Customs officers are only doing their job and it really is a thankless task. All they get is abuse. I look at it more from an anthropological point of view. It's an opportunity to 'people watch', under stressful circumstances and, quite frankly, I have met some extremely colourful travellers and officials, having passed through 136 borders.

I had an Egyptian border guard who pretended to be two completely different people, simply by donning a hat and pair of glasses. He came round the building and through another door. Hey presto, a brand-new official. He even kept up the pretence of having never met me, five minutes earlier, even though I was in a fit of giggles. He knew he had been rumbled, got annoyed and flushed, but could not falter. Brilliant. In the Democratic Republic of Congo, I macheted my way through the centre of the country. When I came to a clearing, finally, the customs officer had not seen a tourist in three years. I was well proud. His official stamp had even dried up, so he wrote, 'Spencer James Conway entered legally', with his signature underneath. It worked. I will never get rid of that passport.

I have had customs who were too drunk to serve me, others who have predicted my imminent death. In Senegal my welcome by the customs officer began with, "If you go to Mauritania you will die, fast.

We in Senegal are nice, but there, you are to be killed!"

I have been arrested and locked up by customs, have stayed at customs officers' houses, been offered drugs by them, and even escaped an attempted kidnapping in Panama. A customs officer in Venezuela, who was a member of a bike club, showed me a route into Colombia, after we waited in vain to clear the bike through legally. We didn't take that option. So, for me, customs are never boring and Peru was about to throw in two more classic characters.

The border in question was a one-horse town, without the horse, but there was a donkey on the hillside, so that will do. La Balsa was the Ecuador to Peru crossing. When we arrived, we immediately doubled the population, so it wasn't that busy. No delays for us on this particular occasion, Ha! As with many borders around the world, the two countries were divided by a river, in this case the roaring Chichipe river, spanned by an iron suspension bridge. On our side of the bridge was a small green and white, breeze-block building, with the yellow, red and blue flag of Ecuador, fluttering outside. It looked like the donkey might have had a munch at the flag. There was also, for our delight, an up-market toilet, but alas no loo paper. Never mind. Give it a miss.

We approached the open door and could see a gentleman, in an extremely bright orange and yellow Hawaiian shirt, sitting behind a battered wooden desk. This was Senor Edison Jose Zambrano and he was the world's happiest official. I knew his name because it was on a sign, on his desk. It covered most of the desk. There was a small space where he could write, and there was a picture of his wife, who had a moustache, and his two portly teenagers, teetering on the table edge; the photo, not the daughters. They all looked as happy as him. There was a large photo of the President De La Republica del Ecuador behind Senor Zambrano. A small table on the left had a vase of plastic roses (Chuquirahua), the national flower of Ecuador. There was also an impressive plastic, Andean Condor statue, in the corner of the room. For some reason, there was a plastic action figure of Spiderman in one of its talons. The doorstop was also plastic, an army green, miniature Galapagos tortoise.

Senor Zambrano jumped up cheerily, and shook our hands, hitting his head on a sign, suspended on chains, which became a swinging 'Policia Y Migracion.' He had a sparkling, white tooth grin but his hair was slicked back sideways, and flat, in the fashion of Adolf Hitler. Luckily, he didn't have the moustache. But he did have a pair of Dutch-orange, tight, silky shorts on, which would have looked good on a 1980s football pitch, in Scunthorpe, UK, but not here. The pair of shin high, Ecuadorian army boots, unlaced and with the tongues hanging out, finished off a very individual look. His ruffled, Hawaiian, unbuttoned shirt, and his 'head-hitting-sign' behaviour suggested there might be a naked secretary in the cupboard, but I didn't really want to pry. It would be nice to get through quickly. Senor Zambrano perused our passports, whilst dancing to some sort of Chinese Ecuadorian music behind his desk. He even swung a passport in each hand, using them as props for his dance. All seemed to be in order and going swimmingly. Suddenly he slammed the passports on the desk, nearly knocking his family off, clicked his fingers three times, shimmied to the left, shimmied to the right, and said,

"Mr. and Mrs. Welcome! I am sorry but it is my lunchtime. You will have to wait some short time. A man cannot concentrate on an empty stomach. What is that noise I hear? It must be a guinea pig, or an empanada, or a Ceviche calling me."

He didn't say that, but the gist of it was he was off to lunch. I wanted to point out that it was only 10.00am, funny time for lunch, but thought better of it.

"Please be patient," he said.

And with that, he was off across the road, to the only 'restaurant' in sight. It was an open-air café, with some red plastic chairs and white tables, plonked in the mud. A torn gazebo, with 'Pilsener' splashed across it, was suspended between bending, straining poles, providing some shade. A woman in a whitish apron, with a pair of breasts drawn on it with extremely large, pink nipples, was stirring a pot of stew and chewing something at high speed. She was extremely overweight, and had to lean far back, like a limbo dancer, almost looking at the sky to avoid toppling forwards. She was a great advert for her street food. You wouldn't want an anorexic pencil serving you. A bit like you should never go to a doctor whose office flowers have died. We watched from the other side of the road as our Hawaiian officer settled down to what we thought would be a quick snack. We also settled down on the pavement and waited, and waited.

After about forty five minutes, thirsty and hungry, I suggested, "Bugger it. Let's go and get some food and a soft drink."

We walked over the hot asphalt road, and were welcomed, highly enthusiastically, by old flowery shirt.

"Yes, yes. Come in. Eat. Drink. It's a long wait."

Funny man he was, as he was the one causing the wait, and we were the ones doing the waiting. It was all great theatre and we settled down for some lunch. It was damn good. We were served a steaming Caldos, or soup, with chicken and potato. I know it was chicken because when Cathy stirred hers, to cool it down, a chicken foot popped out and waved to me. Mine contained a whole head, loitering under the broth, complete with mushy eyes and a Mohican, that rose out of the soup like *Jaws*. Unfortunately, there was about five litres of soup each. She may as well have served it in a petrol drum. You can have too much of a good thing. But we have always been the polite types, who don't want to upset the chef. Rather, rush around the corner and catastrophically explode, rather than be rude and leave food on the plate. So, we got through it.

Our escape was not happening that easily though. To our horror she then brought two orange juices, in glasses as big as our Enduro helmets. It had nothing to do with 'Jugo de Naranja'', it was basically a litre and half each of treacle, a little bit of orange juice and a kilo of sugar. This was followed by a piece of fried chicken with plantains and rice. You couldn't see her over the plates. We fought our way through it. Bear in mind that we both live off half a sardine a day, so our stomachs were the size of grapes. Well, used to be. Just when we were experiencing intense stabbing pains, and were considering folding over double, and collapsing on the floor, she brought the pudding. It was a Torta de Las Tres Leches, a frosted white cake, sitting in a base of sweet milk. Our lives were at risk. Eventually, I was laying on the floor in a semi coma, and she wafted figs cooked in cane syrup under my nostrils. It didn't work, we had to leave. What amazing food, but how could we make it across the road.

Taxi, but alas there were none.

We rolled each other across the road, like pub barrels, and presented ourselves to Flowery Shirt. I am not saying I ate too much, but if I fell over and died, my forensic chalk outline on the pavement would be a circle. How did he stay slim with that food across the road? Hawaiian Harry was not slowed down at all by his mega meal, and danced around and stamped our passports, in thirty seconds.

"My wife is very good cook, no?" he asked.

I should have known it, when I saw her moustache was trimmed identically to Hawaiian Harry's, that they were married.

"She is a very good cook, Senor," I answered, giving the thumbs up.

What a cunning plan. Senor Flowery Shirt Edison Jose Zambrano was always about to go to lunch, coincidentally, no matter what time you turned up. Everyone coming through this border crossing would have to wait hours, or even days, for him to finish his meal. Most would eventually crack and buy something from his wife. Then you got your passport stamp. He got to eat; she had guaranteed customers. Good old family affair. Well done. Amazing food too, which I would have preferred to have sampled after being lost in the Atacama Desert for a few weeks. As it was, we headed off across the bridge to Peru, stamped, smiling, gaseous, and bloated. Good times. What jollities awaited us on the other side. Many. With a wave goodbye to silky shorts, it was a short drive over the bridge to the next group of buildings on the Peruvian side.

The customs officer was dressed in an official uniform, in stark contrast to our tropical island vacationer across the bridge. Diego Romeo Garcia wore a green outfit, with the two red and one white perpendicular stripes of the national flag emblazoned on his shoulder, and his full name on a badge on his chest. He had short curly black hair, a neatly cropped moustache and eyebrows that moved constantly, as if they were asking questions. He was very short, about five foot in boots, on an incline, and very round. (Similar to me at the moment, the last bit.) At the door to Aduana (Customs), we made our introductions. I started to pull out our passports, but he raised his hand in the air to stop me.

"Don't tell me it's your lunchtime and that there is a café over the road, definitely not run by your wife?" I didn't ask.

"I need to take my shower; it is very hot," he said, in a surprisingly high-pitched voice.

He ushered us out of the office and gestured us to take a seat on the verandah, on a tatty, fake red leather sofa, in the shade.

"You wait here, I will return," he said, crossing the road.

This seems to be a theme; customs officers crossing the road to get away from us. On the other side of the road was a solitary, forlorn-looking cedar tree. Senor Garcia picked up a green hosepipe connected to a single standpipe and swung it over the tree and wedged it between the two remaining branches. He then turned it on and proceeded to strip totally naked, folding all his clothes up carefully, and placing them neatly on the roof of a derelict car behind the tree. He then proceeded to lather himself up from head to toe in his full Peruvian glory. He was extremely dedicated in his task and spent fifteen minutes, lather, rinse, repeat. All orifices and nether regions were cleaned to sparkling perfection.

Cathy and I made it very clear that we were not looking, and we earnestly discussed the fluctuating price of free range eggs in Guatemala, or some such subject. We subconsciously shuffled our chairs around, so we basically had our noses against the pebble dash wall. He seemed rather upset that we weren't paying closer attention to his hygiene habits, so he added a great deal of out-of-tune whistling to the scene. A bit like a mating bird, trying to attract a partner. He pulled a yellow, threadbare towel out through the broken window of the car and was just as diligent with drying. It took an age. I grew a moustache, waiting. His neatly folded clothes were left, whilst he brushed his hair to within an inch of its life, styling it in the cracked, wing mirror of the car. He then brushed his teeth. All this was done naked, as he had discarded the towel, once dry. He was not shy to display his crown jewels, his Peruvian meat and two vegetables, but we kept our gaze down.

Once dressed and groomed, he came to the disappointing conclusion that he was well presented enough to help us. He came back over the road and promptly stamped our passports. We were into Peru five minutes later. Mr Garcia either had a germ phobia or was a bit of an exhibitionist. Whichever it was, it was a common occurrence, because Cathy even spotted an internet forum, where a Dutch guy was talking about a Peruvian customs officer who showered naked in front of him. Oh well. No harm done. We all have our little quirks, he just liked displaying his. Believe it or not, between the two eccentric officials and faffing around with the rear indicators, most of the day had disappeared.

In a snap of the fingers, and a twist of the throttle, we were in heaven. We rode through a beautiful, lush green valley, that snaked alongside a winding river. The sheer cliffs cast huge shadows from the setting sun and thousands of bats flew out of enormous caves, dotted along the canyon walls. We took a wrong turn and were rewarded with a 'Not pass with cars' sign painted on a wooden sign. We were too full of food to negotiate rough roads, so backtracked and found the main road. Within an hour it started to get dark so we stopped in a beautiful, almost English meadow and set up our tent next to the river before night fell. We were in a new country and the day had been different. Peru was a geographical marvel from the very first day. Humans are fun; but nature, that's another ball game (pun). All the more pleasant to look at generally. We parked up with the open grasslands on one side, and the river and a backdrop of lush vegetation on the other. After doing a Peruvian shower impression under a tree, for Cathy's amusement, we fell asleep happy and giggling.

It takes all types! Peru time.

Chapter Four
Gigolo Off a Cliff

It's not a very good idea for two African motorcyclists to drive off a cliff, with a Peruvian gigolo, behind the wheel of a suspect van, whilst on the way to a Chinese restaurant, run jointly by a Venezuelan refugee and the gigolo's wife. (Sorry about the sentence length, I am breathless too.) It's not a good idea but we did it anyway. It is not a good move for people who value their future.

I need to backtrack a bit. We were on our way to Los Banos Del Incas, a tiny town famous for its thermal hot baths in the northern Andes of Peru at an altitude of 2750 metres. Cajamarca, the district, was founded by pre-Columbian ethnic groups around 1320 and, surprise surprise, was colonised by the Spanish in 1532. The Battle of Cajamarca marked the defeat of the Inca Empire by Spanish invaders as the Incan Emperor Atahualpa was captured and murdered.

I won't get political, because it is not my thing, but in my experience when indigenous and colonial mix, you end up with the most beautiful architecture in the most magnificent surroundings. Cajamarca lived up to this. The person who we were going to see was not exactly indigenous and arrived in the area a little bit later, 2001 to be exact, but he was already a well-known landmark in Peru. (Haha. 'Landmark' makes him sound quite sedentary or possibly dead.) That was certainly not the case.

David Groves, a traditional Peruvian name obviously, the owner of Adventure Peru Motorcycles, had offered us the use of his house perched on the side of the Andes range, equipped with a motorbike workshop and an in-house mechanic-cum-house sitter, Franco, who was certainly equipped. Actually, to be honest, this story is really about Franco. Some people are imprinted in your memory forever, and others, you have forgotten their name twenty minutes after you have met them. You can't even picture their faces. The difference is a simple one – charisma. Franco had it in oodles or noodles or whatever the saying is.

The Battle of Cajamarca

Franco was destined to become a good friend for life, in the same way as Ashraf the Egyptian, or Carl the Canadian, became. Those of you who have read my Africa book, *The Japanese-Speaking Curtain Maker,* will know who I am talking about. (Quick, subtle plug there. It's a bestseller by the way, in my village: population 200. Proceeds of the next book go to my good friend, Franco. Joke.) Anyway, if you have been camping at altitude, freezing off all your important extremities, then you jump at the offer of a cosy house. (Not literally, of course, because that would be painful.) We hobbled towards this opportunity.

Cathy and I had endured some freezing cold, finger and toe numbing rides. After that type of ride, your camping evening is spent wrapping everything you own around your hands and feet and pretending you are loving it. Every time you speak, to express your enthusiasm and delight, your teeth take over with the chattering, and a cloud of carbon dioxide emission build up between you in the tent. 'Gorillas in the Mist' springs to mind. Sorry Cathy. I am not saying that thirty relentless nights of camping affects your relationship, but we didn't speak for twenty nine.

Camping is the most expensive way to live like a homeless person! We needed this break and David's house was no disappointment. (Sounds biblical.) It was a beautiful Hacienda. Sorry, a quick interruption. Cathy has just turned up with a scorpion in a glass. A baby one. Apparently, they have two hundred children, so our room is a scorpion nightmare. If no more paragraphs are written, you know what happened. Ok, I am back. I survived.

David's place was a delight, a beautiful house made of pink Peruvian stone from local quarries, and covered in burgundy bougainvillea, with wooden outhouses creaking under the weight of vibrant green creepers and flowers. There were multi-coloured lizards and spiders everywhere, which just added to the beauty. The view from the house was endless, overlooking stunning pastures green. (See how I reversed the words to make it more romantic.) Donkeys were wandering aimlessly around the verdant, pristine fields, holding bright yellow flowers in their mouths. OK. Enough. They didn't have flowers in their mouths, but they looked well fed, flealess, and fat. Good enough for me.

Tiny, corrugated or thatched roofed houses were dotted around the valley and in the distance the sheer cliffs of the Andes loomed. At the base, in the shadows, the mountains were angry black, but as you scanned your eyes upwards, the sun fought through, and cast stunning shadows that gouged out valleys running from the peaks. Huge dark clouds moved rapidly across the landscape, creating a never-ending change in the contours of this radical place. The peaks of every mountain were capped with pristine white snow, in a perfect triangle, that reflected off everything like a diamond on a cake. Lower down, the snow slid off the mountain edge, melting, finishing off the perfect image of icing on a cake. A scar spread across the landscape of this perfect view. I was looking at the famous Chachapoyas Road, one of the most revered routes motorcyclists can take, or anyone. We were heading there, but not yet.

David had real sofas and beds and a fridge and a TV. Things we only heard about in rumours, during our travels, so far. David had hot water. The Tenere was definitely going to break down here for a few days at least I knew the bike wasn't running well. Cathy wouldn't listen. She will now. David, the Sussex-born Peruvian was not going to be at his house, but had arranged for Franco to meet us.

Franco was missing in action. There was a pre-arranged key in place. We went inside and turned on the kettle, what a novelty, and stood out on David's balcony soaking up the view and nearly soaking up my first spider bite in South America. (Many more to come, don't worry.) Despite the clear day and bright sunshine it was a pleasant twenty degrees, due to the altitude.

Life was good. It is not always necessary to search the extremes. Sometimes free accommodation must not be scoffed at. I was also acutely aware that Cathy and I had really scraped the barrel accommodation-wise and, quite frankly, I could see Mutiny, on or off the Bounty, ahead. Accommodation and scraping wise; we are talking blood on the sheets, excrement on the walls, no water, used condoms on the floor to slip on, cockroaches, bedbugs and lice, and other biting and flying things, at present unidentified by mankind, or womankind, or trans-lesbo- multinuclear kind either. In short, David's place was a godsend, or not, if you are not religious. This political correctness writing is doing me in, so I do apologise. I am giving it up and writing this book the way I want to. If it offends, I apologise. But not a lot.

Many of you in the Adventure Motorcycle world will know David Groves from the various large Adventure Shows, including the Overland Event, The ABR Festival, the MCN Shows in London and Birmingham. Look out for this top man. He is of medium height, very English (translucent skin), with silver, medium-length Timotei shampooed hair, a great smile, a super warm, enthusiastic personality and a dodgy hip. More importantly, he knows who Percy Fawcett is. This was very important to me. Like me, David was inspired by all the explorers, especially Percy Fawcett. (Yes, related to the sink maker.) I actually have no idea why David, myself and Cathy were all inspired by Percy Fawcett. It must have been his writing and descriptive genius. As my brother Simon so horribly pointed out, bursting mine and Cathy's hero bubble, "He went to the Amazon, got lost, got found. Went back to the Amazon with his son, got lost, never got found. Never found the City of Gold, El Dorado. Failed."

A bit of a harsh critique but true. I still love Fawcett for his blind tenacity. His attempts to find El Dorado, the fabled city of Gold, was the death of him. I suspect, from my experience that he loved the Amazon so much, as did his son, that they faked their deaths and lived with buxom Amazonian women for the rest of their lives. Happy as can be. I respect the fact that this is a warped sexist man's view. They obviously got boiled by natives. The point is, that after reading Percy Fawcett's amazing book, *The Lost City of Z*, it inspired David to visit South America. A good film has been made of his exploits. Fawcett's exploits, not David's.

With South America and the Amazon in mind, David headed to Cajamarca in 2000 to visit a biking friend from the UK who he hadn't seen since they were in their twenties, ninety seven years earlier. (Joke, David.) His friend had settled in Cajamarca.

"That was it for me, Spence. I just fell in love with it, Spencer, and my mind was made up, Spencer."

I am not a repetitive writer; this is how he spoke. Repeating people's names personalises the conversation. What a lovely thing to hear. I wish we could all have that same conviction. How many times have I heard conviction and certainty when someone is talking about their life. Not enough. There are millions of people who don't even realise that there is a better world out there. I don't want to sound clichéd and hippie because that is the last thing that I am. OK. Not a better world, but a better place for them in it. A place where they will feel comfortable enough to pursue their particular dreams and not those forced upon them by their family or their society. I am not saying: be a rebel. I am saying, find your comfortable place in the world but work for it. I hate lazy people. Work is the cornerstone of our society and if I could live my life again I would work harder, much harder. If someone says to me that they are bored, it is possibly the worst thing that they can say. They are insulting the opportunity they have. If you are bored, it means that you have not grabbed the world and its meaning, and you are waiting for something to change, rather than changing it yourself. There is no room for excuses. Action causes reaction. My parents gave me everything. An amazing childhood, an incredible education and a 'you can do anything attitude'. They proved it too. They lived it.

The only thing they could not give me, or predict, was a country I would feel comfortable in. After a life in Africa, UK universities were destined to be a disaster and totally alien to me and Simon. They didn't predict this. And so it turned out. My brother went to Christ's College, Cambridge University, but was more interested in music and Africa. He so wanted to fit in to the intellectual elite that my mum dreamed of. (I have never seen my mother as happy as when she heard that my brother had got into Cambridge.) But it wasn't to be. You cannot tame an African boy. I was the same. I ended up in the UK because of my own failings, not my parents' failings. I wanted to respect the country for my parents but in twenty years I always felt like an alien. I always will. When you don't fit, you don't fit.

As soon as I discovered motorcycles and travel, my life changed forever. It felt like everything in my life made sense. Unfortunately, my dream is expensive. I still want to be the first person to circumnavigate every continent but it is looking less and less likely. Money talks. I am not naïve. Staying in the place where you were born is a necessity for most people, not a choice. Sometimes we just need a push, or a catalyst, that Eureka moment, when you see a better future if you make some brave decisions. Fawcett's story was the death of him, but the life and catalyst for David Groves.

Over a Stella Artois at my house in the UK, before we left for South America, David explained,

"I bought a rundown, seven bedroom colonial house in Cajamarca. I had also met a beautiful Art teacher, and fell head over heels in love… with her etchings, of course. I was a Master Builder (no childish comments please) in the UK, so conversion was no problem for me, and I could do it cheap. I had also managed to save some money working for John Cleese and William Goldman, the director of *Butch Cassidy and the Sundance Kid*. I knew I had to live in Peru but needed a business. I spoke to my mate Dave and we set up Adventure Motorcycle Peru. We ran it for ten years, then I bought land at Huarapongo and designed and built my house, Casa Buena Vista, in two years."

"Tell me about Franco, he seems to be well known," I asked.

David's eyes lit up.

"I met Franco – Franco Guevara Brito – to give you his full name, seventeen years ago. He is one of ten children from a traditional Peruvian Indian family and was raised in Celendin, in the rugged Northern Andes mountain range. He is a super guy and was different, more motivated, more pushed, to achieve something different," said David, a tear in his eye.

I was worried that maybe the end of this story would be Franco's death. It wasn't. David obviously loved the dude.

"I actually met Franco through his Uncle Ennis who was a bike collector and English teacher in Celendin. Franco became the Bradley Wiggins of Peru and was National Champion two years in a row, riding on a bike he made himself in the workshop."

"Not a lazy fellow then Dave," I responded.

"Not at all. Bloody hell. A live wire. He then attained a place at University in Chiclayo and came out with a degree in Electrical Engineering. Not only that, he is a talented motorcyclist and an amazing mechanic," he answered.

"He only had one bag with a T-shirt and some trousers when I met him. Now he is a true friend and my Tour Director."

"Any faults?"

"He is good looking and quite the ladies' man too, if that's a negative," Dave responded. "Very popular with the female clients."

I laughed. I was looking forward to meeting Franco but I was beginning to see two Dave's, because of the lager. Luckily Dave felt the same, and headed home.

Wind forward a year and here we were, on top of the world, well on top of a mountain in Peru, waiting at a petrol station for Franco to come and meet us. Dave was still in Charing, UK, but said we could have his house. We heard Franco from five kilometres away, on what would turn out to be a well-used XT500 with no exhaust. It was quite an entrance and appropriate for a man whose reputation preceded him. He sped up the opposite side of the road, waving to us wildly as he swung round the roundabout, into the station. He stopped the bike and jumped off in front of us, hand outstretched in one smooth Peruvian version, Jason Statham type move. Franco Guevara was a shorter version of all the following people, mixed into one ball of energy – Antonio Banderas, George Lopez, Andy Garcia, Benjamin Bratt and his namesake, Che Guevara. I think he lightly modelled himself on Che, as he had the full mane of hair, the scraggly uneven beard and even the revolutionary beret.

Franco

We both warmed to Franco immediately with his pearly white teeth and genuine grin. He was about thirty five and had a hint of lines around his eyes, a sign of a great deal of smiling, sun and wind. He had a pair of blue, 'definitely mechanics' jeans on, a grey, O'Neill T-shirt with holes in it (from clothes-munching insects), and black, scuffed-to-hell army boots. Franco sported a dark blue bandana, which was failing desperately to keep his hair under control. He had a bandana tied round his right wrist and a chunky silver chain. He had three or four days stubble sprouting on his sun-bronzed face, but not covering the sparkle in his eye.

We received big hugs and rode together to David's house along the most stunning mountain route. A massive fertile, green valley stretched ahead of us as far as the eye could see. On the horizon, the Andes mountains loomed up, 3000 metres, imposing, beautiful, roughly hewn and snow-capped. Down in the valley was the tiny figure of a woman, leading a happily braying donkey, a goat and a dog into the distance. Ant-like agricultural figures hard at work were sprinkled across the valley floor. The odd battered pick-up rolled through, leaving a cloud of dust, and coughing people in its wake. It was a beautiful view and a beautiful house. Although we had been there for a day Franco showed us around more formally and then we headed to the balcony for a celebratory drink. Neither of us were surprised when within an hour Franco was on the wooden table, singing and cavorting around in a ludicrously oversized, fraying straw hat and yellow sunglasses, the frames the shape of two stars. Downing a lager, Franco announced,

"Tomorrow we eat Cuy, guinea pig, you know it?"

"For sure, we know them as pets but not to eat," I answered. Franco raised his eyes and whistled.

"Tomorrow my wife prepare Cuy and the next day after she open Chinese restaurant in town. We go to eat. Yes?"

"That sounds fantastic Franco, thanks so much and great to finally meet up," I said. "Watch that step, Franco."

Oh dear!

The next day, with a sore head and a sore knee, Franco was true to his word. He turned up with his petite and pretty wife, Susan, a softly spoken, elegant woman, and with a guinea pig. A big one. A body-building steroid guinea pig. As big as his wife. At this point I will interject with a few facts for the vegetarians, vegans and general guinea pig lovers out there. It will probably make no difference to your opinion, but it will make me feel better.

The guinea pig, Cavia Porcellus, is a species of rodent belonging to the family Cavidae and the genus Cavia. Despite their name, guinea pigs are not native to Guinea, have not even been on holiday to Guinea, and are not even remotely related to pigs. They actually originated in the Andes and studies based on biochemistry suggest that they were originally domesticated as livestock, as a source of protein and yumminess. They have kiddies every three months, between three and eight, so are totally sustainable, nifty breeders.

For five thousand years guinea pigs have fed rural communities in Peru, Ecuador, Bolivia and Chile, countries deeply and frequently affected by malnutrition and unemployment. The Cuy features prominently in traditional festivals – famously, a cooked guinea pig lies paws up in the celebrated 1753 painting of 'The Last Supper' by Marcos Zapata in the Cathedral Basilica in Cusco. Guinea pigs were munchies for the Andean people long before they became pets in the west. So, who were we to argue. If it was good enough for Jesus and his disciples, it's good enough for us.

The meal was superb and was cut up into a tasty stew. We would not have known it was a guinea pig if we hadn't seen the dismembering beforehand. In fact, Cuy is growing in popularity in high end restaurants and is helping to usher a boost in the return of a traditional and environmentally friendly industry, led by women. Top chefs in Peru and Colombia have brought the meat back to popularity with roasted, curried and even sweetened versions appearing on menus. The squeamishness of foreign visitors facing a deep fried dish of Cuy chactado, has also been reflected in sectors of Peruvian society where the aesthetics of eating a rodent were problematic.

No such thing in Ecuador. The disconcerting thing about Ecuador, that we were to find out later, was that there was no effort to disguise the Cuy. It is served whole, deep fried and splayed across the plate, teeth showing, eyeholes staring upwards, and hands and feet sticking stiffly over the edges of the huge plate. Served with two, grease-dripping, fried potatoes, and anemic green pulses (see picture overleaf).

The guinea pig looked like an animal run over in a cartoon, driven over a few times, thrown on a fire, thrown on a plate and thrown at the customer.

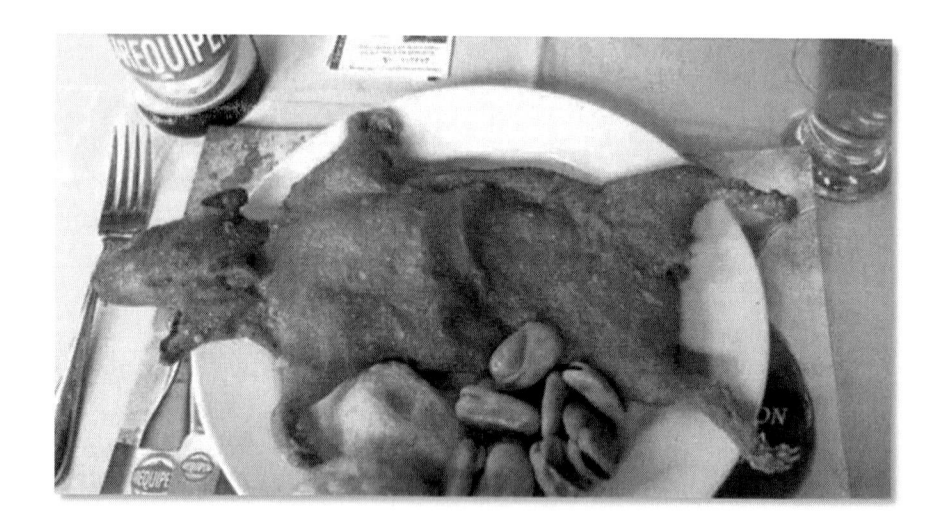

I suspect a lot of foreigners would be 'coy' about the Cuy (pronounced the same). We weren't, and Susan's Cuy was way more cultured than the Ecuador attempts. We had some very deep discussions about life. We went to bed, a real bed, after weeks of camping, full of Cuy and full of joy. OK, enough rhyming. Franco and his wife were superb and, as David Groves said, he couldn't think of any faults in Franco. Unfortunately, we were to find out one of his biggest faults the next day, and we nearly died in the process.

Early the next morning Franco and I headed into the local town, to try and pick up some inner tubes, with Franco as my jittery, over-excited pillion. If you are impatient or in a hurry, never travel with Franco. It took us an hour to go a couple of kilometres. Franco is unable to go past a pretty woman, full stop.

"Stop Spencer, one minute, I need to talk to this girl, she likes me very much."

Two minutes later, "James, sorry, this girl has problems with her moto. I need to fiddle with a few of her parts."

Or something like that.

Five hundred metres later, "You don't have to stop, but slow down. Look at her!"

Franco whistled and shouted his way down the route, but everybody knew Franco and his beaming smile. A difficult guy to get annoyed with. The girls knew full well he was filled with nonsense, but they loved him anyway, and used to blush into their hands. I liked how he gently edged me out of the way, when he was talking to the next girl, so that he could lean against my motorcycle in a James Dean type pose. Franco had swallowed the Dictionary of Latin American Compliments. Some might call it sexist, I just found it endearing and fun as he sat behind me, enthusiastically thinking up his next comment.

"Que bonita." (How beautiful) "Estas buena." (You are hot) "Estas hermosa, Te ves estupenda." "Eres lista," etc etc. Or more simply put and possibly a shade sexist, "Buen trabajo." (Great job). Or more simply, shouting across the road, "Me gusta tu sonrisa!" (I love your smile!) "Eres un Tesoro!" (You are a treasure!).

These compliments were followed by air kisses and did the trick every time. Franco's behaviour, language and mannerisms were in no way typically Peruvian and possibly a great deal of romantic films had been watched. Eventually we made it to the inner tube shop, but not before Franco arranged a tentative date with a street tortilla seller, with three missing toes. Now, polygamy is not really common in Peru in the modern day. However, men having more than one household is tolerated and often expected amongst traditional people. Franco certainly had it covered. Apart from the thirty-seven girlfriends loitering around each corner, we also learnt that he had another wife in Sauce, the fittingly named town his family were from. Franco had a daughter, Sonjha with Susan, the Cuy preparer, but he also had three boys with Ellie, called Etni, Franco and Jim. (Jim was named after David's son.) I refuse to judge, because firstly it is not my society and secondly, I have never seen a happier or closer couple. Franco's fifteen-year-old daughter, who was petite and smooth, like her mother, obviously worshipped the ground he walked on. When she wasn't texting (yes, even in the mountain villages of Peru), she would be saying, "Daddy did this, Daddy knows how to do that, Daddy can fix that."

Great people and a lovely vibe off all of them.

That very evening, after our five-hour inner tube saga, Franco disappeared and returned as his twin brother. Quite a transformation. Now even Andy Garcia looked scrappy and unkempt in comparison. Franco had showered and brushed his jet black hair into two impressive curtains, worthy of the Saddlers Wells stage. He wore a crisply ironed black shirt, a leather necklace with two bright beads on it, clean jeans and some spanking cowboy boots. A beard and eyebrow trim had definitely occurred but had been done badly. He looked like the eagle from 'The Muppets'.

Industrial amounts of deodorant and aftershave had been applied. If you got too close to him, your eyes started to smart. Now the girls of the village could smell, as well as hear, Franco coming. The plan was to go to the grand opening of Franco's wife's Chinese restaurant. Susan had gone ahead, to Spring some Rolls, or weigh some Won Ton soup, so Cathy and I jumped in the back of a camper van, parked at the top of David Groves' extremely steep driveway. Franco jumped in the driver's seat with 'texting daughter' next to him. Franco assumed the predictable driving position; sunglasses, one hand on the wheel, elbow leaning on the open window. He looked pretty cool (if it wasn't a Combi), turned, nodded to us both and said, "Vamonos."

Then all hell broke loose. He kangarooed, or llamad off, at full speed, in reverse, accelerated wildly, clipping the two concrete gate bollards as we went. We careered onwards (well backwards), only just staying on the steep curved driveway. On we went, bouncing and jolting, directly onto the main road and across it, like a bunch of demented lunatics. Cathy and I were both screaming by now. Luckily, there were no cars coming, otherwise we would have been savagely side-swiped and would all be brown bread. Across the road we went and off the other side, into a rough patch of grass, the Combi bouncing violently. We all hit our heads. Then we went over a cliff.

OK. I exaggerate. We went halfway off a cliff, which makes all the difference between life and death, to be honest. Franco and texting daughter hadn't uttered a sound. As the two back wheels went off the cliff, half the Combi dangling in thin air, there was a huge wrenching bang and a metallic tearing, and we came to an abrupt and aggressive stop. I was quite pleased about that. We were hanging there like a pendulum, so I wasn't totally pleased. A rocking Combi on a cliff has been in movies since forever, so we acted appropriately. Cathy and I threw ourselves towards the front. With respect to Franco and text fiend, they remained super chilled. Franco was just sitting there, totally still, sunglasses on, staring straight ahead.

"No problem James. It stops. Big rock."

Well, he was technically correct, the swaying was not too hectic, as long as no one breathed. Franco's daughter was sitting on the edge of a precipice, in a dodgy hippie mobile, texting a friend:

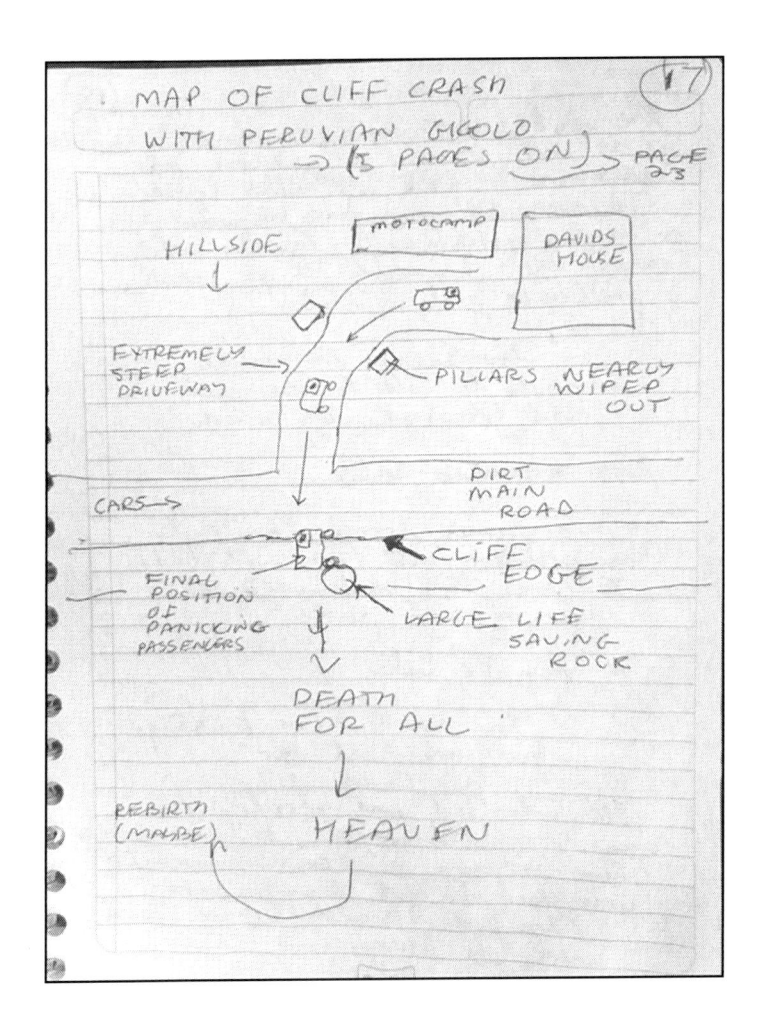

[Hand-drawn map labeled:]

MAP OF CLIFF CRASH
WITH PERUVIAN GIGOLO
→ (5 PAGES ON) → PAGE 23

HILLSIDE
MOTOCAMP
DAVIDS HOUSE
EXTREMELY STEEP DRIVEWAY →
PILLARS NEARLY WIPED OUT
CARS →
DIRT MAIN ROAD
CLIFF EDGE
FINAL POSITION OF PANICKING PASSENGERS
LARGE LIFE SAVING ROCK
DEATH FOR ALL
REBIRTH (MAYBE)
HEAVEN

"Daddy drove of a cliff and we are going to die, so I won't make it round tonight."

Or something like that. Maybe she was texting her mother, "Start the Grand Opening and dinner without us, Daddy messed up."

It was evident that they were not going to move, so I gently edged towards the side of the Combi and slid open the door, to get myself to safety. Sorry, I mean to get Cathy to safety. We jumped onto a rocky ledge, as the Combi slipped and went over the cliff. Sorry, that's the movies. The whole central section of the Combi was grounded on thick soil and the rear right wheel and mangled bumper were wedged against a large rounded boulder. The left wheel was a metre clear of the ground.

This rock one hundred percent saved us all from meeting our Maker. It was not a sheer drop, but was steep enough and long enough for us to roll endlessly to the Pearly Gates. We were very lucky. We all scrambled carefully out of the driver's door and stood up on the main road, surveying the carnage. A pick-up truck with four electrical contractors on the back stopped and a 'Vehicle Recovery Strategy Meeting' began in earnest. Franco was standing quietly, surveying the damage, totally unperturbed and smiling slightly. It could have been indigestion. He then came out with one of the most memorable and classic lines I have ever heard. I said quietly, but forcefully and dramatically, "Jesus Christ Franco, what the hell happened there? I thought we were going to die."

He furrowed his brow, thought for a minute, brushed his curtains back from his eyes, spread his hands out in the air in front of him and announced glumly, "I don't know how to drive car, only Moto".

I knew this could not be true, but answered, "I can see that!"
We both burst into crying tears of laughter.
"OK. Let's fix," he said enthusiastically.

Now there is no way of being polite. The four of them had absolutely no clue what they were doing. They put random rocks and logs in random places, with no appreciation of physics. They just wheel spun the Combi to hell and gone, creating deep grooves in the mud and getting into even more of a Peruvian pickle. I am not blowing my own Zampona (Peruvian wind instrument), but I am good at logical problem solving. They were running around like headless llamas and if I didn't take control we would still be there in the morning, randomly revving and discussing extraction tactics.

I told them my plan and Franco went off to find a pulley, or better, a winch. I commandeered the headless, but super helpful guys, and we built up a massive pile of earth, mixed with large rocks and pummelled it all down with nearby loose fence posts. We then placed scaffolding poles from David's workshop on the mound of tampered earth and rocks. We basically built a platform that extended the road so that the back left wheel was not in mid air. It took us an hour with spades and picks and poles. We then roped up the front of the Combi to the tow hitch of our helpers' pick-up. I drove the pick-up and slowly, slowly, with low revs to avoid wheel spinning, the Combi inched forward. I had to point out to our eager helpers that pushing from the back, on an unstable cliff edge was just a tad dangerous and not conducive to a long future. Bit by bit the Combi edged onto solid ground, with the minimum of scraping. Time for a breather. I suspect that Franco was fairly pleased that the owner of the Combi was more than 10,000 kilometres away. Time for a touch up and a quick bumper repair. (David, I know you will read this, but please don't be angry with Franco. It was not his fault. He doesn't know how to drive).

I don't know if we were insane but after that palaver, we still let Franco drive to the Chinese restaurant. It was hair-raising stuff. Franco looked non-plussed as he mounted kerbs, flattened previously healthy chickens, and had old ladies diving out the way. Apparently, the road was just a rough guideline of where to go, but in no way compulsory to follow, and it was obligatory to ignore junctions and stop signs. Road rules were just an idea that someone had thought up, but were pointless really.

The Chinese restaurant was a bit of a haze. All I know is that there were at least fifty chairs and no customers, except our table of shell-shocked accident victims. The food was bloody excellent and I hope that Susan makes a success of it. Franco drank too much Pisco Sour, (Pisco liquor, lime, syrup, ice, egg and Angostura bitters), dropped his soup and disappeared somewhere with his wife and the chef. Best of luck to them. As long as Franco doesn't taxi prospective customers to the restaurant. Few will arrive.

Susan and Sonjha

The next day we had to head off and despite his slightly unacceptable behaviour, I knew that Franco and I would remain friends. And we are. A top man if slightly off the wall, or off the cliff to be more accurate. It was time for us to head to the Chachapoyas mountains and south towards Bolivia, but not without saying adios to Franco, Susan and Sonjha. The world is wonderful when you are not hanging off a cliff. 'Texting daughter' did stop texting for thirty seconds to say goodbye. Bolivian delights ahead for us. But not before a visit to Cusco and what a visit it was.

Chapter Five
Hiawatha - Jumping into the Fire

Hiawatha was a Native American leader and co-founder of the Iroquios Confederacy. He was adopted by the Mohawk Tribe and became their leader. He died in 1595. Hiawatha has something to do with this chapter. Bear with me.

Something I have touched upon before, in my Africa book, are the dirty words 'colonial' and 'colonialism'. Those words hover around the whole of South America too. Looking at the architecture throughout Central and South America, it is difficult not to see the massive impact that the colonials have had, whether it is Portuguese, Spanish, German or Dutch. The buildings are a wonder of human creativity, so that can't be bad. Consequently, many towns and cities follow a very similar geographical layout, especially in the high tourist areas. The pattern is as simple as this. A 'Centro Historico', which almost always has a large central square, or Plaza, consisting of stunning colonial architecture, from the 1500s onwards. They are normally pedestrian around the Plaza. These five or six streets, with a central church or cathedral, and the main imposing government buildings, are the tourist magnet streets. Simply because of their beauty and history.

It is a double-edged sword, because I am not a fan of tourist areas. It is the same worldwide, whether at the Pyramids in Egypt, the Acropolis in Athens or the Grand Canyon. All places of 'wonder', whether man-made or natural, will attract humans, both the buyers of the experience, and the sellers. These are the places where they sell all the tacky trinkets; the knitted llama keyrings, the miniature bottles of Tequila, the plastic pyramids, the fake artifacts, the novelty T-shirts, hats, plates and mugs, plastic cactuses, coasters, tea towels, plastic animals, etc. All the things you don't want and never will. These are also the areas where you will get harassed by shoe shiners, street artists, drug pushers and tour sellers. Bolivian Tour Guide:

"Hello friend. You want to do tour of Salar de Uyuni Salt Flats. You want to go to train cemetery, very beautiful and interesting. Cocaine, weed, mushrooms."

Peruvian Tour Guide:

" Hello my friend. You want to do tour of Machu Picchu. I give tour very cheap, ecstasy, weed, cocaine, Ayahuasca."

The sentences all come out in rapid fire, with no gap between 'tour' and 'weed'. The 'Historic Centro' is also where all the hotels, restaurants and bars are located. As a result of this tourist influx of money, the facilities are good, the maintenance is top class and the streets are kept clean. It is also where the prices for everything are tripled, and pick pockets help to ease you of your wallet.

We were in Cusco, Peru, the gateway to Machu Picchu. It was no different. Walk four blocks out from 'Historico Centro' and it all changes. Chaos and real life ensues. From the busy, but highly sanitised centre, you are immediately thrown into filth and litter in waves, on the road and pavements, beggars, injured, limping, starving dogs and cats and people. Desperately poor hawkers in filthy clothes sell whatever they can get their hands on; plastic bags of water, phone chargers and cards, a roll of insulating tape, a grubby doll. Everyone seems to be a mechanic, but there are shells of cars and motorbikes everywhere. If they are not mechanics, they are taxi drivers in battered, hardly moving, cars. They are the lucky ones. Buildings are collapsing, open areas of wasteland filled with litter, and homeless people. Paintwork is peeling off buildings, shops are boarded up and those that are open are surrounded by iron burglar bars, curling razor wire, and metal spikes, on all climbable walls.

Chickens and goats run across the road, avoiding the Militia trucks that roll through the area. Men stand at traffic lights, cleaning windscreens with filthy rags and dirty river water. Small children with snotty noses are held out to car windows, by their mothers' outstretched arms, begging for coins. A homeless man jumps out of the skeleton of a broken-down, rusty car, and sits by the bike, asking for money. Plastic bags float past in the wind, dust and sand, going in our eyes. Cracked pavements, cracked potholed roads, half tar, half mud, missing manholes, drains and gutters clogged and overflowing with debris and sewerage.

A man curled up asleep on two pieces of soggy cardboard, a woman with matted hair sleeping inside a black plastic, rubbish bag. A dead cat rotting in the gutter. A mentally challenged young lad, fingering the overflowing, reeking bins, and running off laughing. Loud and distorted music coming from every shack. The smell of hundreds of open fires preparing food. Rickety, colourful buses bouncing past, at impossible angles, full to cloud height with goods. A traffic light, bent at 45 degrees, flickering ineffectually, in its last throes. Posters, yellowing and peeling off walls, flyers advertising a sofa deal lying in the gutter, chickens pecking at the paper. Unidentified green slime, dripping down the walls of buildings, a mountain of soft drink cans being squashed and collected by an old woman, bent like a bow. Smog, smoke, voices, dirt, laughter, dogs squealing, chaos. This was Cusco.

Walk back five blocks and presto. Another world. The comfortable, tourist world. Those of you that have ventured out of these tourist spots, no matter where in the world, will recognise what I am describing. I understand. People want a place where 'all is right with the world, and the locals are so sweet' experience; not a traumatic one. This is the formula throughout South and Central America, and throughout the world. The money driven, tickety boo… everything is perfect, tourist spots… and the rest. Cusco was no different from this formula, of a sanitised centre and impoverished outskirts, despite the fact that it is the gateway city to Machu Picchu, which is listed in the top ten manmade wonders of the world and is a UNESCO World Heritage site, attracting over half a million visitors a year, a staggering 1370 people a day, every day. Good news for the centre of town. Not really for the rest. But Cusco was on our route through the Arequipa, Juliaca, and then onto La Paz, the capital of Bolivia, so we were definitely going to check it out for a day or two.

Cusco is a city in South Eastern Peru, near the Urubamaba Valley, part of the Andes mountain range. The city is perched at 3400 metres, with a population of half a million, and is a sprawling, dirty drive in, the scenes I described playing out for an hour. But the city has an undeniably interesting history. The Killke people occupied the region from 900-1200, prior to the arrival of the Inca, in the 13th century. Carbon dating of Saksaywaman, the walled complex outside Cusco, established a date of 1100. The first three Spaniards arrived in 1524; Francisco Pizarro, aided by another soldier, Diego de Almagro, and a priest, Hernando de Luque, undertook explorations that led to the conquest of Peru. By 1527 they were convinced of the wealth of the Inca empire and took the city in

1533 after the Battle of Cajamarca (David Groves and Franco were not there).

The capital of the Incas astonished the Spaniards with the beauty of its edifices and the length, organisation and regularity of its streets. The great square was surrounded by several palaces, since each sovereign built a new palace for himself.

Through the heart of the capital ran a free-flowing, clean river (how times have changed), faced with stone. The most sumptuous building was the great temple, dedicated to the sun, studded with gold plates. It was surrounded by convents and dormitories for the priests. The palaces were numerous and the troops lost no time in plundering them. The swings and roundabouts of the destruction of history.

Pizarro, the conquering Spaniard, ceremoniously gave Manco, the Incan ruler fringe lands, as the new Peru. Very generous of him; giving them back their own land. He left a garrison of ninety men in Cusco. The melting pot of history led to buildings constructed under Spanish influence, with a mixture of Inca indigenous architecture. Sadly, the Spaniards, like invading armies throughout the world, destroyed many Inca buildings, temples and palaces, presumably as a show of power and dominance. So sad! They used the remaining walls as bases for the construction of a new city. Cusco was the centre for the Spanish colonisation and the spread of Christianity in the Andean world. It became very prosperous thanks to agriculture, mining, cattle rearing and general trade with Spain. The Spanish constructed many churches and convents as well as a cathedral, university and archdioceses.

We decided to stay in the centre of town as we spotted a cheap, run-down courtyard with rented rooms, and some foreign-plated adventure motorcycles. Hadn't seen any of those on our journey. We ended up in a very basic room, but the bike was safe in the courtyard. As soon as we finished unpacking, Cusco exploded into the most incredible hailstorm I had seen in my life; and Swaziland had some spectacular ones. Within minutes the roads were full of millions of rolling hailstones. To the naked eye it looked like snow. The sound on our corrugated iron roof was deafening, and we had a good giggle, trying to hear each other, shouting at the top of our voices, hands cupped. We spotted some pale faces in the courtyard, braving and dodging the hail and drinking beers. We were to find out shortly that these three, Remy, Anthony and Rick, were deranged. In a nice way.

This is the weirdness of the wonderful places and ancient cultures in this world. They spend thousands of years building a beautiful culture and city, that disappears through a twist of history. They then spend the next 300 years surviving on tourism, and the majesty and atmosphere of the place disappears. This is what we face now, YouTubers, Instagrammers, TikTokers, Twitterers and general social media influencers, running around these sites, trying to make the next hit video. This was what Cusco had turned into. A great big Everest queue to Machu Picchu, but without the challenge. Everyone in the world deserves to see these majestic sites, and has the right. I wish they didn't. I realise I am one of them, so this logic fails. You see my point. Along with the tourism, comes the drugs. Now, I understand that this is a big leap in subject, but once again, drugs reared their ugly heads in this chaotic and tourist mecca. That is Cusco.

Dangerous drugs, that sickened us. Before I started this journey and wrote this book, I promised I would not go down the clichéd route of talking about drugs in South America. I failed. I would be lying to you if I ignored it. Let me tell you about Ayahuasca. Stay with me, all will become clear. Or not.

Ayahuasca, also known as yage, is a blend of two plants - the Ayahuasca vine (Banisteriopsis Caapi), and a shrub called chacruna (PsychotriaViridis). You obviously spotted the word 'psycho' in there. They contain the hallucinogenic drug, Dimethyltryptamine (DMT). DMT is illegal in most countries, but in South America, Ayahuasca is an integral part of the life of some tribal societies, pronounced *Eye-a-wass-ka*, for those of you struggling. In 2008, Peru's government recognised Ayahuasca status, saying it is 'one of the basic pillars of the identity' of the Amazon people. Peru's government claimed that consumption of the 'teacher' drug, or 'wisdom plant', constitutes the gateway to the spiritual world and its secrets, which is why traditional Amazonian medicine has been structured around the Ayahuasca Ceremonies. Now I cannot argue this point. To me the problem arrives when tourists get involved. It is not their culture. But they have made it their drug, and quite frankly it doesn't sit right with me.

Ayahuasca tourism is well established and big business now, used by Westerners interested in shamanism, and it has raised the profile of the traditional medicine, worldwide.

"The Ayahuasca trail runs through from Peru and Colombia and is well travelled, with tens of thousands of foreigners taking it every year. It is very dangerous, not just because it is a drug, but because of the circumstances people take it in. They are susceptible to robbery and worse, you won't believe what states people get into, unless you see it," according to Joshua Wickerham, chief advisor of the Ethnobotanical Council.

Traditional Shaman

Scientific evidence of the clinical benefits of Ayahuasca are limited, but advocates say that it has become increasingly popular as a tool to treat post traumatic stress disorder, depression and addiction. (I reckon it can cause post traumatic stress, depression and addiction, but I won't give my opinion. Good reporters stay impartial. That's me done for.) Funny how the ancient and modern world give you drugs, to get you off drugs. Just depends on which are legal at the time in which country.

So, the whole idea is for people to 'explore' their personal development through the introspective nature of the 'hallucinogenic experience'. (What the hell is wrong with work, sport, healthy living, introspection and studying?) Still, I won't give my opinion, rather, let me just describe to you what Cathy and I witnessed.

Enter, stage left, the three Cuy (guinea pigs) of the story. Sorry, the three adults searching for personal enlightenment. That's a bit harsh actually, because I like all three of them, a lot. Remy Weslowski is a Polish/English firework, I think. She is blonde, pretty, small and insane. She is the first player in this Ayahuasca trial and maybe not a good test subject. I suspect that kilos and kilos of any drug, couldn't make Remy more unhinged than she was already. She was 25 but looked 11, never stopped talking, and at extremely high speed. The rare occasions she was not talking, she was laughing hysterically. In fact, she laughed hysterically at everything, but not annoyingly, more endearingly. But I didn't live with her. Remy was obviously well educated and from a well-to-do family (as they say, in good old Blighty), but could be as coarse as hell, and as motivated as any individual can be.

Remy decided to travel around South America, on her own, with a rucksack bigger than her, which is not difficult when you are five foot two, or three, on a good day, at altitude. In America, that is small size. Although she is as mad as a box of piranhas, she has drive, which I respect in any human. Not that they need my respect. I don't want to sound arrogant. I just love people with get up and go, who don't listen to the negativists. (New word, I better look it up.) This little story will give you some idea of her pluck - as they say in good old South Africa, this time. While lugging her unfeasibly large load (I am not talking about your bum, Remy, although we did discuss a workout routine), through South America, Remy met an Australian biker called Anthony. After riding pillion with him for a month, (no rude comments please, we are all adults here), she decided, as you do, to buy a motorbike in a foreign country and teach herself how to ride. She bought a Yamaha 250. On the wrong side of the road for an English girl, which isn't really relevant, because she didn't ride in the UK either. That went well.

She got taken out by a taxi, or a bus, or something, at a crossroads, after a week's riding, and ended up in hospital for a long stretch. Did that stop her. No! For two months she zoomed around Ecuador and Peru. Remy is a very difficult person to ignore, or dislike, for both men and women. It is not because she is small, blonde and pretty; well, yes it is, but she has a huge heart and a contagious enthusiasm that is top drawer. She has 'spark', an appropriate motorcyclist comment. After surviving the roads, and Ayahuasca, (we will get to that) she returned to the UK and became a biker chick, buying a Yamaha 600. We went to a bike show together in the UK, a few years later, but my Tenere broke down on the way, so we didn't really go together. Cathy and I limped home, embarrassed.

Anthony, the Aussie biker who Remy linked up with, was doing the 'trip of a lifetime', riding through South America for five months on his Honda XR 600. I made that bit up. No idea what bike it was. A Kawasaki KLR 600, I think. Sorry Anthony. Anthony, not Tony, was tall, well built, with a hairstyle, rare amongst bikers. Take Elvis hair, in his prime, double the volume and sheen. He had the beard though, the rite of passage for every backpacker, just like braids for the girls. Oh, and barefoot. That wouldn't go down well in Waitrose, in the salad aisle, but apparently OK if overseas. The beard thing when travelling, doesn't really have the same impact now, as it is the fashion to have a beard, even for women. So now, you have to either grow a beard, on a beard, at least three foot long, or be clean shaven, to be different. Anthony went for the beard, but manicured; good curveball. He was very neat. He was very keen on telling people, within thirty seconds of meeting them, that he was a male model. There is no doubt that he spent more time in the mirror in one day than I had spent in my lifetime. Still, he looked the part, whereas I looked like an old, feral loon, who had just stepped off a desert island, after years alone. He was a really good guy, and had us in stitches because he was one of these:

Me: "I have travelled through 134 countries."

Anthony: "I have travelled through 400 countries, naked, pulling a chain, balancing a frisbee on my head."

If you had broken your arm, he had broken his in nineteen places; falling out of a plane, and then landing on a bus, that went off a bridge. He landed in the river and was attacked by a crocodile. He killed the crocodile with his belt buckle and made himself a hat from the skin, and a handbag for his ex-girlfriend.

Anthony and Remy

If you could bench press a hundred and twenty kilos, he could do three thousand, with his thumb.

Despite that, Anthony was a kind-hearted and gentle man. Thumbs up.

The third cast member in this scenario was Rick, a thirty-year-old Canadian, covered in tattoos. He looked like he had been in prison for ten years for murder. I never asked. Joke. He was wiry as hell, with a skinhead, soft spoken, a direct, look-you-in-the-eye dude. I liked him a lot, and he knew a lot. Fun to hang out with. Sadly, soon after the Ayahuasca fiasco, Rick heard that his grandmother was critically ill. He headed back to Canada on the next flight. I wish him the best. A man with a lot of knowledge and humble as hell.

The setting was a courtyard in our grotty hotel. We had a concrete floor, a banana bed, one curtain, an outside toilet, and once again, free fleas and bedbugs. $5, sorted. We didn't want to spend too much time in our room, and after the Biblical hailstorm had subsided, we hung out with the motley crew, who were frying sausages on a makeshift barbecue on the floor. We learnt that the three of them were preparing for an Ayahuasca experience that very evening and were going through a cleansing ritual. I asked if we could come along and witness.

"Not far to go, they are coming here," Remy answered.

I thought that was a bit strange. A spiritual cleansing in a backpacker backyard. Not too conducive to reaching spiritual plains, or planes, never before reached. I kept quiet. They said we could come. I wish we hadn't. It was an off-putting, verging on repulsive experience. It wasn't the three amigos' fault, although they definitely would not have liked their parents to be there. It was the sickening con artists that turned up that made my blood boil. Firstly, a hippie American lady of about sixty, with dirty hair and nails, turned up with an appropriately dressed, and predictably dressed, shaman. He had the robes and the beads and the long, straight, luxuriant hair. He had perfected the quizzical, deep look, leaning his head sideways and looking to the heavens, furrowing his brow, as if in deep consultation with nature and the spirits. He wanted the audience to hang on his every word. Personally, I had seen it all before, when Swazis in the villages, quickly hide their mobile phones and briefcases, change into skins, hiding their Nike trainers. Tourists were coming through, and the tourists had to believe, by pure luck, that they had stumbled upon a traditional Swazi wedding. This was the same. Cheap theatre. Quick bit of acting, dancing and wailing, some cash, off go the tourists happy, back to normal life. Simples.

The American actress-con-woman spoke absolute spiritual mumbo jumbo, otherwise known as bollocks, for a good fifteen minutes. Her dressed-up sidekick, the actor, sorry, shaman, nodded at appropriate times, to add solemnity to the proceedings. He sat, cross-legged in the 'serene Indian in harmony' position. He tried his best to act like a shaman, but I was watching him intently. It was fascinating. Sometimes his guard slipped and you could actually see him getting distracted. He was definitely thinking about his next woodwork or carpentry project; on the building site he was returning to on Monday. Quick bit of bonus shaman money from the weekend, that's all he was worried about.

Nothing spiritual here. At times I saw a flicker of embarrassment on his face, as his partner-in-con spewed more 'balancing the system', 'harmonising the body' tripe. The next stage was to cleanse the body of its toxins and bad energy, in preparation for ingesting the Ayahuasca, in the jungle, the next night. This involved Remy, Rick, Anthony and a late entrant, Rafael, who was from Argentina and travelling on a 310 BMW. He reminded me of Franco, the Gigolo off a cliff. He also had short legs. I gave the con-woman and the con-shaman the evil eye throughout, making them uncomfortable, but making my ethical position clear. I wanted them to know that their transparency didn't fool me. I hate bullshit dressed as spirituality, or worse, dressed as religion. It is called sacrilege, a violation of the true sacred things in this world.

The victims had to ingest a 'spiritual solution' that would purge their negativity. They were made to drink what I knew was salt water, mixed with a spoon of sugar, and a dissolvable vitamin effervescent tablet, readily available in Boots the Chemist, in your local high street. How do I know this. I had inside information, from a turncoat, guilt-ridden shaman (an ashamed shaman), from Milton Keynes. If you have ever been dumped by a wave, in the sea, and have swallowed water, you know it can make you feel sick. They were made, wrong word, chose, to drink six litres of this each, in under two hours. Of course it is going to clear out your system. Lunacy! The next hour of our lives were wasted, watching the three of them rushing to the toilet every ten minutes, either to vomit or violently release their bowels. Backpacker toilets are not the most soundproof. It was not a very elegant or civilised way to behave and I couldn't help feeling angry with the whole bunch of them. The two shamans, because they were con artists, and my three friends for lowering themselves to this. Maybe that's a bit harsh, but it was not pleasant to witness. More importantly, I was genuinely worried about them, for the night to come, where they would head into the jungle, for the real Ayahuasca ceremony.

Let's imagine this is the plan for your 18-year-old son or daughter; go to a foreign country, take some super strong drugs, that you have no clue of the effects. Then go into the jungle with a bunch of strangers, in a foreign country, for the night. What could possibly go wrong? Actually a lot. Sadly, not only have people gone missing in the jungles of Colombia and Peru after an Ayahuasca ceremony, people have died from a reaction to the drug. There is also no doubt that people of a fragile mind, or delicate disposition, are at a high risk of going bonkers. (Technical term.) The drug made headlines last year when a British coroner confirmed that Henry Miller, a 19-year-old from Bristol, had died from taking a dose, during a shamanic ceremony. The coroner urged the Foreign Office to provide a standard message, warning tourists. Miller's story may serve as a cautionary tale to any of you considering this 'trip'.

Miller had attended one ceremony where he drank three cups of yage, but told his family he felt nothing. Two days later, he attended another ceremony, but rapidly fell ill. He was carried by two teenage tribesmen to a local clinic. He died on route. The tribe that administered the Ayahuasca apologised and levied a punishment of nettle-whipping for the shaman and some of his family.

OK. Huge questions remained in my head, especially after what we had witnessed. I was worried for our friends. Cathy kept council as usual, but I could tell she was super uncomfortable. We had seen the total, unregulated trade in the drug, answering to no formal authority. I have seen phone numbers of shamans passed between travellers, left on hostel notice boards, plastered on street walls. A proliferation of websites have sprung up, promising you enlightenment, and escape from the drudgery of life. In many hostels, the staff help travellers to arrange their trips into the jungle, some lasting several days and costing hundreds of dollars. Online, people share their experiences and recommendations on forums such as Lonely Planet.

I met another shaman called Victor. He administers Ayahuasca, and claims it helps with asthma, leukemia and cures many mental illnesses. This, I cannot stomach. Giving people with terminal cancer, false hope. Others may argue that it is still hope. It's a murky subject with many points of view and opinions. I have mine. I am against it. But it is not part of my cultural heritage either. Victor said, "Ayahuasca is part of my ancestral heritage and deserves to be shared with the world."

In my cynical head, this translates to: "Tourist dollars deserve to be shared with me".

"It is precious and curative," he said, dressed in a colourful poncho type overall, with a necklace fashioned from Caiman teeth.

"It taught us to defend our land and protect it (how exactly, I was thinking) and, of course, we are open to other people learning about its spiritual and health-giving properties. I want people to appreciate it,"

Victor concluded solemnly.

'I am sure you do, and gullible people pay through the nose for it,' I didn't say. Relations between South America's indigenous tribes and Western visitors have been tested in recent months (as I write this in 2021). In April, a Canadian tourist, high on Ayahuasca, killed a faith healer in Peru and was lynched by villagers in response. Forty-one-year-old Sebastian Woodroffe inexplicably killed an eighty-one-year-old indigenous medicine woman, Olivia Orevalo. A minute and a half long, a mobile phone recording of the lynching was posted on Facebook. It showed two men dragging Woodroffe by a noose around his neck as others looked on. His body was later found buried nearby. Evidence came out that Woodroffe was extremely unstable, and was taking prescription, anti-psychotic drugs and tablets for depression. Along with Ayahuasca.

Matthew Dawson-Clarke had been working on a luxury yacht charting the waters of the Mediterranean and the Caribbean. He had saved some money and flew to Peru and then travelled to Iquitos, a centre for Ayahuasca ceremonies. The man from Auckland went looking for spiritual and personal growth. He would never come home. Matthew's mother heard of his fate, by phone, late on a Sunday night. It was an emotionless voice on the other end.

"I got this really heavy-accented woman that came through, saying, 'Is that Matthew's mother?' She said to me, simply, 'Your son is dead. Sorry for your loss.' My life stopped that day, forever."

After taking Ayahuasca, Matthew went into cardiac arrest within fifteen minutes. He was given CPR, but it didn't work and he was deep in the rainforest. He had no chance. You may think that I am being a bit dramatic. Of course; not everybody dies from Ayahuasca. Many do, however, get sexually molested and raped. There are many reports, often multiple ones, about particular shamans and their sexual offences, but they are all still working.

They have the perfect excuse, "She was unwell before she came to me, and anyway, she was on Ayahuasca. She imagined it."

Pretty difficult to disprove. So, if you don't die from an overdose, get murdered, raped, molested or robbed, it is safe. Oh! Apart from the side-effects; tremors, nausea, vomiting, diarrhea, hypothermia, sweating, motor function impairment and muscle spasms. Those are just the physical effects. I would be lying if I said I wasn't worried about

Remy, Rick, and Anthony, and we were both mightily relieved when they returned from their jungle ceremony. They looked bedraggled, but otherwise unscathed, just a bit startled and tired. Remy on the other hand was still stark raving mad, dancing around in a canary yellow T Shirt, bike boots, and not much else. Hadn't really affected her then.

The startlingly obvious thing that became clear over the next few days was that none of them were enthusiastic about the ceremony. Remy said, rather weakly, that it 'helped her work out some issues from her past', but it sounded like she had read it in an article. No conviction. I think they all know that they had been conned by a fake shaman. We had heard that to become a respected traditional shaman, it takes twenty to thirty years of training. We also heard that foreigners were being trained to become shamans in a week, so they could lead a ceremony. Farcical. We all knew what the American woman was, with her dressed-up partner, but it was more comfortable leaving it unspoken. Especially as they had each shelled out $175 for a hangover, with zero enlightenment.

Cathy had no such etiquette about feelings. Whilst our three amigos were recovering in the courtyard, under the shade of a tree, their wallets slightly lighter, Cathy offered this, "I was down at the traditional herb market, in the Indian area, this morning. Opposite, there's a shop called Carmen that sells guinea pig and chicken. Anyway, they were selling Hiawatha for less than $2, even with instructions of what to do."

"Hiawatha?" I asked, thinking; if they are selling small North American Indian Heroes, in the market, I would know about it.

"The drug these guys took, Spencer." "Oh! Ayahuasca," I laughed.

"Exactly. High-a-wa-tha... or however it's pronounced. They could have saved $173 each," Cathy said, making herself ever more popular.

None of the shadow dwellers had any energy. They just shook their heads weakly. I am totally aware that because the focus of this story was Ayahuasca, my depiction of the three amigos' characters may have suffered. They were all great people, interesting, intelligent and informed. The focus on their Ayahuasca ceremony may have shed them in a bad light. It shouldn't, they had their reasons. We are all different.

It was time for us to jump on the Tenere and get the hell out of Dodge. Cultural events awaited us throughout Peru. Plus, we needed our particular buzz-tough roads, nature and motorcycle therapy. As usual, we were not disappointed by any of the three.

All was superb, until we crashed in the Bolivian salt flats.

Tidy luggage, tidy mind. Twelve years, 170,000 km, same Army sausage bag

Volcanoes constantly loom over your progress, as South America is part of the 'Ring of Fire', which runs down the west of South America and has 1000+ volcanoes. Above: view of Osorno Volcano, Chile, from Condor Man and the Smoked Trout's carpark. Below: baby volcano in Peru

Adventurer and camerawoman, Cathy Nel. Above: packing up the gear before a cloudburst in Colombia. Below: filming wildlife in Amazon hideaway, Brazil

6.00am Brazil: Ready for another day, and toilet break before entering the Amazon

The expedition so far scrawled on my pannier

Chapter Six
Surviving the Salar

The Salar de Uyuni, in south-western Bolivia, near the crest of the Andes, is the world's highest, largest and most beautiful salt flat. At 3656 metres and spanning more than 10,800 square kilometres, it is a magical place, another planet; a Mecca for adventure motorcyclists, and the world traveller in general

But I need to interrupt this introduction, because by pure coincidence, as I was writing these first few sentences of the chapter in June 2019, I received a phone call, here in Mexico, from my father. He told me that two students from our tiny village in Kent, UK, had just died on the Salar de Uyuni salt flats. According to *The Independent* newspaper,

> 'A pair of British teenagers have been killed after their car flipped, while exploring the world's largest salt flats, in Bolivia. Freddie McLennan and Joe Atkins, both nineteen, died in the crash on Saturday night, while a third British man was taken to hospital with serious injuries. The twenty-two-year-old Bolivian driver, named locally as Alberto Barco, also died. McLennan and Atkins were both former students of the five-hundred-year-old Cranbrook School, in Kent, and had been travelling after completing their A' Levels. It is believed the car flipped over a number of times. Unconfirmed reports state that the driver was speeding and under the influence of alcohol.'

The experience of driving on the Salar is always likened to visiting another planet, especially when it rains and the salt pan becomes a huge, drivable mirror. It is a special experience, no doubt, but there is a very real, dangerous, and often tragic side to these tour expeditions.

Travel publisher Lonely Planet warns: 'Travellers should take extreme care in choosing a tour operator, when visiting the salt flats. Fatal accidents are unfortunately not rare."

That is a serious understatement, and also does not take into consideration people in private or hire cars, and motorcycles. The blame cannot be thrown only at tour drivers. It is a complicated situation on the Salar, and a grave one. (Excuse the weak pun.) Let me quote a few more headlines, the first from Reuters:

> 'Two Israeli tourists were killed and another sustained serious head injuries, when the jeep they were travelling in, overturned on the Bolivian salt flats. The Bolivian driver was also killed.'

Another:

> 'Five tourists were killed at Bolivia's famous salt flats, after the vehicle they were in overturned. Three Belgians, one Italian and a Peruvian died. Two injured, were transported to hospital. Police Commander Col Rodolfo Salazar, told the Associated Press, that the driver lost control due to excessive speed, and was not a legitimate guide.'

One more:

> 'Uyuni; Bus flips on Salar. Two French and a Belgian killed. The victims were identified as Marie Soulif, 58 and Marcelle Gilberte, 48, and Ben Bollon, 28, of Belgium.'

There is no beating around the bush (not that there are any on the salt flats), now that I have personally witnessed the Salar chaos. The drivers are often drunk, or high, and speeding. Many vehicles have seat belts removed, to fit more people and to look 'adventure-like', have bald tyres, tired and untrained drivers, no medical supplies, no long-range radios, and no protocol for emergencies. A lot of the drivers keep themselves going by chewing coca leaves, which cannot be good in the longrun, when drivers have been chemically stimulating themselves, to stay awake for days.

They are not the only culprits. The central problem lies in the fact that the Salar is treated as one huge playground for cars, motorcycles and bicycles. All rules are taken away. There are no roads, there are no signs, no traffic lights, no speed limits and no police to enforce these non-existent rules. Just a flat, 10,000 square kilometre race track. Added to that, a lot of people succumb to the freedom and desolation, and decide to ride around naked, at high speed. The salt is an unforgiving, hard as concrete, abrasive surface, and I know of at least two bikers who have had extensive plastic surgery. By all means get naked, and film it, if you so desire, but do not do it on a motorcycle.

Two more absurd rituals have sprung up amongst bikers. I urge you not to follow suit. The first is to try and ride for one minute, with your eyes closed. The second is to try and break your top speed. Need I say more? Both recipes for disaster. Please guys, the Salar is a once-in-a-lifetime experience, do not make it your last one.

In case my annoying preaching has not hit a chord, here is a letter I received, during my research. The writer is a nineteen-year-old French girl, who wants to stay anonymous. Here is the letter, unedited:

'Sorry to disturb you, but I read your article in a travel magazine, about the Salar de Uyuni. I wanted to thank you for pointing out the dangers of travelling in the Salar, independently and unprepared. But more I want to thank you for pointing out the care needed, when picking out tour companies, in any country. I wanted to tell you our story.

'We started our Salar de Uyuni trip on Sunday 13th July, at sunrise, a day tour on the salt flats, and then to the train cemetery. Our driver was late and seemed tired, or worse. When we were halfway to the Incahuasu Island, we were overtaken by a jeep, travelling at high speed. There was a driver in the front, and six tourists in the rear, crammed in, with rucksacks, gas cylinders, stoves, bags of food, and large bottles of water, loaded on the roof rack above them. Just like our jeep. They suddenly turned, for no obvious reason, lost control, and started skidding sideways, all about thirty metres from us. The jeep was top heavy and flipped, over and over again.

'Bags and food and bodies were flying everywhere and our driver had to slam on brakes too. We all watched in slow motion. Of course, we were the first at the scene. As we jumped out of our jeep, we saw a man climbing out of their overturned and crumpled jeep. His whole head was red, from a large gash above his ear, and he was limping,

but he seemed reasonably OK. Then we turned around and there were bodies everywhere, people wailing everywhere. My partner and I went to the nearest person, who seemed critical. It was the driver, who at that time had a weak pulse. My partner gave him breath of life and I did the compression on his chest. He had a very large open wound on his head and he was dying. We continued but we could not keep him alive. He died within five minutes of our arrival. Another two, we found dead in the back of the jeep, a Belgian man and French woman. It was obvious they had died on impact. So, there were four alive, but in a bad way. We looked after a Belgian girl who had severe facial lacerations and extensive injuries to her knee and hands. She was twenty seven and married to the dead Belgian in the jeep. The scene was hell, luckily enough, other jeeps stopped and there were two Uruguayan doctors who more or less, took control of the situation. There was no assistance from the Bolivian drivers or guides.

'None of the jeeps that stopped had a radio transmitter or satnav phone to make contact with the emergency services. Luckily a German traveler had a sat phone. Three hours passed and no ambulance came. The doctors decided that we had to get the four survivors to hospital, and we assisted in loading them. This was the worst part, as they were in such pain. One of the French women died on route to hospital. She probably had internal injuries, and time killed her. Not receiving any pain relief over this long time frame made it a more painful death than you can imagine. We will never forget that day. Luckily the Japanese and German guys survived, just. The Belgian girl was transferred to La Paz, and will most likely undergo reconstructive surgery, for life. She did not have much face left.

'We are so, so angry and upset about the chain of events, and felt strongly we wanted to highlight it to you. First, all jeeps had no seat belts. Secondly we were going fast, and they overtook. I was told that the driver was a mechanic and not a tour guide. He had been told three or four times to slow down, but apparently took it as a joke and started zig zagging. Thirdly no guide had a radio, satnav, basic first aid kit, blanket, nothing. Keep in mind that thirteen people have died in May; this leads to a death toll of seventeen in two months. This must not continue. Thank you. Ride safe.'

Wow! What a sobering and hardcore letter. It took me a long time to respond.

In any country, when tourists are involved (having the time of their lives), a disaster will inevitably become worldwide news. I agree totally that something has to be done about the tourist safety issue. But there are also the unreported local people that die on the Salar, trying to cross it in a three-hundred-year-old unroadworthy car, or by bicycle, or on foot, badly prepared for the incessant sun and its reflection off the bright white, unforgiving salt. Although it is at high altitude, the Salar can become an oven, as Cathy and I were to find out. Water, and lots of it, is vital. Without it, you are doomed within three days.

So now that I have cheered you all up, and put you off ever going anywhere near the Salar de Uyuni salt flats, let me try and explain why so many people want to visit this spellbinding place, one of the most incredible places on the planet, in my opinion.

All bikers, and many other people in the world will have heard of the Bonneville Salt Flats, in Tooele County, in north-western Utah. These salt flats are 19 kilometres long and 8 kilometres wide, creating an area of 40 square kilometres. Motor car racing has taken place at the salt flats since 1914 and there are five major land speed events that take place at Bonneville, including cars, trucks, and motorcycles. Despite its fame in 'vehicle event' terms, in geographical terms the Bonneville salt flat is just a baby. The Salar de Uyuni is a staggering 100 times bigger than Bonneville, covering 10,582 square kilometres and stretching 130 kilometres across. Following rain, a thin layer of totally calm water sits on top of the salt and transforms the flat into the world's largest mirror. This phenomenon itself is worth travelling across the world to see. That is a lot of salt to cover with water; 10 billion tonnes, to be exact, supplying 70 percent of the world's salt. Of course we ate some, with our sardine sandwiches. Check your table salt now, it could be from Bolivia. Some places defy description, that is why I have included multiple photos from the Salar. But I will still try and describe the experience, and the calamity it nearly was for us too.

The Salar was formed as a result of transformations between several prehistoric lakes that existed around 40,000 years ago, but all have now evaporated. It is now covered in a layer of salt a few metres deep. The average elevation over the entire salt flat changes by less than a metre. It is the flattest place on earth.

Cathy and I were blown away by the spectacle (not by the wind, because the Salar is also one of the stillest places on earth), as we made our way to one of the two islands that exist on the Salar. These are remnants of volcanoes and can be seen, jutting out of the landscape, hours before you reach them. It seems strange calling them islands, when there is no water in sight; islands in a salt sea. The main island, Incahuasi, stands proudly for all to see from far around, and we reached it after several hours of awe and wonder at the beautiful hexagonal shapes created by the salt. It was pristine. The island is dominated by giant cacti, and has colonies of viscachas; rock rabbits with large, silly ears, sprinting around.

We found a cave, and camped in it, building a fire to keep warm from the chilly desert night. The best wake up I ever had, staring out at the empty Salar. Sitting up in our cave, looking out of the rock crescent exit, was like being in a space ship, looking down on a planet that you had just arrived at. One giant leap… for Swazi kind.

Yes, the Salar is officially a desert, but like most deserts, what a lively one it is. We saw flocks of stunning pink flamingos, on absurdly blue lakes. Every November, the Salar de Uyuni is the breeding ground for three South American species of flamingo, feeding on the abundant brine shrimps; the Chilean, Andean and rare James flamingos, named after me - not. If you are a bird loon, the Salar is up there as one of the top locations for twitchers. About 80 species of bird are present including the horned coot, Andean goose and Andean Hillstar (cool name). There are also Andean foxes running around.

All these animals and this whole natural wonder is in danger. Why? Salt, of course. Bolivia denies that they are mining to the extreme, but because we rode off the designated route, we came across hundreds of massive trucks, ripping the Salar to pieces. This is not the only problem. The Salar also contains large amounts of sodium, potassium, lithium and magnesium, as well as borax.

With an estimated 9,000,000 tonnes, Bolivia has 17 percent of the world's lithium resources. Lithium is vital in rechargeable batteries for mobile phones, laptops, digital cameras, electric vehicles, pacemakers, toys and clocks. It is also used in vaping devices, E-bikes, electric toothbrushes, tools, hover boards, scooters, and for solar power backup storage. Lithium and its compounds have several industrial applications too; including heat resistant glass and ceramics, lithium grease lubricants, flux additives for iron, steel and aluminium production.

As you can see from the list of uses, lithium is fairly important, and even more so now, in the cyber era. Bolivia officially states that 'no serious mining is at present on this site'. Bulldust. We have seen it. American and Chinese trucks, hundreds of them, creating a huge scar, that increases in size, exponentially, daily. The Bolivian government has been accused of ransacking the country's vast lithium reserves, concentrated in areas inhabited by indigenous Aymara people. The Altiplano Puna plateau is home to the 'Lithium triangle', salt flats that stretch across Chile, Argentina and Bolivia, and hold over 75 percent of the world's supply of lithium.

After a night in our cave, the evening spent chatting with long-eared rabbits about the fate of the Salar, the fate of the indigenous, and indeed the fate of the long-eared rabbit, we rode around to the other side of the island. There was a group of Bolivian men, sitting round a small shop, drinking coffee and chewing coca leaves, a double-strength, wake-up remedy, whilst warming themselves up around a small log fire on the ground, as the mist rose off the Salar. Despite being a massive tourist magnet, I respect the fact that the Salar has very few facilities. They have two smelly Salt Hotels, completely built out of... you guessed it, salt blocks. They should be avoided, as they never solved their sewerage disposal problems, and you will gag if you book in there. It is just not worth it for the novelty of sleeping in a salt-made building. To be honest the hotel just looks like dirty snow.

The island has toilets, a little restaurant serving llama stew, and a shop, the size of two telephone boxes. Love it. Hope it stays that way. Not a lot of amenities for 12,000 square kilometres. We bought four litres of water and some chocolate and it was time to head west, to the edge of the Salar. Don't go off the designated route! Wrong decision number one. We did.

Imagine the Salar as the shape of a pancake, which it is. If you cut it from north to south, and from east to west, thereby creating four equal slices of pancake; that is the extent of the road network. It is easy to intentionally stray from the two tracks. The road, needless to say, is not a road. It is just tyre prints, lightly obvious, in the salt, breaking up the perfect hexagons. At times, it is just a hint of where to go, rather than a road.

Also there is no perspective in the Salar, and it plays tricks with your mind. Because there are no landmarks on the salt; no trees, no buildings, no hills, no people, nothing; it is impossible to judge distance. Hence, the famous photos people put up of themselves, standing on a giant Mars Bar, or holding their motorcycle, or boyfriend, in the palm of their hand. (Nothing new with the last one.) The only visuals are the two islands in the center of the salt pan, and another row of mountains and a volcano, on the northern periphery of the Salar. I thought these would provide enough visual orientation for us to ride off the main tracks, get some solitary time and footage, and presto, head back.

We drove about 30 kilometres north west, away from the main thoroughfare. We quickly collected brilliant footage and photos for the TV series and book, in pristine salt, and perfect, blue sky conditions. You will be surprised to hear that the Salar only goes to 21 degrees. That fools you. It feels much hotter. The problem is the constant reflection off the salt and the absence of shade. We were both as brown as chestnuts within two hours. I even burnt my face so badly through the helmet (looking like a reverse panda), that three days later, I peeled off an entire layer of my face. And I am from Africa. The sun was relentless, and four litres of water was not a lot. It was time to head back to the island. Turn the bike, point it towards the volcano in the distance, and ride. Simples. Not quite.

We were cruising along merrily, and had a catastrophic blow out. I do not use the word catastrophic, lightly. We were doing about eighty kilometres an hour, and the inner tube decided to blow, so violently, that it actually took the tyre off the rim, and must have been heard by half of Bolivia. Now, I have been riding for nearly fifty years and I have never heard of a whole tyre coming off the rim. Unless you ride it for many kilometres on a flat tyre. Let me tell you, it was a shock, especially when you are humming 'Stir it up' by Bob Marley inside your head, and feeling super relaxed.

There was a massive bang, that nearly took my wig off, followed by a total loss of control. When I say that, I am not exaggerating. My top bike skills kicked in, and I just let the bike go. It's not as though we were going to hit anything, or anybody. But, to my surprise, the bike started snaking more and more, and I was getting seriously worried. I was losing control, and if we came off now, at sixty or seventy, onto concrete like salt, we would be in serious trouble. I decided to put a bit of back brake. It helped a bit, and we started straightening up. Just as I thought we had it sorted, we hit a small mound of salt, the bike flipped sideways, and I jammed my left bike boot heel into the ground, and pushed off, to keep us upright. It worked, but jarred my leg, straight through to my hip, and I knew that I had an injury. I heard Cathy make a pained, grunting noise at the same time, and knew she had felt the shock, through her back. I struggled to keep the bike straight, the tyre sliding all over the show. Eventually, after a serious fight, I brought the bike under control. I was impressed with myself, and just when I thought I was a superhero (but with heart in my mouth), and had diverted an imminent prang, with broken bone consequences, I got a slap on the back of my helmet:

"When the hell are we going to stop?"

Jesus, woman, have some respect for the rider's skills.

We eventually came to a halt, without coming off, but only because I was ordered to. Then we fell, sideways, slowly. My legs gave in, and turned to quivering twigs. I could not hold the bike up. It was nerves, not fatigue. We crumpled onto the Salar. Normally we laugh, when we have a minor tumble but, on this occasion, I think we both knew how close we had just come to disaster. Not death on impact, but a much slower one. Lying there, injured, with no water, and no shade. You are in peril. Many don't realise the hazards of exposure to the sun, regardless of the temperature. In the modern world (or whatever the politically correct term is), for most of our lives, we avoid direct sunlight for long periods of time, without realising it. We go from a shaded house, or verandah, to an air-conditioned car, walk down the shaded side of the street, into a climate-controlled office. The brief time we choose to be in direct sun, we are incredibly prepared. We have sunglasses, caps, hats, umbrellas, mini fans, little battery-face fans, light clothing, sunblock, timed periods of tanning when on holiday, strategically placed showers, with many iced drinks involved. Most hot-climate cultures have a siesta period, where they all escape from the sun.

We did not have those choices. We were still in a very serious position. Cathy quickly pointed out that we had lost one of the bottles of water during our swerving, and that it was hot, and there was nobody around. I love positivity. All due respect, we have been travelling together so long, that we just kick in to our respective, agreed roles. Cathy decided that we were not going anywhere, so set up the tent. I was not sure if that was good survival skills, or just showing her confidence in my tyre-changing skills. It was a perfect survival decision, of course. I wrapped a white T-shirt around my head, to reflect some of the sun, and to keep the sweat out of my eyes, put on my one dollar, fake, 'Raybin' sunglasses, and set to work.

There were thin metal strands poking through the wall of the tyre, which needed to be fixed. I clipped them all with some pliers, pushed them back in, as best as I could, and then covered the area with three layers of duct tape, to avoid another puncturing. The tube had to be checked. That was not difficult: it had a livid tear, about four centimetres long; obviously where it had dragged, after the blow out. It is possible to fix those, by stitching the tear with fishing line, or a similar strong twine, and then patching over it.

Mr. Organised had a spare. All went well. I had the new tube fitted, in the blink of a desert lizard's eye. No, I didn't. It was an absolute nightmare. I did not want to pinch the new tube. That would add other issues, which we did not need. The sweat was pouring into my eyes, from my salt-encrusted face, stinging so much, that it was hard to see. The glare of the ground made my eyes water even more. I was staggering around, like an idiot, twisting the tube, not lining up the valve, etc. All the things a beginner struggles with. It was adrenaline, working negatively. I needed to chill a bit. I had to follow my own maxim, that had got me around Africa:

"Day by day, border by border, nothing lasts forever."

I burnt this into my head, and even said it on camera, to force myself to relax. I went to the tent, where Cathy was lying on the ground mat, spread-eagled, helmet still on.

"Lie on the salt, it's incredibly cool."

I did, and she was right. After a sip of water and a bit more body cooling, I wiped my eyes clean of sand, sweat and salt. I had gathered my thoughts, and was no longer a headless Salar goose. My hip was aching, but that was for another day. I ventured back out, to finish the repair in the glare. Never work on mechanical issues when angry or frustrated. You will make errors, and probably scrape knuckles. After more tussling, I nailed it. But the compressor that connects handily to my battery, decided to expire. I took it apart and put it back together, three times. I felt like crying, but that's not manly. The fourth time, I took it apart quickly, and threw it on the salt, smashing it. Lost my cool. Again. (I did pick it up. Only leave tyre prints and footprints, people.) I should have changed the compressor in 2011. Oh well, retrospect.

After much discussion (shouting at each other about dying), and cooking ourselves slowly in the tent, over six hours passed, without even a sniff of a vehicle on the horizon. There were none coming this way and we knew it. We had water for the night, but tomorrow would be grim. After soft-spoken deliberation, no swear words involved, Cathy decided that we should ride out of there, on the flat tyre, luggageless, in the direction of the main island, with Indiana Jones music playing. I disagreed totally with her survival plan: I wanted ACDC. I am being flippant, because it is the way I cope. We were in a serious situation. We could never walk forty kilometres or so, in this terrain, with a few sips of water, and injuries.

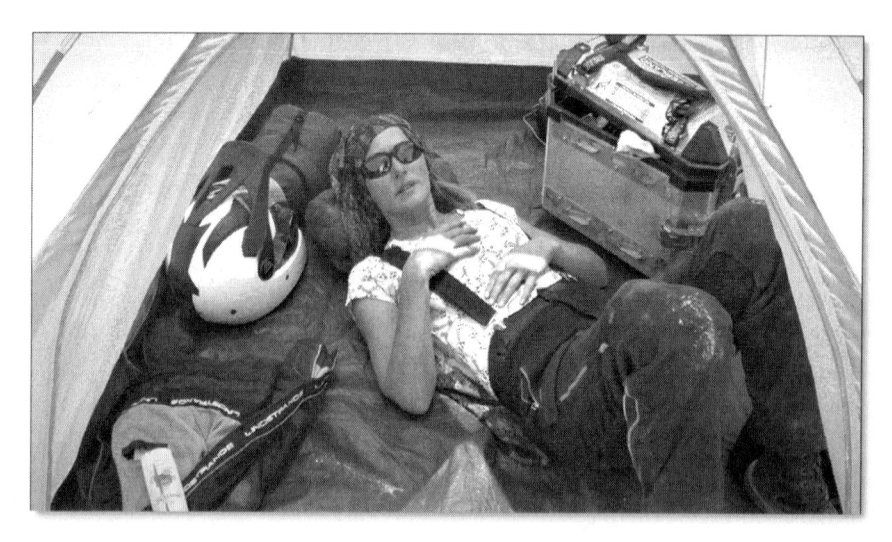

We had no choice. We jettisoned everything, to try and lighten the load on the flat tyre; our panniers, our clothes, our cameras, our sleeping bags, rolling mats, blow-up Queen-size mattress (OK, we didn't have one of those), everything, except our Yamaha T-shirts and sweat shirts, which I had a use for; I stuffed the flat tyre with as many clothes that I could, to try and give it a modicum of rigidity. I made a pile of all the possessions we owned, covered it all with our open tent, and we made our wobbly wheel way towards the island of hope.

It was a torturously slow, but at the same time, amazing journey. Peaceful beyond belief. Another fascinating feature of the Salar is that sound does not travel. There is nothing for sound to bounce off, no obstacles, and it quickly disappears. The only sound was the light reverberation in our helmets, as we crossed the hexagonal salt shapes. It was almost hypnotic, and the lack of visual stimulation, made the brain act weird. Well, it did mine. I had to concentrate, and my eyes were straining against the glare, despite my wonderful Fox goggles. (Go to my website, for special deals on Fox clothing, boots etc... just joking.)

We rode for four hours at walking speeds, and slower, my arms shaking from the instability of the bike, and my wrist tendons burning. It was getting bad, but I did not want to complain. Eventually the island became a reality, not a never-ending illusion in the distance, staying the same size, forever.

Not like when I did a poo, a few hours earlier. I had no choice but to obey nature, but as we travelled away from the scene of the crime, I could still see my poo, a long way off, in this pristine, totally flat landscape, in my rear view mirror. It haunted me, that a couple from Manchester might come here, for their wedding, saved up for a lifetime trip, and come across my Swazi poo. Not acceptable. I had no choice but to turn back, scrape a layer of coarse salt from the Salar, and cover the offending ejection. Cathy laughed, but approved of my thoughtfulness.

Inevitably, it started to get dark as the Salar gets, which is not a lot. The huge blue, night sky, with light wispy stars, and spotlessly clean air, acts like a huge nightlight. The wind-battered flags, planted at Incahuasi island, by various nationalities, started to take form, and we could make out a few people, amongst the cactus fields on the island slopes. It was a total relief to weave up to the island, our single wheel track snaking off behind us into the desert. To say it was a total relief, really is the understatement of the century. If we had come off the motorbike at eighty kilometres an hour when we first had the blowout, we would be dead. If we had been going slightly slower, we would have crashed, been badly injured, and then died. If we had been mildly injured we would have lasted a few days, and then we would have been dead. We were both shattered from our day's activities, more mentally, I suspect, and managed to scrounge a concrete bench, outside the shop to sleep on. All good. Tomorrow is another day.

The next day was action stations. We knew from experience that there would not be many people stealing our things, as there were not any people, but no point in tempting fate, and the next morning, before sunrise, I headed out with three jolly Bolivian guides in their truck. I assumed that we could follow the bike track back to our things. No such luck. The entrance road to the island was a spaghetti network of tracks. There was no way of finding the bike tracks. I would just have to guess the direction. I guessed badly, and after a full day of searching, we came back empty-handed. The same on the second day. Nothing. Just try and digest that. I was with three guides, with more than forty years' experience on the Salar between them, and we couldn't find a tent, in nothingness. It truly is a vast place, and if the tent had been us, we would have passed our expiry date.

On the third morning, after persuading the guides to give it one more try, Cathy saw us off. As we were leaving, she pointed at the peak of a volcano, and said, "Two inches to the left of that peak, just go straight towards that point."

That is exactly what we did, and an hour later, we spotted a green hump in the distance. It was not a sick camel. It was our tent and gear. To this day I will never forget the guides' reaction. When we jumped out to load the stuff, they all leapt around, and we all hugged. Brilliant people. They never asked for a penny, for two and a half days' searching. Unbelievable, contrary to many of the horror stories I had heard about guides.

On the way back, I said to the search crew, "Keep a straight face when you see Cathy, and we will pretend we didn't find anything."

Did they hell. As soon as Cathy came out to meet us they all smiled and whooped and thumbs upped. She had somehow got the direction perfect. Why Cathy didn't say that on the first day, is a mystery. I think it was pure luck. Cathy disagrees. That night we were put up in the back of the restaurant and the next day drove to the town of Uyuni, with the three amigos, and fixed the puncture. It was time to leave the Salar and head to the sand dunes of Tupiza, and onwards to Chile. We said our goodbyes to the guides, with many hugs and hand slaps, and yes, I did insist on giving them expenses. Chile awaited, but not before one more visit; to the Dakar statue, made entirely of salt. The Paris Dakar Rally is another huge reason the Salar is an iconic place for adventure riders to visit, including me. Some of the most incredible photos of the Dakar racers, were taken by helicopters, high above the Salar.

As you will read in Chapter Eight, involving an eccentric Polish fellow, I have filmed the Dakar, and been obsessed with it, since childhood. The Dakar Rally ran from Paris, France, to Dakar in Senegal from 1979 to 2007, until it had to be moved, because of security issues. The race continued in South America until 2019, when it was moved to Saudi Arabia in 2020, because of money squabbles between the organisers and the four countries involved; Bolivia, Peru, Chile and Argentina.

The stage that roared through Uyuni was one of the most anticipated sections, because of its visual beauty and stunning TV scenes. It was also fast and demanding, because of altitude. It will forever remain one of the most iconic stages of the rally and the Bolivian government took full advantage of the media coverage to boost tourism in the country. The Dakar monument created in 2014 has become a symbol of the desert and a must see. We were seriously underwhelmed. It is small, and not particularly well made and, like the hotel, the only intriguing feature is that they are made of salt. The local communities seized the opportunity and sell souvenirs made of salt, in the shape of the Dakar symbols mainly. They are extremely tacky, but I love it. One ambitious fellow even sculpted a full size Dakar car from salt. An ambitious salt sculptor, but not the most talented, I must say.

I will never forget the Salar, and the kindness of its people. Spending time on another planet is seared in the memory forever. No wonder the Salar is a famous location for hundreds of sci fi films, including *Star Wars: The Last Jedi*. If you ever get a chance to visit this spectacular place, be wary; but be polite. Be tidy, be prepared; food, water and shadewise. Do not be tempted by challenges, and leave the speeding to the Dakar riders. Respect the distances. Oh, if you see any miners, be unfriendly. Having said that; who wants dinner without salt, or a mobile phone without a battery? That is the proverbial dilemma. Beautiful places often have other riches, that lead to their downfall.

As for Cathy and I, dunes beckoned us ahead, but unfortunately before we got to the border with Chile, I was destined to dislocate my kneecap and jeopordise the success of our circumnavigation. After all my preaching about safety and preparation in the Salar de Uyuni, I did exactly the same. I made the mistake of going off road, and I mean off road, badly prepared and mentally not with it, and we both nearly paid dearly. Unforgiveable really. I was about to make another wrong decision.

Chapter Seven
Butch, Sundance, Tequila and Tupiza

Ten years ago, I was negotiating a really brutal road in Angola, the Serra de Leba Pass, which is a predominantly broken-up asphalt, winding pass, through the mountains. I decided, however, to take the dirt road, next to it, more technical, but less harsh on the tyre rims. It was frequented by goats, cows and other four-wheel drive animals. It was great. After eighty kilometres of me, and goats, and cows, and me, I met up with some astonished soldiers at a road block. Commandos, no less. (Hate war, love that word.) They had taken the day off school, and had dressed up in soldiers' outfits, and were conning people for money. That was my take on it. The leader of the con group, Abilio (Eagle) Da Silva was eleven. Probably not old enough to be an eagle. An eaglet, or fledgling, maybe. Much older than your average Colombian policeman though. They looked extremely smart, with camouflage outfits, red berets and red neck scarves. The bright red totally cancelled out the effectiveness of their camouflage, but I wasn't about to question their attire, or jungle survival skills. They had 'Angola Commando' badges on the upper arms of their shirts, with the red and black flag of Angola, with a machete and hoe emblem, underneath. (A step down, intimidation-wise, compared to the Automatic Kalashnikov (AK47) and a bayonet, sported by the Mozambique flag. Very welcoming, when you cross the border.)

Our bunch of road blockers looked quite intimidating, for a kindergarten group, but I refused to give them any money, when it was demanded; in a lackadaisical way, I must admit. Instead, I asked their main man, eaglet, for some contributions for me and Cathy, because we were arguing with each other, broke, hungry, thirsty and depressed. They all laughed at my audacity. But it worked, as usual. I have used that line in many countries, and Cathy always squirms, but it has never failed. Boss man looked at me, quizzically, nodded his head forward, a few times, in disbelief, and then burst out laughing. He offered me a beer. The bottle was bigger than him, and definitely more mature. As they were all swigging beers (which goes well with loaded machine guns), I felt under pressure to be sociable, and drank it, at two in the afternoon, with 180 kilometers to go. Madness.

As soon as I left the friendly pre-school roadblock, I realised I was not up to scratch. English understatement. I gave up riding, quickly. I was weaving all over the road, and after eighteen stupid, regrettable, kilometres, of one eye closed, torture and stupidity, I set up my tent, in the bush. What an idiot. I don't know if it was the guilt at my stupidity, building in my mind, or the alcohol, but I couldn't even negotiate a pebble. One bottle of Luandina Lager had ruined my riding skills, and a broken leg in the Angola bush is worth two in the hand. Sorry. Lost my proverb thread there; a broken leg in Angola would be bad news. I swore to myself that I would never, ever, again, drive on alcohol. Roll on eight years and I made my second grave mistake. I mixed a Tequila hangover with off-road riding. Not good.

After the insanity of the blowout in the Salar, we decided to take it easy, in the nearby town of Uyuni. We had little choice as we were waiting for a replacement tyre for the one that was destroyed in the Salar de Uyuni. They only had baby tyres for sale in Bolivia. We waited for DHL (Drop it, Hide it, Lose it) for ever, and a day. You pay them to deliver a parcel, at an address in Bolivia, and two weeks later they deliver it, somewhere in South America, with a similar name, and say it is nothing to do with them. The worst courier company in the world. You can tell that I am not sponsored by them. Actually I was, but not anymore. After six weeks, DHL (Do nothing, Hang on, Lie) turned up with the tyre. But it was for a bicycle. Joke.

Our plan was to ride to Tupiza, a road that had not been built yet. No worries, it was desert riding. But before that, unfortunately, we were to bump into a very dangerous couple. We were walking down the road in Uyuni, looking for a shop that sold chillies and ginger, fighting off people selling salt carvings, and tacky Dakar trophies, when we spotted a BMW1200, with two posh people next to it, eating scones and drinking tea from a porcelain tea set. OK. I exaggerate. I loved this couple. It was Tom and Lorna, who we had met three years earlier at the MCN Motorcycle Show in London. After my circumnavigation of Africa, I ended up giving presentations at various motorcycle shows, including Horizons Unlimited (HUBB), the wonderful Overland Event in Oxford, organised by the force of nature that is Paddy Tyson, eccentric Nick Sanders' Mach Festival in sunny, bright Wales (sorry for sarcasm Nick, I lived in Wales for two years, and never saw the sun. I became an albino), and the MCN Shows in London and Birmingham.

The MCN Motorbike Show in London was my first big show. I had to stand on stage, and talk about my adventures. I was like a fish out of water. Having so many people around me, asking questions and praising me, was all too much. I had become feral during my travels, and crowds were intimidating. I wanted to be alone, in the bush. I couldn't cope with the complexities of humans. I fought off panic attacks. It was a struggle. I felt guilty, not feeling comfortable amongst other motorcyclists. I wanted to relate and inspire. I realised that open space and escape were what I sought. This spotlight on me was the opposite of what I wanted, but I had to commit to the people who had supported me. An alien I was, even to other bikers. After my talk, I was at the side of the stage, concentrating on breathing, and not keeling over, when Tom and Lorna came up and poshly told me their plan. They wanted to know my opinion. (My opinion was; never travel round the world and then commit yourself to crowd scrutiny. They are opposite sides of the emotional spectrum: crowds and freedom.)

Tom and Lorna intended getting married and wanted to travel through Colombia, Ecuador and Peru, on a BMW GS, for their honeymoon. Both were so clean cut; about twenty five, gleaming white teeth, rugby, sailing, plum in the cheek, Pimms o'clock, jazz ensemble type people. I worried that it would be too much of a trip for them to bite off. But, as my blind friend, Rajiv said, "Don't judge by the look."

I enthused and enthused, until I could enthuse no more. It was a welcome distraction from my panic attack, but also because they were so keen. I want everyone to travel, especially on motorbikes, so I have all the time in the world to try and encourage it. Roll on a few years, and they had only bloody gone and done it. Here they were, in Bolivia, many thousands of kilometres from 10, Worcester Lane, Worcester, Worcestershire, United Kingdom of Great Britain. (That is not their real address.) Rajiv was correct. Don't judge by appearance. We hugged, enthusiastically, even though I am an emotionless, tough biker. We chatted for four hours, the connection was still there, and we decided to meet for dinner, as Cathy and I were off in the morning ('off' in more ways than one, we were to find). I felt like I had in some small way contributed to their leap of faith to be there. I was so relieved to hear them rave about how amazing their trip was, interrupting each other, with enthusiastic stories. It was wonderful. Tom and Lorna certainly had balls; well, Lorna didn't, but you know what I mean. That is the reason for getting on a stage, and sharing my stories. Give people the push and confidence, to go on that adventure of a lifetime. We discussed this topic over numerous tequilas, in a bar with eight stools, which soon became sixteen, in my vision. I also noticed that they were clear bottles, we were being served from, with no labels, which is always suspicious. Tom and Lorna were dangerous. As a strictly lager drinker, I couldn't cope. I had to make like Donald, and duck. It was too late.

The next day, at 7.00am, I was dead. I decided to say nothing. My head was groggy. A stupid and irresponsible decision by me, and once again, I put Cathy's life in danger. I am ashamed to admit this particular episode, but I guess, writing warts and all, means warts and all. If there is a God, He either has a great sense of humour, or He is a brilliant teacher, because He popped one of the most difficult rides ever, on our plate. We left Uyuni, and the first thing we had to face was a demonstration about housing shortages. There were about fifty people blocking the main road out of town. That was easily solved. We just headed straight into the desert, which was hard-packed dirt, bypassed the demonstration, and rejoined the road. We had long since stopped worrying about demonstrations and roadblocks. South and Central America live off demonstrations and marches. Each town has on average, fifty demonstrations a day. If they don't have a particular cause on a given day, or hour, or thirty minutes, they just make them up. 'Small dogs' rights', 'One-legged, dyslexic fisherman's rights', 'Lesbian fruit bats' rights', etc. We have been through many roadblocks, and everyone has always been great, which is more than I can say for most demonstrators' singing voices. But never a sniff of aggression. I sometimes ask, what all the fuss is about, but often, the people in the crowd have no idea what the demo is for. They just want a break from everyday routine, and a bit of singing practice, which they sorely need.

The road from Uyuni to Tupiza is 226 kilometres long, which seemed a reasonable distance. But if you factor in it was 30 degrees, in full bike gear, through the desert, on an unfinished road, maybe we were optimistic. Actually, let me be clear. It is not an unfinished road. It is not a road at all. There are just hundreds of random tyre prints, heading into the desert, which quickly disappear, and then it is almost guesswork. The fact that it was also on the Dakar Rally route should have rung alarm bells. The first 50 kilometers were bone-jarring boulders through a flat desert environment.

This was obviously the first layer of the new road, they were constructing. It was hard. After that the road turned into heavenly dirt (see picture on previous page). But it would not last.

Tupiza is at an elevation of 2850 meters, and the landscape transformed into a dramatic, red escarpment, which jutted ruggedly skyward, from the coarse, rocky, thorny terrain. Another serious issue was that the eagles, soaring high up, in the craggy mountain tops started swooping down, and attacking me, and red-faced vultures wanted to headbutt me. They were not remotely interested in Cathy, only me. It had never happened before and it was happening every fifteen minutes. I was perplexed and Cathy was in hysterics, quite enjoying me being dive-bombed by carnivorous birds of prey, nearly as big as me. It was only a matter of time until we got 'swooped' off the bike. When an eagle's wing actually hit my arm, it was time to stop. We jumped off the bike, and Cathy turned to me, crying with laughter and said,

"Spencer, in ten years, you have never attracted birds. Maybe it's your jacket, those orange fluorescent pieces might be catching their eye."

It sounds absurd but Cathy was bang on. It was a new jacket from my sponsor, Lindstrands. I unpacked the pannier and got a permanent black marker from the bottom section, and blacked out the fluorescent orange stripes. It took two coats, but looked pretty good. I never got attacked again. If any of you have had a similar problem, I would love to hear about it. The problem was that I had just altered a jacket that I was supposed to launch for my sponsors Jofama, Lindstrands and Halvarssons, including photoshoots. I had to send an email to head of marketing, and a good friend, John Lagerway, to explain,

"Dear John, I am so sorry but I was getting attacked by birds of prey, because of the fluorescent stripes on my new Lindstrands jacket, so I had to black them all out, with permanent marker. Obviously, the jacket looks very different. Sorry."

He replied, "Spencer, we never expect anything normal from you, so don't worry one bit. But if all the customers want the black version, you are in trouble. You don't need help to attract birds. Stay well you two."

Typical John. Superb.

So after solving the bombing birds issue, we pressed on, struggling, but happy. I was pretty keen on seeing Tupiza, not just because it's a Dakar Rally town, but also because I knew that Butch Cassidy and the Sundance Kid met their end at the hands of the Bolivian army in Tupiza, ending their notorious string of bank robberies. I had read all about them as a child. (I loved reading about criminals, bank robbers, serial killers, athletes and explorers.) I felt a bit Butch Cassidy, riding through this landscape, except I had an iron horse. I whistled in my helmet, the only cowboy theme I knew, 'The Good, the Bad, and the Ugly'.

Robert Leroy Parker, better know as Butch Cassidy (or Mike Cassidy, George Cassidy, Jim Lowe, or Santiago Maxwell) was a man with quite a CV. He was a farm hand, cowboy, butcher, gambler, thief, train and bank robber, ladies man, and leader of the Wild Bunch. All these occupations, unsurprisingly, made him an official 'outlaw'. Butch Cassidy had no intention of ever following the law. While working on a cattle farm as a teenager, Robert met a man who would alter the course of his life forever. Mike Cassidy, cowboy by trade, outlaw cattle rustler by choice, seems to have indoctrinated the restless Robert into the lucrative business of stealing livestock.

Not surprisingly, by eighteen he was imprisoned in Laramie, Wyoming, for horse and cattle rustling, and bank and train robbery. He served eighteen months and was released in January 1896. Cassidy and the Wild Bunch's notoriety grew, as they racked up a staggering average of $35,000 per robbery. Although the Wild Bunch probably only robbed four banks, four express trains and a coal company, they were soon blamed for every robbery in the Northeast. It was Cassidy's meticulous planning that made his robberies so successful. Little was left to chance. Butch and a few selected gang members would spend days, sometimes weeks, scouting a robbery site, and the best escape route. Wisely, they always chose the summer months for all the holdups, when the weather was favourable for eluding posses. (One of my mother's favourite lines from a film; 'This posse is so useless, they couldn't even find themselves'.) Butch was more organised, even training the gang's horses to stand completely still, as they practiced vaulting onto them from behind, in preparation for a bank escape.

It appears that Cassidy also avoided killing, right until the very last few days of his life. Although shots were fired during escapes, Butch was never known to have shot directly at anyone during a holdup. The closest Butch ever came to harming a robbery victim was when he used explosives, to force his way into an express car. A few express messengers were injured in the blasts, but not seriously. The gang always warned the victims before they used dynamite, and were wise enough to protect themselves, by hiding behind cargo.

The powerful railroad companies were soon on the trail. Pinkerton detective Charlie Siringo called Cassidy, "the shrewdest and most daring outlaw of the present age".

Cassidy participated in criminal activity for more than ten years, but the pressure of being pursued by law enforcement, notably the famous Pinkerton Detective Agency (later to become the FBI), forced him to flee the United States. A break for the Pinkerton agents seems to have been the result of one of Cassidy's legendary larks. In 1900, some of the Wild Bunch were in Texas visiting their favourite brothels. They decided to get a formal portrait taken as a joke. This photo (opposite) of the Sundance Kid, Will Carver, Ben Kilpatrick, Harvey Logan, (Kid Curry) and Cassidy, was a rare error for him. A Wells Fargo agent recognised the outlaws when the photo was displayed in the photographer's Fort Worth studio windows. It was soon on wanted posters throughout the west.

By 1900, it appears that Cassidy was tired of life on the run. He visited a lawyer, curious to see if he could get a pardon, if he gave himself up. When he was told it was impossible, Cassidy replied,

"You know the law and I guess you are right. But I am sorry it can't be fixed some way. You'll never know what it means to be forever on the dodge. Guess I better carry on."

And he did.

The Wild Bunch pulled off their last major robbery at the National Bank of Winnemucca, Nevada, on 19 September, 1900. Now called Butch, after his brief job as a butcher, and Cassidy after Mike Cassidy the cattle rustler, he fled with his accomplice, Harry Alonso Longabaugh, known as the Sundance Kid, and girlfriend Etta Place. It was not long before the trio were accused of bank robberies in South America. They travelled to Argentina, in 1907, and then to Bolivia, to the town of Santa Cruz, a frontier town, in Bolivia highlands. Their story was that they wanted to settle down as respectable ranchers, but that wasn't the plan: yet. Letters written by Butch from the time, suggest that the pair were looking for the proverbial, 'last job payday', to buy a ranch and retire. Aren't we all.

It was while laying low in Tupiza, that Butch learned of a payroll to be transported by mule, near Huaca Huanusca (Dead Cow Hill), fifty kilometres northwest of Tupiza. Twenty-two kilometers from Tupiza is Salo, a rural community where Butch and Sundance pitched up, seeking a bed in a local posada, the night before the robbery. From Salo the road climbs sharply, on a dirt track, to Huaca Huanusca, where the pair hid on a rocky outcrop, overlooking an expanse of scrub land, dotted with cacti, rocks and thorn trees, a raw and unforgiving terrain.

As Carlos Pero encouraged his mule to lumber up a rugged, dusty track, high in the Andes mountains, on the morning of 4 November, 1908, little did the courier for the Aramayo, Francke and Cia silver mining company realise, that his every move was being watched.

Pero later recounted that after cresting a hill, he was 'surprised by two Yankees, whose faces were covered in bananas (sorry, spellcheck), bandanas, and whose rifles were cocked and ready to fire. The pair robbed the courier of the company's payroll and disappeared into the cacti-dotted desolation of southern Bolivia. Witnesses saw them three days later in a small mining town nearby, where they were lodged in a boarding house owned by a miner named Bonifacio Casasola. Fortified by a meal of beer and sardines (at least they have good taste in fish), they tended their animals, and bedded down for the night. Casasola became suspicious of the pair because they had a mule from the mine, identifiable from the company's brand on the mule's bum. (I don't know about you, but Butch and Sundance don't strike me as meticulous, well planned, and super intelligent, on this occasion.)

Casasola notified a nearby telegraph office who called the Aboroco cavalry. Three soldiers were dispatched under the command of Captain Justo Concha, and they told the local authorities. The soldiers, the police chief and some of his officials surrounded the lodging house. As they approached the house, the bandits opened fire, killing one of the soldiers and gravely wounding another. A proper cowboy firefight ensued, and the building was riddled with bullets. Eventually silence fell, and there was no returning fire. The authorities waited overnight, and in the morning cautiously approached the room. They found two bodies, with numerous bullet holes to their arms and legs. One was slumped against a wall and had a bullet hole in the forehead. The other body, lying on the floor in front of him, had a bullet hole in the temple. The police speculated, judging from the positions of the bodies, that Cassidy had shot the gravely injured Longabaugh to put him out of his pain, then killed himself. Now, that is a sticky end in Tupiza.

Apparently, the colonial town square, overshadowed by the bleached wide façade of the cathedral, looks unchanged since the days in 1908, when Butch and Sundance were casing the local bank. The bank still stands today, with a wild west-style cantina, across the square. However, before we got there, we were facing our own sticky end, as the road had not been improved since Butch Cassidy rode it, and we had a challenge ahead.

There are three stages in an adventure rider's day. The first is the warm-up period, when you start the day's riding, where you are a bit groggy and stiff from the previous day. Then you warm up to your style, and the road difficulty, and you hit what every motorcyclist wants: the 'zone'. I don't want to sound hippie and obsessed with the sport, but this is when man and machine are one. It is that wonderful feeling when you are loose and relaxed, going with the bike and not fighting it. It is when you are braking well, changing gears smoothly, cornering well, controlling the weight of the bike. Cathy knows exactly when it's happening, and moves with me. She is the world's best pillion. It is the only time in my life where I think about nothing else, but conquering a difficult road. Being hyperactive, I find it impossible to switch off my mind. Day and night is spent struggling with a multitude of thoughts, about my life, my family, my commitments, my guilt, my life mistakes. When I am in the 'zone', I am truly free, mentally and physically. Riding is very selfish, and highly addictive, and I admit it. It relieves the clutter in my brain. Jeremy Kreoker's book, *Motorcycle Therapy*, is perfectly titled. I really don't know what I would have done without motorcycles. I don't know what I will do without them.

Like any sport, after hitting the 'zone', then it's the comedown. This is when you start getting tired, and small 'hints' and mistakes start creeping into your riding style; missing a gear, slipping off a foot peg, hitting that rut you normally wouldn't, braking too hard, etc. This is a dangerous time, because it is near the end of the day, and physical fatigue is setting in. But worse, is the mental switch. You start thinking about the end of the day, relaxing, a nice meal, and showers. You have taken your eye off the ball. You are no longer mentally in the desert, you have already arrived at your destination, and it will be reflected in your riding. I am guilty of it, as much as the next person, but if you can recognise it, and know when to stop, you are halfway there. We were facing the comedown stage by one in the afternoon, the riding was so draining. The road disappeared into desert sand, and the temperatures were scorching in the valley floors, even at this altitude. Despite drinking two litres of water each, we were still dehydrated, and running out of water. We pushed on for four hours, the odd llama caravan, or a solitary camel, running away from the engine noise, little explosions of dust from his hooves, marking his route. That, and the occasional tin mine, one of the few distractions to the wild, unyielding scenery. There were numerous twisters that built up, and whipped across the landscape. Sometimes we stopped, and watched them crossing the road, at high speeds, disappearing towards the horizon, before the next one whipped up. We also had three or four river crossings and were soaked with sweat, and soaked up to the knees from the rivers. We still had fifty kilometers to go to Butch and Sundance town, when disaster struck. It was inevitable.

When you are riding in deep sand, you have to keep the acceleration up, the front wheel up, not hesitate, and let the wheels move freely, to keep forward momentum. Never grip the handlebars hard, give them play, and never snatch at the brakes. After that speech; we were hauling along nicely, when we hit a deep pothole of loose sand. The front wheel dropped, and dug into the sand, twisted sideways, and off we flew, with very little dignity. Cathy managed to push off from the foot pegs and throw herself clear. I, on the other hand, decided to slow the right side pannier's descent with my right knee cap. My knee cap decided to relocate, a little further to the right than it should have. An acute patella dislocation occurs when the kneecap pops sideways out of its vertical trochlear groove, at the knee joint, and can no longer move up or down. This locks the knee, and pulls the ligaments out of place, often tearing them. That's what happened to me, and it looked horrible.

When things go wrong, and look initially bad, I am seriously over the top, with doom prophesies, for about two minutes; then rationale kicks in, when I hear Cathy's dulcet tones. I was rolling around in the sand, clutching my misaligned kneecap, and screaming like a girl, sorry, that's sexist; like a boy. "Right that's it. It's all over. My leg is buggered. It's finished. All done. The dream is over. We may as well go back to England and go on unemployment benefit and live on 'one minute' noodles, for the rest of our lives. I can dig some trenches, lop some trees, or unblock some drains, in freezing Kent. No problem. We can watch other people enjoying themselves on TV; after my operation of course. Finished. Buggered."

"Calm down, stop being a drama queen," was Cathy's response.

That stopped me rolling in my tracks. But it did not change the fact that we were in 30 degrees, the last shady tree was 3,000 kilometers away, and my kneecap had a different view of the world than it normally had. There had not been a single vehicle, the whole day, so waiting for Godot was not an option. It was time for me to hop up to the plate, and be a superhero. We had to drive the 46 kilometers to Tupiza, which is exactly what we did, but not without a modicum of pain. I had to ride with my right leg, stiff, out in front of me, like a Hitler salute with your leg. It was another two hours of moaning, but we made it to Tupiza. We booked into a hovel (no, I did not misspell hotel), and collapsed on the bed, exhausted. A rat as big as Mike Tyson ran straight up Cathy's leg, over her breasts, and out the window. We just looked at each other, and sighed. Then we fell asleep.

The next morning, when we left the room, I nearly fell two floors, as the whole banister collapsed, when I leant on it. The owner wasn't happy, but nor was I. Nevertheless, we thanked her for the rat hovel, and went in search of a truck to take us, and the bike, back to Uyuni. As was our luck, Alberto Quispe, the driver we procured, was suicidal. (After I have finished this book, I am writing a guide to hospital care in Africa and South America. I have done ample research.)

But we still had to get to the hospital and the 226-kilometre trip back was the worst journey of our lives. I was weakened by sun, bad decision guilt, Tequila, and a repositioned knee, and Cathy was weakened by a stupid boyfriend and by a jolted back. We bounced our way to Tupiza, hitting our heads frequently on the roof of the Combi, leaving numerous dents, as Quispe ramped every little bump, or dune. Sometimes he careered off the raised road completely, down a steep slope, and into the desert, before righting himself. He was constantly on his mobile, having a passionate discussion and, at one point, he started crying. Not good for his vision or concentration. He also never looked at the road.

He was either looking at Cathy, in the rear-view mirror, or he was rearranging his bald patch. He was as keen on Cathy as Oscar El Jefe Acosta, the Cartel gang leader in Cordoba. We nearly rolled and died at least five times, but I kept my eyes closed, and found God. We made it, but upon arrival, my knee was swollen like a basketball. The hospital staff were excellent. They unceremoniously repositioned the offending patella, injected me with cortisone, gave me enough anti-inflammatory and pain killers to solve a giraffe's infected throat, or a blue whale's toothache. The doctor's final sentence was the nail in the patella though:

"No riding for six weeks. It is a bad injury."

Fat chance! Seven days later, with my leg strapped like Tutankhamun, we were bouncing our way back to Tupiza in another truck, thankfully with a less depressed driver, to retrieve the bike and carry on to Chile. The drive was much more serene, as Walter was no younger than one hundred and eight, so we felt more confident of getting to Tupiza. But not before we saved a Belgian European Union diplomat, hitching from Uyuni to Tupiza, with no water, from certain death. That's another story.

Did we make it to Butch Cassidy's death place? Yes we did. It was haunting and emotional, and atmospheric. Despite the fact that the house the two gangsters died in was a ruin, and filled with llama excrement, made no difference. There were even bullet holes in the walls. I had fulfilled one of my childhood dreams. Strange though it is. I stood on the bank of the river that Butch Cassidy and the Sundance Kid had their last bathe. I looked out, over the mountains, that they looked over, and imagined life in those days. I don't care if I am in a location where David Livingstone was looking at a waterfall, or Percy Fawcett was struggling through the Amazon, or Che Guevara was trying to motivate his rabble of soldiers. When I feel part of history, I feel alive.

The next plan was to visit another iconic event, which would hopefully involve less death. The Dakar Rally was running through Bolivia and Argentina. We had to be there.

Chapter Eight
The Bi-Polar Pole and a Joey

It is difficult to imagine life getting anymore strange than standing in the middle of a South American desert, with five thousand people cheering, while our last-minute-recruited Polish cameraman sprinted across a sand dune, naked, followed by half of the Argentinian Police Force. Cathy and I were styling it up, as usual, in a top-quality hotel, 'hotel' being a ridiculous compliment to this establishment. We were in San Juan, a modern city with wide, tree-lined avenues irrigated by canals, from which it derives its nickname: Oasis Town. The city is in a fertile valley, surrounded by rocky, mountainous desert. It was such a smart city, that it was quite a struggle for me to find a place so bad, but when costs dictate, it can be done.

Our room was a small outhouse on the roof of a Hotel El Dodgy, which I presume used to be a storage or laundry room. The only other use for the roof area was for the washing line, where the decidedly, World War Two-like sheets and blankets were hung. For some unknown reason, there were also twelve truck tyres, five shop mannequins, with various limbs missing, and a cardboard cut-out of Queen Victoria. Queen Victoria was waterlogged, and lay on the concrete, depressed and deflated.

Her Majesty had been assassinated on this roof. Our humble abode had free bedbugs galore, cockroaches, wet blankets (common, and my one nightmare), no toilet, no running water, and an inebriated, rusted fan, hanging dangerously from the ceiling. It was close to 30 degrees, despite the altitude, so evidently, we slept well. The bed was a bit on the small side for one, let alone two. But if you stay stiff and still, you can sleep. Not one of my strong points.

There was also a rat in the room, who decided that one corner was his hangout. I thought that rats were supposed to constantly run around - surely the word scurrying was coined especially for rats. It was rather disconcerting when he just sat in the corner, staring us down. It rather freaked me out. I solved the problem by imagining him with red, square sunglasses on, and I named him Yasser Ara-rat. I didn't really mind him after that. This was a psychological technique that Cathy taught me.

She told our children that if they were ever scared of an animal, they should give it a cute name. Five-year-old Feaya had a run-in (luckily, not a full mugging) with a spider and a pre-existing fear of hairy Arachnids, courtesy of her uncle and grandmother, who both made Usain Bolt look slow, if a spider appeared. However, as soon as she named spiders, 'Charlottes', after that, she was fine.

We woke suitably unrested, sweating like miners, and nauseous. We had food poisoning and Cathy had come off worse. I was not remotely surprised as the previous evening we had bought some dodgy street food that was about three hundred years old. The meat was green, but the hue was hidden well in the dark. Luckily for me, Cathy had been

A Tuareg tribesman of West Africa, inspiration for the iconic Dakar logo

hungrier, and my eyesight better. There was no way she was doing anything but horizontal today. The problem was that this was not just any day. The world-famous Dakar Rally was coming through. I had secured a wonderful position with the world's press and camera people, in the Exclusive Press Area, on a towering, rocky outcrop with a flat, high plateau above a spectacular river crossing.

For those of you that have been living on a different motorbike planet, the Dakar Rally is an off-road endurance event, with heavy emphasis on the word endurance. The terrain traversed is much tougher than that of conventional rallies and the vehicles used are typically true off-road machines, rather than modified road vehicles. The race involves huge sand dunes, mud, camel grass, rocks, boulders and erg. (Google time, I was not clearing my throat.) Unlike a lot of rallies where much of the route can be blocked off and monitored, the Dakar throws in other hazards including terrorists and camels. Both are dangerous, believe me.

A famous Dakar rider and friend, South African Joey Evans, broke his back in a devastating motorbike accident. In October 2007, with two races left in a regional off-road racing championship, and his sights set on a win, Joey crashed his bike at the start of the race and was ridden over by almost the entire field of racers. Teeth shattered and his back broken, Joey woke up spitting out his own teeth and unable to feel his legs. Two specialists agreed that Joey would never walk. The third wanted to fuse his back to take pressure off his spinal cord. But the specialist also gave him hope. His spinal cord was not severed but was severely compressed and there was a chance he could regain some movement. As it was, Joey was paralysed from the neck down. But the married man and father of four girls was not ready to give up. He then spent two years enduring intense recovery and rehabilitation. Joey not only learnt to walk again, he even got back on his bike, lifted on by incredulous friends.

This was not enough for Joey. He decided that anything was possible and even with his broken body, he believed that it was only his mind that could hold him back. He set his sights on entering the Dakar, and told only his wife.

"I saw myself crossing the finish line and over the ramp. I envisioned the end, repeatedly. This created a mind-set that it had already happened. I just had to follow the path that would get me there."

But that path was studded with setbacks. To qualify for the Dakar, you need to submit a CV with a set number of long-distance rallies and endurance races, at least one of which must be on the international circuit. To meet the criteria and to get ready for the race, by 2013 Joey was competing in 500km and 1000km races. It had taken him many years to get back up to that level, but in 2014 disaster struck. Joey hit a cow at high speed in KwaZulu, Natal. This is where the reader goes "for God's sake" or "I think someone's telling him something". Joey ended up in hospital, this time with broken ribs and a shattered arm. The recovery would take six months.

"It was devastating. When I woke up and could feel my legs, I knew I could handle anything else, but I still questioned everything I was doing. What was I putting my family through? And for what? I asked my wife, and she said that I need to be me."

A year later Joey was back at Amageza, a 5,000km rally through Botswana and Northern Cape. He followed that with his international race in Morocco, sent his entry in to Dakar and was accepted. Now he just needed 1.1 million rand ($71,900). I could go on with the setbacks, but Joey being Mr. Motivator - he raised the money.

Joey entered and completed the Dakar, ten years after his initial accident, in 2017, and is a total inspiration. Never, never, give up. But that was not enough either, this time God had other plans. In his next rally Joey hit a camel. Camels, in case you have not met one, are big and hard, and Joey came off worse, with a split head and superbly spectacular, multi-purple bruising. The camel had the hump (sorry), but Joey like the superman he is, finished the rally. Once again, the man recovered.

In his next rally, he sadly hit an elephant. OK. That last sentence is false, but I think you get the gist. Joey epitomizes the type of lunatic that enters this mad rally, and I cannot sing his praises enough. Joey has written an amazing book, brilliantly entitled *From Para to Dakar*. It is almost irrelevant what pursuit/sport/job etc. that Joey undertook. He speaks to everyone about overcoming obstacles in your life, no matter what they are. He is also extremely humble which makes the potency of his never-say-die attitude even more powerful. It is inspirational, dedicated people like Joey that are the only ones who will get a sniff of this amazing event, a rally that was started by the 'interesting' Thierry Sabine. Now you will get a glimpse of what Joey bit off. What a challenge.

In 1976 Thierry got hopelessly lost in the Tenere desert whilst competing in the Cote Abidjan/Nice rally and decided that the desert would be a spectacular location for a rally. He chose a route from Paris to Dakar in Senegal and the world's most difficult rally was born. One hundred and eighty two vehicles entered the inaugural rally in Paris with seventy four battered machines. Surviving the 10,000 kilometre trip to the Senegalese capital. Cyril Neveu holds the distinction of being the event's first winner, riding a Yamaha motorcycle. (Yay- maha- my favourite brand since I was two months old.) The event rapidly grew in popularity, with two hundred and sixteen vehicles taking part in 1980, and two hundred and ninety-one in 1981.

Tragically, Sabine was killed when his Ecureuil helicopter crashed into a dune in Mali during a sudden sandstorm, at 7.30pm on Tuesday 14 January 1986. Also killed on board was the singer-songwriter Daniel Balavione, helicopter pilot Francois Xavier Bagnoud, and journalist Nathalie Odent. Sabine's ashes were later scattered at the Lost Tree in Niger, which the rally thereafter described as the Arbre Thierry Sabine. Many Dakar racers go there to pay respects. Sabine is by no means the only tragedy.

Since 1979, seventy-six people have died as a result of the Dakar. Among the thirty one competitor fatalities, twenty three were motorcycle-related, five car-related, one truck-related and two competitors died as a result of local rebel conflict. The Dakar has received criticism because of its high mortality rate, with the *Vatican Paper*, of all the famous journals, describing the event as the "bloody race of irresponsibility". The event understandably received criticism in the 1988 race, when three Africans were killed in collisions with race vehicles. Forward wind to 2008, where the rally was to start in Lisbon. The event was cancelled amid fears of terrorist attacks in Mauritania following the killing of four French tourists in 2007. There were also unsubstantiated reports of riders getting shot at in Mauritania. This is not really a good thing for any motorcyclist's future - a bullet.

These rumours ended up being properly substantiated in the most horrific of ways. On 13 January 1991 Charles Cabannes, a support truck driver for the Citroen Factory team, was shot dead by rebels, at the side of the road, in the small village of Kadeouane. His co-driver, Joel Guyomarch, escaped with a superficial bullet wound. The killing was not claimed by any rebel organisation in the following days, but was believed to be related to the conflict between the Malian Army and Tuareg Rebels. Organisers cancelled the following two rounds, and the Malian Army escorted the competitors passing through the country. That is what I lap up. I am, and always have been, an extreme sports/ adventure lover but it was the Camel Trophy and the Paris-Dakar Rally that really ignited a little boy's imagination, living in Kenya. So, I was not going to miss the world's best riders rocketing through the desert.

I was not going to miss the opportunity of filming it either. Problem. The beautiful camera woman had been floored by San Juan Revenge, and I desperately needed a replacement human. Enter, stage right, Slavic, a Polish fellow who made a fruitcake seem like the sanest of cakes. But what a nice cake he turned out to be, in the end. We had met him briefly outside our room, the previous evening, where he was cleaning the chain and sprockets of his BMW 650 Dakar, with a pink toothbrush dipped in petrol. Judging from his stunning white teeth, he evidently had another toothbrush. This morning, Slavic was sitting downstairs, in the communal kitchen, examining every single corn in his cornflakes, with a grimy spoon. I greeted him, sat opposite and explained my dilemma. Slavic was about sixty-five plus and looked like Robert de Niro, except left in the oven a bit longer and with a more bulbous nose. It must have been his eyes that reminded me of De Niro because you couldn't really see much of him. He had a huge grey beard, which spread out across his BMW T-shirt like a sun dial, a similarly massive mop of grey hair, another sun dial, silhouetted against the blue sky. His face was garnished with thick lensed and framed black glasses that seemed to be constantly steamed up and greasy, even when he was riding. Added to this he was bright red so looked like an extra who had just stepped off 'The Black Pearl' and was about to explode. However, Pavel was quick to volunteer as cameraman. He had such a great, trusting face, and beaming smile so I stupidly agreed. I did not know at that stage that he had more personalities than the village I lived in in Mexico, luckily most of them super nice. Every time he spoke, he squinted for emphasis, and his eyes watered and he leant forward to share his words of wisdom; and his rather aromatic garlic breath. Still, it was excellent of him to offer to help, so I rushed upstairs, mopped the food poisoning victim's brow and whispered suitable kind words of love, affection and sympathy, and we were off.

It turned out that the junction outside had become a meeting place for bikers who wanted to head to the Dakar. We left in a group of six bikes. I was quite pleased to be riding with a few others. It was a novelty for me. There was a Dutch couple in their early twenties, suitably blonde and good looking. The husband was an ex-policeman and now worked as a bouncer in Rotterdam. He was quite keen on threatening imaginary people, and very enthusiastic about telling us how he could kill six people simultaneously with his thumb. He should meet Ayahuasca Anthony. I steered clear. There was a German couple in their early one hundreds, who spent most of their day huddled over a GPS and maps. I only really saw the top of their heads. There was another German guy, with clichéd round spectacles and unfeasible tallness, on a Honda 500 with a see-through tank. Dieter must have been six foot eight and even on his tall bike, his knees were warming his ears. Then there was me, alone on my Tenere. Pavel had agreed to take a clean-cut, enthusiastic, teenage Dakar fan as pillion. So that made seven.

We headed off and all was good for about eight hundred metres. Then it all became odd. I saw Pavel pull up ahead of me and jump off the bike, redder than ever before, with steam coming out of his ears and nose. He was gesticulating at the young Argentinian and obviously berating him for something.

"I cannot ride with you, you stay here, you make me crash. Fuck, shit, thank you, no, goodbye," said Pavel.

Apparently, the young lad had been squirming around in the saddle and making it difficult for Pavel. I could not blame the pillion because in this short distance, I had noticed some worrying traits in Pavel's riding. He had already gone straight through a red light, and his acceleration was erratic, to say the least. One moment he would be ambling along at a snail's pace, then he would suddenly accelerate, and be off like a ferret on coffee.

"You can't just dump him here Pavel. There is nobody around."

"This man is no good on the moto, no good on back, no good," he replied, gesticulating wildly in the air to some invisible God.

"OK, but we are in the middle of nowhere," I pleaded with him.

Slavic was having none of it and after some strange conversation about being 'let down by the world', I realised this situation was not going to be resolved. As I was wondering about the next course of action, a battered pickup kangarooed towards us. I flagged them down, asked if they could drop the traumatised pillion back in town, they agreed, and it was done. Crisis averted.

Now it got weirder. As we were exiting the city, it became glaringly clear that Slavic was stopping at every green light, and going through every red one. After pulling up alongside and quizzing him with my arms and eyebrows, he just rocketed off. Then he would wait at a vital junction, and rocket off again. As soon as we hit the dirt he turned into the most amazing rider, I must admit, and disappeared down an arrow straight road, in a cloud of dust, up to the horizon, over a hill, and gone. We continued and met up with Slavic at various splits in the track. At least he was waiting at strategic points, but were they strategic points? After eighty wrong turns and an extremely circular route, we tied Slavic up and left him by his bike, with a little bit of water and a mango. No! We did not. We eventually arrived at the river crossing. I am convinced to this day that Slavic found the river crossing by pure luck, and would have continued for days, until he shrunk to nothing and died of thirst. The location was superb, the atmosphere electric. The Argentinians had pulled out all the stops. If you have ever been to an English country fair, multiply the stalls by a thousand, and add five thousand screaming Argentinians and Bolivians, a sprinkling of Germans, Dutch and the unhinged. Add smoke billowing asados; an

Argentinian barbecue of ludicrous proportions - picture three cows upside down. Next to each other, cooking. Not for vegetarian Dakar fans, this one. Add thousands of litres of Quilmes beer, zillions of litres of Mendoza Red wine from the nearby hills, international flags fluttering in the breeze, and the smell of fuel in the air and there you have it… not an English country fair at all. The whole scene was divided in two by the river and the road crossing.

On one side of the river were the 5000 fans partying like there was a pandemic called Covid coming soon, as well as some high-powered vehicles, and on the other side was a cordoned-off section with Winnebagos and four-by-four trucks, with tents and tarpaulins and barbecues. Important people were running around, with radio mikes and high-speed, important walks. I was so excited. We found a spot with a view of a sweeping bend, on the approach to the bridge and water crossing. I had the stills camera and I showed Slavic how to use the handheld Panasonic HD camera, and taught him the basics of how to do a piece to camera, and how to film the riders, preferably not pointing the camera into the sun and never zoom, etc. It was Neanderthal-basic instructions, but it was better than having no cameraman at all. Slavic seemed to concentrate and take it all in. But that was before he turned from hippie Robert de Niro into Captain Barbosa.

Picture this. You are set up with all the bigwigs of adventure filming, NBC, Fox Sports, Redbull TV, etc. and the anticipation is palpable, the atmosphere electric. Everyone is making last-minute sound checks, and radios are crackling, announcing the imminent arrival of the fastest men in the world, on two and four wheels. The danger element is, of course, always there. Most fans are aware that this is a difficult section, and that many people have died trying to complete the Dakar. It is a strange, morbid attraction, the morals of which I will not go into now. I will always be an avid defender of extreme sports, whether it is surfing, kayaking, rock climbing, solo ice climbing, sky diving, rafting, BASE jumping, ultra-distance running, free diving, caving, wing suit flying, whatever. Overcoming adversity and stretching the mind and body to its limit make people, and me, feel truly alive. Let it flourish. Love it all. Back to Dakar. As I was fighting off a desert wasp who wanted to hurt me, I heard the crowd starting to stir, somewhat muted at first, but then they started clapping, and then screaming. The race was on. The riders were coming first, followed by the four-wheelers. My plan was to do a quick piece to camera, then swing round to the sweeping bend and follow the bikes through the water crossing. I would use the stills camera; Pavel would do his best on the HD Panasonic Film camera.

"No panning bru, keep the camera still and let the subject pass."

I turned to Slavic to give him the thumbs up about the plans that were in my head, and he was nowhere to be seen. I spun round and looked down the slope of the riverbank, to where the epicentre of the crowd-stirring noise was coming from. There was Slavic, on the river's edge, close to where cars and bikes would be hurtling through at 150 kilometres an hour. He was bent over double, performing a moonie to the opposite riverbank. For those of you that do not know what a moonie is - if you look in the Dictionary, it will say:

'A moonie is when a Polish motorcyclist shows his lily-white bum to a crowd of five thousand spectators at the Dakar Rally, causing untold distress and embarrassment to another unnamed motorcyclist, who probably wants to disappear into an abyss.'

My cameraman, and therefore, in the sandy eyes of the Dakar organisers, my responsibility, was showing his worst (back)side to the world via TV, not to mention to the large, well-alcohol oiled, crowd, witnessing his revealings, and loving it. I ran down the hill super-fast, shouting

"Slavic, Jesus Christ, man. What the hell are you doing? This is a conservative, non-bum exposing country."

Slavic pulled up his trousers, managed to look a bit sheepish, or llama-ish and said, "Sorry, I thought it was funny and get the crowd much happy."

"Yes, if you were eighteen, out at a party in a Polish University town. Come on man, pull it together."

'NAKED DESERT RUNNER FROM POLAND CAUSES DAKAR CRASH.'

Those were not the headlines in *La Nacion* newspaper the next day, but they could have been. Guess what Slavic did next. After following me a few steps up the hill, he turned and bolted back down the dune, removing his boots as he ran. He then sat/fell and simultaneously removed his motorcycle trousers, and underwear, quickly and impressively. He stood up in his white T-shirt, and stained white socks, his proud belly sticking out from underneath his BMW shirt. He then gyrated his hips in a circular motion, displaying his Polish jewels to huge applause. Did I mention 5,000 people, now it was 8,000. By this stage, the organisers were livid, and Slavic had unsurprisingly caught the attention of security, and the Police who were armed to the hilt, and rapidly approaching.

Surrender was not an option in Slavic's head. Freedom! Now he was naked William Wallace. Off he ran, at Dakar speed, across the dunes, not before taking a quick detour across the road, crossing the route of the soon-to-arrive competitors. He ran down the line of spectators, arms in the air, like a World Cup winning striker, before peeling off across the desert, with many uniforms after him. Success and fame would be short-lived, and he was rugby tackled by five men, much like a streaker at an English football match. Except, in a desert, and no football to be seen. The crowd were cheering on hysterically, and when he was tackled, undoubtedly causing friction to his tackle, there was a collective 'Ahh!' of disappointment that he had been caught. He escaped for a final time from the clutches of the law, and received a 'Champions League goal reaction' from the crowd. This was followed by a red card; Pavel was finally taken down. With all due respect, the police were remarkably civil and led Slavic off to a metal container in thirty degrees and locked him up, to frazzle to death. We realised that our biker friend was struggling a bit, and that him, and his Polish sausage, were in danger of frying, so all the bikers sprang into action. After splitting up, we eventually located the container over a kilometre away, behind some dunes. We managed to persuade the police to get our potty Pole out of the container. They agreed, but only to move him to the holding cells in town. They made it clear that he would be released the next morning. Maybe.

Cathy spent the night worrying, phoning various dead ends, and trying to find out on the internet where Pavel could be. At 6.00am we were up, and after numerous phone calls and red herrings (not sardines this time), we eventually located Slavic's whereabouts and got him released. When he arrived at the squat, evidently traumatised by his evening's accommodation, courtesy of the Argentinian taxpayer, he turned into Jean Claude van Damme and just wanted to karate all of us.

"You leave me, you leave me to die, shit people bad bad."

We tried to reason with him, but it didn't work. He was too traumatised and all over the place.

"You left me with police, I kick you," as he swung at my shins.

I jumped up and performed a Polish restraint manoeuvre that I learnt in the Selous Scouts. I tried to explain to him that I was not the naked desert runner, he was, and it was his choice. I tried to reason with him, explaining that Cathy had been on the case since the minute he was rugby-tackled in the desert.

"Foreigner shits," was his retort.

That made me laugh. Difficult to be more foreign than a Polish dude in Argentina. He was not thinking straight, and we all made light of everything and cracked a few Quilmes to mark his freedom. Pavel was still extremely tense, but after a few manly biker hugs, things eventually calmed down with a modicum of tranquility restored.

Let me now twist this story on the head and tell you why it is the feel-good factor story that Sam Manicom asked me to write. On the surface, this is a story of danger, death, tragedy and obvious mental issues. What is it that links someone like Joey Evans to Pavel? The only obvious link was their love of motorcycles and the Dakar. That is a tenuous link. The link that joins them is the tenacity to never give up, albeit for different reasons. I stayed in contact with Pavel, and he admitted freely that he was struggling from grief and some mental health issues. On top of that, and thank God, mental health issues are not such a dirty secret anymore in this world; several well-known adventure riders have also admitted their struggles with mental health. Without wanting to be contentious, and forgive me if I offend, or you do not fit into that category; many people seeking extreme adventures are often running away from something or trying to resolve issues, or trying to find something meaningful about themselves, and the world. I was so pleased to see the emergence of mental health issues in the motorbike world and the fact that The Overland Event, to name one example, is backing the Mental Health Motorbike Support Group UK (MHM). In the light of Covid and the way it has affected human interaction, this subject will only become more important to cope with through the right channels.

Pavel not only returned home and pulled himself together. He told me that the support he got from bikers, not only with us, but throughout South America, had literally saved his life. He said he was sorry to have caused us grief.

"Not a problem," I said, and meant it.

He went on to surprise me. Pavel had returned to Poland, controlled his issues, and had also set up a Mental Health Support Group for Bikers. It had proved extremely successful and had saved Pavel, to boot. He was planning to bring a group of twenty bikers on a three-week tour, culminating in watching the Dakar. During our many conversations, he once let it slip that he had raised over 80,000 Euros to support mental health schemes. So, on the surface, you can see me as slightly taking the mickey out of someone with my story of Pavel, but it is not the case. It was comedic at first, but then worrying. I cleared it with him before I submitted this chapter, and we still celebrate our love of travelling and bikes, and life, and adrenaline and hardship, and experience and stimulation, and friends. And small subjects like the complexity of the mind.

Joey and Pavel made me realise that when you are worrying about yourself and your reactions to life, always think about what others are going through. A man with no feet cannot understand the complaints about uncomfortable shoes. The survivors and never-give-up people are my heroes. I am not one, but I do know that the difference between success and failure is to keep trying one more time and if that is not enough, a hundred more times. From these two men I learnt to travel with a more open mind to the struggles of others and to be more accepting of those who stray from the norm, and chase their goals, no matter how different they may be. My life is easy. Complaints must stop, and my love of fellow humans and this beautiful planet must be multiplied. This Dakar Rally, on the surface was amusing, deep down it was a Eureka Humanity moment for me. Pavel's struggles were so different from Joey's almost self-inflicted ones, but no less impressive. We all have our mountains to climb, some higher than others and some need to do the climb with a pebble in their shoe. These two men, during Dakar week, made me realise that we need to celebrate our differences and support each other and cherish each other, help each other succeed, acknowledging our strengths and weaknesses, but living life to the full. I was not doing that. I was too cynical to trust people. These two also compounded my motto:

'Day by day, border by border, nothing lasts forever.'

This is a maxim that I have been living by since 2009. Luckily, the future comes a day at a time. This is my point. Take life in little chunks and savour them. 'Nothing lasts forever' is about the good and the bad, so suck up the first and overcome the second. 'Border by border' means keep moving forward in life. I was learning all the time. But open-mindedness to others is another vital key to a decent life. As Stephen Fry, the English genius said in an interview:

"I have no idea why people talk about dysfunctional families as though it is unusual. Eighty percent of people are dysfunctional. How are their families going to be normal if we judge them by the standard, expected, circumstance and behaviour."

I concur with this. My mother's sister committed suicide, my wonderful grandmother had callipers on her legs and spent a lot of her life in a wheelchair. She never complained and was a ball of sunshine. Other family members were institutionalised. My mum's Uncle Bert was run over by a steamroller. It's 100 percent true. Do not ask me the details, and do not be embarrassed to laugh. He obviously was not quick off the mark, or it was a Dakar steamroller.

So, dysfunctional, I have an inkling of that. This is what I believe the Biker Code is:

'Do not judge, and always help others, wherever possible. Our differences are our strengths, not a hindrance. Try to be the best version of yourself, and focus on achieving your own personal goals, not ones that other people want for you.'

I try to live it, but fall short all the time.

Chapter Nine
Condor Man and the Smoked Trout

The Osorno Volcano is absolutely spectacular. It is exactly how a child would visualise a volcano, and probably draw one, very badly. Osorno is a peak of beauty, rising in perfect symmetry, topped by a cap of brilliant white snow, often backed by a pure blue sky, the horizon unspoilt by any other peaks, only the majestic Osorno. Osorno had it all. It dominated the skyline from 100 kilometres away, and never seemed to get closer. The volcano literally loomed over you, and breathed over you, and dwarfed all nearby features. Maybe I am exaggerating. I am a volcano nut. In the same way as I am an archaeology and anthropology nut. I appreciate the ludicrous amount of time these geological formations have stood guard over our efforts.

Volcanoes have some sort of mesmerising effect, no matter how beautiful the surroundings they are in. I feel the same about rivers. Both are God's dominant forces, and can't be ignored. Osorno is the supermodel of volcanoes. Second place goes to Mount Fuji in Japan, and a distant third is Kilimanjaro. Other aesthetes of Vulcanicity, (nothing to do with Star Trek) and geologists may disagree. These are my first, second and third volcano choices. If you disagree, you evidently have no understanding of volcano aesthetics.

Osorno is a 2,652 metre, conical, stratovolcano in the Los Lagos region of Chile. It stands on the southeastern shore of Lake Lianquihue, an amazing black sand shoreline to camp on, with incredible views of the volcano. The lake is a massive 860 square kilometres and an impressive 300 metres deep. The area is a mesmerising combination of natural beauty, man-made, landscaped Germanic lawns, and pristinely painted buildings. Perfect asphalt, pothole-free roads lead up to the volcano. The nearest town, Puerto Varas, dates to 1853. It was founded by German immigrants who settled on the shores of Lake Llanquihue, as part of a government colonisation project. Yes, Chile was so empty, they had to persuade people to come. The whole area surrounding the lake is just like Germany, only more so. There are German bakeries, signs for Eisbein and sauerkraut, there are sausages hanging everywhere, and even German Eagle motifs on some of the shop fronts. Everything ran like clockwork, the shops, the banks, the road sweepers, everything. No surprise there, the famous Germanic precision.

This area and the volcano is worth riding to, from all corners of the world. (Even though the world has no corners, stupid quote really.) It is possible to ride the first two thousand metres up Osorno, and after that, it is every man for himself, or every woman in this case, as Cathy hiked to the top. I chickened out, in a quivering pile. Who would believe that I used to be in the Swansea Coastguard, and was a Cliff Rescue Instructor? No more do I have those genes, or guts. Must be guts, because you can't get rid of genes. I am a fan of heights no more.

Osorno is a happy, active volcano with at least eleven historically noted eruptions. Note the word, eruption, we are not talking, puffs of smoke here. Despite these high temperature eruptions, the upper slopes are almost entirely covered in glacier, sustained by the substantial snowfall in the very moist, maritime climate. I love this volcano more because it is mentioned in my favourite book, *The Origin of the Species*, by Charles Darwin. A genius he was.

During the second voyage of *The Beagle* in 1835, a famous ship, (but badly named, after a non floating, fat dog with questionable intelligence: sorry Pepper), Darwin was lucky enough to witness an eruption of Osorno, which impressed him greatly. Lucky fellow. I would love to have been there, discussing eruptions and evolution and other light subjects. On a more banal note, and to rid you of visions of intrepid explorers, Motorola used Osorno volcano as the backdrop for their most popular promotional advert and photos for their best-selling PEBL mobile phone. Millions saw the vision of Osorno, and bought phones, like Lemmings. Luckily, not so many came to the real place.

The last time that Osorno erupted was in 1869, but that doesn't mean there haven't been mild explosions that affect people for hundreds of kilometres, but don't make the news. I saw it in Ecuador, in Argentina, in Mexico, where people keep partying, as stairwells collapse beneath them.

"Oh. Another earthquake. Fifth today. Ooh, another eruption."

Chile was on the list of dodgy earthquake spots. I should have known that as it was bang in the middle of volcano and earthquake belt. Someone who had been heavily affected by an eruption of Osorno volcano was Condor Man, the maddest person ever to live at the base of a volcano. Possibly the maddest person ever to be allowed to roam free in this world, but the owner of the most amazing restaurant, with views of Osorno of which God would have approved.

Guy, pronounced Ghee (like the Indian cooking lard), was the oddest of odd people, from Oddsville, Oddland. But, not being judgmental, we both found him... odd. Guy was a six-foot two-inch Dutchman, with hands as big as shovels and arms that reached the ground. He had long, curly hair, blonde with grey streaks, that looked like it had been in rollers. He also had large, blue, piercing eyes. They would have been piercing, except for the fact that one eye was a lot higher up on his head than acceptable. On his forehead, basically. I never made, or even thought about making, Cyclops jokes.

Guy was wearing blue towelling shorts, that would have been rejected in the '80s for being too tight and too short. He had homemade flip flops, seemingly fashioned from an old car tyre. I was used to this in Africa, but it was a first for me in Latino countries. His feet and toes were incredibly long and splayed. They reminded me of Maasai feet, so the sandals were appropriate. He had a white T-shirt with one of my favourite shepherd quotes on it. (Not the writer, the goat herder.)

'Get the flock out of here.'

Guy had deep lines on his face, filled with volcanic dust. Because of his enthusiasm and verve for life, I guessed his age at 27, but when I got a closer look... 63. Guy owned a single room restaurant, in a spectacular setting, on the lake edge with a view of Osorno on the other bank. The car park was very optimistic. It was a flattened area covered in pea shingle (horrible on a bike), with space for about 200 vehicles. When we pulled up Guy came jogging out with his sidekick, a portly Chilean with the traditional name, Malcolm. Malcolm had a moustache but his straight, jet black hair was cut more like an Inca chief.

It was a strange look. He was a foot shorter than his lanky friend, but he was constantly jumping up and down, for no reason, so it was difficult to guess his height. Both of them were manic as hell. Malcolm was obsessed with the camera on his new mobile phone, and spent the whole two hours of our visit taking photos of everything Cathy did. He wasn't as interested in me. If she took a sip of a drink, he was there, snapping away. When she went to the restroom, he followed her, snapping away, until Cathy had to say, "Hmm, excuse me, I need the bathroom."

He backed off apologetically, but was back at it a few minutes later. He kept sticking the camera in our faces, even when we were eating, blocking the route of food from our plates to our mouths.

"Look, look, mira, mira, photo perfect, no?"

We nodded enthusiastically and he carried on with his art. He was batty, but Guy was insane. He was one of those gangly types who never seem to get used to their own coordination. He was like a spider monkey, on spirits. He lumbered around, swinging his arms skyward, and in circles, as though he was trying to keep his balance. He also had a strange tick. When he was emphasising a point, he would raise his right arm, parallel with the ground, and shake his hand and fingers violently, from side to side.

Guy handed us a menu each and then announced, "We don't have anything on the menu, except the bottled water and beer. But I do have a dish ready, if you would like to try."

We both nodded in agreement.

"Whatever you have, that would be great," Cathy said, flashing a pearly white smile.

"Right," shouted Guy, clapping his hands together loudly, giving us both a fright. He spun on his heels, and nearly fell sideways off the verandah and into the lake. Luckily, he bounced off a support beam, regained his balance, and was gone behind a curtain. Malcolm disappeared outside to try his new camera phone on landscapes and unsuspecting animals. Thank God.

Cathy and I were stifling giggles about this eccentric pair. Their enthusiasm was great, actually. Now, I am not a food buff of any sort, but I swear to God, we were shocked. After fifteen minutes of banging and mumbling and singing, from behind the curtain, Guy came out with the two most beautiful plates of food we have ever seen. The plates were pristine white china, raised slightly at the sides, and in the shape of a teardrop. On the thinner end of the plate, was a tomato, cut and shaped exactly like a rose. There was a beautiful mixed salad, and nestled next to it, was a perfectly presented piece of smoked trout, with garlic butter melted over it. We were given a side dish of fresh, crusty bread, and butter squares, lemon slices and two majestic two-foot salt and pepper cellars, made of a beautiful smelling wood.

"I make the bread myself and I catch the trout here," Guy said, pointing out to the lake.

"I also have a smoker at the back, I build myself, with Marcom." His sidekick's name had changed slightly, but I didn't pull him up on it.

The food was unbelievable and was followed with a mango mousse and homemade truffles, with edible, local flower petals, sprinkled over the dish. Looked and tasted amazing. We are talking about a place that looks like a roadside café, meanwhile, what is produced inside is Michelin star food. Get on down there, Gordon Ramsay. Unbelievable.

Guy and photo snapper were pacing around the table, gauging our level of delight. They were drinking Santa Carolina, Chilean Sauvignon Blanc. I happen to know, because I looked at the label, that this wine has been produced since 1875. By the time we left, Guy was on his second bottle and had dispensed with the glass, swigging earnestly from the bottle, with his left hand, and flapping his free hand around in front of him.

As often happens with people, we were surprised by Guy entirely. He was a proper dude. Not only is he a fantastic chef, he also grows grapes for wine, bakes cakes and sweets, has completed the Dakar Rally and The Roof of Africa Rally, and has saved his son (Mushroom - that's what his name sounded like), from being taken off by a Condor. Yes, indeed. You heard it right. A three-year-old Dutch boy was nearly taken off, over the Chilean mountains by a Condor, never to be seen again. Guy saved the day. This is what happened and I will try to include the sound effects, which is difficult in a book and takes particular talent.

Before you snigger, Condors are serious business. Condor is the common name for two species of New World vultures. There is the Andean Condor (Vultur gryphus), which unsurprisingly, inhabits the Andean Mountains of South America. The Californian Condor (Gymnogyps californianus) is found in the Western coastal mountains of the USA and Mexico. The Condor is the largest bird in the Western hemisphere. They can grow up to 40 pounds in weight and have an incredible wingspan of up to 350cm (10 feet). The adult plumage is uniformly black, with the exception of a frill of white feathers neatly surrounding the base of the neck, which is kept meticulously clean. As an adaptation for hygiene, the Condor's head and neck have few feathers, which exposes the skin to the sterilising effect of ultraviolet at high altitude. The ancient relative of the Condor (Argentavis magnficens), fossils of which have been found from the Pleistocene era, was the largest flying bird ever with a wingspan of seven metres (23 feet).

The modern birds are not slouches, and travel up to 250 kilometres a day, in search of small Dutch boys; sorry, I mean, carrion. They prefer large carcasses such as deer or cattle, which they spot by soaring high on thermals and looking for scavengers, who they easily bully away from the carrion. Other scavengers also find it difficult to rip through the hides of these bigger animals. In the wild Condors are intermittent eaters, often going many days without food, then gorging themselves on several kilogrammes of meat. Gorging is the right term, because they often eat so much that they are incapable of taking off.

So how did a three-year-old get to Chile? In a nutshell, forty years ago, in Amsterdam, Guy used to steal loaves of bread from the delivery area at the back of a bakery, and sweets from a delicatessen near his house. He would sell the sweets to his friends at school, and the loaves to their parents. This was his heady introduction to the world of crime. He decided crime wasn't for him, but money-making was. He left school and sold ovens and cooking utensils to Algerians and Somalians. He then decided to travel, and backpack around South America. The beauty of the continent haunted him, especially the crisp, clean air and beautiful mountains and the lakes of Chile. Life passed by, for thirty or so years, until he returned, met a Chilean woman, got married and set up a restaurant near a volcano. As you do. Then along came Mushroom. Back to the story.

Six months back when Mushroom was barely three, Guy decided to strap him to his front and scale a nearby peak, which looked like a stiff trek, but not too daunting. After three hours of hard slog and rock scrabbling, they came to a large flattened rock, that needed to be scaled to reach the summit. After a few curly-hair raising slips, Guy pulled himself and Mushroom over the final rock, and came face to face with an angry Condor female, sitting on a nest. At that point in the story, Guy put his bottle of wine on our table, his eyes widened. He spread out his arms, to show the Condor's impressive wingspan, made whooshing sounds, flapping his arms slowly, and started running round and round our dining table.

"The Condor saw Mushroom and went for him, to eat," said Guy, looking at us manically, for a response.

At this point Guy stretched his arms out in front of him, opening up his fingers, like Condor talons. Malco, whose name was shortening by the minute, was following him around, taking photos of the flying Dutchman Condor, and showing them to Cathy for artistic approval. Guy was not getting enough attention, so decided to up the ante.

"So the Condor came straight for my son, 'whoosh,' and tried to take him from my front pack. 'Whoosh.'"

He demonstrated by soaring down on an innocent, unsuspecting piece of lettuce on Cathy's plate, grabbed it in his talons and flew off around the room. He then mimed, "No, no!" whilst reaching his arms to the heavens.

"That Condor, it wanted Mushroom, I tell you truth, Spencer and Katy," as he continued on his flight path around the restaurant walls. Then he stopped dead and announced, "I fight it off, with both hands".

He demonstrated, flailing his arms wildly in front of him, as though he was an epileptic being attacked by a swarm of bees.

"The Condor take his jacket, but I hold on. My son is alive. Life is good now. I have my son, my wife is at home making essential oils, and tonight I will make more mushrooms with her."

I didn't have the heart to say that Condors are not birds of prey, they are scavengers, and eat from other predators' kills. I didn't say that the Condor was probably scared stiff when she saw a two-headed human pop up, right in front of her nest, and was probably trying to get away. I kept quiet. It was obviously a big moment for Guy, and he felt proud that he had saved his son's life. We were highly entertained by the gentle, but off-the-wall Guy and his happy snapper, but we had to head off to find a campsite before dark. We left, waving happily and promising to return. As we drove off, I looked in the rear-view mirror. Guy was still swooping, and Malcolm was snapping photos of our rear as we disappeared around a corner. We continued on for half an hour skirting the lake. I am glad I didn't rudely burst his bubble because, forty kilometres further on, we were stopped by a road block. We got chatting and told the police about our delicious meal.

"Ah, Condor man," said one of the police, nodding his head slowly.

They waved us on.

A few weeks later we received 317, yes 317 photos, taken by Mal, the snapper, all of them useless. We also received some photos of Mushroom, presumably to prove to us he was real, and not a fig tree of Guy's imagination. As is so strange with travelling, and social media, we met Guy and Malcolm for two hours, but we still talk two years later. Guy is doing great, his wife Martha has another Mushroom in the oven and Mushroom One is, well; mushrooming. (Do not quote me on Malcolm and Mushroom's names, I could have misheard.)

The meeting with Condor man was seriously entertaining and we would undoubtedly be back for more culinary delights, and Condor stories, but we had been sidetracked. We had to get to a campsite near to the base of the Osorno volcano, so that the next morning we could try and summit. Before we got there, I was to fall off the bike, in front of two seven-year-old policemen at a roadblock, and would eat a cockroach. More of that later, or maybe not.

Our peculiar fascination with volcanoes began in Ecuador when we camped near our first volcano together in South America, Cotopaxi. I had ridden past Kilimanjaro, in Tanzania, during my Africa circumnavigation, but never really took it in. I was too busy trying to make the world's worst TV commercial, for Optimax Laser Specialists. In return for free eye surgery and ten quid, I agreed to film an advert at the base of Mt. Kilimanjaro. The director had to have the classics; the savannah, Acacia thorn trees, Mt. Kilimanjaro, and zebras, obviously. It wasn't the easiest thing to film, but you can check out the results in my Africa TV series or on YouTube. Consequently, I don't count Kilimanjaro as my first proper volcano experience.

South America is certainly the place to go, if you are a volcano hunter. Why? Because it has the Andean volcanic belt that stretches through Argentina, Bolivia, Chile, Colombia, Ecuador and Peru. It is formed as a result of subduction of the Nazca plate and the Antarctic plate underneath the South American plate. South America has 174 volcanoes that have had historically noted eruptions, and up to 1000 more, dormant volcanoes. Littered with volcanoes. Our first, sit down, take in and enjoy, volcano was the incredible Cotopaxi, which is a stratovolcano located fifty kilometres south of Ecuador capital, Quito. It is the second highest summit in Ecuador, reaching a spectacular, permanently snowcapped, perfect cone peak of 5,897 metres. It is going in my top four list.

The first recorded ascent of Cotopaxi was by Wilhelm Reiss and Angel Escobar in 1872. Cathy and I had no intention of repeating this feat but we knew, from research, that we could ride up to at least 4,500 metres, on a dirt road, set up camp there, and see what the morning brought. Since 1738 Cotopaxi has erupted more than fifty times, resulting in the formation of numerous valleys, formed by Lahars (mudflows), around the volcano base. It made for wonderful riding and all the time, Cotopaxi was in front of us. After a hard hour riding, on slippery gravel, we came into the most beautiful valley, dotted with a couple of buildings. This must be the first campsite. There was no one around, just a rudimentary hut, with an outside sink, with no water, a toilet locked with a rusty bolt, and a long-eared rabbit watching us, from a purple flowering, gorse bush. Not a problem for us, as we had a tent, we had some snacks, and plenty of water, and the great outdoors as a loo. (Buried afterwards, good citizens.) If we got hungry, there was always long-eared rabbit stew. A dream was about to come true. We were going to fall asleep under the stars, with a volcano as a backdrop, and we would wake up to its shadow against the rising sun. It was wonderful and huge. Just consider that on a clear day, Cotopaxi is clearly visible to the residents of Quito, fifty kilometres away. It is part of a chain of volcanoes around the Pacific plate, known as the Ring of Fire. We felt ant-like-insignificant, staring up at this peak. It is very humbling to feel small, but a part of a much bigger thing; the grandeur of huge mountains, the raw power of an ocean wave, the vastness of a desert, the energy of a plunging waterfall, the power of nature. It is something to behold and Cotopaxi is a prime candidate for evoking those ant-small feelings. The thing about nature is its timelessness and power.

Cotopaxi has a lot of character. The last eruption lasted from August 2015 to January 2016. The volcano was closed to climbing until 7 October 2017 but this is constantly under review. We felt privileged to be there, at an altitude of we later found out was 3,800 metres. It did get bloody cold in the night. The base, where we were, is a staggering 23 kilometres around. Cotopaxi has one of the few equatorial glaciers in the world, but the fact it only started at 5,000 metres, meant we were not going to touch it.

Cathy was beginning to feel light-headed and short of breath, and so was I, in a more manly way of course. So going higher was out. We had made the mistake of going from almost sea level to 3,800 metres in a day. Athletes and climbers stop off and acclimatise. We rushed up there like idiots. It wasn't to be the last time we had altitude problems, through our own fault.

My favourite line about Cotopaxi, was uttered by a politician on Ecuadorian TV, three days before we went there,

"The volcano is in a very abnormal state, and is not acting like a normal volcano," he said, stone-faced, seriously, on national TV. Apparently, this year alone more than 1,000 earthquakes were recorded around Cotopaxi and emission rates of sulfur dioxide reach a staggering 20,000 tonnes per day. (Not good, cough cough, and all that.) The volcano is ready to blow again at any point, to be Frank, Bruno. I have no idea why that is categorised as 'abnormal'. That seems like exactly how a volcano should behave, in my opinion. However, the government estimates, because of this abnormal behaviour, that 300,000 peoples lives are at risk from the volcano in the provinces of Cotopaxi, Tungurahua, Napo and Pichincha. I don't want to trivialise this warning, because Cotopaxi has a moody history.

A tragedy occurred here on Easter Sunday 1996, when an avalanche partially buried the Refuge we were currently in, and buried dozens of tourists. The glacier above the Refuge was weakened by an earthquake that had shaken the entire province of Cotopaxi, for several days prior to the avalanche. But you can't keep people away from beautiful places. In the warm midday sun, a huge portion of the ice wall broke loose. Being Easter, and great weather, there were many day visitors on the mountain, who were buried in the ice and snow. Those inside the Refuge broke windows on the downhill side to climb to safety. We walked slowly round the Refuge, trying to imagine the horror. There is quite an atmosphere at the base of Cotopaxi, whether you know about the tragedy, or not.

Thirteen people died on the slopes that day and eighty six were injured. It was clear from where we were standing, that this valley was directly in the line of fire, and consequently, highly vulnerable to future avalanches, eruptions and earthquakes. I don't call that much of a 'refuge', if you are going to get buried in millions of tonnes of pyroclastic flow.

The volcano is not finished yet. On 25th July, 2021 there was a massive eruption of ash and steam, that spread more than 100 kilometres. Future eruptions are a massive threat. Latacunga, the regional capital, is holding its breath. Latacunga is located in a southern valley of the volcano. The city has been totally destroyed, twice, in recent history, and built again from scratch. Wise, brave, resilient and a bit foolish. H.G. Wells even wrote about a Cotopaxi eruption, with a tumult of lava reaching the coastline in a day, in his short story, 'The Star'.

Bearing in mind that the earthquakes and volcanic eruptions are only ever heard of in the news, if there is catastrophic damage or loss of life. The day to day struggles of people living in volcano zones is not often reported. Guy, the Condor man, showed us photos of his restaurant, the carpark, road and mountainside after a minor volcanic blast in the late '90s. Everything was covered in a layer of fine ash, more than a metre deep. It took more than two weeks of shovelling and cleaning, to get any semblance of normality back.

All is possible it seems, with volcanoes, but luckily there were no eruptions, earthquakes, landslides, avalanches, pyroclastic flows, ice storms or wind storms while we were there. But we had another problem. Cathy woke up in the middle of the night with a splitting headache, disorientation and shortness of breath. She hadn't improved. She had altitude sickness. We were also poorly prepared, with sleeping bags that wouldn't keep you warm in Bermuda, and Cathy was beginning to shiver badly. Some people saunter up to 7,000 metres, others collapse at 2,500 metres. We are the latter. Altitude is our nemesis. The only solution was to go down, quickly. I packed up the camp, like an SAS master and we were off, within twenty minutes. Not before we both turned to the volcano, and Cathy burst into tears. Cathy rarely cries, so I knew she must be feeling very ill. Her comment surprised me.

"I don't want to go. I am so sad, that's why I am crying. Not because I am sick. It is so beautiful here and I want to stay forever," tears streaming down her cheeks.

I felt the same. We headed off, pensive, but keen to clear our heads at lower altitude. This place would not only be in our hearts forever, I knew we would be back. There was a final twist in the tale. We were one of the last motorbikes to ride up to the Refuge at Base Camp, Cotopaxi, if not the last. A French rider turned up a week or so after us and acted like a moron, a word I don't use lightly. Bear in mind that Cotopaxi is a national park with clearly designated, unobtrusive, dirt roads and walking trails, leading up to the pristine base of the volcano. There are beautiful, elegant plants and flowers everywhere. It is natural and understated. Access is provided, but no shops, tar roads, street signs or telegraph poles. This gentleman used the flat, lush plain, below Cotopaxi, full of mosses, wild flowers, animals and insects, as his own personal motocross track. He ripped the place to pieces, was arrested and thrown in jail. Good.

Cotopaxi is now closed to motorbikes for good and the wonderful experience Cathy and I had, riding to the Refuge, will not be repeated by other bikers. Shame on you. Much love to Cotopaxi. We were defeated, but we had Osorno volcano in our sights.

But first, don't pass the jail.

View of Osorno volcano from Condor man Guy's carpark

Chapter Ten
Chucky and the Triceratops

San Martin jail in Cordoba is in a state of total collapse, and is the worst prison in Argentina, if not South America. Last year, inmates held 60 hostages in protest at the gruesome conditions. Harrowing scenes from the riot were broadcast live on television, showing hostages being slashed and stabbed on the jail roof, with dead prisoners sprawled on the ground, killed while trying to flee the mayhem inside. At least eight people were killed; two prison officers, a policeman and five prisoners. More than 40 others were seriously injured. Relatives visiting prisoners were caught up in the violence, including women and children, five of whom were badly injured.

The prison authorities said that the inmates overpowered the guards, took their weapons and then found additional arms in a storage area. They also used makeshift knives and set the prison on fire, using mattresses. The area around the prison became a battleground too, as shots from the jail whistled through the streets, hitting houses and smashing windows in the densely populated San Martin district. An eleven-year-old girl, waiting for the bus from school, was killed instantly, when she was struck on the forehead by a stray bullet. Experts blamed the uprising on the insanely crowded conditions, where prisoners lie like sardines in the cells, and the exercise yard has no room at all to walk. The prison houses more than 2,400 prisoners and was originally built in 1881 for 400 inmates. Tempers at the prison, frayed by the sweltering, 40 degree summer heat, in concrete airless rooms, were further aggravated by the prison's water supply being cut off. Toilets were un-flushable and quickly overflowed, the urine and faeces baking in the stifling heat, and even overflowing into the canteen. Inmates had to sit in poo and eat their rations. Too grim!

The Mayor of Cordoba, Luis Juez, admitted that the situation was one of terrible anguish, and that the subhuman conditions threatened to escalate to a state of total collapse.

This was not an isolated experience. Trouble has flared regularly for over 100 years. In 1971 a riot, also caused by overcrowding, left 17 dead and 50 injured. In 1997, the police and army raided the prison, trying to smash a cocaine ring that was operating from inside. It didn't work and it is easier to score drugs now in the prison than it is in the streets.

Cathy and I were about to spend two days with a hardcore Cordoba prison gang, led by the boss, 'El Jefe', Oscar Acosta, who unfortunately fell head over heels in love with Cathy. Awkward. We came into the town of Rio Cuarto, a sweltering dustbowl, 200 kilometres south of the city of Cordoba. After a gruelling seven-hour ride, both our bike suits were soaked through, and we were as parched and sunburnt as an albino in the Sahara, without a paddle, or an umbrella.

The main street was quiet and the central plaza was deserted, but we did spot a small shop, on a weedy, overgrown roundabout, with a group of men, sitting outside, under a corrugated iron cover, held up by four squiff poles and frayed blue rope. There were five men on beer crates, sitting around a short, portly gentleman, in a cowboy hat, who was bizarrely holding court, astride a stack of eight sun-bleached, cracked, off-white, plastic chairs. As he became more animated, his feet swung back and forth, like a child on a swing. It would have been comical, if he didn't look so bloody hard, and evil.

Senor Acosta had piggy eyes, a bulbous nose, and squashed up cheeks that collected in creases under his eyes. He had a scar running from his lip, up past his eye, and disappearing into his thick, black hairline and a thin, neatly trimmed moustache, that relayed a bit of self-love. He was wearing jeans, a red and black chequered cowboy shirt, and pointed boots, that looked way too small. His feet were about the size of my six-year-old daughter's. I am sure if he stood up, he would fall over. All the group were drinking bottles of blue labelled beer, called Quilmes, the national beer of Argentina, and in my humble opinion, the worst beer on earth. It smells a bit like liquidised boiled eggs, and tastes worse.

We pulled up in front of Oscar Acosta and his gang, stopped the bike, removed our helmets and greeted the group. Oscar jumped down from his great height, and the group immediately stood up, except for one guy of about eighteen, who fell backwards over his chair, hitting his elbow on the concrete window sill of the shop. It sounded painful and was probably cracked. He let out a yelp, but was ignored, and they rushed to greet us and offer us crates to sit on. A small hobbit-like character they called Chucky, wearing baggy green tracksuit pants and a red T-shirt that was so long it looked like a dress, offered Cathy a fresh orange juice, and he handed me a beer.

They were all extremely animated and welcoming, but I was on a mission to find somewhere to camp, and asked them if they knew of anywhere. Oscar Acosta, who spent the whole time staring at Cathy, waved his hands in the air. "No problem my dearest friends, we will finish this beer and I will take you to where you will sleep," he said, scrunching up his miniscule eyes even more.

It sounded like an order, rather than an offer, but we thanked him kindly. After brief introductions, and a very rapid Quilmes, Oscar Acosta beckoned us to jump on our bike. He mounted a black and red Argentinian-made Motomel CG 150 motorcycle, and careered off down the road, almost hitting a cartoon-looking donkey with furry ears and a fringe, as he waved enthusiastically for us to follow. Although the bike was small, his feet were still far from the ground. Every time he went round a corner, he flailed his legs wildly in the air and nearly went off the road, and on one corner, sent three chickens scattering for cover, feathers flying. The inevitable happened, and Oscar Acosta hit a pothole at full speed, bounced a metre above the seat, and when he came down, his motorcycle was no longer there. He landed on the dirt road, stood up, patted the dust off his bum, wiped his hands on his belly, gave us a smile and a thumbs up. He retrieved his motorbike from the bush, straightened the handlebars through brute force, and left an indicator and mirror on the road.

On he jumped, and careered down the road once more. After falling off two more times, we eventually arrived at a stone gate and a long boulevard of dead trees. I hoped that Oscar Acosta did not notice the vertical streaks of clean skin on my dust-covered face, when I took off my helmet. I had been crying with laughter at his riding antics for the whole journey. It was like letting Basil Fawlty loose on a motorcycle, but worse. He didn't seem to notice the streaks coming from my eyes and pointed proudly at a sign at the end of the boulevard. It was a Dinosaur Theme Park. South and Central America are obsessed with them. A dinosaur park usually refers to a theme park in which several life-size sculptures or models of prehistoric animals are displayed. Dinosaur parks were to play an integral part in our camping plans throughout South America. So, where did it all start?

The first dinosaur Park worldwide was Crystal Palace Dinosaurs, which opened in London in 1854. From 1977 to 1991 the largest dinosaur park was Traumlandpark in Germany. The Jurassic Park films evidently led to an explosion of theme parks worldwide. South and Central America pushed it to the extreme and there are literally hundreds of Dino parks with such names as The Beasts of Patagonia, Museo Paleontologico

Egidlio Feruglio, and not forgetting The World's Best Dinosaur Park, which quite frankly could have been the worst. Do not think of Spielberg-type effects when imagining the South American parks. Think more, children's cartoon, 'Barney the Dinosaur'. They are truly horrific and kitsch.

Under the entrance arch to the Chubut Dinosaur Park, Oscar Acosta fell off the motorbike in front of the ticket office, and left his bike lying in the dirt. He approached the rickety wooden desk and broken window, that housed a glum looking, thin-as-a-reed, scowling woman, in a gypsy bandana. Oscar Acosta, stated to her, pointing at us:

"These two are staying here for as long as they want. Free."

She just nodded silently and we were in. I don't think she had much choice. I didn't ask any questions. Free accommodation is my favourite price. Oscar Acosta wobbled down a dirt track, and then came to a halt, proudly pointing to the first exhibit, a Brontosaurus. Brontosaurus, means 'thunder lizard', a wonderful name. I think my next bike might be called that. Or maybe it's a good name for Cathy. Anyway, a Brontosaurus had a long, thin neck, and a small head adapted for a herbivorous lifestyle. They had a bulky torso and a long whip-like tail. They were truly massive fellows. Adult individuals weighed up to fifteen tonnes and measured up to 22 metres. If that means little to you, they weighed about the same as 250 adult men, or 312.5 women, and were the length of at least 20 strapping, Argentinian gents.

The only similarity of the exhibit to a real Brontosaurus was that it was life-size. That's where the resemblance ended, extremely abruptly. It looked like a child had grabbed a piece of neon green chewing gum and had stretched it into some sort of random shape, whilst blindfolded. The head was devoid of eyes and had less definition than a cotton bud. It was the saddest looking Brontosaurus I have ever not seen. As a child, even with a vivid imagination, I would have been in tears at the disappointment. The Brontosaurus was not the worst exhibit in this park, in fact it was the best. These places are traumatic for children.

As we rode slowly through the park, we were met by one-eyed dinosaurs, made of papier mâché, their horns broken off. All the dinosaurs were a ridiculous colour. They were a bit like Caribbean dinosaurs, their skin was the colour of the tropical houses you find all over that area, neon green, bright yellow and other cheery, luminous-type colours. It looks great on the wall of a sun-drenched Caribbean house, but when you paint your dinosaur exhibits with the same colours, it doesn't have the same effect, and can only be upsetting for small children, hoping to meet a real dinosaur. It's all the adults' fault, buying sub-standard products. I happen to know that certain cheap Chinese, brightly coloured paints, of extremely low quality, are available to the South American market. Hence the silly dinosaur colours.

On our lefthand side was another feature that goes hand in hand with dinosaur parks; water parks. I hate them. These are the huge fibre glass, soulless, spaghetti water slides, in various shapes, running in to different pools of various sizes. Lots of screaming and shouting and sliding goes on at water parks, but not at this one. Its glory days were long past. There was one empty pool which was covered in slime, and had been taken over by sick-looking lizards. The second pool was full, but was a septic tank of filth and litter. The third pool, which had the biggest slide, was in reasonable order (well, it had water in it), and three boys were in the shallow end, throwing a frisbee to each other. The 60-foot water slide had a floor panel missing, a third of the way down, with plants growing out of it, so if anyone used it they would fall 30 feet onto concrete, and expire. If you didn't get TB, E coli, salmonella, camplobacter or norovirus from the water first. Or, boring old gastroenteritis. I admit to a phobia of public swimming pools. I never use them. I swim in the sea, a body of water that is cleansed by nature. In a swimming pool I cannot help thinking that I am sharing a bath with another hundred people, involving snot, dead skin, coughing, sneezing, cuts, infections, athletes' foot and those lovely people who like to urinate in pools. I don't think a pile of chlorine the size of the Great Pyramid would lure me into a pool now. I was worried that Oscar Acosta was going to insist we swim, but luckily, he felt the dinosaurs were more noteworthy.

He led us past various unidentifiable blobs of dinosaur, many of them missing limbs. He pulled up next to a grass verge, where there was a bumpy clearing, watched over by a Tyrannosaurus Rex. He was remarkably badly made. He had horns, and the canopy throne of bone, that I found so thrilling when I was a child. But sadly, he looked seriously scared, cross-eyed, and had legs that were way too long, and was in definite need of a dentist, and looked pregnant with octuplets. There were no claw details, vein and skin details, nothing anatomically accurate. It was a blob T Rex. Oscar was impressed.

We were ordered by 'Senor, I won't Acosta you' to set up camp in the grass clearing and then go back to town for dinner and some more horrific Quilmes. We accepted the order, I mean, invitation, happily. It would be rude not to thank Oscar publicly, in front of his group.

We set up the tent in ten minutes, beating the world 'putting up a tent record', and decided to have a lie down. We were both asleep in ten minutes. I think we would have slept for the next fifteen hours, if it wasn't for five skinny, tan-coloured bush puppies who invaded our tent, and tried to sit on our faces, and get in our sleeping bags. They were a bit like the dinosaurs. You could tell that they were supposed to be labradors, but they had not quite appeared in the world correctly. Their legs were more sausage dog. When they all started passing wind, due to all the excitement, I decided to evict them. I crawled out of our unnecessarily small tent, to see where the puppies had come from. There was a small, defunct, brick barbecue under a tree, and the puppies' mother had dug a hole under it, and deposited them there. She had obviously just popped off for a break, from the relentless breast feeding, as the puppies were well fed.

I grabbed a litre bottle of Eco De los Andes water and walked around the super realistic Triceratops, that was guarding our campsite. I splashed my face with water, trying to wake up, so we could head into town. I noticed that the Triceratops was cunningly made of reinforcing bar and plaster. Sadly he had cracked in the sun and had holes in him. I peered through one of the holes, got the fright of my life, and jumped high in the air. Chucky was staring back at me from inside the dinosaur.

"What the hell Chucky!" I exclaimed, jumping backwards again, and nearly squishing a puppy.

"Sorry James, I was waiting to take you back to town for food, and I fell asleep."

"No problem," I managed to stammer.

If any of you reading this have had this experience, chatting to a Cordoba gang member inside a Triceratops, please email me.

After my initial shock at finding a gangster inside the stomach of a dinosaur, and then squeezing out of his belly, we followed the afore-mentioned gangster back to the scene of our original meeting. But not before he took us to the town square to show us a statue of the founder of the town, Arnoll Gutierrez. There was a 15-foot, faux marble plinth, the base surrounded by dead flowers, and some sort of water feature, that evidently had not worked since the revolution. The statue of the town hero was in gaudy spray-painted gold, and poor old Arnoll Gutierrez was about the size of an action man toy, perched unimpressively upon high. A gold plaque was screwed to the plinth, extremely squiffily. But it was the message that was presented, that had me laughing:

'Arnoll Gutierrez, town founder died from alcohol abuse.'

Wow! What an epitaph. Surely they could have thought of one of his more positive attributes, like town planning, or fundraising for undernourished indigenous children.

After our cultural tour, we returned to the motley crew, who were still on the Quilmes lager. All of them were louder than an hour before, except one. The silent one. I will get to him.

El Jefe - Oscar Acosta - had resumed his position atop many plastic chairs, and was waving a gold gun around, which was slightly disconcerting. Cathy was waited on hand and foot, but when Oscar Acosta decided to spoon-feed Cathy some stew, while staring longingly into her eyes, I'd had enough. I grabbed the spoon and said, "Come on man, that's ridiculous, that's my woman."

I am not sure if I said that, because it sounds a bit too cowboy-style for me, but I did say something to set boundaries. Which is difficult when you are talking to a gang leader. Cathy defused the whole thing by telling The Boss to get off the pile of chairs and share them around. I cringed. He immediately did as she said. The gang all looked shocked. Chucky giggled. Maniacally.

"So why do they call you Chucky?" I asked, knowing full well that he resembled the doll in the Stephen King film.

"It's because he likes to cut people up," was the unexpected answer from the silent eighteen-year-old, Isandro.

That shocked us both and silence reigned for a minute. I decided to jump in at the deep end, as is my style. All six of them, apart from the obvious coverings of gang tattoos, had livid scars, more than thirty of them each, running parallel up their forearms and I couldn't ignore it any longer. "Why do you all have those cuts?" I asked.

Janik, a man who stared at the floor more than anyone I have ever met said, "Every time one of our gang gets in trouble with the police or army, or with rival gangs, or gets killed, we all cut ourselves," he said, without looking up.

Bloody hell! They must get in trouble a lot. This was so beyond the realms of what Cathy and I knew as normal, but it is super important not to judge. We are all dealt different cards. Just as it couldn't get more odd, Janik suddenly burst into tears.

Cathy put her arm on his and said, "Hey, what's wrong?"

He bowed his head and his shoulders convulsed.

"His girlfriend killed herself last Thursday evening," said Cyprien, a smooth-looking Al Pacino type.

Bloody hell! What next?

Well, next was that Chucky decided that he wanted to go to the local booze house and that I was to accompany him. I looked at Cathy for approval and could see she was fine. She had her 'humans are fascinating' look on. Not a problem and we headed off walking down the road. Chucky kept staring at me and shaking his head in disapproval.

Eventually I stopped and said, "Have I done something wrong?"

"Yes, you are too tall, I can't walk next to you."

"No problem, Chucky, I will come down to your height."

I bent my knees to almost 90 degrees, so that my six foot four could become fit foot nothing.

"That's better," said Chucky.

So it came to pass that I walked three hundred metres at Chucky height, and my thighs were burning to buggery by the time we made it to the shop. No point in upsetting a slasher. Chucky ordered 2,000 beers, ten packets of Virginia Slims, and a couple of head-sized, sticky buns. Chucky did not pay for anything. The shopkeeper was very happy not to argue with my vertically challenged friend. Luckily, on the way back, Chucky forgot about being offended by my height. That was a bonus, because I felt a slight niggle in my right leg, and cramp coming on.

We made it back to the group and luckily Cathy was still being treated like a Queen, waited on hand and foot. Unfortunately, El Jefe had decided that we were going to stay at his ranch in the mountains the next day and we were going to sojourn there for a month at least, all for free. "No problem, we show you hospitality."

At this point, the fifth member of the crew, called Screwdriver, if I remember correctly, piped up randomly,

" I am a street fighter, a boxer," he said, clenching his fists, and grimacing. "OK, Screwdriver, calm down," I didn't say.

"You see this scar on my head. I won a street fight and the bastard decided to stab me in the back of the head with a broken bottle."

Screwdriver was covered in tattoos, but the type that looked like they had been wiped with a cloth, before they had dried.

"Jesus Christ that's terrible," Cathy understatedly said.

"What did you do?" I quivered, I mean queried.

"I shot him," was the answer.

Screwdriver had a mole on the side of his face, that was covered in hair, and looked like a mini forest. I had no idea how to respond to his comment and found myself looking at his hairy mole. I went into some sort of trance, and only came out of it when I saw murderer Screwdriver looking at me accusingly.

"Are you looking at my mole?"

"No, definitely not. I never noticed that huge growth on your face. Relax. No need to add to your tally of killings."

The 'Silent One' to me was the saddest of the group, and this was the first time I heard him speak:

"Leave them alone Screwdriver, you acting like shit, man."

"Have you ever shot a gun?" said Screwdriver, ignoring the 'silent one' and staring at Cathy.

"Yes, many times in South Africa," Cathy replied.

I knew this was true as we all have some sort of gun training in Southern Africa and on top of that, Cathy's father was a Police Officer and involved with Protection Services.

"Have you shot anybody?" Screwdriver continued.

"Not yet," was Cathy's reply.

That seemed to stall Screwdriver and luckily the conversation changed. But not to cheerier subjects.

Gaeetan Cordoba, with the same surname as the prison he had just been released from, was the only member of the group to unnerve me, despite the fact that we were in the company of murderers. Gaeetan was twenty and good-looking: the browning teeth, the yellowing drugged eyes, the lank, thinning hair, the bad skin, that afflicted the other gang members, was yet to affect him. But he seemed so utterly distraught with life, and angry at the same time. His expressions flickered from a blank 'stare into space' look, to an intense 'I want to kill someone' look, and no wonder. Later in the evening, he told us his story and it was a typical 'born with no hope story', and it didn't get better.

Gaeetan's father, Michael, had been killed in a turf war when Gaeetan was two, so he had no father figure. His mother was a crystal meth addict, so he had no mother figure. At thirteen he was homeless and on the streets, and joined a shoeshine and bicycle riding gang, who robbed people on their bikes and sold drugs through the shoe shiners. At seventeen Gaeetan was caught with a small bag of marijuana. He was jailed for eighteen months in Cordoba.

He was beaten and raped and was only saved when El Jefe, Oscar Acosta, took him in, and protected him in jail. After the gang were released at different times, they gravitated towards this town (which I have named wrongly out of respect), where Oscar Acosta's business dealings were based. They now all worked for him, along with another forty men. I was not stupid enough to ask what his business interests were, but I would bet my bottom Argentinian peso that they weren't legal, or very nice.

We agreed to go and stay at Oscar Acosta's ranch in the mountains, and after more horrific stories of life in Cordoba jail, we went to bed, sobered, despite the Quilmes lager. I can in no way condone any of the gang's actions. After all, they are immoral and criminal people. That's why they were in jail. But we were treated with the upmost respect, and they all bent over backwards to welcome us. A snap-shot of lives so different to our own. Many people have tragic, violent and dysfunctional upbringings, full of upheaval, insecurity and torment. How are they supposed to turn out? I am not excusing any of their actions. Society fails without laws. But putting a seventeen-year-old in a violent prison, for a few joints, is criminal in itself.

We made the decision not to visit the mountain ranch the next day. It is not beyond the realms of possibility that we would accept the hospitality for the weekend, be treated like royalty, and then be given two suitcases, to transport to Europe. It has happened before to innocent tourists and will happen again. We were not innocent tourists though. Cathy and I were not looking for careers as drug mules. Either that, or Cathy had been picked as a new wife for El Jefe, and I would end up the drug mule. Maybe neither of these scenarios would play out, but we were not willing to find out. However, we had experienced great hospitality and there was no way we were going to be rude, and just disappear. We packed up our tent, gave the puppies some sardines, and went back into the centre, to make our excuses.

When we arrived, the whole crew were busy loading fruit and vegetables, or some similar product, onto four pick-up trucks. We were given big hugs by all, and when we announced that we had to head off straightaway to meet a cameraman in Santa Fe, they all looked genuinely disappointed. As we left, the Cordoba gang stood in a line, waving us off - 'El Jefe', Oscar Acosta, Chucky the slasher, 'falling over' 18-year-old Isandro, 'stare at the floor' Janik, Screwdriver, and good-looking, tragic Gaeetan Cordoba. As we were leaving, Oscar Acosta handed us both a cup and silver straw, the necessary equipment for making the traditional Argentinian tea, called Mate. We thanked them kindly for the present and rode off towards Chile.

We were both silent for a long while. How long will that gang stay out of jail, or stay alive. We will never know. Life is madness. On to a lighter subject: the cave of dodgery.

Chapter Eleven
The Cave of Dodgery

Cuevas de Las Manos, or Cave of Hands, is a series of caves and a complex of rock art sites in the province of Santa Cruz, Argentina, 161 kilometres south of the town of Perito Moreno. It is named after the more than 2000 hand paintings, stencilled into multiple collages, on the rock walls and ceilings. Several waves of people inhabited the cave, as evidenced by some of the early artwork that has been radiocarbon-dated to around 7300BC. The age of the cave paintings was calculated from the remains of bone-made pipes, used for spray painting the wall of the cave to create the stencilled outline of the hand collages. The site is considered by scholars to be the best material evidence of South American early hunter gatherer groups. The site was last inhabited around 700AD, by ancestors of the Tehuelche people. Argentinian surveyor and archaeologist Carlos Grandin and his team conducted research on the site in 1964, that would continue for 30 years. (Sounds like a cushy contract to me.) The importance of his discoveries led to the site being named a UNESCO World Heritage Site in 1999.

The main cave is 20 metres deep and the paintings span about 200 by 650 feet (60m by 200m). The art is some of the most important in the New World and by far the most famous rock art in Patagonia. The artwork not only decorates the interior of the cave, but also the surrounding cliff faces and exterior. Of the 2000 hand images, most are painted as negatives or stencilled, alongside some positive handprints. A survey in the 1970s counted 829 left hands to 31 right. This suggests that painters held the spray pipe with their right hand. Some fingers are missing, which could be due to amputation or deformity. Others argue that it was the use of sign language, bending fingers to convey meaning.

Apart from the hands, there are also depictions of human beings, guanacos (Llama guanicoe), rheas, felines and other smaller animals. There are geometric shapes, zig zag patterns, representations of the sun, and hunting scenes. There are repeated scenes of Guanacos being surrounded, suggesting this was the preferred tactic to capture them. This includes scenes with the use of Bolas. Bolas were weapons, designed out of cord, with weights on either end. When thrown at the legs of larger animals it trips them. Similar paintings, but in smaller numbers, can be found in nearby caves. There are also red dots on the 30-metre-high ceilings, which archaeologists believe were made by submerging their weights on the Bolas in dye, and throwing them upwards. The binding agent for this paintwork is unknown to this day, but the mineral pigments include iron oxides, producing reds and purples, kaolin producing white, natrojarosite producing yellow, and manganese oxide producing black.

The exact function, or purpose of this art is unknown, although some findings suggest it had a ceremonial or religious purpose. Others argue that the hands are indicative of the human desire to be remembered, or to record that they were there. That so many people contributed to the artwork, for thousands of years, suggests the cave held great significance. In modern times, the caves served as the inspiration and setting for the best selling children's book, *Ghost Hands*, by T.A. Barron.

Sounds intriguing and amazing, doesn't it, so when Cathy and I saw a sign which read 'Cueva de Las Manos', we were more than excited. We very rarely do anything touristy; one, because of the price, two, because of the expense, and three, because of the impact it has on the sites. So, this was a bit of a treat, but one we still felt guilty about.

We had read that the number of tourists visiting the site had increased exponentially since it was made a world heritage site. Like the idiots that us humans can sometimes be, the biggest threat is graffiti, and people stealing pieces of painted rock, as well as touching the artwork. Silly behaviour.

The sign for the Cueva de Las Manos was less than impressive. The caves were first 'rediscovered' in 1941 by a wandering monk (they seem to have a 'habit' of wandering, another cushy job), and the sign looked like the monk might have painted it. It was wooden and rotten, the letters had faded to nothing, and it was leaning at 45 degrees, away from the road. We were surprised, considering archaeologists have been studying the caves since the '60s, and it had been on the World Heritage site list for more than twenty years. We were expecting an entrance, maybe a touristy archway, or something more imposing than a wilting, indecipherable sign. We preferred it that way, keeping the tourist impact to a minimum. We turned left, off the main highway, and the road immediately turned into a windy, sandy track. As we turned the first corner, we were met with the gaze of a desert fox, perched on a large round boulder. He watched us slip past, only moving his head, to follow our progress. After five kilometres of deep sand, and the consequent over revving, clutch slipping, foot paddling, general sweating and swearing scenario, we laboriously made progress, under the watchful eye of foxes, hawks and rabbits. We came to an outcrop of rocks and the road hardened, into compact dirt, as we started climbing. After five minutes, we were at the ridge of the mountain, in the distance we could make out a wall, or once upon a time, a wall.

The road dropped steeply into a dry valley. We could make out an open clearing, between God-strewn boulders, a car park, devoid of cars, and a tatty mobile home, with no wheels, slumped in the dust. We rode down the steep slope, wheels sliding all the way, and pulled up outside the 1820s Winnebago. The monk had been at his sign writing again. There was a piece of wood, hanging on a dirty rope, on the side of the mobile home with 'Recepcion' spelt out on it, in red electrical tape, that was curling at the corners from the sun. Below it was a crudely spray-painted silhouette of a huge hand. Inside the palm of the hand, written in electrical tape, it said 'No tirar basura' (Don't throw litter).

The door was missing so I banged on the side of the caravan (or whatever it was) and it nearly caved in. A rapper from New York came casually sauntering to the entrance. He was dressed in baggy-to-the-floor blue jeans, a baby blue Miami Dolphins jersey, with the number 13 on the front and the name, Marino, on the back. It reminded me of Johnny Dollar's 'uniform', our chum from Bogota. He had a gold chain, a black Nike baseball cap and a pair of Nike trainers, that the 'youth' would stab you for.

Luckily our tour rapper, sorry guide, who turned out to be twenty-six, was an excellent guy called Santino Perez. He was not chewing gum, did not have a handkerchief tied round his head, under his cap, and he didn't give us the downward v sign, that would all have been too clichéd. Santino invited us into his caravan which, having now been in it, I am downgrading to a hut. He was in a very cold, leaking hut and served us some very cold coffee in leaking polystyrene cups. The three of us stood nose to nose, as most of the hut was filled with junk. There was no room to swing a chihuahua. Santino was from Mendoza, the wine region of Argentina, and had moved down here to be nearer to his brother after an industrial accident. Santino lost the sight in his right eye and maimed his right hand when a pressurised container exploded. Two of his colleagues were killed by a jet of boiling steam. Santino was slightly further away and his burns were not so serious.

As is so common worldwide, Santino did not receive any form of compensation. There were 'irregularities' (a favourite excuse of corporate snakes) in the company's insurance policies and serious negligence in the Health and Safety procedures. A roundabout way of saying, 'We are not paying a penny to anybody'. Now, Santino lives and works with his brother, who runs an Asado restaurant in Calafate.

Santino works at the Cave of Hands on Saturdays, for a bit of extra money, and for: "Un poco de paz y tranquilidad y algo de espacio James." ('for a little peace and quiet and some space'), he commented, while writing out our small yellow entrance tickets, identical to Church raffle tickets in the UK.

I understood. It was a beautiful place, and exactly what Santino said; tranquil. I couldn't help but notice, after seeing my ID, I was immediately called James, by Santino. This has been my name for almost eleven years, throughout Africa and South America. Ninety percent of officials pick up on the James, many adding 'James Bond', with a smile and a thumbs up. I don't mind. Spencer seems too difficult to grasp.

We received our official tickets, stepped out of the now-downgraded shack, and Santino pointed us in the direction of the caves. 2000 individual handprints and other rock art. Should be impressive. As Santino stepped down from the caravan, I noticed he winced, and as we walked, I could see his right leg was damaged. That must have been one hell of an explosion. Santino pointed rather sheepishly to a gap between two boulders, where a crude, string-bordered pathway, led.

"Follow the numbers and that will take you in the right way. Enjoy."

Off he went, back to the chilly shack.

Well. Where do I start? How do I start? There were no cave paintings, there were no stencils of thousands of prehistoric hands and animals. In fact, there were no caves. There were no *cuevas* and no *manos*. No cave and no hands, at the Cave of Hands. Very peculiar indeed. The cave was, in fact, just a very large overhang, with a dusty concave area underneath. It was evidently a favourite hang out for the local cows, judging by the flying saucer-shaped landmines, they had deposited, liberally, from their posteriors. We stepped in gingerly, not wanting to slip on cow pats, and not wanting to hit our heads on, what I had read, was a thirty-foot ceiling. This ceiling was no more than twelve foot. Of the 839 handprints that scientists have studied in detail, 839 were missing. The other 1160 were also missing. Gone were the hunting scenes. There were a few blotches of red, here and there, on the rock face, but nothing to resemble a hand. There were other mysterious smudges in white. I think they were bird poo. We wandered around the cave, that wasn't a cave, for all of three minutes. That was four complete circumnavigations. Nothing. We followed the path around the side of the cave, but there was nothing. There were random wooden cubes, painted red, with numbers on them. They were obviously supposed to mark out some wonder of archaeology, some fossil, or pot, or sketch. But there was no explanation and nothing discernible from the natural landscape, let alone signs of human activity, habitation and art classes.

I was actually in hysterics. My mum would have loved this. Cathy also saw the funny side and we walked around with pretend magnifying glasses, examining the amazing cave art. The icing on the cake was when we were leaving this incredible UNESCO World Heritage Site. As we wandered the last section of the four-minute path, we spotted a piece of writing on the rock, about six inches long. It said, 'Michel 1949'. I kid you not, there was a modern information plaque underneath it, which said, 'Modern Rock Drawing'. The bare-faced cheek of this place. My stomach was sore by this point. We made our way the three metres to the humble reception to be greeted by a flushed and embarrassed-looking Santino Perez. Surprisingly, he wasn't dealing with hoards of tourists, so could spare us a minute of his time.

I approached him with a smile. "Santino, this is not the Cave of Hands," I suggested.

"This is the Cave of Hands, James," he said, trying to look baffled by my comment, but failing.

"Well, where are the 839 hands and other rock art?" I continued. "Where are they? I have seen them with my very own eyes, all over the internet." I regretted my phrase, as he only had one eye, and was looking at me with it, worriedly.

"They are there, but not so clear," he said, waving in the general direction of the cave.

"Not so clear, that's an understatement," I said jokingly, looking him directly in the eye (singular).

He then announced, looking rather pleased with himself, "This is Cueva de las Manos 2."

We both burst out laughing and Cathy said, "Santino, it's not a movie with a sequel. Where is the Cave of Hands?"

He caved in, "111 kilometres from here," was his immediate response.

Excellent. We had come to the worst imitation of the Cave of Hands, it was physically possible to do. As attractions go it was the worst in the world. It made the Cordoba dinosaur parks look good. They didn't even bother to make any fake handprints. It would take a group of people, with scaffolding, a day to spray paint 2000-odd hand prints, and make them look old, with a bit of dust. It would also help the cause greatly, if they could have found a location for the Con-Cave of Hands, that actually had caves.

There was no way that we could be angry with Santino. He was a nice guy, a bit of a con artist, and not a good one. I took the Michael Mouse out of the whole set-up and he took it really well. He offered us the couple of dollars back from the entrance fee, but we declined. We wished him luck, gave him extensive tips on how to improve the con, and we were gone.

But that's not the end of the story. We met up with Santino's brother, Agustin, almost a year later, in an absurd coincidence that happens from time to time, when you are constantly on the move. He told us that Santino only stayed in Calafate for another two months after we were there. He came to Agustin one night, telling him, "I was sitting on a rock when a gorilla came up to me, and started to speak to me, through Jesus." (A long way from the Congo; the gorilla, not Jesus.)

The upshot of his strange vision/conversation was that Santino felt compelled to shave off all his body hair. He proceeded to tell his brother that he was commanded by The Lord to walk from Calafate to Buenos Aires, a mere distance of 2732 kilometres. He also donned a robe and carried a small pebble in his mouth during the journey. We never found out if he found enlightenment, found Buenos Aires or if he ever stopped walking. A world full of oddity again.

Chapter Twelve
The 'No You Cannot' Ischigualasto/Talampaya National Park

Try saying that after a couple of Tequilas, or before. I am sure that ninety percent of you have never heard of this place and you are lucky. I have to tell you about this National Park, not because it is one of the natural wonders of the world, but because it is the worst National Park in the world, bar none. First the worst Dinosaur Park, then the worst Cave of Hands ever created, and then this. I really am not complaining. All of life's rich tapestry. So, what made Cathy and I take a 160 kilometre detour to the strangest place we have ever been to? I feel really bad writing about this (but obviously not bad enough) because I had the National Park Director in tears and basically crumpled on the floor, a broken man, by the time we rode off. I hope he doesn't read this book. It may be the catalyst that throws him over the edge towards committing sewerage pipe. I jest. We ironed things out...

Ischigualasto National Parks are located in the northern part of Central Argentina, comprised of two adjoining protected areas. The Ischigualasto Provincial Park in San Juan Province (60,369 hectares) and Talampaya in the Rioja Province, jointly covering close to 300,000 hectares, west of the Sierra Pampeanas. It is a beautiful area of warm scrub desert, along the Eastern Andean foothills. Against this backdrop of stunning mountains, the area is a scientific treasure of global importance. ('Global importance'; bear in mind these words when you hear about the extensive and organised facilities the Park provides.) The Park harbours a basin consisting of continental sediments deposited during the entire Triassic period. This basin boasts an exceptionally complete record of plant and animal life in the geological period from roughly 250 million years to 200 million yeas ago. Amazingly, this represents the origin of both dinosaurs and mammals in the same location. If you are not excited enough yet (I thought this was a book about motorcycles!), you will be now.

Six, distinct sedimentary formations, contain the fossilised remains of a wide range of ancestral animals and plants revealing the evolution of vertebrates and detailed information on paleoenvironments (try sticking that word on your helmet), over the 50 million years of the Triassic Period. Most exciting, it records the dawn of the 'Age of the Dinosaurs'. (I bet you were singing a famous song just then.) The ongoing scientific discoveries in the area are daily occurrences and invaluable for evolutionary biology and paleontology, plus super exciting for Geek riders, of which I am a paid-up member. Furthermore, for the significance to research, the area has important archaeological value, such as 1,500-year-old petroglyphs. The rich diversity of fossils includes some 506 known genera, but also a staggering amount of species of fish, amphibian, reptile and mammalian ancestors that we knew nothing about until recently. This includes the early and excitingly named Eoraptor, named after the donkey in 'Winnie the Pooh'. Not.

No denying, it is a stunning place to drive towards, and the excitement of seeing dinosaur fossils made the journey even more exhilarating. There were soaring sandstone cliffs rising 200 metres into the clear blue sky, and further into the park, white and multi-coloured sediments created a stark and unforgiving landscape.

This was the Valle de la Luna, or the Valley of the Moon. Another world, that reminded me of the weirdness of the Salar de Uyuni Salt Flats, or the desolate areas of Patagonia. We rode through Clint Eastwood land, sparse desert vegetation, characterised by xeric shrubs and painful-looking, bum-skewering cactus, interspersed with depressed-looking, shrunken trees. Bonsai by mistake.

We rode steadily for two hours, constantly hoping to see the park entrance, but to no avail. It was 4.10pm and we knew that the outer gates closed at 5pm. The chances of getting there in time were looking slim. No big deal but it would be a night in the desert with very few provisions, only four litres of water and two cans of sardines in Salsa Picante (chilli sauce). So organised we are! Wouldn't it be nice to have an organised campsite for an evening and live it up. Ha!Ha! Fat chance. We rode through flat, red lands, with mountain peaks rising in front of us, no sign of life. Then we spotted two small dots in the distance. I wish they had stayed like that. As we got closer, we made out the shapes of two massive rucksacks with legs. That's all we could see, until we passed the walking rucksacks and pulled up. It was two German girls who had decided to walk the 160 kilometres to Itchy Giraffe National Park, or whatever it is called. I thought we were tough.

"I am Mia," shouted the short-haired one with the massive arse.

"This is Sofia," she ordered, challenging me to disagree, pointing to the even shorter one, hair and height wise.

Before either of us even had a chance to be friendly, sharing water, travellers' greetings and stories, Mia launched into a lesbian/Germanic rant, which I personally thought was unnecessary. I was scared of the two of them before the tirade, and I am nearly two metres tall. In high heels.

"We have much water. We are organised. We have enough for five years. We have chocolate bars, energy bars, fruit bars, Mars bars, Jupiter bars, hydrated meat bars, back-up soya bars, prison bars, burglar bars, trendy bars, rehydration salts, emergency rationing and military survival training for eight years. We have been planning this trip from before we were born, before our parents were born."

I raised my eyebrows.

"Why are you looking at us like that?"

"Is it because we are women?"

"You don't think we can do this?"

I had no answer for this defensive couple. I thought they were superb, but didn't get the chance to tell them. She was off again.

"We have GPS, latest version, compass, binoculars, maps, flash drives, memory stick, copied and stored, and recopied. We have YouTube, Facebook, Instagram, TikTok, Twitter, Pinterest, LinkedIn, Snapchat, Reddit, Flikr, Qzone, Meetup and QQ. We have flares, Spot tracker system, blow-up sleeping bags and pillows, tent, tarpaulin, cooking stove, mosquito nets, Mace, cattle prod, an emergency horn, an inflatable Conference Centre, and some lesbian reading material."

I nodded.

"Do not nod at me like that. You man bastard. Do not judge us, like our parents do," she shrieked, not.

Mad as hell, these two. They made it clear that they would not accept even a solitary peanut from someone with a penis. They didn't want us there and scowled, muttered goodbye, held hands defiantly, and stomped down the road as only Teutonic lesbian rucksacks can. Oh well! It takes all types. They didn't want us in their zone. Fair enough. I feel like that most of the time. Plus, they were no way going to make the grand 5pm gate shut-off time. Shame. What a pity they weren't going to be our campsite guests, stabbing me in the arm because I turned over their Tofu at the wrong time on the barbecue.

We arrived at the gate at 5.08pm. Were we welcome? No! The guard made Mussolini seem liberal. Senor Matias Gomez was extremely thin, almost anorexic, with a long, pointed nose a Concorde would have been proud of, and a neck as long as an ostrich. He was dressed all in black, which although imposing, was a bit silly in the sunshine. He had bowed legs and absolutely no posterior. It gave him this weird, leaning forward, off-balance, pecking posture. A weird man and angry with the world.

"The gate is closed," he stated, before I had time to take my helmet off. I tried my best.

"We stopped to help some dehydrated lesbians. We are only eight minutes late. We took a two-hour detour and we are tired, hungry and sunstruck. Please can we come in,'' I pleaded.

"No," was his 'extended' answer.

"Please, we can pay for the entrance fee."

"The office is closed till tomorrow," was his response.

"Maybe we can pay you cash and you can give it to the ticket office in the morning."

He perked up considerably and just like that, we were in. Don't pay bribes children, it sets a precedent and encourages illegal behaviour. As most of you know from my last book, *The Japanese-Speaking Curtain Maker* (now available in user-friendly Kindle. Subtle marketing there), I refuse to give bribes and have even spent some time in jail in Ghana for refusing to pay a speeding ticket. Snails were overtaking me in Ghana, when I got the speeding ticket. But, on this occasion I rationalised it. We were tired and it made no difference if we paid him or the ticket office. We were let in, to the black hole, that is the Itchy Giraffe National Park.

As soon as we entered the park, it reminded me of a gypsy encampment where I stayed in Romania. There was a large open, dusty carpark, devoid of any vegetation. On our left hand was a row of what I can only describe as trinket shops. No. Sheds, which I will come back to. On our right was another dusty clearing about the size of two football pitches. The site was devoid of shade, devoid of toilets, lights and amenities. The only thing it wasn't devoid of was solid, scorching, unlevelled ground. It was a clearing in the desert, open to death from the sun, within a few hours. This was the campsite. At the far end of the plot was a prefabricated, sad and gritty, sorry, grotty, looking café and next to it, a corrugated iron airplane hanger which had the word Musum (Museum) painted on the side, probably done by a blind person. We headed towards the campsite to set up before the sun went down. There was one other tent, about forty metres away, and that was it, tourist-wise. Luckily, it wasn't the Teutonic pair.

We tried to put up the tent. Would the tent pegs go in? No! I bent five using a rock as big as Trump's ego, but to no avail. I gave up. Cheap Chinese tent pegs are no match for scorched Argentinian soil. I tied the guy ropes to various parts of the bike and on the other side to a piece of rebar, safely sticking out of the ground, ready to impale an unwary biker. There was nowhere flat for our tent so we just cleared the obvious rocks and boulders out of the way. It was to be a corrugated kip that night. Lastly, I put four medium-sized rocks inside the tent, one tucked into each corner, to prepare us for the vicious Argentinian winds that whip up at night. We didn't want to be those 'two bikers that floated off'. I didn't do a good job with my erecting. The tent was squiff and saggy in the wrong places and the poles were bending all over the show. It looked like the Museum sign writer had put it up. It would do. We headed over to the shop/café to get some provisions.

Riding all day creates a whole different level of hunger. We were met by a vertically challenged, portly woman who was having trouble looking over a very grubby counter. She was as gushing and friendly as Matias Gomez, the Gatekeeper.

"Hello, can we please get two coffees," I asked in a super friendly manner.

"No coffee."

"Oh! OK, no problem. Is this a restaurant?"

"Yes," she said, as emotionally as Arnold Schwarzenegger on valium.

"Great. Can we see the menu?" I enquired hopefully.

"No menu, no food, closed," she replied.

"So, this is a shop and restaurant but we can't buy food or drink?"

"No, only water," she said, pointing at a row of eight, dusty plastic bottles. About the only thing that we make sure never to run out of.

"Is there another shop here ?" Cathy asked.

"No."

"Are you open for breakfast tomorrow?"

"Not open tomorrow or next day, only Saturday. But closed on Saturday to fix shop smelling. Then closed Sunday."

OK. We lose. We thanked her for exceptional service, as we were not going to eat until Monday and maybe not even then. We decided to head to the row of trinket shops. Most of them were closed due to lack of enthusiasm, except for two stalwart shopkeepers. There was a middle-aged ginger, freckled and white as a sheet, bearded and beaded Argentinian fellow, whose mum was probably Scottish, sitting glumly on a plastic crate. (Plastic crates are chairs in over a hundred countries in my experience.) He was selling bangles and necklaces and various dinosaur figurines, that were the worst I had ever seen. Most were plastic, the size and type that children get in Kinder Egg surprise packets, save for two, that were lizard-like and of higher quality.

Children play with these trinkets for five minutes, until they swallow them and die. Actually, these were worse than Kinder Egg toys. It was difficult to see what type of dinosaur they were. Melted in the moulding, I guess. The only other type of curio he offered were dinosaurs made from 'the very stones of the National Park'. They really should not have bothered. None of them looked anything like a dinosaur either. In fact, you couldn't even say; "I want that cow, or that pig, or that Triceratops." None looked like any animal I had seen on this earth. Once again, the same designer as the dinosaur theme park in Cordoba. I picked up one of the figures, to show my appreciation. It looked like a lion crossed with a hippo and its head promptly fell off. No food and no dinosaur curios for us. I did spot a bottle of crusty-looking wine and some homemade biscuits. Good enough for a classy evening by our tent.

"Can I please have that bottle of wine and packet of biscuits, I asked, pulling out my smallest note.

"No," he answered.

There seems to be some kind of 'no' theme going on in this Park. I was taken aback.

"No change," he said.

Well, he wasn't keen to make a sale. So that was that. End of discussion. No merriment and biscuits for us. We headed back to the beautifully manicured, dustbowl, facilityless (new word) camp site, when a guardian angel in a white Ram pick-up, stopped and leant out the window.

"You guys want some steak and bread and cheese, we are heading off now."

I nearly hugged the guy but he looked like a Canadian lumberjack, so it probably would not have gone down well. We headed back with a smile. Of the fifty pitches or so, there was only one barbecue. It was a rusted gasoline drum, cut in half, welded to some reinforcing bar, as legs. My favourite kind of 'braai', as we call it in Eswatini. The barbecue had seen better days and was as unstable as me, and the tent. We carried the crippled barbecue back to our bent tent and the centre fell out as we walked. Dealable with. I headed off to get charcoal or chopped wood from Senor Matias Jackdaw Gomez. Every campsite in the world sells charcoal or wood.

"No," was the answer. "Can I collect wood then?"

"No, it is forbidden," was his helpful reply.

"How do I cook then?" I pleaded, hands outstretched.

"Not possible."

Well. I wasn't having any of that. We had a steak to cook, and although I regularly eat raw steak, with salt, Cathy is not as keen. I collected as much firewood as possible and loaded up the barbecue, after a brief repair to the base with rebar. Just as the coals were getting to that perfect stage for cooking, the whole of the remaining base collapsed, depositing all the coals on the ground. The barbecue 'equipment' then leant alarmingly, and slowly fell to the ground. Time for some African boy ingenuity. Never will this steak escape. I went and found a wide, flat rock, larger than the piece of steak. I then placed all the coals in a semicircle and put the rock in the centre, with a dash of water on the upper surface to boil off any dodgery. After ten minutes the rock was hot and sterile, and presto, we had a griddle. Soon, we were sitting on the ground savouring the smells of the steak fat sizzling. My Swazi hot rock was working a treat and has been adopted by top restaurants throughout South Africa. I lie, I got the idea from the Spur Restaurant chain in South Africa. We nibbled on our starter, the three rolls Mr. Lumberjack had given us. Life was good.

Cathy decided to head over a nearby hill to take some photos. Enter Senor Gomez and Senor Gonzalez. Funny pair. Seems like they spent their time ordering around troops that actually didn't exist, so take it out on the rare visitors instead, when frustration sets in.

"No collect wood," said Senor Gomez, pointing at my juicy steak. I noticed a glimmer of interest from both of them about my cooking methods. Senor Gonzalez, who for some reason kept staring at his own eyebrows, or tried too, asked, "Where is your wife?"

I pointed over a nearby hill. "She is over there taking some photos," I replied.

"No," they said simultaneously.

"It is prohibited to enter there," added Gomez.

"So we are confined to this little, arid, shadeless clearing, and if we step over the last camping pitch, we will be shot?"

I didn't say that. I said, "No problem. I will go and get her," and turned to go.

"No," they said simultaneously. Some kind of "no" double act. "It is prohibited."

"So, my wife is not allowed over the hill, but she is over the hill and I am not allowed to go over the hill to get her?"

They ignored me and started shouting across the plain.

"Senora, Senora."

They had just as much chance of being heard in England. It was windy and Cathy, as you might have guessed, was on the other side of a hill. They got bored, shook their fingers at me, not simultaneously this time, but alternating. They headed off, mumbling semi-angrily.

"She must not go again and no more fire time," said Senor 'Stare at my own Eyebrows' Gomez, his parting pearl of wisdom.

He had a last, jealous glance at my juicy steak and I am pretty sure he licked his lips.

"No, you can't have any."

And they were gone.

Cathy came back thirty minutes later, with some beautiful photos of a desert fox. She was in hysterics when I told her about the Gomez and Gonzalez stand-off.

"This place is hilarious. I am sure you are not allowed to work here unless you say no to everything."

Despite all the 'no's' and officiousness, we were in great spirits. The sun was setting, the air was beautifully clear and crisp and the temperature a balmy 24 degrees centigrade. In the distance, massive red mountains cast spectacular shadows on the plain. Our desert fox decided to reappear, silhouetted against the clear orange sky. He was sitting, motionless, watching us like a hawk. No; like a desert fox that wanted sirloin steak. Cathy, the hardened criminal, stepped over the firing squad line and fed a juicy morsel to the fox.

I headed off to find an ablution block. I was successful. No word of a lie, there were twenty-two toilets and only three showers. I walked along and counted, believe me. When the place is busy, there must be a lot of pooping going on and not much showering. Surprisingly, there was no water in the showers. I went up to the entrance gate, where the two Stalins were standing in the shade of the entrance hut, sipping on cans of Quilmes Lager.

"Sorry, there is no water in the showers?"

"No," was the answer.

I headed back to the tent, giggling, not angry. It's all fun. Stay dirty. No big deal. Drink water, eat biscuits and tomorrow, head into the Park. We slept, not like logs, and woke up groggy but excited. Time to find dinosaur stuff. We wandered up to the main gate where there were two comatose guards, surrounded by crushed cans of Quilmes Lager. (I am sure I know them.) Not a lot was got out of them. Luckily, a lady with a moustache and no eyebrows, and a Christmas bauble in her ear, for some unknown reason, was at the ticket reception.

"Can we pay to go into the Park on our motorbike?" I asked.

"No, only with a tour, no motos."

"I understand. Can we book a tour?"

"No, no tours till Monday," she said, not raising her eyebrows, because she didn't have any. But she did stare at the corner of the ceiling as she spoke to me. Maybe a spider.

So no tours, no fossils for us. We took a 320-kilometre detour to see nothing. I wouldn't have missed it for the world. We had actually laughed a lot at the surreal happenings. It was a blast. One more event happened before we left the welcoming Park of 'No to everything'.

We had not lost hope. There was still the Dinosaur Museum to visit. Although not the same as seeing the fossils and bones in situ, it would still be pretty cool.

"Can we have two tickets to the Museum please?" I asked a guide, snoozing on some gunny sacks at the entrance.

"No. It is closed," he said, pulling his cowboy hat back over his eyes.

I burst out laughing. I love this place. How do people survive out here and what do they do all day? We made the not-too-difficult decision to pack up and head south. As we were getting our tent unpitched, sorting out our panniers and weight distribution, checking oil, coolant, tyres and brakes, the basic daily routine, a very tall, well-dressed man with a clipped moustache approached us. Stepped off the Orient Express by the look of it. He was about sixty. His hair was gelled back and sideburns neatly trimmed. He sported a pristine dark blue suit and white shirt with cufflinks, and shiny, dust resistant, black shoes that looked about a metre long. He turned out to be the Director of the National Park.

I am one hundred percent not the complaining type, as many of the people I have moaned to, can testify. I couldn't help regaling him with our Park experience. It was not in a 'Disgusted of Tunbridge Wells' sort of way. It was more just something to chat about, on the spur of the moment. Or so I thought. But when I think about the conversation I summarise below I can't help, in retrospect, feeling very guilty. It was so unlike me. After all, Cathy and I are totally used to roughing it, with no facilities whatsoever. I just found it hilarious that one of the most famous National Parks in South America, and a World Heritage Site, attracting zillions of visitors (that's a rough estimate), was so unbelievably disorganised. So, to sum up what a horrible person I am,

this is what I said in précis form, without punctuation as it seems apt.
Could we get into the Park easily? No.
Could we buy food or drink anywhere? No.
Could we buy wood or charcoal? No.
Could we collect wood? No.
Could we shower? No.
Could we use the barbecue? No
Could we have some shade at campsite? No
Could we buy curios? No.
Could we walk around freely? No.
Could we visit the Museum? No.
Could we visit the Park by motorcycle? No
Could we book a guided tour? No.

The well dressed gent called Senor Benjamin Fernandez listened to me intently. I was obviously not as rude as summarised above. I coated it in humour because I really didn't mind one bit about the Park's shortcomings. We had a blast and it was undeniably a beautiful spot. But my last comment to Senor Fernandez, I did mean seriously:

"You have recycling bins everywhere of different colours. When I was out last night around 11pm, looking at the full moon (not in a vampire way), I saw one of your staff, with a quad bike, loaded with more than twenty black plastic bags of rubbish. He came back without them, ten minutes later. I went to look and you have a mountain of garbage and plastic in the desert. I think that's pretty shitty."

Sometimes I can be so eloquent.

Instead of defending himself, or getting angry, or even apologising, Senor Ben did something I did not expect in the least, and caught me totally off guard. I was mortified and wanted to crawl into a hole in the ground in shame. His bottom lip started quivering, then his cheeks reddened and started twitching and he let out a few whimpers. His shoulders started shaking uncontrollably and he burst violently into tears. He bent down on his haunches, sobbing and slapped his thighs hard, with his open hands.

"I have big problems Senor, big problems."

I had no idea whether he had just found out that his wife was having eight affairs simultaneously, or what, but it was a radical reaction. I wanted to give him a hug, so I did, and he was racked once more with tears. We ended up chatting for more than two hours and we are still friends to this day. Basically there was no money coming in to the Park, or it was being filtered away. He said all the staff were in mutiny mode, because wages were always late. I found this very strange as it was a designated World Heritage Site. But nothing worked and there was a good chance that the Director would top himself or shoot all the employees in a siege/hostage situation.

Luckily he didn't do that. Over the years we have talked frequently and there were a whole load of personal issues bringing Senor Ben down, when we met him. Out of respect for him, I will not go into detail. He resigned last year, moved to the wine region of Mendoza with his wife and started a small vineyard and cheese and wine shop. I have never heard him happier. I learnt another massive lesson. Always realise that every single person has a history and issues, some of them radically serious, but hidden to the world. To bring someone, and their job down, the way I did was cruel. I won't do it again, ever, to anyone. What I took as light-hearted moaning, was more serious to Mr Ben. Always try to look from someone else's perspective.

We left the Park with hugs from the Director, but I was in thoughtful mode and the next hundred kilometres passed in silence, and a blur. Do not hurt people. I felt bad and because of the nature of what we do, ride in and leave, it is so much better when you leave a good feeling for everyone.

Forgive me now as we make much more than a 100-kilometre jump. More like two thousand. Although Brazil makes up half of South America I am focusing this chapter on another iconic section, crossing the Amazon jungle. That was my biggest aim when I knew we were going to Brazil and another childhood dream. The reason I am not discussing the five-month traverse of Brazil is a simple one; it will make a book of its own. I hope you enjoy this little dip into the Amazon proper.

Chapter Thirteen
Amazonas and the Ghost Road

Like all sports, if you do them properly, Adventure Motorcycling (yes, in capitals, it deserves it), has iconic tests; iconic routes, that everyone wants to do, and few achieve. I like to chase these routes, It is what keeps me going. Why would I ever ride on a motorway? To me motorcycles are for sport, not for cruising. I know I am making enemies as I write this. I am not putting down the cruiser, or anyone on two wheels. We all want slightly different things from our motorcycle.

I may as well be in a car, commuting to work, in comfort, with aircon, the radio and a sandwich. Motorcycles are not transport. They are a feeling. They are the ultimate symbol of freedom. Nobody likes a motorbike overtaking them on a motorway, or any road, for that matter. Why, I ask. Because they are having freedom, and an alternative life, rubbed in their face. Competition. The speed of modern life. With men, the macho response kicks in, and they try to race you. Basic and silly. Strangely, women can be even more vicious. If you pull in front of a woman at a traffic light, be prepared, at best, to be rear ended, and not in a nice way. At worst, she will run you off the road, and reverse over you, to make sure the job is done, no witnesses. Whoops, lost it there for a minute. I have not worked out the psychology of why a hairy biker, with a loud exhaust, and a big smile, is such a threat to society. Motorcycling is peace, escape from judgement, and above all the freedom to appreciate nature, alone.

Adventure motorcycling is escaping people, testing your body's coordination and strength, getting fit in the process, and just enjoying our world. It is the same with many solitary sports. Long distance runners have hundreds of kilometres to just think. Don't underestimate this. It is just the road, the pounding of your shoes on the pavement, and the way your body is coping with it. It gives you time to sort out your head, your commitments, your lists, your family, your bills, your worries, while at the same time, strengthening your body. Kayakers feel it, sky divers, surfers, free divers, climbers, trekkers, Dakar riders and cross country skiers. The list goes on, but the elements are the same. Sport is seriously underrated, and should be compulsory, for everybody over six months old. As should military service, at three. Joke. But we have become way too sedentary, and it is time for the fitness fanatics to stand up to the burger fanatics. All fast food sellers should be fined.

People who play team sports are a little bit different from the solitary loons, like my Dad, the marathon runner. They share the common goal of getting fit, as the solitary sports person, and the thrill of mastering a skill, and improving their times. But they are happy in a group, and often get, and need, validation from their teammates. What all sports do though, is give you that respite from thinking only about everyday life. You are focused on what you love. Test your body, free your brain, and breathe. Ready for real life again. It's hard to go back to the humans around you, everywhere, without respite. You can escape that pressure through your sport. It just makes me want to ride forever. Put on my helmet, shut out the world, and test myself on the world's toughest roads. Why? Ask any lunatic. It's freedom.

When I hear about the Tenere desert, the route through Mauritania, the Moyale bandit road in Kenya, the road of Bones in Siberia, the Danakil depression in Ethiopia, and, the off-road Ethiopian Highlands too, my heart races, and I want to go there. There are different levels of difficulty, but nothing beats Africa. The toughest roads I have ever been on were in the Democratic Republic of Congo, and more than ten other African countries, before any other country, in Europe, South and Central America, get a look in. That is just the way it is. Africa is the hardest continent to deal with on a bike. 'Africa is not for sissies', as the increasingly popular T-shirt says (available on my website...). Oh, and Mexican back tracks, in the rainy season. They are brutal.

There is another level of road, that is hard, and famous, for a reason, but not up there with the tough routes. They just became famous, for some reason, usually for their high death toll, before they were improved for tourists. Still challenging to experience, whether on a bike, a motorcycle, on foot, or in a truck. Do not catch buses on these roads. They tend to crash, and kill hundreds, flying off cliffs, like lemmings, but less bouncy.

These are the Death Road in Bolivia, the Wind Tunnel of Doom Road

30 flat tyres in 20 countries. Top, Salar de Uyuni blowout

Below: Ecuador thorns

Joey Evans, the Camel Collider and Dakar hero in action

Dakar Rally racers on the iconic Salar de Uyuni Salt Flats

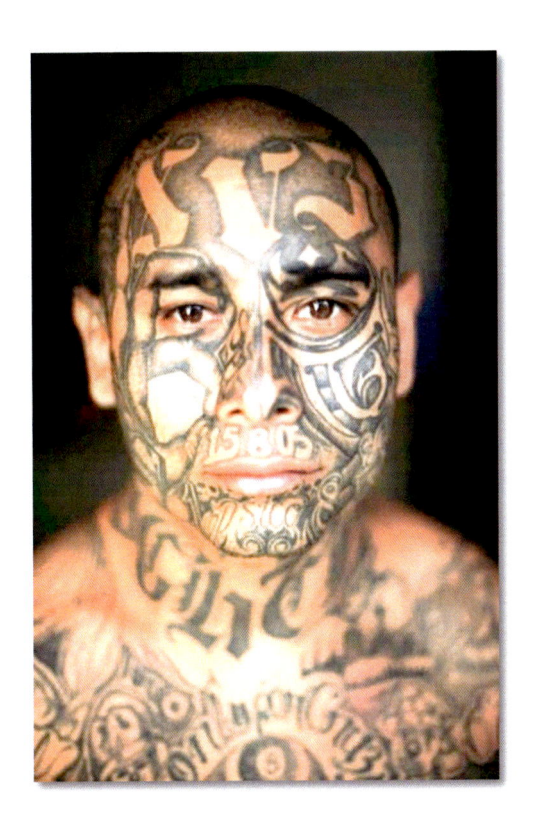

Two sides of South America: top, Cordoba member from the Chucky and the Triceratops gang; bottom, the friendly Military Police of Bogota, Colombia

Left: whether it is Atacama, Patagonia, Sonora or Sahara… desert riding is one of the most energy-sapping environments

Above: Ushuaia in Argentina, the world's southernmost city, nicknamed 'the End of the World', and the halfway point of the trip

in Patagonia, the Devils Trampoline in Colombia, the Georgetown to Lethem Mud Road in British Guyana, the Uyuni to Tupiza Sandviper Road in Bolivia and the one I want to talk about now. The BR319 Ghost Road, in Brazil. The BR319 has a special place in my heart. This was the first time, since Africa, that I nodded to myself (if that is possible), and said out loud:

"You are a proper explorer and adventurer. Well done."

You, against the road, nobody around, jungle everywhere (obviously Cathy was there, but for me, that is alone. We have been together so long, and had such amazing times, that we merge into one). Heaven, for me was the Ghost Road. It cuts straight through the Amazon jungle, from the eastern Venezuelan border with Brazil, west, through the centre of the Amazon, for thousands of kilometres of nothing; but beauty, solitude, and peace; until the Peru border. The Ghost Road was one of the best times of my life. I would do the whole trip again, despite the hardship.

The introduction to the Amazon, and the jump-off point into the unknown, is the town of Realidade. Try and Google it. It is a ghost town, on a ghost road; but it does exist. Realidade has a rickety, middle-of-nowhere feel; a succession of dodgy bars, rough as hell motels, truck workshops, evangelical churches, and little wooden houses, on dirt roads, that turn into a quagmire of slush, and slipperiness in the rains. In the last few years it has grown, and now has a school and a health clinic, in a boom driven by the lucrative businesses that destroy the jungle; illegal logging, cattle ranching and soya bean production. The BR319 is threatened by another twenty Realidade towns, and that will be its death.

The BR319 is an 870-kilometre, federal highway, that links Manaus, Amazonas, to Porto Velho, Rondonia. The highway runs through one of the most pristine parts of the Amazon, a rainforest that covers half of Brazil, and covers an area, the size of the European Union. (We are crossing it, yay.) It was opened by the military government in 1973, but soon deteriorated, and by 1988, was impassable.

For half of the year, the road is a mud bath. In 2008, work began to repair the highway. The idea was to provide an alternative to boat travel along the Madeira river, that was less dangerous and costly. The project never really got off the ground, and the BR319 once again became the most difficult route.

Although bridges were replaced, the route is brutal and traffic is sparse, in fact there would be none, except me and Cathy this year; hence the name 'The Ghost Road' (see photo above).

The Indians were against the development of the road, and still are. The Ghost Road is surrounded by extensive protected areas, including indigenous territories of the Mura, Munduruku, Apurina and Parantintin tribes. (No, I did not make up Paranormal Tintin.) The area is sparsely populated by families who live largely by subsistence agriculture. There are 18 indigenous villages peppered around, originally, far from the main road. But many of the illegal secondary roads that scar the landscape are within touching distance of the territory of many of them, including a group of around 40, up to now, isolated indigenous people. The same old story. They are probably descendants of the Juma people, who survived a massacre in 1964. The encroachment on traditional people and their way of life, will only worsen, exponentially.

As an adventure motorcyclist I am glad that the Ghost Road is unsuccessful; so far. As soon as a quality asphalt road, is built anywhere, it immediately opens up the area to deforestation, exploitation, and destruction. It is a sad fact, that the only places unspoilt in this world, and the most magical, are those that we cannot snake our way through, in trucks, destroying as we go along. The Ghost Road, if improved, would open up the central and northern portions of the Amazon to the migration of land grabbers (grilerios), precious mineral prospectors, oil and gas seekers, loggers, cattlemen, individual squatters (posseiros), and organised landless farmers. Not to mention, the criminal element of this world, who want to disappear.

Luckily, the engineers who built the Ghost Road, were not super keen on construction, or on doing a good job, and were unfamiliar with the terrain. The bridges were badly constructed and we risked a fall into muddy waters on several occasions.

The lack of proper drainage systems quickly crumbled the inadequately thin layer of asphalt. Annual floods have continuously washed away the rickety bridges. There are more than thirty wooden bridges: a crossing point for crocodiles, who love adventure motorcyclists; as the meat is soft, and they are easy to digest. Except for me of course, because I am as hard as hell.

The lack of maintenance lends to a beautiful sight; full size trees growing in the centre of the road, huge bunches of white, blue and yellow wild flowers spilling onto the asphalt, covering half of it in parts. The road started off with promise, but quickly the asphalt started breaking up, splitting into huge, sun-baked cracks, that could knock you off the bike.

We ended up winding back and forth across the road. Things deteriorated further, and the scars started joining potholes, that were half filled with water. It had obviously rained recently. Further on, the tarred surface had disappeared, for large stretches, and we were faced with a patchwork of joining potholes, jarring us to the core. Huge lianas covered the road in parts, dragged down by huge trees, that have collapsed and rotted. The debris makes for constant, small, slippery, speed bumps. It sounds like a minor complaint; riding over a jungle vine, but they are lethal, covered in a slippery moss, and will take your back tyre out, in the blink of a marsupial's eye.

The road was overgrown, and in parts was just a path, but it was still negotiable. The road would have been reclaimed by the jungle long before we got to it, if not for one thing; the digital era found its way to Manaus; the city needed a fibre cable for internet access. The BR319 had a new function for a while. A cable was laid along the entire 880-kilometre stretch, and the telephone company of Embratel maintained it; for a while. This led to a slight improvement in the road, and the surreal sight of satellite masts, with neatly trimmed grass borders, in the middle of the Amazon proper. They are pretty plush places to camp. They have been cleared slightly, you get a piece of lawn in the jungle, to pitch your tent, so you can see the creepy crawlies coming to kill you, from metres away. If a jaguar comes, I could quickly vault over the fence that surrounded the mast, and give Cathy instructions on how to behave and respond to the jaguar.

At times we met up with the Amazon river and the jungle sprung to life with humans. There were rusted ferries, chained to rotted posts, on the bank, having evidently not ferried passengers for a good 20 years or so. Many are taken over by the jungle, the odd chicken, popping out of a door. Small wooden boats carrying passengers, or catches of fish, briefly race the bike, their 15-horse power engines, shooting plumes of smoke, into the air, the motor screaming. They keep it up, nevertheless, and when they realise that they have no chance against the Tenere, they stand up and wave. There are rickety restaurants, on the banks, selling Espetinhos; skewers of meat, and a variety of sweaty, depressed-looking salads. Dead, rotting trees lay everywhere, between the wooden houses; home to guinea fowl, cattle and buffalo, foraging between the waterlogged trunks.

Then we were out, the village gone in a flash, the scurry of activity, a memory. It was hours and hours of nothing, just us and the bike and the Amazon. How could life possibly be better. The electricity and wires were the only reminder of humanity, and often they disappeared, meandering, through what is, presumably, an easier route. It is a telling statistic, that ninety percent of trucks, still load onto boats, to negotiate the BR319 section. Only the tough ten percent of truckers, and us, try the road route. Furthermore, during the rainy season, the road is totally impassable, and is closed by the army. It is a preventative measure. They don't want to spend their time digging out trucks, full of sugar, and thirsty people, in the middle of nowhere.

On we pushed, risking flat tyres and cracked rims. There was the odd ranch, a gate and a rusty sign, announcing a turnoff into the jungle deep. What brought these people to these places? I can appreciate remote. But there is remote, and remote. The ranches have names that reflect the hopes of the new settlers, in this most beautiful, but most difficult of places to live; 'Sitio Bom Future', or Good Future Ranch. 'Sitio Nova Vida', or New Life Ranch, Big Hope, Rich Earth, and God Provides, were the signs of false optimism. We never ventured down those tracks.

We also came across a Seventh Day Adventist Church, lovingly built out of breeze block and a bit of plaster. I peeked inside, through the handkerchief-sized window. The interior was easily big enough for a midget priest, and two slim worshippers. The exterior was lovingly painted white, with blue edging, but there was not a town, a settlement, or even a single wandering person, to convert, in sight. It was very odd.

Maybe that church was strategically placed, for a final prayer, because after that, the road deteriorated, beyond my wildest dreams. And not nice, wild dreams either. I love the word, deteriorated, so English, and understated. The road collapsed, not just on one side, but often on both, leaving a skinny channel to ride on. I had a bit of fun, pretending that I had lost control, at the steepest drop-off point. The asphalt was more a collection of broken puzzle pieces, and I was frankly relieved when it disappeared altogether. Broken asphalt, with sharp lips, is more harsh on a tyre than a dirt road. It was slow going, technical, but we were alone, so it was serene, and an adventurer's dream. I could go back there right now, build a cabin, and become a weirdo hermit.

The road ceased to be a road, and became an overgrown track, for about eighty kilometres, a lot like the Democratic Republic of Congo road. It was odd to negotiate your way through jungle, and suddenly come across a random piece of asphalt road, with remnants of a painted, yellow line on it, that divided the once pristine highway into two, civilised lanes. Good for you, nature. Fighting back. Thick, strong grass had dug its roots into the highway, and huge slabs of road, could be spotted, way down, in the jungle valleys, forced apart, and downwards, by the power of a plant. For hours we rode, on a ribbon of road, the jungle encroaching on both sides. Magic.

For the seven days it took to cross the Amazon, from east to west, we were soaking wet for the whole time. Not from rain, because, thank God and his cousin, there was none. I think, in the rainy season, it would have taken us a month. We were soaked from sweating. It collects in the seat of your trousers, chafing you in private regions, to the point of sandpaper sore. Insects are constantly stuck to your face and visor, and a few end up being swallowed, in a surprise, bitter, gulp. Potently acidic insects land in your eye, and sting you to tears. You are constantly getting bitten, and have to just ignore it, and ride.

Your socks become soaked in sweat, and ride down your boots, bunching around your toes, in a soggy mess. Your gloves are soaked. Stopping at night, to camp, our feet were shrivelled and cracked, and our toes looked like old grapes. The dye from our boots turned our feet black, and accentuated the deep cracks in our heels. Our fingers were red, shrivelled and numb, from the vibration of the bike. We tried drying out our bike suits, boots, gloves and socks by hanging them up. To no avail. It is so damp in the Amazon. No surprise there. We put talcum powder between our legs, and in our socks, and back on went our soggy gear, for another eight hours of duelling with the BR319. The talcum powder ends up as a solid lump that you chip out of your motorbike trousers, at the end of the day. We were constantly itchy, day and night. Red sores build up on your body, but you are too scared to scratch them, in case some evil-looking, grinning, Amazonian, flesh-eating worm comes out. So, you ignore them. It is easier. I ended up with a boil, two months later, on the side of my foot. I dug it out, with a knife, a la Rambo, and a weird cocoon came out. No idea to this day.

Camping was hilarious. We pretended to sleep, got up in the dark to pack, and were off at first light. It was better than lying there, as a meal platter for mosquitoes, and other armoured, pincer-type fellows, who even David Attenborough would have problems identifying. After three days, sleep deprivation starts to set in. Your eyelids become heavy, whilst riding, at about 2.00pm, a weird experience for me, as I am hyperactive. There was no time to be sleepy. It is dangerous. The bridges were in good shape, but consisted of lethal planks, full of moss and slipperiness, with gaps between them, for the front tyre to drop into, and jettison two soggy people.

This is exactly what happened to two friends of ours, Lisa and Simon Thomas. But worse. Simon rode onto a bridge, and it collapsed, taking him and the bike on a journey downwards of twenty feet. He broke his back, but didn't damage the spinal cord. Miraculously, Lisa towed Simon and his bike out of the jungle, and he recovered. In Simon's case it was pure bad luck. All ended well, and they are both now renowned adventure riders, who present their amazing stories at all the same Bike Shows and Events that we do. Respect to them. Most of those horrific bridges had been fixed when we crossed, and it was still dicey.

There is a technique for crossing wooden bridges, but not one for falling through. Approach it in first gear, get some torque, then into second. Keep a steady throttle, for forward momentum. Choose your path, and commit to it. Look where you want to go, not where you don't want to go. There is hazard fixation syndrome in humans. The brain fixates, and you will end up hitting that pothole, or going into that crevice, or flying off that bridge, that you are concentrating on. I made up the name of that syndrome, I think, but it exists, believe me. It is like every single thing in life. Focus on the negative, and it will happen. Focus on the positive, and it might happen. Which is a better option. Look at the end of the bridge, the end of the plank, past the pothole, and commit. There is plenty of time for hesitation and self-back patting, when you are across the obstacle. Same with life.

After that speech about riding skills, let's get back to the road. The next morning, we woke up and it had rained. Serves me right, for being so righteous about riding skills. It got worse, as we headed into a mangrove, waterlogged section. The road degenerated into black coloured puddles, as big as lakes; smooth as glass, the trees above us, reflected perfectly in the road. It was beautiful. The track then transformed into vivid red mud, sprinkled with bright red puddles, glistening in the sun. We rounded a corner, and a tree had been felled by a storm. There was a large burnt scar, on one side of it. I assume it had been struck by lightning. It was too large to ride over, and we could not skirt it, as there were steep, slippery banks on either side. We managed to lift the front wheel over the log. It was like holding onto an already slippery machine, which was then covered in Vaseline. We were laughing, which drains all your power, but managed to get the bike balanced on the log, on the bash plate, both wheels flailing aimlessly on either side. If wheels can flail. Sounds a bit human to me. Get a grip.

After a bit of grunting, we just pushed the bike over the other side, into the mud. It gave us time to laugh a bit more, but obviously not good for fuel spillage, etc. Sometimes you do not care. Until you meet another ten trees, and another seven slippery bridges. Then it's taxing. But we were crossing the Amazon jungle, from east to west. What was there to complain about. Life could not be better.

Always space for a quick moan though. The next day, both of my wrists were burning, from constant clutch and accelerator changes. I could not feel any of my body from the waist down, due to the constant jarring, from my dodgy old, one cylinder bike. We both had raw knees from our bike padding. We came to a bridge that had collapsed into the river. Our only way through was to ride, next to the bridge, cross the river, and up the other side. It was a struggle up the other bank, and the clutch began to smell. Not a good sign. We weaved and revved our way up, Cathy pushing from behind. (As it should be in an equal relationship, before all this 'the man must push'.)

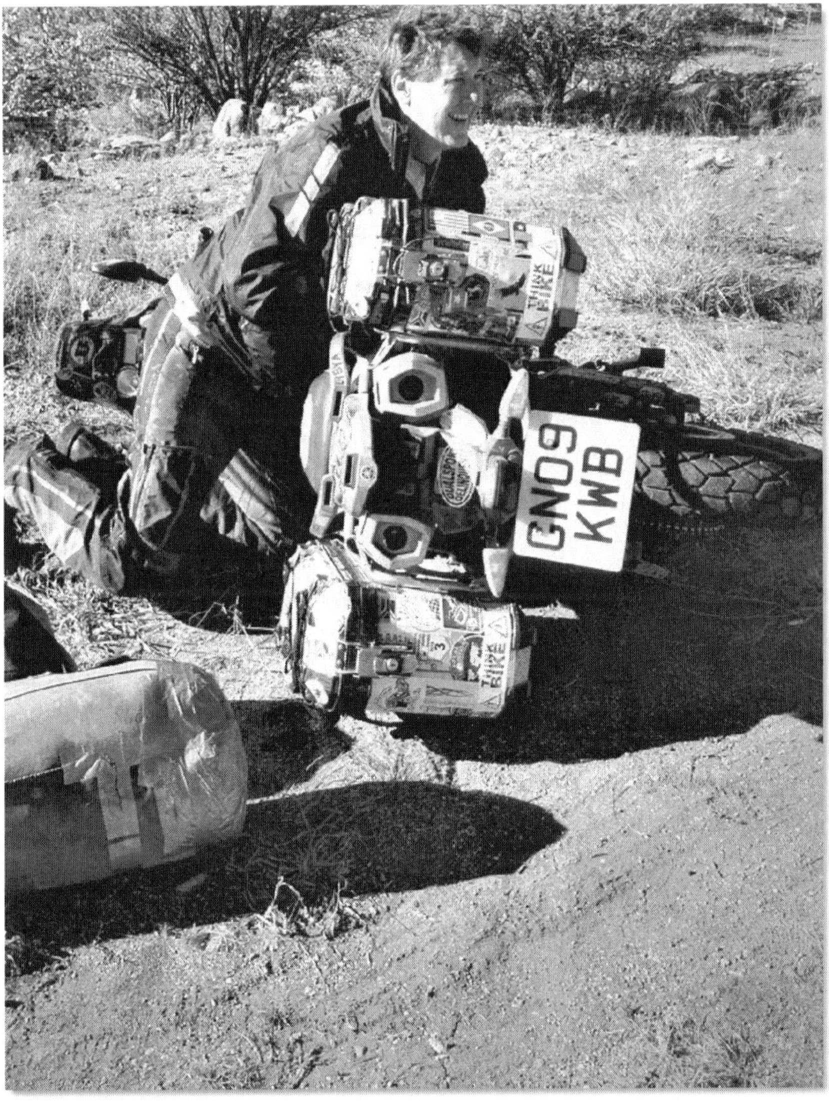
GN09
KWB

At the crest of the hill, I was so relieved that I drove straight over a fallen branch, and a thick thorn went straight through the tyre and into the tube. A flat. Wonderful. Within thirty sweaty minutes, Cathy had changed the tube; OK, we had. It is important not to lose momentum, and focus towards your destination. Not that we had one.

Civilisation reappeared for a short time, the road widened, but became a washboard of corrugations. Not only were our fillings in jeopardy from the road, so were our teeth. At one point teeth loss was the least of our worries, as we were passed by hunters, riding on skeletons of motorbikes, brandishing guns, as well as bows and arrows. I did not stop to ask the if they had poisoned tips to their arrows. Then they were gone, in a flash, and we were alone again. By five o'clock, we were too tired, and I was making riding mistakes. It was time to stop but too late to avoid hitting a pit which sent me flying and shaken, but not stirred, onto the side of the road. Cathy stepped off without a sign of injury and slapped me in distress!!

After this mishap I totally failed to put the tent up properly. I didn't realise how tired I was. We crawled into the soggy, saggy tent. A tapir walked past. Macaws, toucans and howler monkeys made sure that our seven minutes' sleep was intermittent. The only memorable part of those seven minutes was a cockroach decided to take advantage of my snoring, and crawled into my mouth. It woke me up, quicker than a fire alarm. I was spitting and gagging cockroach legs, and green, squidgy abdomen. I had no interest in sleep after that, especially as I had been sweating for all the seven minutes, and my sleeping bag was like being wrapped in a sweaty cabbage. I felt like a moody Lebanese snack. (A quick tip: if you do not wash your lips, your mouth and brush your teeth when camping, cockroaches come in the night and nibble the food from the corners of your mouth. If no food is found there, they will explore further, between your teeth.) That can cause cold sores. Any children reading this; I bet you brush your teeth like lunatics from now on. You don't even need to be camping, kids. The 'cockroach gnawing' could happen in your own bedroom. Brush your teeth.

The next day was dry. Dust, dust and more dust. What a strange and constantly changing terrain. We hit a brutal, corrugated road again, which shook every bolt on the bike, and gave me a few loose screws too. To add to the collection. We still had a crash to deal with, on the final day; before extraction by the SAS.

Joking. We got out of there on our own. And we saw a sloth. I decided to brew up coffee, and get to know the sloth. It was excellent. Cathy had a chat with the sloth and put him in a tree, away from the road, and safer from anacondas. Invigorated, we went over a rise, and came across a puddle, spanning the road. I hit the puddle, in a caffeine-induced frenzy, and immediately realised that it wasn't a puddle. It was a bottomless lake. There could be a family of crocodiles in there, plus their extended family. The front wheel promptly disappeared, and kicked to the right. The bike flipped forward, in the air and we were ejected, rodeo style. I went sideways, past the handlebar, and landed in a mound of mud, in the centre of the 'puddle' and sank. What!? I couldn't see a thing and my gloves had gone. I looked round. No Cathy. Then, this helmet rose out of the red water. It was the creature from the red lagoon. Red mud and streams of water poured out of Cathy's helmet, revealing some very startled, blue eyes. We both burst out laughing. The bike was submerged. After rolling around a bit, and throwing mud pies at each other, we eventually got the Tenere out of Lake Placid.

" Are you seriously OK, Cathy? That was quite a prang."

" Of course I am. Loved it. And I needed cooling down."

Top woman. Love that girl, love this road, love this motorbike, love this life.

Little did I know that for fourteen days, the entire trip through the Amazon and Ghost Road, and more, I had been suffering from malaria. I had caught it at the Swiss camp, on the return section of our Venezuelan loop. Jeremiah, the owner's son, was unrecognisable, having had malaria, whilst we were in San Cristobal. He was literally half the man he used to be, having lost thirty five kilogrammes. He was a haunted man, covering himself in mosquito repellent, and surrounding himself with burning cardboard boxes, to keep off the mosquitoes. I think he had lost it, more than just physically. When my symptoms of malaria started, I just thought I was getting soft, or old. I had a splitting headache, and I was constantly tired. The sun hurt my eyes, and I had no appetite at all. My riding was below par. Even canned chilli sardines could not tempt me, so I knew things were bad. The reason I tell you this story is not because I want sympathy, or that I want accolades like, 'what a tough guy'. It is because Cathy uttered one of the most memorable lines I have heard a 'nearly dead' man receive. (Cathy is full of 'Clintina' Eastwood quotes). I was riding two up, in 35 degrees, day after day, sleeping rough, and eating little. Meanwhile, Malaria Man was me. I thought I was being stoic, maybe uttering the odd, "I don't feel quite myself today, a bit under par."

But, in reality, Cathy tells me, I was acting like the classic male with man flu, moaning it up, to the maximum. Amazing how two peoples' perceptions are different. My perception is more accurate. On one particularly testing stretch of road, a muddy red road, at an angle, ready to spit us off into the jungle, I was burning up, hallucinating, being all malaria-like, and drifting in and out of consciousness. Whilst riding. Not good. I was sore all over and felt like I had been run over by one of Escobar's hippos. I decided to meekly confess:

"I really feel terrible and I don't know if I can carry on riding."

Cathy's extremely sympathetic response was; first the helmet slap, as usual, and then the reprimand (don't forget the South African accent):

"What are you talking about? We are in the middle of nowhere. I need a real man, not a wimp. Pull yourself together."

That shut me up, quick, sharp, and in retrospect, was exactly what I needed. The comment totally motivated me, much like the one Carl the Canadian, made, many years ago, when I crashed in Kenya:

"You will never make it round Africa."

Shamed and inspired, we persevered, as swiftly as tortoises on tranquilisers. Think of a new analogy, Spencer. I had plenty of time to deal with malaria when we were out of the Amazon. We did get out. Keep moving forward is the key. I did finally collapse, a jibbering, shaking wreck, but the pep talk got us out. I then succumbed to near rigor mortis, followed by an impersonation of a plank with epilepsy. I went down quite spectacularly, and theatrically (Richard E Grant would have been proud), in the street in Huanchaco, on the coast of Peru. Luckily, a long-haired traditional healer, wearing what looked like a plastic bag from Waitrose, and some beads from Ikea, magically produced a bottle of ointment, and covered my back in it. I almost immediately stopped shaking, and felt a warm glow, almost a burn on my skin. It was Deep Heat from Sports Direct, but I will give him the benefit of the doubt, that it was a thousand-year-old traditional recipe, handed down by his forefathers. It stirred me enough to jelly fish into a taxi, throw up everywhere, and pass out. I apologised profusely to the taxi driver, and promised to reupholster his whole town.

The next thing I remember very clearly was being jubilant when my results came in. "Ha ha Cathy. I told you I had malaria. Fantastic. I told you I wasn't a wimp," I announced, then fainted.

Five days later, thanks to the amazing Peruvian doctors and nurses, I was sorted. Except when I got the bill, which left me in need of a triple bypass, so there was no point in recovering from the malaria.

Chapter Fourteen
Tarantulas, Cane Toads and Hell Town

The Amazon and the BR319 had ticked all the boxes I loved; remoteness, tough riding, pristine jungle, no people and incredible animals. Although I am from Africa, and devoured books on African explorers, I also had an obsession with the Amazon.

I read and re-read Percy Fawcett's diaries. The unforgiving Amazon has claimed the lives of many adventurers, but perhaps none so famous as Colonel Percy Fawcett, who disappeared in 1925, while on the trail of a mythical Lost City. One of the most colourful figures of his era, Fawcett had made his name during a series of harrowing, but groundbreaking, mapmaking expeditions to the wilds of Brazil and Bolivia. During these travels, he formulated a theory about 'the Lost City of Z' (recently made into a brilliant film of the same name), which he believed existed somewhere in the unexplored Mato Grosso region of Brazil.

In 1925 Fawcett, his sixteen-year-old son, Jack, and a young man called Raleigh Rimmel, set off in search of the fabled lost city. But following a letter in which Fawcett announced he was venturing into unmapped territory, the group vanished without a trace. While conventional wisdom suggests the explorers were killed by hostile Indians, other theories blame everything from malaria, to starvation, to jaguar attacks. All are a possibility for their demise, which makes the Amazon so dangerous, yet so exciting. Some have even speculated that the men simply went local, and lived out the rest of their lives happily in the jungle. This is my favorite theory, but seems doubtful, considering Fawcett's love for his wife, Nina. Whatever the cause, the group's disappearance captured the imagination of people around the world. In the years since Fawcett disappeared, thousands of would-be adventurers have mounted exploratory missions. As many as 100 people have died while searching for some sign of Fawcett, or the city of gold, in the darkness of the Amazon.

Despite my fascination with the Amazon, I had no intention of dying there. I just wanted to experience one of the last wildernesses. The Amazon really is one of the last strongholds for indigenous people, as well as for many animals, insects and plants, and the BR319 cuts through a jewel in their habitat crown. I am not going to become a tree hugger, so I will just give you one sentence.

The Amazon jungle has two important organs; the lungs of our world. Without it, we are doomed. The Amazon is losing the equivalent to three football fields every hour, twenty four hours a day. The animal and insect losses are too rapid to document. Why? Destructive humans. Seventeen percent of the Amazon, in the last five years, has been decimated. No other animal on this precious globe of ours could come anywhere near causing this rate of destruction. Even if beavers had chainsaws.

I have always thought of adventure riding as so much more than the motorcycle. It is the whole package, as they say, and if you are missing one of the links, the chain is pointless. We should always be sponges, soaking up all. It is, of course, the adrenaline of conquering bad roads, and coming out, unbroken, on the other side. But that is a frankly privileged goal. It is the exhilaration of unpredictability, it is the next majestic view, that makes you gasp, and clench your fist in the air, with a "Yes, this is amazing!"

It is smiling in your helmet, and stretching your jaw muscles, saying out loud, "I want to do this forever."

It is the ever-changing landscape and, with it, the ever-changing challenge. It is the freezing cold mornings, packing up the frost covered tent, heading out as the sun is rising over the hills, warming up the landscape, in a moving blanket of sun, no one about. It is waking up, writing some of my book, and going, "Yes, another day".

Those three words can never be underestimated. Although I love England dearly, I spent fifteen years in dead-end jobs, working outside, in often miserable weather. I never said those words, ever. I never felt them. It is the fresh air. It is the people you meet, those chance encounters, with people from a different world. It is the history of the place, the stories, the building of culture, the monuments, the natural wonders, the strange customs that you struggle to understand, sometimes, but in time, totally understand. It is the different food, the different clothes, the nuances of greetings, the etiquette of greetings, the variety of jobs, some you never knew existed.

It is soaking up the last rays of the sun on a high altitude pass, the rains, the scorching deserts, the sandstorms, the wicked winds, the flash floods, the lightning, the intense cold, burrowing into the tips of your fingers and toes. The sweats, the shivers, the insects, the animals, the diseases, the dangers and, of course, the biggest encounter: with yourself.

My favourite encounters, however, are with animals. They leave the longest impression with me. I have drifted further away from humans than I could ever have imagined, and closer to, and more fascinated by, the other animals on this planet. It is strange because people frequently say to me, having travelled to so many countries:

"You must get to know so many people, and adapt to so many cultures, and have millions of friends."

Not true. It is the opposite. I have become a hermit, who cannot deal with people. I have become a person who has panic attacks, when giving a talk or a presentation. It is a problem I never had before. I cannot travel on underground train systems anywhere in the world. I cannot be in shopping centres, croweded streets, night clubs, parties, noisy places, and so on. I have almost become a feral member of this world. I do not want to take orders from anyone, but that is the reality of life, you have to answer to someone. I just want to be on my motorcycle, riding, and soaking up my interactions with animals, filming, photographing, and writing books. I want to inspire people to travel and see this world. I want my grandchildren (no sign of those right now, hint hint), to be inspired. Sadly, life is not that basic. And it costs. I did not realise that one of the side effects of being alone, in the bush, is that you forget how to be sociable, and connect with all the complexities of other people. It is too overwhelming for me: animals are simpler, more true, direct, no bullshit, readable, and trustworthy (maybe not the last two).

The reason I have not harped on about my animal encounters (unless they were catastrophic), is because I am aware of the 'holiday snap' syndrome. This is where Uncle Ron and Aunty Betty come back from their two weeks in Kenya, full of 'joie de vivre'. They regale you with 11,000 photos of an elephant's rear end, 9,000 of them out of focus. Or at least, that is what they say it is, as there is no way of confirming it from the photo. Just when you think you have escaped, they have the coup de grace; the close-ups of mating lions.

"'Very, very rare in the wild," says Uncle Ron, looking to Aunty

Betty for confirmation. The same problem. The mating lions are indistinguishable from the surrounding bush. All you can see are the other twenty trucks, that are also convinced that they are witnessing a rare lion mating encounter. It can't be that rare, or there would not be many lion cubs running around, would there? Looking at photos of the rear end of an elephant, disappearing into the bush, from two hundred meters, kind of loses its impact too. You need to be there.

Having said that, and going totally against my own philosophy, just a quick interaction with a snake, or even a gecko or hummingbird, is enough to lift my day. Seeing animals in their natural environment is a privilege; seeing them in a zoo, is a curse, for them, and us. The BR319 was a dream, as was all the Amazon. Another surreal twist in my life is that I am allergic to every biting creature on earth, but love them all. God certainly has a sense of humour. He said:

"Let's make this guy allergic to all animals, but he is attracted to them, like a magnet. Let's see what happens."

He didn't actually say that to me. He told a friend, who told me. So be it. Adaptability is the key. Keep the love, even with things that are trying to kill you. Even if they do kill you.

Our first encounter was on the very first day, only 100 kilometres from Belem, the city of mangoes, the gateway port to the Amazon. We had just hit a slippery section, so we took it slowly, snails overtaking us. Around a corner we witnessed a scene that an arachnophobic would keel over instantly, and die from. There were a few tarantulas on the road…

A few thousand. I am not scared of spiders, but what started as a few crossing the road, that we had to weave past slowly, progressed to a carpet of tarantulas, spanning the width of the road, in a column, twenty five foot wide. We had to stop, or it would be carnage, squished spiders flying off our tyres. The amazing thing was that they started attacking the wheel of the bike, and rearing up. The plucky fellows made two grown adults balance precariously, with their feet up on the seat of a motorcycle. It took more than ten minutes for them all to cross the road. I looked up 'herds of tarantulas' on the internet. Nothing to panic about. Starting in late September and running through mid October, the Amazon tarantulas appear en masse.

They are looking for love. Males appear from their burrows to find female spiders. They were possibly a bit touchy with us because love is a risky game for male tarantulas. If they are smaller than the object of their affection, and she does not fancy him, and is hungry, he quickly becomes a meal, rather than a mate. If you find a tarantula, do not be afraid. You can even go extremely close. No one has ever died from a tarantula bite, and while a nibble will hurt, they will not sink their fangs into you unless you scare them. I know all about that, after scaring one in Mexico, that was in my shorts. He bit me on the bum, but that is another story.

Our next encounter was more tranquil, to say the least. We came across another sloth crossing the road. It is absolutely true that they move slowly, painfully slowly. They even blink slowly. We decided to move him, otherwise he might get hit by the truck coming through here, next Friday. I picked him up in my biker jacket (he looked pretty good, head a bit small), and deposited him next to a Eucalyptus tree, ten metres into the jungle. We sat with him for about twenty minutes. I made lots of 'don't rush' jokes, but he was not impressed. I can also report that sloths are not keen on 'sardinas con aceite' - sardines in oil.

On our second night camping in the Amazon, we walked into a Stephen King film. As the sun was setting quickly, we had to set up camp in a military way. We were far enough away from the river (the famous one) about fifty meters, to be safe from crocodiles and anacondas. I wasn't really worried because I might have considered sacrificing Cathy to see an anaconda, I was so desperate for the experience.

We sat on a log, next to the small fire we had built, enough to give us a flickering, distorted view of our surroundings. On our left was the river, and on our right a beautiful tree. Around the base of the tree, the ground started moving, and out popped the biggest toad I have ever seen in my life. Both Cathy and I stood up off the log and stepped backwards. This is from two people, who clean lions' teeth with toothpicks. As soon as this giant cane toad showed his face, the ground erupted around us, like lava. Every step you took, a toad would pop up. I can sometimes exaggerate. Within ten minutes there were 200 of them; realistically, 1,000 surrounding us, with military precision. They were everywhere, it was a totally toad terrain, as far as we could see into the distance. Their eyes glistened, the warts on their backs sparkled and shimmered in the moonlight, as they slowly surrounded us, for the kill. They just had to wait until fatigue set in. We had to sleep at some point. Then they would pounce, or hop, in their case, and then drag us to their lair. We managed to survive the night, toadally in one piece.

You think I am exaggerating, because I just admitted that I sometimes do, but if you were an expert on giant cane toads, like I am, you would know, that they are prolific breeders. Females lay single dump spawns, with thousands of eggs. Its reproductive success is due to opportunistic feeding; it has a duct unusual to anurans, it has both living and dead matter. The success of their reproduction was evidently clear to Cathy and myself and, even worse; we were surrounded by thousands of brothers and sisters. Inbred giant cane toads. To make matters worse, they are by far the world's largest toad, with biceps. Some specimens reach thirty centimetres, easily covering this page, with its belly alone. They are super impressive, super ugly, and did not leave us alone all night, so we left early morning. That was not to be our last encounter with giant cane toads. Before we left the Amazon, we were to see a levitating one.

We had days and days of nothing but us, the animals and insects, and they were some of the best days of our lives. We took it slowly, filming, and interacting with the wildlife. I entered some sort of trance-like Nirvana. This jungle was everything my little boy's mind had read about and dreamt of, fifty years ago. We were followed on the bike by flocks of green and red parrots, and were swooped and squawked at by green, red and yellow macaws. We rode through clouds of tropical butterflies. Toucans eyed us from the treetops. We saw eagles, buzzards, bats and iguanas. Crocodiles and caimans eyed us from the river, and its banks. Flocks of thousands of egrets, perched in trees, giving the impression that it had snowed. Hummingbirds buzzed around us, during our sardine sandwich breaks, woodpeckers busy drumming nearby. Giant moths landed on our helmets, and stupidly burnt themselves on our bike engine. At night we saw thousands of fireflies, lighting up the jungle. Possums scurried past, bullet ants, fire ants, smiley ants and centipedes, checked out our feet. Every fifty meters was like a botanical garden. Never ever will I forget it.

Eventually we came across a derelict bus stop. No buses had stopped there since I was born. Yes, it was derelict, but it was a sign of humanity, and a signal that the BR319, and our special journey, was coming to an end. I was immediately brought down psychologically, about the whole civilization thing, facing people again. The Amazon had stolen my heart, beyond words, and Cathy enthused all day... so I know she felt the same. I decided to do a funny news report, to lift the vibe, where I would pop up inside the bus stop, lamenting the imminent arrival of humans. The bus stop frame would be the frame for my TV screen. Time to report on cane toads, taking over the world. By this stage I had done more research on the fascinating lives of cane toads, so was confident of nailing my news report. I found out that the cane toad has highly toxic poison glands, and even the tadpoles are highly toxic. They are particularly lethal to wild and domestic dogs, who are naturally inquisitive. So not only are they vicious little buggers, they are also considered a pest and invasive species. No hope then.

I am not making the following up. The 1988 film, 'Cane Toads; An unnatural history' is still a Top 10 bestseller worldwide. OK, I exaggerate; in Australia. It documents the trials and tribulations of cane toads. Either the cane toad is way more interesting than even I imagined, or Australian TV is extremely dull.

As I was about to impart these fascinating facts to camera, Cathy shouted, "Jesus Chris, what is that?" as she jumped back, in more than alarm.

We were sitting in deep grass, which is not clever in the jungle. In the long grass, less than a metre from Cathy, was a giant cane toad levitating back and forth, with its head and legs in the air. What the hell!! Then the cane toad levitated a few more centimetres. All became clear. He was in the mouth of a massive, ebony snake. I grabbed the snake by the tail and pulled him out of the long grass, so that we could film him. He wasn't happy, and who could blame him. I was so ecstatic, because I had just been complaining about the lack of snakes in South America. He eventually spat out the toad, and this was my sign to back off. I let him go. He retrieved his meal, and headed into the bush.

I know that the fear of spiders, snakes and heights are the three biggest fears on earth, so I apologise. If you are one of the millions who suffer from Ophidiophobia, a fear of snakes, don't go to a place I learnt about from the Amazon Indians. About twenty-five miles off the coast of Brazil, there is an island that no local would ever step onto. The last fisherman who strayed too close was found days later, adrift in his boat, lifeless, in a pool of blood. The mysterious island is known as Ilha da Queimada Grande, and is so dangerous to set foot on, that the Brazilian government has made it illegal to visit. The danger comes in the form of the Golden Lancehead snake, a species of pit viper, and one of the deadliest snakes in the world. The Lancehead only grows to just over a foot in length but there are an estimated 5000 on what is unsurprisingly known as 'snake island'. The snakes became trapped, when the rising sea levels covered up the land that joined it to the mainland. The ensuing selection process allowed these bird-eating snakes to rapidly adapt, and thrive. Access is only available to the Brazilian Navy, who vet the island to see if any adventure motorcyclists have tried to get there on a homemade raft. Actually, despite the reptile nut that I am, I might give that island a miss.

The Amazon jungle and the BR319 are more than enough to satiate any animal lover's dreams. I have done the bullet ant attack in Ecuador. Leaving the ebony snake to his cane toad meal, I really thought that animal drama was over. Now it was time for fire ants. My crime? I picked up a piece of wrapping, with a small piece of ham in it. The fire ants were feasting on it, quickly transferred to my hand, and attacked it.

Fire ants are in the genus Solenopsis. There are over two hundred species but the most common names are the tropical fire ant, red, and or, ginger ants (don't be childish). Don't mess with their venom, and don't mess with their survival skills. During Hurricane Harvey in Texas, in 2007, clumps of fire ants, known as ant rafts, were seen in groups of more than 100,000 individuals (who counted them?), who held hands, or feet, or pincers, and formed a temporary structure, to float on, until finding a permanent home. Not only are they tough survivors, they bloody hurt. My arm was burning, and quickly swelled up to splitting point. In about five percent of cases, fire ants can kill.

They can cause a severe allergic reaction, where the throat swells up, and you die. What makes them even more annoying is that, unlike many insects, one fire ant can sting multiple times, which makes them particularly dangerous to children and pets. Luckily I was neither of those, and my normal extreme reaction to stings and bites didn't either. No need to stab myself with an EpiPen this time. I just had a fat accelerator hand for a day, and a strange hole on my hand, that became infected over the next month. It eventually scarred over. I didn't want to die without a few scars and I have certainly succeeded in that.

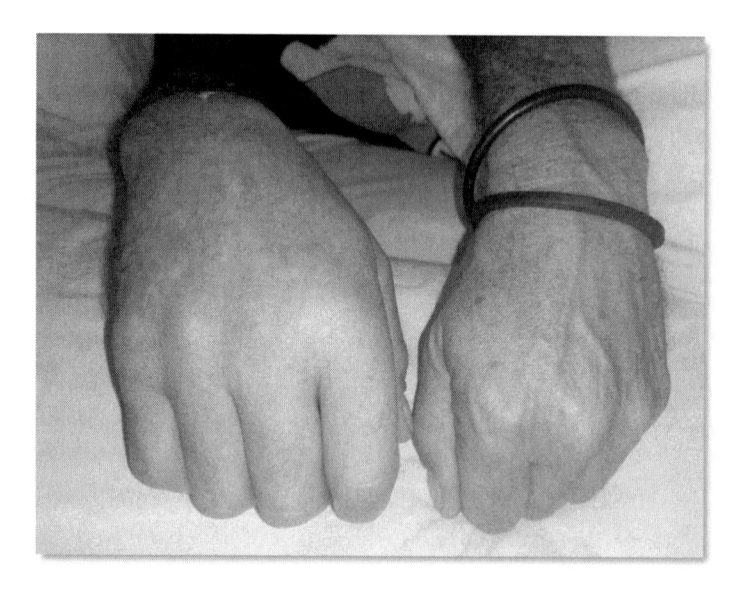

On we went towards the border with Peru. The riding was harsh, especially with my sausage arm, but perseverance is the hard work you do, after you get tired of the hard work you have done. I live my whole life by mantras, and it helps. A lot. I would turn around right now, and do the whole Amazon again. But we had other Tilapia to fry. Always onward.

After dealing with the brutal, but unspoilt and pristine BR319, Ghost Road, we drove into a hell, made by man. After hundreds of kilometres of red jungle road, nothing but the bike, Cathy and I, and the Amazon animals. We were jarringly reminded that there was another animal in the world: man. The 'first contact' with man we had was the smell and taste of burning plastic as we rode straight into a huge plume of dense, black smoke. Our eyes were smarting and it was difficult to breathe. We turned a slippery, red mud corner and ahead of us were kilometres of garbage, in a huge clearing in the jungle. On the left-hand side of the road, the whole area was on fire, tonnes of rotting, melting waste, the smoke reaching high into the sky, and blocking out the sun, in a perfect post-apocalyptic scene.

On the righthand side, the dump was fifteen foot high with filthy refuse. Hundreds of young boys and girls, and elderly people too, with scraps of material tied over their mouths, to deal with the stench, scrabbled through the waste, trying to salvage anything of value. They are known as 'catadores', and survive by fishing out plastics, metals, cardboard, and other recyclables from the dump, to sell to middlemen. They rummage through detritus, knee-deep in reeking mud, watched by massive vultures, who loiter and hop around the children, angrily grabbing scraps of food that are uncovered. There were rats, cockroaches, mosquitoes and huge groups of flies, bunched like some obscene cloud, above the dump. Most of the 'workers' were no older than fifteen. A few adults were amongst them, and the sprinkling of elderly decrepit, bent-over people was grim as hell. None of them had protective clothing. They were in rags, and flipflops, many getting injured. Nothing looked of value.

We waved, as we always do, but there was no reaction from any of them. Blank, grim looks. The problem of rubbish disposal is something I saw throughout Africa and to a lesser extent, in South America, and to a great extent in Central America. Peru and Guatemala are covered in plastic, much of Africa is covered in open, landfill sites, with plastic bag trees, children swarming everywhere, and vultures in equal numbers. As humans, we are supposed to be at the top of the food chain. If our children are rummaging through other people's waste, we are far from being civilised. There are a staggering 20,000 children living on landfill sites in Brazil. Brasilia, the capital has acquired a feature on its landscape that should be a national disgrace. A few miles from world renowned buildings stands the largest open garbage dump site in the world. It is growing rapidly, and at present, wait for it, is more than 300 acres, roughly the size of 300 football fields. We know we have gone wrong somewhere, in society, when there are street demonstrations by the 'garbage children', to allow them to keep working in these cesspits. It is because they have nothing else to do to earn a living, as some make money by fashioning what they retrieve into articles for sale!!

Sorry for tangent, back to our present situation. The smouldering heap of garbage was on the outskirts of and introduction to the worst town I have ever seen, in my life, and I have seen bad. Bear in mind that I have been through the Democratic Republic of Congo. You may remember my description of Cusco, in Peru, and my description of Kinshasa. This place was worse than both.

Imagine your normal life, in your normal house. You have good roads, gas, internet, electricity, water, garbage disposal, a bus, a taxi, an Uber, government benefits, a post office, a convenience store and a neighbour to moan to that the post was late. You have garbage trucks that miraculously make your waste disappear at three in the morning, while you complain that their truck woke you up. You have a bus for your children to go to school on. If all else fails, and your complaints fall on deaf ears, you have a multitude of ombudsmen, local radio stations, and corner gossip neighbours to talk to, and 'um and aah' about. If you run out of complaints, you can always discuss the terrible weather, and what the lack of rain has done to your roses.

Let's add two years of no rain to the grim scenario. You are facing a drought in your comfortable, predictable world. Remove the emergency services too. Hospitals, ambulances, firemen, garbage disposal, police and your local shop. Gone. Remove all of these amenities we take for granted. No sanitation system, nothing at all. You try and make your garbage disappear. It won't happen. Then add; no law, no policemen, no rules, no slap on the back for being a good citizen. I will not name this town, but suffice to say, it is near Lethem, the rough and ready border between French Guiana and Brazil. Enough said.

We rode through, wide eyes full of smoke and sadness. We did not speak all the way through this town. I know that we were both listening to the engine, the tyres on the road, trying to block out our thoughts - how can human beings live in the most squalid and frankly, inhumane conditions that we were seeing. Using the word 'inhumane' really means nothing in this context. Animals would never be so filthy, or ruin their environment, to this extent.

After negotiating the expansive, repulsive, gag-inducing rubbish dump, we were then faced with rows and rows of armoured police trucks and military vehicles, parked alongside the road. There were at least ten riot vehicles, huge grey trucks with 'Militar' emblazoned on the side, and a riot grill covering the windscreen, windows and lights. The side windows were mere slits, and the roofs had four massive mega phones and a red light mounted on them, all covered in riot proof mesh. There were more than twenty pickups, with seats and a 16-person riot squad in the rear of each. They were dressed in black, with bullet proof vests, body armour and black helmets with flip-down visors. All of them had IA2 Assault rifles, Colt and Taurus handguns, batons and mace. No tasers for these guys. Not hard-core enough. Hundreds of riot police also lined the road, getting a final briefing in huddled groups of twenty. They were obviously not after the local pickpocket. This looked like a classic 'guns and drugs raid'. Brazil suffered a record 64,000 murders in 2019, a mind-blowing 175 deaths a day, 45,000 of those involving firearms, so this is one serious problem, not isolated to this hell hole.

We were waved through by a masked military gunman. They probably wanted us through, and out the other side, before the poo hit the proverbial fan. As we made our way slowly through what seemed like a war zone, we saw some locals had been stopped and were being screamed at and hit with rubber 'whips' about four feet long. The scene was getting grimmer by the minute, so it was eyes ahead. On the very outskirts, the obligatory dogs, injured, ribs jutting, and almost hairless from mange, sniffed around in the hope of some scraps, to keep them alive for another day. I can't look at these dogs, it's horrific. This was getting more and more like the port scene in Kinshasa, in the Democratic Republic of Congo. I knew we had to get out.

On our right were a group of four ramshackle huts, sliding down a riverbank, twisted and mangled bits of corrugated iron and wood. Another police roadblock had been made temporarily, with two banana trees that had been hacked down, and dragged into the middle of the road. The masked, sunglass-wearing Militia at the banana roadblock were as grim as everyone else. No smiles, no greetings, just,

"Where are you going?"

"Peru."

"Go now, quickly. *Esta cidade e perigrosa.*" (This town is dangerous.) He cleared his throat, pulled his mask down and spat, "Go now, go."

He gestured aggressively down the road.

We needed little persuasion.

One hundred metres later, we entered the town fringes. Jesus Christ. First impression, no improvement. Mountains of plastic bottles, beer bottles, multi-coloured Brahman beer cans, squashed neon green Guarana Antarctica cans, the popular Brazilian drink made with extracts of, surprisingly, Guarana. There were separate piles of Coke cans, Yoki crisp packets, rotting fruit, broken glass, used nappies, used toilet paper and rotting animals. Massive black buzzards, with livid red heads, leapt and swooped about amongst scrawny, nearly featherless chickens. Filthy people, barefoot and obviously on drugs, were brushing the birds aside, as they scavenged amongst the litter, competing with cat-sized rats. The heady and putrid smell of methane, sulfur and ammonia, the gases produced when bacteria breaks down organic waste, made the air thick, and the eyes stream. That's the warm up. The 'town' itself, consisted of houses made of bamboo and wooden pallets, that were all sinking into a river of garbage, stench and death.

Imagine a river; not a romantic, picturesque, 'let's sing about the Danube' river, where children frolicked in the sunshine and paddled in the shallows of a crystal clear mountain stream. No siree! Take a stagnant, thick brown sludge of a river, with zero movement. Then clog it up with human excrement, and anything that has died in the last five years. Fill this with as much garbage as you can possibly muster, until the river has disappeared. Only the almost indiscernible movement, and the odd release of a fetid bubble of water, or gas, gave any clue that there was a river under the scum. The stench was rank, and we were both gagging. The smell was permeating through our face covers, and I eventually vomited. A woman was serving a green slime stew to someone, while stepping over a head-split-open, rotting goat, its open stomach alive with maggots. It was too much for me. I pulled over and had a quick clean-up, and on we went, past the houses of horror.

We have this town. It has an obscene death sludge river going through the centre. How do we make it worse? Well, it's obvious. Build houses on stilts, above the sludge. That is exactly what they did. All of them were slipping into the sludge. Everyone was living at an angle. It would be funny, if it wasn't so incredibly tragic. The houses were ready to dump their occupants into the slurry. There were people openly smoking crack cocaine from homemade pipes, huddled by the road. The asphalt road through the centre was no longer asphalt. It was a broken-up quagmire of rubble, puddles and litter, much like the river. I prayed that we didn't get a flat tyre. I was not the biggest fan of this town, and we also knew that they were about to be raided, by an army. Not a good place to be.

The buildings only got worse. I have never seen houses so badly built and in such a ludicrous location. It looked like a man, or woman, with no building experience, had been given a variety of rotten timber, and scraps of metal and been instructed to, "Build a town out of this."

"Oh, and on stilts above a river, full of disease."

The result was as expected, but worse. Many buildings had collapsed into the river, and had now turned into floating pontoons that hawkers swarmed onto, balancing precariously. Makeshift pallets were thrown between collapsed houses, so they could walk above the slurry. Nobody looked happy, everyone looked dirty at best, drugged or deformed at worst. I say this rarely. I never want to come back here again. Dante's *Inferno* step aside.

But we still had to get out, and it was slow progress. The road ahead wasn't spared the detritus. It was littered with broken bottles, dead birds, indistinguishable animals, squashed flat and crisp-dried in the sun. There were bolts and nails and metal scraps peppered along the route and the inevitable happened, We got a flat tyre and we were immediately surrounded by people selling rotten, battered fruit, popsicle-shaped plastic bags of water, crack cocaine, in tiny plastic wraps and marijuana wrapped in palm leaf strips.

I fixed the tyre in record time and we continued on through burning piles of wood, a group of children kicking a flat, half-moon-shaped football. Twenty metres on, another group of children threw handfuls of soil into the potholes in front of us and asked for 'Road repair money'. On our left, a stick of a man pulled a catfish out of the sludge. I have no idea how a fish could survive those conditions, let alone the people who ate him. Catfish are the hardiest fish and live and thrive in the dirtiest conditions. I don't think the people were thriving.

The collapsing town continued for two more kilometres, and on the other side we were met with the same scenario; rows and rows of Militia and police. It was only then that we learned why they were there. A young officer waved us to the side of the road. He was evidently a bike lover, and a bike owner, as he immediately started asking questions about the engine, the stickers and the panniers. It was a relief.

After a brief chat, I felt brave enough to ask, "What is happening here. What are you guys doing?"

His answer was sobering. "There were two murders here yesterday and they cut off a woman's hand."

"My God! Why?"

"Drugs Senor, always drugs. You go now."

With pleasure.

Within thirty minutes we were back in the Amazon jungle, in total silence, at one with nature, helping another sloth across the road and into a nearby tree. He was in no hurry. Nor were we now. Towns like that make me want to escape all human contact. Ten nights of wild camping was in order. The best kind of accommodation for an adventure motorcyclist, and my favourite price. But sometimes camping is totally out of the question and we found a superb alternative when camping is not an option. LOVE MOTELS.

Chapter Fifteen
Love Motels

Experiences like sleeping out in the Amazon are cherished. As an adventurer you have to be adaptable to where you stay, especially in built-up areas. Jungles have their hazards, but they are of the animal and creepy crawly kind. In the towns and cities, it is important to find a fairly secure location, preferably where the bike can be locked inside, or in a secure area. Otherwise I spend all night guarding the bike and end up with sleep deprivation. This is why I have to sing the praises of the phenomenon that is the Love Motel. Drum roll. We didn't spot any in the Amazon jungle but in Latin America, Love Motels (get used to the capital letters, they are important), are huge business, and for logical reasons.

Many couples live with their parents well into their late twenties because of financial constraints. Understandably, most do not want to perform their sexual manoeuvres next to the room where Abuelo is getting ready for bed, or Papi is watching the game on TV. Not conducive to passion. Then, of course, there are couples who want to role play, or just go a little wild, and to be honest they are also a great place to sneak off for a steamy affair.

The Love Motel industry started in Japan but has spread (hopefully not in the sexually transmitted disease way) throughout the world. The history of Love Motels goes back to the seventeenth century in the Edo period in Japan, where inns and teahouses started to provide discreet entry to their venues and even built secret tunnels to allow an even more discreet exit. Modern Love Motels developed from these tea rooms. By the 1960s the widespread introduction of the automobile caused an explosion of the concept of discreet venues, where couples and lovers could meet away from the confines of a crowded family home.

By 1961 there were more than 2,700 Tsurekomi Inns in Central Tokyo alone and by 2019 they were pulling in a staggering revenue of more than $60 billion. South America has adopted Love Motels with fervour and are difficult to escape (not in that way). They are a totally accepted part of Latino culture and it's not uncommon to see giant billboards hanging on bridges or off rafters in local bars, advertising the delights and, of course, discretion.

The openness of Love Motels can be jaw-dropping when first encountered, but you quickly realise, as a scrooge traveller, that they are cheap and clean. Cathy and I were forced into using their facilities when in cities because it is almost always impossible to camp. In fact, after a few basic errors of etiquette, we became reasonable experts on Love Motels. (Always use capital letters for Love Motels and when you say the words, your voice has to go as deep as possible, a la Barry White, and stretch out the word Luuurve.) Love Motels differ widely in quality and seediness but there is a basic set-up and structure that is good to know to ease the shock factor. I certainly embarrassed myself.

There is an inner courtyard which is made up of rows of garages, which either have massive pull-across curtains or in the more upmarket establishments, remote controlled doors operated by the reception, much to my frustration on a few occasions. The rooms are situated directly above the garages, connected by an internal stairway. This ensures that you don't need to show your horny faces again. So the deal is, you drive straight into the garage, like Valentino Rossi, run up the stairs, hanky-panky for a couple of hours and then leave. I didn't realise this. At one particular Love Motel in Brazil, named The Snake Pit, if I remember rightly, I stood outside our garage sipping my tea and cheerily saying,

"Morning... " "Good Morning... " "Lovely day... " to the amorous couples and Ladies of the Night coming and going. Strangely, management were very quick to complain, as was Cathy, and we were banished to our room.

"You can't act so English, Spencer. You don't stand outside Love Motels in South America, or in any continent for that matter, and greet the clients. It's weird," Cathy reprimanded me, giggling.

"I was just being friendly and welcoming," I said, rather weakly.

Cathy was right, of course. There was an incognito code here and when in Rome do as the Brazilians do, or whatever the saying is. My etiquette quickly improved and I became a dab hand (bad choice of phrase) at melting into the background, like a ninja. Anyway, to the interior and décor.

Most rooms in Love Motels have themes whether it be dungeon, jungle, maritime, fantasy, spaceships, moonscapes, or whatever strikes the fancy of the owner. We saw a cartoon-themed Motel with Mickey Mouse hanging off the roof. Strange. The Love Motel San Felipe, Brazil was predictably called 'The Anaconda' and had a wall surrounding the property that was fifty metres long. It was adorned with a 49-metre long fluorescent green and orange anaconda who had a demented smile on his face. His eyes lit up red when you drove past. Considering his head was about the size of a car, as tacky murals go, it was impressive. All the rooms were plush, carpeted jungles with gold vine-shaped taps and animal and jungle fauna murals. Or so we were told. That one was a bit too expensive.

Love Motel architecture is not exactly subtle or tasteful, with buildings shaped like boats, UFOs, castles, sharks, octopi and other marine life and usually lit with enough neon lighting to impress Las Vegas or Lapland at Christmas. One Motel in Argentina was actually an ornately painted and bejewelled skull, and patrons drove through the mouth to enter the courtyard, while the teeth snapped at your car. They looked like dentures, so it wasn't the biggest turn-on. Modern Love Motels tend to be a lot more bland and understated and often can only be spotted by the lack of windows.

The interiors are often highly tacky. Almost all rooms in Love Motels have a chaise longue, or massage chair, or canoodling couch, or love-making sofa, or whatever the technical term is. It looks like some serious acrobatics can go on in these rooms for the sexually malleable. Most also have love swings, if you want to try and Tarzan it up while you fornicate. Another Brazilian Love Motel called 'Pop Life Luxury Suites' had not one, but two pole dancing areas in each room. Presumably so you could have an impromptu competition. Cathy wasn't keen so I tried my hand at pole dancing for the first time, in my full bike gear and my size twelve Harley Davidson concrete boots. I won't give up the day job. It didn't go well, especially when I decided to go upside down when I was more than halfway to the ceiling. I tried again without the boots, but a bad workman cannot blame his boots. It gave Cathy some amusement and gave me an elbow injury that I carry to this day. Cathy also got a few photos; fond memories to show the grandchildren. Or not.

The beds are also extremely large, about the size of the mats that people land on when they jump five storeys out of burning buildings in American films. They are also very dangerous beds. They vibrate uncontrollably on anything over control setting 7 (I have been told) and can bounce you off. The situation is made more complex by the fact many of them are water beds. Because of the bed size you have to brave mini tsunami waves coming towards you if someone jumps on the other side. They are also covered in some sort of plastic, so if you approach it with a bit too much amorous intent, you will slide straight off the other side, onto a purple carpet or some such garish colour. If you are really fast, you can slide off the bed and straight into the jacuzzi. In retrospect, everything is actually designed to make it difficult to stay on the bed. A bit like the *Titanic*, which also happens to be the name of quite a few Love Motels. I am not sure if a 'sinking feeling' is the right emotion to conjure up when you meet your lover. Maybe they stand in the showers with their arms outstretched.

Another salubrious spot in Colombia was a Love Motel called 'Nels Executive Suite'. We evidently could not bypass it, as it is Cathy's surname, and may have been a distant relative who Cathy could claim some family ownership or shares, or something. (Not my idea, but always up for a bonus in life.) Or a discount for having the same surname. We had no luck on any counts. At Nels, not only were the undersheets plastic, but the main sheets were imitation silk. Every time you moved in the bed, they collected so much static they electrocuted you. It was also impossible to keep them over you. They would just suddenly fly off and stick to the wall or ceiling, or wrap themselves round a ceiling fan. (Or so I heard from a reliable source.)

All Love Motels have televisions, sometimes more than one, many as big as a small semi-detached house in the UK. The choice of programmes on every channel is graphic, naked human interaction which would scare the hardiest gynaecologist. There is a great deal of groaning that is totally out of sync with the actors, and what they are doing. At least the language selection on the remote is not vital. Another rather disconcerting feature is that next to the bed, on either side, is a mounted toilet roll to clear up over-zealous fluids. When you first enter the rooms, the bathrooms look like crime scenes, as the toilet seat, the sink and shower are covered in yellow tape, with the word 'Disinfectado' written boldly and repetitively along it. Good to know. Another common feature is padded walls (don't ask me), and large, ornate, dangerously positioned mirrors on the ceilings above the bed, for better observation. There are speakers mounted in the headboards so you can experience multi-surround sex sounds. Most of it was totally unintelligible and distorted. It was a bit like being in a crowd scene from *Ben Hur*. If you splash out (pun), you can land a room with a generous circular jacuzzi with a bucket-size, rain-water-mimicking shower head above, and thousands of different jets and bubbles of different power and color, shooting out from underwater. And space for ten guests. I am old. The thought of ten guests shatters me already. Many rooms offer dozens of different light settings and colours and bed positions. By the time you work out all the controls, gadgets, nozzles, bed positions, etc, it is time to leave and anyway, by then you are too tired for any form of carnal encounter.

There are also menus next to the bed; make sure not to eat the Strawberry Love Lube or the Pina Colada Oil. The menus offer standard soft drinks and beers, but also a selection of sex toys, stallion condoms in various flavours, vibrators, anal intruders and fancy dress outfits. (Glad they don't have anal extruders.) One particularly well-stocked motel called the Sunset Marquis Motel had a menu called the Love Store. They offered no less than nineteen different sex toys, including the 'mariposa (butterfly) vibrador', the 'matrix vibrador' and the 'poseidon multi speed vibrador'. Let us not forget the 'tutti frutti super orgasmo gel estimulante femenino' and the 'Ligatura contractora'. (Don't ask me.) Their most expensive sex toy was the 'SC Adventure Rider'. No it wasn't.

If you are keen on going down the nurse, fireman, super-hero, magic wand fairy, lace teddy or blackout mask route, it can be sorted. I already had my Adventure Motorcyclist fancy dress kit on. Whips and chains and fluffy pink handcuffs can also be rented or bought. Goods are ordered by phone or intercom and are mysteriously delivered through a hatch, directly into your room, with not a person in sight. One doesn't want coitus interruptus, or interruptus coitus if you are Spanish.

An important thing to point out is that Love Motels are rented by the hour, so most couples pay for a couple of hours. (They don't cater for men's performance times, with what would be more realistic six-minute bookings.) So when I asked to book in for 10-12 hours, I got some raised eyebrows. I just made some tiger noises and said, "You know, I am a real man, Wink wink."

They loved it and giggled. Actually an increasing number of Love Motels are getting used to renting rooms to 'Economy-saving foreigners' for the night, so not so many eyebrows are raised nowadays. Love Motels are also extremely common, peppering the sides of highways and scattered throughout business districts and densely populated areas. Although they do hide behind large walls and are discreet with their customers and all that goes on inside, as said before, they announce their presence with gigantic, garish signs, highlighting names like 'Hotel Love Time', 'Te Adore', 'Sin City', etc. In Japan they go for different names; 'The Hide and Seek Club', 'Naughty Kitten', 'Capricious Ponytail', 'Hello Clown Hotel', and my favourite, 'Legend of the Ignorant Feigning Beaver Hotel'.

Once you get over your initial reserve, or not, Love Motels are great. They are a cheap alternative if you can make do without the personal waiter, heated pool, water slide and all the mod cons some offer. They are a perfectly acceptable part of Latino culture, especially in Colombia and Brazil and usually have no links to brothels or sex-working establishments. Clients may, however, take a prostitute or escort to a Motel much in the same way as a standard discreet hotel. Although totally accepted, they do still strive to protect your privacy and anonymity, which is kind of nice. Lobbies are dimly lit and attendants operate behind privacy screens. Almost all the rooms are without windows. They evidently don't want Adventure Motorcycylists staring through opposite windows, commenting on the weather and offering tea.

After being on the road and camping for months, these hotels really are a sanctuary of safety and relaxation in a city environment, an environment that neither of us is keen on. Also the bike and all our gear is safely locked up for the night, which is unusual for us and lends for a good night's sleep. Furthermore, if you are worried about cleanliness, you really don't need to be. It's all about perception. Any, and all hotels, are used for sex, Love Motels are just more upfront about it. Love Motels are held to the same health standards as any other hotel. From my experience many are cleaner. Once you leave, housekeeping is in there, in force, like a SWAT team. All towels, sheets and dodgy robes are sent off, the rooms are disinfected to standards a German hospital would aspire to, and everything is swathed in crime scene tape. The final bonus is that the staff are always so normal and friendly and welcoming. They are normal men and women of all ages. It's not the seedy sex industry; so no greasy overweight guy with a slipping toupee, greedily snatching your money and dribbling through a stained, smeared glass partition. No peeling scantily clad adverts on the wall. It is all very civilized, 90% of the time. Don't blame me if you get the 10% one. Of course, it's not a bed of roses. In the cheaper places they do have very thin walls. You may have to fall asleep to a chorus on either side of you, generally grunting men and 'oohing, aahing' women who are verbally extremely enthusiastic. That's about the worst you will have to deal with.

Chapter Sixteen
Butterflies and Colonialism

There are no Love Motels in French Guiana and to be honest we didn't come across much love either. We entered French Guiana through the southern Brazilian border at Olapoqu. Brazil and Guiana are not friends, and that is putting it mildly. The tension we felt when crossing the border was instantly palpable and reminded me of the crossing from Eswatini (formerly Swaziland) to South Africa. You move from a beautiful vibrant, friendly country, into one where 'something is wrong'. Apologies to my South African friends. South Africa is my second-most favourite country in the world. It is difficult to describe a vibe, or an atmosphere, of a place. It needs to be experienced, and our first hour wasn't so welcoming. Brazilians are also not welcome in Guiana. The country has gone so far as to ban all imports from Brazil, which is a bit harsh.

However, two years ago French police officers were shot dead by a gang of Brazilians, involved in illegal gold mining. A 32-year-old corporal and his assistant were involved in Operation Harpy Eagle, designed to control illegal mining in the area. Two other French police were seriously injured in the battle. In April last year more than 100 Brazilian artisanal gold miners were imprisoned in French Guiana, in apparently grim conditions. Last June, a Brazilian boatman was shot dead by French police, on French territory. It was alleged that he was transporting clandestine products to one of the illegal gold mining areas. No evidence was produced and this did not go down well with the Brazilian government.

There is no doubt that massive illegal mining is occurring, but it is by a multitude of nationalities, including French Guianese. Apart from violent skirmishes on the borders and in the jungle, Guiana accuses Brazil of poisoning their country with mercury. The substance, used to separate gold from other materials, is highly toxic and is dumped into rivers and pits, playing havoc with the food chain and damaging the health of plants, animals, fish and humans. Illegal miners use as much as one kilogramme of mercury to extract one kilogramme of gold. The World Wildlife Fund has estimated that 30,000 kilogrammes of mercury is being dumped per year, much of it in protected national areas and indigenous reserves. In the upper Maroni River, a third of local communities are suffering from mercury contamination. It's not just the Guianese. As many as 15 million people in South America, Africa and Asia are suffering from mercury poisoning.

Illegal gold miners and smugglers

Those of you who know nothing about Guiana, may be wondering why I am talking about 'French Guianese', and 'French territory', in the middle of South America. Nine countries in South America are Spanish-speaking and one, Brazil, is Portuguese. Evidently these are colonial languages if you go back 500 years or so, but all are now independent states. In French Guiana, it is different. They speak French, but it is not an independent country. It is the only territory of mainland South America to be an overseas department and region of France. Strangely, it is therefore part of the European Union and the currency is the Euro. I am sure this colonial-type structure and slave history doesn't ingratiate them with Brazil either.

French Guiana was originally inhabited by indigenous people; Arawak, Kalina, Galibu, Take, Wayampi and Wayana. The first French contact is recorded as 1503, but they did not establish a durable presence until colonists founded Cayenne in 1643. The first concerted effort to colonise was in 1763 and failed utterly. The settlers were subject to ridiculously high mortality rates, given the numerous tropical diseases and harsh climate, for which they were totally unprepared, both physically and mentally. All but 2,000 of the initial 12,000 settlers died. (Sounds like the Scottish settlers in the Darien Gap.) But they persevered and Guiana was developed as a slave society, where planters imported Africans as enslaved labourers on large sugar plantations. Slavery was abolished in 1794, but in 1946 French Guiana became fully integrated into the French Republic, as it is today. The country has the highest GDP per capita in South America. This statistic is totally misleading. Believe me, French Guiana is far from equal and is a shockingly divided country, which is not too pleasant to witness.

Apart from the clashes with Brazil, and the history of slavery, there are two other factors that have affected the social and economic structure and vibe of this tiny nation, up to the present day; one, that it has a space station and two, that it was also a penal colony for French criminals. In my opinion both these facts tarnish the atmosphere of the country. (Sorry my French friends.) I have insulted two nations in one chapter. This is going well.

The Guiana Space Centre (Centre Spatial Guyanais), also known as Europe's Spaceport, cannot be ignored. Within an hour of arriving we were driving round a huge perimeter, with twenty-foot, diamond mesh fencing, topped with curled barbed wire and security cameras every twenty metres. It was like approaching Area 51. There were smartly dressed, egret-white-skinned French security guards, with scissor-trimmed beards, scowling at us as we rode past their security check points. There were search lights on scaffolding towers, and uniformed men with sniffer dogs. At the main entrance there was a huge concrete bollard blocking the road, but a turning on the left had a small supermarket on the corner. We stopped and bought two bottles of Evian, and two 'pains au chocolat'. Yes! Evian water and croissants in South America. We sat on the pavement outside, in the shade of the bike to eat and drink French fare.

Opposite us on the pavement edge was a man of about sixty, with a wispy beard, a pair of stained jeans tied at the waist with string, and a tweed suit jacket, four sizes too big wrapped around him, and also tied with string. Somehow, the jacket had bunched up around his chest. He was taking sticky plant seeds, that looked like mini coronaviruses, from the shoelaces of his battered trainers, and slowly placing them in a line, next to him, on the pavement. He had very hairy eyebrows, which rose a good few inches every time he looked up. He had sad eyes.

A large Renault people carrier came out of the Space Centre and pulled up outside the shop, in the parking space partially taken up by 'Sad Eyes' feet. Four young French gentlemen got out, two in white overalls and two in smart suits. The driver pushed 'Sad Eyes' foot out of the way, with his foot. 'Sad Eyes' looked up, a bit shocked, and asked them for some change for bread. Three of them ignored him completely, pretending to be glued to their latest iPhones. The driver, with a thick, but highly manicured and sprayed beard, and aggressive, deep-set eyes, turned back, said something rude and spat on the ground in front of the prone man. 'Sad Eyes' just bowed his head to the road. It is incredible how someone with no money, almost becomes demoted to non-human status, so unimportant that you look at them like they are poo on your shoe, treat them like a lesser being, or at best ignore them as an embarrassment. Sickening to me.

Cathy grabbed my arm, because she knows me well; but I was up. I confronted the driver and told him exactly what I thought of him. He wasn't impressed. The whole group stopped. I had my helmet in my hand, just in case things escalated, but it petered out with some handbag swinging from them, before they went in the shop, muttering Gallic threats to me and my entire family, all of which I understood. I speak French.

As soon as they were in the shop, we went over to 'Sad Eyes' and gave him some Euros, which is unheard of with us. He immediately burst into tears. I nearly did too. With huge smiles he went into the shop and came out smiling, laden with bread, cheap plastic cheese (that had never been near a cow), and water. Superb. Fabian was a lovely, gentle man. No abuse was necessary. We left Fabian, with a hug, and within ten minutes drove straight into the French Guiana version of the Tour de France.

The Tour of Guiana, formerly known as 'Le Tour du Littoral', is an annual, nine-stage bicycle race that connects the main cities, Cayenne, Kourou and Saint Laurent du Maroni. The tour expanded from purely

Guiana entrants, to become international in 1978, with more than ten different nationalities. We were heading out of Cayenne along the main, smooth tar, well-maintained road, with neat, spacious houses dotted along it, when we were guided by a traffic policeman, angrily, onto the hard shoulder, and then down a dirt road, to allow the peloton to pass.

The first three minutes were incredible. I love sports, and any athlete at the top of his game, is an exciting privilege to watch, especially live. The first twenty riders were strapping, professional examples of dedication and hard work. The next 100 were serious cyclists, pushing themselves in the heat. Sadly, as a spectator sport, it leaves a bit to be desired. It takes all of two minutes for 120 fit athletes to zoom past. Then come the less than professional. Then the strictly 'fun' people. Then the 'I will never do this again' brigade. Respect to all of them, it's great. But after thirty minutes in the sun, in bike gear, watching men and women, with pot bellies, in tight lycra; at some point the wonder and awe wears off.

The race was evidently not going to end for a week or so. After losing five kilos each, sweating, and whining, at the side of the road, we were finally waved down another dirt detour, that according to angry official, would bring us out on the road to Suriname, our next mini country. This is where is got interesting. The nice houses disappeared.

The asphalt road disappeared. The road names and street signs were not here. There were no manicured lawns and strategically placed trees. The neat painted shops disappeared. The smell of baguettes and cakes disappeared. The well-dressed French, in massive, gleaming 4x4s were gone. The road became a muddy potholed mess, and we were going fast, if we were going ten kilometres an hour. We were basically paddling with the bike, as they say in the trade. There were no white people anywhere, anymore.

A different country altogether. On our left we passed a building 'development', for want of a better word. There were rows and rows of tiny houses, square and concrete and baking in direct sunlight. A whole plot of land had been razed to the ground, devoid of all vegetation, and beauty, and 200 of the ugliest houses you can ever imagine, were crammed onto the dry, sun-baked space. They were boxes. The windows were tiny, like sighting holes in a turret gun. There was an open sewer running along the length of the road, between us and the development. Cans, plastic bags, blocks of wood, scrap metal and dead animals (a scene often encountered but to which you never become accustomed), clogged up the canal. The houses which were presumably once white, were now green with slime and fungus. The jungle was reclaiming the houses. Many had cracks down their entire walls that you could fit your fist into. Makeshift wooden poles, acting as scaffolding, was holding up some walls, alarmingly leaning groundward, ready to collapse. Washing was hanging on trees. Dogs and cats were aplenty, as is another curse of poor places, and pigs and goats scrabbled around in the debris on the canal edge, snorting and bleating.

Everyone waved and smiled everywhere we rode. We smiled back too, but underneath, we couldn't believe that there was such a sanitised, white, French-money-soaked area, and a hidden, poor, Creole, traditional area. We saw the very rich and the very poor, during our brief visit. One group was white and French and rich, and the other was poor and black and indigenous. No other way of putting it. We saw enough, believe me. Even without this detour, it was obvious in the capital city, Cayenne, that things were odd. Every position of authority, from policeman to bank managers, to government officials, to tourist guides (joke on the last one, they don't exist), were all white, French men. No French women either. It was very noticeable and unpleasant. We went into roadside cafes that were full of white people. They looked at us in our muddy bike gear, as though we had committed a crime by joining them in their haven of colonialism. There were no signs saying 'Whites only, and then only certain ones'. There was no need. It was obvious from the reception we received that we were not welcome.

It is not rocket science (sorry, I could not resist), to see that the massive amount of money swirling around from the Rocket Launch site, is staying in the hands of the French. The same with the general structure of society in Guiana. A large part of the economy derives from jobs and business associated with the presence of the Space Centre. But does it improve the lives of the local people. No! When I speak about the atmosphere of a place, you have to see the little snippets; kicking Fabien's foot out of the way, rude orders in shops, hooting aggressively at Creole people, raised eyebrows, racist comments about 'untrustworthiness', 'laziness' and 'differences'. We heard it all, in the space of a few days. And bear in mind that we were brought up in southern Africa, so we know a little bit about racist people, although they are in the minority in southern Africa, thank God. But the French in Guiana are up there with the most shocking, colonial, racist dividers; between Caucasian French recent imports, and the ethnic Creole. French Guiana was one of the only places in the whole of South America where the police were rude at customs and at roadblocks. They had imported European officiousness, petty one-upmanship, hierarchy and divisiveness, to a South American country. All good to look down on two scruffy motorcyclists. But racism. That's another story. I despise it.

Once again; all of this for gold, minerals, and whatever you can exploit. The same with the 'European' Space Centre in Guiana. Although located in South America, it is the nearest 'European' country to the equator. The closer a rocket launches from the equator, the more effective the launch, since the earth's rotation helps with the rocket's trajectory and velocity making it 2.5% more effective than launching in Europe, and hence, cheaper. Whilst the station does not launch humans into space, it is famous for sending supplies to the International Space Station and several communications satellites. A pity they can't send supplies ten kilometres down the road, to people who are obviously frozen out of society. The second reason is that as Guiana has a coastline, the sea is suitable to receive rocket debris, and hopefully not kill too many locals. This country does not sit well with me.

French Guiana's penal history doesn't improve my view, but oddly, it is one of the main reasons I wanted to visit. During operations as a penal colony, France transported more than 80,000 prisoners to the infamous Devil's Island. Fewer than 8,000 made it out alive. I heard about this island, like many of you, I suspect, through a book called *Papillon*, that totally entranced me as a teenager. It was written by Henri Charriere, and was made into a blockbuster film, starring Dustin Hoffman. The film did nothing for me, and neither did the recent one, but the book let my imagination soar. To me, the book was a masterpiece, that made me want to visit those sweaty, inhospitable jungles, Charriere so expertly described.

As you know, Cathy and I do not do the tourist attraction thing, and everything is done on a budget that a church mouse would be proud of, but there was no way I was not visiting Devil's Island, even if we had to pay heart-attack inducing prices.

Devil's Island (Ile du Diable), Ile Royale and Ile St Joseph were the three islands that were the most notorious part of the penal colony and operated from 1853 until after the Second World War. Sadly, Devil's

Island was out of bounds, but we managed to visit Ile St Joseph. The overgrown ruins of the solitary confinement cells where prisoners were chained to the walls were too much for me. It was overwhelming. The memories of reading *Papillon* as a teenager, in my bedroom in Swaziland flooded back to me. And here I was. Thirty years later. The boy who dreamt of slashing through the Amazon, had not only done that, but had made it through almost every country in South America so far to get here. We even took a sneaky detour out to sea, in a no-go zone, so we could see Devil's Island in the distance. That was even more exciting. OK, I know I am odd.

Prison dormitory, 1947

What an atmosphere oozed across that stretch of sea. I will never forget that day my reading world collided with my real world. I gave myself a brief pat on the back. Every day I spend more on this earth, the more I want to know. I am like a sponge, soaking up water, but miraculously I am never waterlogged. It is wonderful.

The Charriere story was one of many that sparked me to try to explore as much of this world as possible before I die. I read voraciously, ever since I was knee high to a cockroach, and it was always explorers and adventurers. Fiction never interested me. I saw it as a waste of time. I had my own imagination. I wanted to read about real people, who had pushed the limits of human endurance, often verging on lunatic, suicidal and irrational behaviour. I read about every seafarer; Bartholomew Diaz, Vasco da Gama, Columbus, Cabot, Magellan, Amerigo Vespucci and Sir Francis Drake.

Because I am from Africa, my favourites were Diogo Cao, Richard Francis Burton, John Hanning Speke, David Livingstone, Heinrich Barth and Mungo Park. I made sure not to miss out on the polar explorers. I must admit to following the polar explorers with a little bit less verve as I am not a cold weather fan. I am hesitant to go near an ice cube in my fridge. Anything less than 100 degrees is cold for me, and needs to be endured. All the more respect to Roald Amundsen, Vivian Fuchs, Edmund Hillary, Tensing Norgay, Robert Peary, Robert Falcon Scott, Ernest Shackleton and more cold weather loons. They did not escape my awe, but I was never going to follow in their icy footsteps.

The final category are the living explorers, the likes of Sir Ranulph Fiennes, Sir Chris Bonnington, Eric Larson, Ed Stafford, Andrew Skurka, Jessica Watson and Sir Spencer James Conway, to name a few. I just need to think of something ludicrous to earn that title. But there is a further category. These are people who are not explorers or adventurers by profession. They are not geographers or botanists, searching new routes or plants. They are not evangelists or government officials. They may not be people with a sound moral compass. They may even be out-and-out criminals. But they endured, through some of the most extreme situations a human can find themselves in. These are the survival stories that were also a staple of my childhood reading. My childhood consisted of sport, explorers, adventurers, criminals and survival stories. I lived them, I dreamed them, especially survival stories.

The story of Henri Charriere takes the award; for the hardest, most persistent nutcase to grace our planet. Devil's Island was a penal colony from June 1852. It held criminals from France convicted by a jury rather than by magistrates. Devil's Island became known as one of the most infamous prisons in history, and one of the worst prisons in the world. While in use, until the astonishingly late date of 1953, inmates included political prisoners (such as 239 republicans who had opposed Napoleon's coup), and the most hardened of France's thieves and murderers. Most died from disease and harsh conditions. Sanitary systems were basically non- existent and the region, much as it is today, I might add, is mosquito-ridden and infested with endemic tropical diseases. Prisoner on prisoner violence was rife, as was murder. The only exit from the island prison was by water and very, very few convicts escaped. Henri Charriere was one of the exceptions.

He was born in Ardeche, France and had two older sisters. His mother died when he was ten and his father was nowhere to be seen, five minutes after the impregnation of Charriere's mother. At 17, in 1923, after a brutally poor childhood, Henry enlisted in the French Navy and served for two years. After that it was pretty much downhill for this dodgy character, as he joined the Paris underworld. He wasn't very good at it. On 26th October 1931 Charriere was accused of the murder of a pimp named Roland Le Petit. Surprise, surprise, Charriere strenuously denied this slur on his character, but was sentenced to life on Devil's Island, including ten years hard labour. Just to get him into the swing of things, evidently. Charriere was having none of that and who can blame him. Not a bright future. A month later, on 28th November, he made his first escape attempt and was joined by prisoners Andre Maturette and Joanes, who would accompany him throughout much of his time on the run. Thirty seven days later, the trio were captured by Colombian police (they are everywhere those Colombian police), near the village of Riohacha, and were imprisoned. Charriere subsequently escaped. Don't worry, you will get used to it, escape is a Charriere theme.

During an extremely heavy tropical downpour, he made his departures out of a weakly slatted, toilet window, and fled to La Guajira peninsula, where he lived and was adopted by an Indian tribe. He spent several months living with the indigenous people, but felt he had to move on, and make a different life for himself. (Tell me about it.) This was a decision he would regret. He was quickly recaptured and sent back to Devil's Island, where he was put in solitary confinement for two years. Yes, you read that right. It is easy to brush that sentence off, but two things come to my mind. One. How can we possibly treat other human beings like that and use the words 'civilised' and 'society', in the same breath. It is depraved, no matter what someone has done. Many were actually sentenced to death by guillotine, but at least Charriere escaped that end! Secondly, how in God's name can anyone not come out of two years solitary, a gibbering, drooling idiot? Well, Charriere didn't. He was made of sterner stuff.

After his release from solitary confinement, Charriere was thrown in prison for a mere seven years more. During this period, his spirit remained unbroken, and he attempted to escape several more times, resulting in increasingly brutal responses from the French guards. In a fantastic escape and survival story, Charriere finally achieved his permanent liberation, in a truly spectacular fashion.

He jumped off a cliff and used bags of coconuts as a makeshift raft, to ride the tide from the island, and escape the sharks that loved weak-prisoner snacks. Miraculously, Charriere made it to the mainland, but a fellow escapee died in quicksand, as they landed on the French Guiana coast. After meeting up with some Chinese escaped prisoners, they bought a boat (as you do), and sailed to Georgetown, the capital of British Guyana. After a year, a bored Charriere (even I would want a quiet life by now), joined another group of criminals and escaped convicts in another boat, with the intention of reaching British Honduras. With luck a bit like mine, they sailed straight into a cyclone and only managed to reach Venezuela, which I think is pretty impressive, and a good choice, under the circumstances. However, they were arrested and sent to a brutal penal settlement in El Dorado, Bolivar State. (By coincidence, Cathy and I had stayed in the same mining town, El Dorado, ten months earlier, as discussed in another chapter. We were greeted warmly by the prostitutes, drug dealers and gold miners but it was rough as hell when we were there, so God knows what Charriere faced.)

After a year of imprisonment, Charriere was released and given identity papers on 3rd July 1944. Five years later, he was given Venezuelan citizenship. He married a beautiful Venezuelan woman (that's not difficult, they all look like supermodels), called Rita Bensimon. They got on great and were truly in love, which is a bonus.

Imagine being in a loveless marriage after what he'd been through. Still, he should never have murdered someone.

Charriere opened restaurants in Caracas and Maracaibo, in Venezuela. He was subsequently treated as a celebrity, even appearing on television programmes. Charriere finally returned to France, visiting Paris in conjunction with the publication of his memoir, *Papillon* (butterfly in French), Charriere's nickname because of his butterfly tattoo. Prisoners on Devil's Island also collected butterflies for export to France, so the name had double significance. The book *Papillon* promptly sold 1.5 million copies in France. It's amazing the lengths to which you have to go, to become a bestseller. Getting attacked by bandits in Kenya is so boring. My little dig. The book received widespread fame and deserved critical acclaim. It is considered a modern day classic. 239 editions of the book have since been published worldwide, in 21 languages. The book was adapted for a Hollywood film in 1973, starring Steve McQueen and Dustin Hoffman, as well as another in 2017, starring Charlie Hunnam and Rami Malek. Charriere also published a sequel to *Papillon*, called *Banco*, in 1973.

Left: Charriere with butterfly tattoo, and above: in 1970

Papillon has been described as the 'greatest adventure story of all time' and a 'modern classic of courage'. The best-selling book prompted a French minister to attribute the moral decline of France to 'miniskirts and *Papillon*'. Hilarious. Charriere also played the part of a jewel thief in a 1970s film, 'Popsy Pop', directed by the French director Jean Vautrin and translated into English as 'The Butterfly Affair'. It did not look likely that Charriere would be up for an Oscar at any time soon so he resumed writing. The French Justice System issued Charriere with a pardon for his murder conviction in 1970. On 29th July, 1973 Charriere died of throat cancer in Madrid, Spain.

Having seen Devils Island, which was numbing and sobering, we both became introspective and frankly, we both felt really down. We made a mutual, gloomy decision to ride on to Suriname, a country which many of us could not point out on a map. I know a big factor for heading to the border was the atmosphere in French Guiana. It was not dangerous, we were not mugged, threatened or even shouted at. It was the 'divide and rule' attitude.

"We are superior," is a comment I will never entertain; and I heard it from a café owner in Cayenne.

The beauty of the bike. We have the freedom of rapid escape. Onwards Iron Horse, to Suriname.

Chapter Seventeen
Suicidal Tendencies

Crossing Suriname ended up being a three-hour ride and we were in and out before the blink of a sloth's eye, so I really cannot enlighten you on much about this country. The three-hour crossing is not surprising, as Suriname is just under 165,000 square kilometres and is the smallest sovereign state in South America. My memories are of lush tropical rainforest and the shock of hearing people speaking Dutch, in the middle of the jungles of South America. In 1954 Suriname became one of the constituent counties of the Netherlands, but in 1975 it became an independent state. Suriname is considered to be a Caribbean country, culturally. Dutch is spoken by sixty percent of the population, the rest using Sranan Tonga, an English-based Creole language. I am a child, I admit, but I couldn't get over a Hindi guy, with a Caribbean accent, speaking Dutch. It was superb, but the crucial point is that it didn't have any of the oppressive colonial vibe of French Guiana. So, apologies Suriname, for a less than in depth analysis of your beautiful country. Three hours is not long enough to be Mr. Knowall. Into British Guyana now. What a melting pot.

I always like to start my chapters with something uplifting, and inspiring, to draw the reader in, so I was a bit slow with this one. Let me remedy that. The World Health Organisation, last year, cited Guyana as the country with the highest suicide rate in the world, with 44.2 suicides per 100,000 deaths; more than four times the global average. Black Bush Polder, a rural community, is known as the 'suicide belt' of the Caribbean. Reasons cited are poverty (40% of Guyanese are below the poverty level), the pervasive stigma about mental illness, access to lethal chemicals (I am quoting from someone; what the hell does that mean, 'access to lethal chemicals'), alcohol misuse, interpersonal violence, family dysfunction and insufficient mental health resources. I agree with the first bit; the other words are just hot air for, 'we are in a bad way'. We shall see.

I admitted, in the last chapter, to an obsession, starting as a child of five, with explorers and adventurers, and extreme sportsmen, and pushers of the norm. Now I have to admit to a fascination with another genre, that came at a slightly later age, thirteen; true crime, murder and serial killers. Please don't get the wrong impression. I don't want to kill anyone. I cannot watch any violence on television. In fact, it is a big reason why I have not watched TV for more than 25 years. (I did watch my TV Series though.) What interests me, is not only the psychology of the perpetrator, but also the mind frame of the people who followed these psychopaths.

Sadly, Guyana's reputation as suicide capital of the world, was cemented by a truly evil man, called Jim Jones. I admit, that part of my morbid fascination with Guyana (I think morbidity lives in everyone), was that I wanted to visit Jonestown, the scene of a horrific suicide pact, and the subject of many books and documentaries, some of which you might be familiar with. In 1974, the Guyana government leased 1,500 hectares of land to the 'Peoples Temple', an American new religious movement, led by the pastor Jim Jones. The settlement, informally called 'Jonestown', eventually grew to a population of over 2,000 people, mostly followers from the United States.

In 1978, Guyana received worldwide attention when 909 people died in a mass suicide, by drinking cyanide-based Flavor Aid. A day prior, US congressman, Leo Ryan, had visited and toured the settlement as part of an official investigation. His report was expected to be dire. As he was preparing to leave the Port Kaituma airstrip, a group of Peoples Temple members pulled up, and opened fire on the visiting delegation, killing Ryan and four others. The murderers, somewhat comically, if murderers could ever be comic, arrived at the airstrip on a tractor and trailer.

The delegation had left hurriedly after Temple member Don Sly (unfortunate name, not to be trusted), attacked Ryan with a knife, which was thwarted. Later that day, 909 inhabitants, 304 of them children, died of cyanide poisoning, all of the bodies found near the settlement's main pavilion. This was the greatest loss of American civilians in one day, until the September 11 atrocities. The FBI later recovered a forty five minute audio recording of the mass suicide in progress. According to escaped Temple members, children were given the drink first, by their own parents, and families were told to lie down together, and say goodbye. Insane beyond belief. Mass suicide had been previously discussed on the site, on a regular basis, in simulated events, called 'White Nights'. Following the mass suicide (which I would class as murder, especially the child victims), Jones was found dead on the floor, resting on a pillow, near his favourite deck chair. He had a single gunshot wound to the head, apparently self-inflicted. A cowardly way out for an awful human being.

Jim Jones, cult leader and murderer of 900 men, women and children in Jonestown Guyana suicide pact

Jonestown is a village in the Demerara-Mahaica region, famous for its sugar. It was only forty kilometres north of Georgetown, but because of the relentlessly torrential rain, creating instant, slippery rivulets in the road, we decided to head south. I was peed off, not making it to the suicide site, but I won't harp on about it, or you might think I am odd. I didn't makes it to Devils Island, where Papillion was incarcerated and tortured, and now I never made it to Jim Jones suicide site. I am such a loser when it comes to morbid tourism.

Guyana decided to throw at us another difficult road, the toughest, bar the Ghost Road in Amazonas, and the Tupiza road in Bolivia. We thought we could get from north to south in one day. Ha! We hit Guyana in the rainy season, and was it spectacular? Yes. Even the Yamaha Tenere 660Z, 2009, 'super reliable, deal with any road' bike, was moaning and overheating. Pleasant, hard-packed, red dirt roads, turned into unpleasant slippery, red rivers. A great day's ride through the national park of Guyana, turned into a sixteen-hour ordeal of night riding, before we turned up at Prince Charles's place. Yes, you heard right. The future king of England owns this jungle. (That is jumping the gun a bit, and if you jump the gun in South America, you will end up brown bread.) Let's rewind.

You will not be surprised to learn that British Guyana was a former British colony, the clue being in the name. I still find it difficult to come to terms with the fact that we went out of Spanish-speaking Paraguay, into Portuguese-speaking Brazil, into French-speaking Guiana, into Dutch-speaking Suriname, into English-speaking Guyana and then eventually out, to Brazil again. It is even more complex than that. Although Guyana is the second least-populated country in South America, after Suriname, there are ten official indigenous languages, as well as English; Hindustani, Spanish, Portuguese, and some Dutch. The strange dice-throwing of colonial times. Guyana was part of the British West Indies, until independence in 1966. Maybe England was feeling generous after their World Cup Final win. Another random twist of fate and another result of colonialism is that British Guyana is famous amongst philatelists. Guyana postage stamps were first issued in 1850 and these stamps include some of the rarest and most expensive stamps in the world. The unique British Guyana 1c Magenta sold in 2014 for $9.5 million. I am not trying to make light of colonialism with this fact. I only bring it up because when we were parked up by the side of the road, having a water break, a random Eastern European fellow wandered out of the bush.

This was Zein, from Latvia, who was an avid stamp and butterfly collector. (So Zein was a philatelist and a lepidopterist.) He didn't have khaki shorts, a pith helmet and butterfly net, but his enthusiasm for both subjects was intense. Zein (which means fragrant or beautiful bush - maybe he was trying to blend into the jungle), said that Guyana was the ultimate Mecca for stamps and certain rare blue butterflies. (We had seen hundreds of blue butterflies in the last hour, giant ones too. Didn't seem too rare to me, but I kept quiet.) Out of one of his many voluminous pockets, Zein pulled out a thermos of coffee. We took turns sipping from the screw cap cup, while he regaled us with tales of Hesperidae, Nymhalide and Paplionidae, that he had nearly caught. It was all Latvian to me. My butterfly collecting days, when living in Kenya as a boy, were short-lived, as I was not keen on formaldehyde, or sticking pins through bodies, or the dark basement where my parents kept their skewered spiders, butterflies and beetles. Zein had been to Guyana no less than fifteen times, so was obviously an accomplished pin pricker. As he packed up and headed into the bush again, I said, "Good luck, but I don't think there are any 1c Magenta left in the wild."

He didn't like my joke, which I understand, and gave us a weak smile and a wave. Good luck Zein.

Our mission now was to helmet up, brave up and head down the legendary Georgetown-Lethem Road. It leaves from the coastal capital, a colourful centre with a lively market, directly south to Linden and then to the border town, Lethem. It is a 421-kilometre stretch, which doesn't sound a great distance, but it is mind-blowingly difficult in the rainy season, and not to be attempted.

We were about to do it in the rainy season. If I didn't have bad luck, I wouldn't have any, is a saying that springs to mind. I said the 'legendary road', only because it is legendary to Cathy and me. I am yet to meet an adventure motorcyclist who has done this route, although I know many must have. Every adventure motorcyclist seeking out a challenge should put this route on their list. It is tough, incredibly beautiful and euphorically rewarding to complete. An overwhelming 80% of Guyanese territory bisected by the road, is classified as wilderness, much of it only accessible by boat or plane. This is what you ride through. I will not lie, you need to be an advanced off-road rider, with hundreds of years' experience; or just go for it, like me. The area along the road was sparsely inhabited. A variety of Amerindian tribes live and work in these dense jungles, and we caught glimpses of small hut settlements, as we slid our way southwards, but we were alone. It was wonderful.

The road fooled us, as many do. It starts from Georgetown, as a perfect, smoother than an Amazonian baby's bottom road, and by the time you get to Linden, some 103 kilometres away it is a slippery mud track. Luckily, before we hit the real chaos, we stopped for some street food. It was stewed meat with cinnamon peppers, and a sauce called cassareep, made from cassava root. The dish was called Pepperpot, and was top class. We were refuelled and raring to go. That didn't last long. The road turned 'challenging' to put it politely. I love it. The bonus of tough roads is that the human traffic decreases, and the animal sightings increase. Within an hour we had chatted to two black caimans, inexplicably tanning, by the side of the road, saw a giant otter slide down a bank, and a tapir's bum disappearing into the undergrowth. To top it off, we were followed by inquisitive eagles along the road, until they soared off, in search of slightly smaller game. You drive slowly, because it's difficult. But it opens up your vision to all the smaller animals and insects, negotiating the road crossing. I don't like squashing giant crickets and tarantulas with my tyres. Non-asphalt roads always have a different atmosphere, and the animals and insects are safer.

Like many places in the world, there are calls to asphalt the whole route. Others argue that two million acres of pristine rainforest and savannahs will be opened up to development and destruction. This is the age-old question of balancing development with conservation, especially in the Iwokrama Forest and the Rupununi savannah regions whose biodiversity continues to astound. On the other hand, you cannot expect any country to run without a good road system. If you are spending sixteen hours travelling a few hundred kilometres, with no guarantee that you will reach your destination, it spells disaster for most businesses. Conservation is almost never the winner. I understand totally. Money always talks. Today's protected zone is tomorrow's high-rise development, as soon as the negotiations, and money, are handed over, or under. I was a witness to Africa being tarred by the Chinese, literally and figuratively. I hear it may be possible soon to circumnavigate Africa, without going on a dirt road. Sacrilege, but good for the economies of Africa. There is no stopping it. From a purely selfish biker point of view, I don't want any roads surfaced.

On the same subject, but a Conway tangent (that's not a fruit from Ireland), I really don't understand why the Pan American Highway is the Holy Grail for adventure riders, Alaska to Argentina, on a sealed, asphalt road. I think that is the worst possible route. We avoided the Pan American highway for 100,000 kilometres, and when we had to use it, to get to Santiago, Chile, for an emergency, you could have been on any motorway in the world. I feel the same about Route 66. It is iconic, but it is touring, not adventure motorcycling.

Oh dear. I am going to make enemies. I don't talk much about motorcycles and routes in my books but, when I do, it is because my excitement levels are through the roof. Let me counter the Pan American and Route 66 comments by saying, sorry. No disrespect. Different riding, that's all. For those who criticise my books, because I don't give enough tips to motorcyclists (I just made that up for dramatic effect, no one has criticised yet), here we go.

My adventure motorcycling routes are the BR319, Ghost Road, in Brazil and the entire route through the Amazon jungle from east to west.

My second is through the centre of the Democratic Republic of Congo, through the Maquela de Zombo border.

My third is the Moyale, northern Kenya road, near the border with Somalia.

My fourth is the road directly after Death Road, in Bolivia. Death Road is a proper tourist con by the way. Be prepared for roadblocks to extort more money for the next stage of the road, and be ready to buy a 'I survived Death Road T-shirt'. The road directly after touristy Death Road, leaving from the mountain town of Coroico, is a gem.

My fifth adventure road is from the Salar de Uyuni salt flats in Bolivia, to Tupiza, a sandy section of the Dakar rally.

My sixth are all deserts I crossed, the Sahara, the Mauritanian and the Namib deserts, not to mention Patagonia. Sand riding and wind. Tough stuff. Not for sissies.

My seventh adventure road is any road above 4,000 metres, especially volcanoes, and twisty Peruvian, endless passes.

My eighth is Mexican mountain backroads, the locations of which I will reveal, for a small fee. This is a part list that I will come back too. Don't say I don't give tips on adventure roads. Oh, and this one, the Guyana Glue Road. This was no ordinary road, or ordinary ride. It was a constantly changing road, more like a river.

Crossing the initial river Essequibo; no problem. Slide through mining towns of questionable pedigree and safety; no problem. Cross rickety bridges, threatening to implode into the chasm below, cross rivers again on tiny canoes, wobbling with the bike; no problem. The boat crossings were relief from the constant red mud, glued to us and the bike. Our tyre was bright red and swollen. A bit like Cathy, (sorry), hanging on for dear life, while filming. On a flatter, easier and dryer stretch I had to get off and de-clog the chain.

Getting to Lethem was the only gateway to Brazil, but bloody hell, was it difficult. One of the pleasures of not doing any research is that you face everything with an open mind, and you don't have any preconceptions about your route. This road nearly changed my whole philosophy. I might become Mr. Researcher. Not. This road even defeated the locals. Unheard of.

Normally, when you are in tears, soaked to the skin with sweat, and dejected, huddled by the side of the road, a family of four will ride past, waving, on a 125cc, Chinese motorbike, the engine smoking, but moving forward, and off over the hill. That made me feel 'over the hill'. The overtaking didn't happen here; I was really proud. Not a single vehicle overtook us on that sixteen-hour journey. Either I was an off-road God, or they were all stuck in the mud; mud that was building in attitude, especially with the heavy rain that soaked us, not to the skin; but beyond.

It turned out that everything on two wheels, three wheels, four wheels, eight wheels, or four hooves, or two feet, were all stuck, and we ended up being the stars of the show, humbly moving forward, at a clutch-burning rate of 15 kilometres an hour. At this spectacular speed, I expertly calculated that we would make it to Lethem, the border with Brazil, somewhere in the next two years. It's not as though Lethem was going to be a treat to arrive in either. It only became a town in 2018. It is still seen as a remote area, and has a massive population of 1158; when Cathy and I arrived, population, 1160. Cue, Clint Eastwood music, and dust bowls, and tumbleweed.

Lethem lies on the Takutu River, which forms the natural border with Brazil, opposite the town of Bomfin. Everything felt like a border to us, it was so harsh. The road was not empty, like the Ghost Road. People had no choice. There was only one road. We did have long stretches of nobody, but when you met a bottleneck in the proceedings, it was total mayhem. Five or six minivans, or 'Combis', as we know them in southern Africa, were negotiating absurdly slippery, steep roads, all the time, the rain bucketing down, and making the next attempt even less likely. We sat at the bottom of many of these hills. They certainly improved on the African occupancy levels. Twenty five people in a 15-seater in Africa, you turn a blind eye. (The eye you lost in the last Combi trip.) The minivans here, double the occupants. The drivers would accelerate like lunatics, get halfway up a hill and slide backwards, past us, and career further down the hill, onions and people flying off, smiling all the way. The enthusiasm would not be killed, but this time, everyone in the Combi was outside, and pushing. There was lots of wheel spinning, lots of muddy faces, lots of laughs and minimum progress.

Knee-deep in mud, in the jungle, pushing a van in the rain, whilst the driver burnt out the clutch: great people. As smoke billowed out, convinced that it was about to explode, over the hill it would go. The wonderful thing is that all the people in the 'saved' minivan, all trudged back and helped with the next mud-victim vehicle, all their footwear, huge blocks of red mud. This happened on a number of occasions, and I felt guilty, rocketing past, sorry, sliding past, our arms and feet flailing, desperate to keep up the momentum. We rode past people praying to the Lord, but I had to keep the throttle going, or we would be in the same boat. Evidently, not a boat; but stuck. We were caked in red mud, the Tenere was caked in red mud, and it got worse. The rain started in earnest, huge droplets, in huge slanting sheets battered us, and stung our cheeks. My goggles were steamed up, my clutch arm was burning, as the clutch would be soon, but we pushed on. We started passing vehicles that had given up for the day, passengers bedding down in the minivans for the night, to see what tomorrow's weather would bring. We pushed on and saw not a soul until we came round a corner and faced a scene of sliding carnage. An extremely steep winding road had been carved up into furrows of 'No go'. Four minivans had attempted the climb, none with success. A green and white minivan, with a stencil of Rambo on one side, complete with machine gun and bandana, had slid sideways more than fifty metres, and was now wedged against a tree, the driver's door caved in. They were well and truly stuck. We slithered up the hill, in first gear and parked up, so we could help the mud-afflicted minivans.

The twelve occupants of the Rambo van were huddled forlornly on the side of the road, under a tree, that was giving zero shelter. They were being watched by an inquisitive, bright green parakeet, who also looked a bit weather-beaten. What a soggy dejected bunch. I was loving it. Four men were trying to bounce the van sideways, away from the tree. They had as much chance of bouncing the Titanic off an iceberg. Amongst the bedraggled group, we spotted two pale faces, a young German couple, the first travellers we had seen in Guyana. They weren't very perky. The girl was shaking, and verging on hysterical, refusing to ever get back in the van.

"He is a crazy man, this driver. Four times we crash. We will all die."

I had a look at the van, and must confess, it was in need of a team of panel beaters, not to mention, a better artist. On the opposite side to Rambo, was another stencil, of Bob Marley, with 'One Love' written under it. Faces were evidently a problem for this artist, as Rambo looked like Dame Edna Everage, and Bob Marley looked a bit like a sheep with dreadlocks.

Her boyfriend, the clichéd, round glasses, wispy goatee, and single braid with beads type, was pleading with her. "We are in the jungle and it is getting dark. We need to stay with the group."

She put her muddy head in her muddy hands and wept. I decided to make my motivational speech.

"I don't think you guys are going anywhere today, or maybe for a few days. You will need to be towed out of here, and there is nothing that can tow you. The dry season will be here in the next few weeks. I am sure you will survive. Anyway, if the minivan does get going, at least there are no cliffs you can go over. The worst that can happen is you can overturn. I am sure all will be good with those bald tyres. You have Bob and Rambo to protect you. Good luck, "Viel Gluck, seh dich spatter," I said in my best German, and we were off.

Mist was gathering around the fringes of the jungle, and spilling onto the road, in rolling blankets, that played tricks on the eye. The rain continued unabated. The sun was disappearing, dipping low in a blast of orange light, forcing its way through the mist and rain. That was its last blast. Then it was dark. Real darkness is something that very few of us have experienced, in the developed world, without realising it. There is always a street lamp, a lit-up building, a shop sign, or a car's lights; there is always a light source. In the jungle, with no civilisation, no artificial light, when the rain is torrential and the cloud is thick; dark means dark. No beams, or shards of light for us. A solid wall of blackness. Instead of rivulets of ochre red water running in our direction, nature had another plan. Run rivers across the road, with slippery, plankbridges to cross. There were gaps in the planks big enough for the front wheel to drop into and eject Cathy and I over the handlebars. The next obstacle to face were giant puddles, that in England, would be classified as ponds; at a stretch, lakes. We came off three or four times. A little further on, the road surface changed and it got a little lighter with the last burst of sun. Mud was now brown and sticky with ruts and puddles either side. It stopped raining so we decided for a change of clothes and a clean up!! Joke! Pointless really. For a short rest actually. I took off my bike gear and sat barefoot in a puddle. Relief!

After soothing our feet, which had their own heartbeat they were so sore, we rode on, the sweat from our bodies drying and cooling us, and then the rain started again, running down our necks, soaking us once more. We started shivering uncontrollably, in spasms. Your body starts jolting, and my fingers were numb around the bars. Guyana means 'land of many waters'. No kidding. From all directions. Not a problem, if you have lights. The Tenere headlight was useless. It was facing towards the sky, like an air raid search light, the road ahead, pitch black. No choice but to stop and adjust it. I duly snapped the adjustor knob off, so had to stuff a sock behind the light, at the top, to lower the beam. It worked a treat. It was like following the light from a burning cigarette, or from a gloomy candle. Must sort that out. This was getting dangerous. I was all for stopping, spreading the tent over the bike, and sleeping on the ground, crying, underneath it.

It was a no from Cathy: "Keep going, take it slowly, we will get somewhere."

"We are somewhere," I didn't say.

I repeated in my head, 'Day by day, nothing lasts forever'.

On we went. What can go wrong in the 3,710 square kilometre Iwokrama National Park. Just when it couldn't get darker, it did.

The whole roadside was now dominated by tall, tropical trees, easily 30 metres high, with a dense green canopy, red-faced spider monkeys leaping from one to the other. We could only hear them, but I knew from earlier in the day that they had cheeky little red faces. All light perished. This jungle is considered one of the four most pristine, along with the Congo, New Guinea and the Amazon. Wouldn't be so pristine if we died in it. Just as I was beginning to predict crashes in my head, not a good thing; we finally saw the light.

It had been an incredible sixteen hours of riding. No wonder Sir Arthur Conan Doyle based *The Lost World* on the Guyana landscape. Although we hadn't seen Goliath bird-eating spiders or Gladiator tree frogs, two of my bucket list creatures, it had been an amazing experience. The distance covered? Too embarrassed to say. I am not embarrassed to say that when I saw a light twinkling through the trees, fatigue washed over me, and I was spent. Stoic Cathy was silent. We pulled up into a clearing. On the left-hand side was a thatched, two storey cabin with a simple criss-cross balustrade, encircling a verandah, that had solid wooden steps leading up to it. This was the Iwokrama National Park Police Station. On the left-hand side, in a clearing about fifteen-foot square, with a path leading to it, was a less auspicious building; the long drop toilet. For those of you not familiar with this; you dig a hole as deep as you possibly can, put a seat on it, and some sides, for modesty. You poo in the hole, cover it in a scoop of sand, job done. After a few years, the hole fills up and reaches your bum, so you cover it up, and find a new poo venue. Sounds simple enough. Through extensive and painful research, I conclude that they are never clean, and are a wretched experience. Hopefully I wouldn't need to visit this one, as we had eaten nothing.

The most basic 'long-drop' possible, dug by me at a campsite

We approached the cabin and a very smart fellow emerged at the doorway. How any human could stay that pristine in a rain-drenched, tropical jungle was impressive Michael Williams was decked out in a khaki suit that was half-police, half-game ranger style. His buttons were shining, as were his black shoes and lapels. (The next morning, when the sun was shining, I could see little reflections of my face, in the tips of each of his shoes. I looked like a colobus monkey. That's how clean they were.)

Michael and his equally glistening colleague, Mr. Persaud, were superb and offered us the holding cell for the night.

"Welcome to Iwokrama, you picked a fine night to travel, Lucille," said Michael. I added the Lucille bit.

He removed his hat and extended his hand to Cathy, on the slippery wooden decking.

"Welcome to Prince Charles's Place. You just missed him, he was here two weeks ago," he added, pointing at the floor, where Prince Charles stood.

"Well, what a shame that we missed him, maybe he would have enjoyed a spin on the motorcycle," I didn't say.

"Wow. Great. Why was he here?"

"Conservation," said Mr. Persaud, gravely serious. Hunting, in other words then? I didn't actually ask.

Before I could respond, Michael Williams offered us a lifeline. "You are welcome to stay here tonight. The rain is expected to continue abated for the whole evening."

I wanted to say 'unabated', but correcting people tends to lead to a frosty friendship.

"Fantastic. That would be excellent."

"You can sleep in the holding cell at the back. There is a single bed in there."

The room was everything we dreamed of, and less. The bed was built by an anorexic, trying to be more anorexic. It was basically one plank, balanced on bricks, with a cut-out piece of foam, balanced on the top. Being the gallant type, I offered the bed to Cathy and settled down on the floor. We were both soaking wet, but Cathy had a blanket, to cocoon her misery. I just lay on the floor, head on the wooden floor, watching the multiple eyes through the sizeable gaps in boards. It was only spiders and scorpions, discussing the method of attack, on such big prey. I fell asleep for ten minutes, then woke with cramp in my hip, a sore neck and freezing cold. I had no choice. I grabbed the plastic tarpaulin, folded it in half and lay down on the floor. I then rolled towards Cathy, as quietly as possible, until I was a big, blue, soggy, sausage roll human, motorbike boots out one end, head out the other. I fell asleep, eyes were watching me. Both Cathy and I bring up this jungle sleep often. It was the best night's sleep either of us ever had. Sixteen hard hours of riding, then sleep in a jungle hut. Nothing beats it.

The next morning, we woke to sunbeams streaming through an emerald forest, and two grinning guards to meet us. A red road, full of puddles and slipperiness, snaked ahead of us. What a life. We thanked the police for their overnight refuge, and headed off. Not quite. I was already feeling super-negative about my riding. I was like an out-of-control salmon for the whole of the last two days. I needed a pep talk. Wasn't going to happen. Michael gripped me firmly on the shoulder, not a good thing between men.

"You must ride very safe. Nobody has come through. I was on the radio. While you were sleeping, nobody passed. You are tough, but look after Lady Catharine."

Lady Catharine. I liked that, but never told Cathy. No point in giving her ideas above her station.

"Don't worry, Officer. Cathy looks after me. Keeps me under control."

Michael laughed and Mr. Persaud grimaced. As we were riding off Michael shouted, "If you have a big tree, you need a small axe," with a big thumbs up.

He didn't know what he was talking about, and nor did we. That's how I like life.

There was no one else, all the way to the border. When your foot pegs are so slippery that you can't hang on to them and your boots are soaking wet, and inside, your socks are curled up by your toes, caked in mud. When your bike trousers weigh ten kilos, and the protective kneepad has rubbed your knee raw and your jacket is soaked and hanging off you. When your helmet is soaking wet, on the inside, from sweat and rain and your goggles steam up, so you can't see anything. When you feel Cathy holding on, as you tackle a steep, rutted road. When you both need water, but want to get somewhere. When you both have mud in your eyelashes and at the corners of your mouth and you take off your goggles, you look like a panda from the dust. When your back aches from thumping corrugations. When your face burns from the sun and wind, and rain. This is motorcycling. Then a Honda C90 with a five-year-old boy overtakes you, one hand on the accelerator, the other on his hip, mobile phone wedged between ear and neck, with four passengers, six melons in a net, and a bag of potatoes. It ruins all your delusions. Ego swings and roundabouts.

Just as I was getting tired and starting to make mistakes, the landscape dried up, the jungle slowly thinned and faded behind us, and the scene opened up into the Rupunini Savannahs, dissected by the Kanuka Mountains. The Savannah encompasses 5,000 square miles of untouched grasslands and swamplands. There are a few Amerindian villages dotted around and some ranches, worked by vaqueros (cowboys), some of whom are descendants of 19th century Scottish settlers. Them again.

The Savannah had no intention of giving us a respite and the road turned into a rock-hard, dirt ordeal with unrelenting washboard corrugations, that rattled out our dentures. I exaggerate; Cathy lost a filling and every bolt on the bike rattled loose. To add to our woes, we were very low on fuel, and no way would we make the border. Luck was on our side, and just as the bike was about to go on strike, we spluttered round a bend and came across a huge corrugated iron hangar. Underneath it was a gentleman of about sixty, in the world's largest sombrero, working on the engine of a Cessna crop-spraying plane. He must have fuel. We lurched up, he turned his head, stopped working, and approached us with a number 22 spanner in his hand, but a smile on his face. All went well as he happened to have a 25-litre drum of petrol, and a hose. Bonus.

"Where are you from?" he asked, after sucking on the hose and siphoning the fuel into our bike.

"South Africa," Cathy replied.

He stopped what he was doing.

"South Africa, South Africa bastards. You know Hendrik Coetzee, do you know him, do you?" he quizzed us animatedly.

It was a bit like saying, 'I know a John Smith in England, do you know him?'

"Um, no Sir, it's a big country," I answered, taken aback by his vehemence.

"He steal all my money, my grain and my truck. He had a plane, we went into business and he take everything. All. All. Bad people."

I felt like telling him we are not all bad people, there are Hendriks everywhere, but I didn't.

"So sorry about that," was all I could think of to say.

He ranted on as we paid him, and thanked him. He was still going off, when we had our helmets on and we're riding away.

"If you see Hendriks Coetzee, tell him I kill him."

"Will do," I said cheerily, waving goodbye and giving Angry Sombrero the thumbs up.

We were not going to be invited to lunch and we were definitely not added to his Christmas card list, but at least we could get to the border town of Lethem, into Bomfin in Brazil, and then a short run to Venezuela, the last country in our circumnavigation. Talk about saving the best till last. Wonderful Venezuela, with beautiful people and a beautiful landscape was about to become one of the most challenging months of our lives and our favourite country in the world. Before we get to Venezuela I would like to veer off on a bit of a tangent, which is unheard of for such a straight thinker as me, but while it's on my mind.... Something that has blighted my life from the age of one day. Accidents, mishaps, injuries and animal and insect attacks. All summarised in two words; bad luck. Not a good trait when you are on a dangerous machine in dangerous places for most of your life. I would never change it.

Chapter Eighteen
I Am an Accident Waiting For a Place to Happen

I am fully aware that the cards I have been dealt are ridiculous. But I have to take it in good humour. Him upstairs decided to make me the most accident-prone person ever. If I saw me in the distance, I would run. I am a bad omen to all. It is so absurd, that if I wrote a book about my accidents and injuries; human, mechanical, insect, acts of God, and animal-wise, it would make the Bible and Encyclopedia Britannica combined, look short. Consequently, I am forced into the situation of listing all of these mishaps, in… well, a list, over the next few pages.

I will elucidate on the more interesting, near death experiences, because they are all my fault really, so you can mock my decisions. First let's get over the magnitude of my misfortune. Bear with me. It gets fun. Actually, a 'bear with me' is probably the only animal not involved in these stories.

If they had invented ADHD when I was young, I would have had it. In fact, most modern clinical psychiatric labels; like tri-polar, multiple personalities, hyperactive, paranoid, unpredictable, socially inept, bad egg, socially disorientated, insomniac, maladjusted, difficult, confrontational, different, deranged, misunderstood, wayward, genius. OK, I added the last one, but all the others would have applied to me, or possibly were named after me. I feel for my parents, but they made me who I am, and I am proud beyond proud of that.

When I was a young boy I would hold my breath, for no particular reason I can remember, until I turned blue and passed out. Doesn't look good for your parents in a crowded 'Children Deserve Clean Air Too Club'. Another trait was to randomly do headstands in the street. It didn't matter if we were at the local shopping centre in Kenya or walking down a muddy road in Swaziland, or strolling down the Champs Elysee in Paris, or outside the Van Gogh Museum in Amsterdam. Headstand time.

I would disappear, and my parents would rush back, finding me balanced in mid air, pedestrians politely going round me; or I would be against a wall, with small stones embedded in my head, and a demented smile on my face. My folks, to their credit, never made a big deal about this. It was more like the English, understated reaction: "Spencer, come along now. Enough of that."

I was a disaster attracting disasters, since birth. I think they knew it. Simon, my elder and only brother, thank God, by three years physically, but definitely only one step behind me mentally (joke bru), just stayed quietly in the background, making notes on his pad, on how to put me in the poo with the parents later on. I have no sibling issues whatsoever... have I mentioned, when my parents went out? Simon used to take all the shelves out of the fridge, and lock me in there, until I was 'Stalactite Spencer'. Anyway, enough of that. Or Simon would make me put socks on my hands, as boxing gloves, and re-enact Muhammed Ali fights. Then he would just knock me out. A stab in the dark; Simon had cast himself as Ali in this little scenario, and me as the secondary, less skilled boxer. Oh, and hold me down, and tickle me until I wanted to die. Or cover my face with a pillow until I was about to expire. OK. Now we are getting childish and dramatic. I bet all you younger siblings got the last two.

Simon was the best brother... I ever had. There was another time, when he put vegetable oil on my bicycle brakes and hand grips, when I was preparing to impress a girlfriend with my wheelies but I won't mention that. He also used to lock me out of the house as soon as my parents went out, or away, even if it was for a few days. As soon as he saw the dust from my parents' returning car he would open the front and back door, and act like a choir boy. Which, by coincidence, he was. But I won't harp on.

I will try and summarise each disaster (those caused by Simon respectfully cast aside, and never mentioned), so we can get back to discussing good routes, valve clearance, cushdrive maintenance and important things like; will the new Harley Davidson adventure bike cut the mustard, and where does the saying 'cut the mustard' come from. Things like that.

Oh and tyre pressure, life's pressure, etc. The saying 'cut the mustard' comes from; well, nobody seems to know. Cut the mustard is exactly what I did, when entering 'The World's Most Accident Prone Person Competition'. I won easily, by eight accidents. Not just the Mexican quarter finals, I won the Whole World Competition.

On the next pages is my list. I can't help laughing.

1. I contracted Hepatitis A at eleven, from a cut in a dirty river. It only kills seven people a year, so I would be seriously unlucky to kick the bucket. That was the diagnosis of the doctor in the Swaziland Clinic. His eyes were close to his hairline, and I think we were all worried that they would disappear behind his head, if we disagreed with his diagnosis. I was put in isolation for 14 days, got loads of attention and was fed ice cream constantly. Fun at that age. I whizzed around in a wheelchair, running over nurses. They loved me, with my child, bowl-cut hairstyle, and innocent, 'I didn't run you over eyes'.

2. I had a tonsillectomy at thirteen. I had tonsillitis every year for five years. Enough was enough. They had to be whipped out. Fun time. Same routine. My doctor was six foot seven and was called Doctor

Stephenson. I only remember that because my favourite doctor in Swaziland was Doctor 'take one of these a day, I do' Steven's, with a similar name. Ice cream, good times for the throat, and lots of sympathy.

3. I fell twenty feet out of a massive tree in our garden in Swaziland, onto my head, like an arrow. I was in a semi-coma for three days, the quietest period of my parents' life since my birth. I fell at thirteen. I was probably egged on or pushed by my brother, Simon, but there was no concrete evidence from any of the police or detectives involved, so I will have to let that one go. And there was no concrete either, or I would be dead.

4. I rocketed down a steep fairway and ramped off a golf course tee on a dodgy bicycle, to impress my brother and his pretty Sri Lankan girlfriend, Chantal. Actually, to impress her. I fancied Chantal in an innocent, ten-year-old way, so was trying to impress her. (She ended up having brittle bone disease and spent a lot of her life in plaster casts, a bit like me.) I wasn't too successful with my stunt. The bike rocketed into the air, a bit like in the E.T movie but the bike and I parted ways, high in the air. I followed the rules of gravity and landed on my head, like an even more efficient arrow than the previous accident, not quite embedded in the ground, but close. Four days in hospital. Loss of memory and an unexplained increase in intelligence, personality types and risk-taking behaviour ensued.

5. I was fifteen and preparing for a presentation at Waterford School on snakes of Southern Africa, so visited my local library in Mbabane, the capital city of Swaziland. I broke my right leg wiping my feet on the slippery wooden steps of the library. I fell down the stairs, to utter library silence, as is the law. I was noisy. People were less than responsive or sympathetic. I didn't mind breaking my leg that much, but that night I had tickets for a Johnny Clegg and Savuka concert. I was not going to miss that. Clegg who died in 2019 was a South African musician, singer songwriter, dancer, anthropologist and anti-apartheid activist. His music was a huge part of my life when I was growing up. As was Lucky Dube, the reggae star who was shot in the head in his car, in a robbery. Luckily, more luckily than Lucky, I had

the cast fitted rapidly and off I went to the concert at the Royal Swazi Convention Centre. I danced at the front and it was brilliant. I was a bit out of order but I don't think security wanted to rugby tackle a youth with a broken leg. Plus, I danced well, not as well as Johnny Clegg, but not bad.

6. I broke my left leg this time, at sixteen, in a rugby match against a bunch of mad Welsh farmers, when I was at Atlantic College, in South Glamorgan. It was minus 200 degrees, pouring with rain, and the only spectators were two bored sheep and my geography teacher, who was the coach. My obese Physical Education teacher was the referee. I was attacked by a double-legged Welsh kamikaze tackle, and the big bellied, rugby player came off better. I had only just gone through a late, gangly, growth spurt and should never have been on a rugby field, especially in Wales, where the rugby is Godlike. I had the legs of a stork and the arms of an ant. I needed an operation in Bridgend Hospital. I underwent a carbon fibre ligament replacement. It was a proper operation, that only a tough, skinny sixteen-year-old could survive.

7. At eighteen I was heading to the local butcher in Swaziland to buy some Boerewors, Pap and Chakalaka for a braai. (You may need to Google Boerewors, Pap, Chakalaka and Braai if you have never been to Southern Africa.) I slipped on a white line in the centre of the road, where they tend to be, in a typical Swazi thunderstorm, a total deluge of rain in blinding, stinging, sheets of water. I was on my beautiful white and red Yamaha XT500. My leg got caught under the bike, so rapid and unexpected was the slip. There was a woman behind me in a smokey Datsun Sunny. She jumped out of the car in a panic and asked if I was alright. Of course I was. I managed to kick start the motorbike with a broken leg. How, I still don't know. I rode home. I went to the Mbabane Clinic the next day and found out that I had two breaks. Small fry stuff.

8. I was stabbed with a pencil in the stomach, by my brother. I still had the graphite in my stomach muscle, fifteen years later (but not the grudge, obviously), then it popped out, for some reason. The pencil is stronger than the sword, as the famous saying goes. No mal intent, for sure.

9. At sixteen, on a school holiday in England, my brother Simon and I got various jobs gardening, window cleaning, rubbish clearing, etc. The idea of taking strong English currency back to Swaziland motivated us. It didn't last too long. On the way back from the second day's gardening work, my brother swung a spade around his head, which had been kindly lent to us by our grandfather. He had inherited it from his great grandfather, who had inherited it from an unknown fellow. It weighed more than me, and would last another three hundred years minimum. "Imagine if the end came off," Simon commented.

It did, and hit me in the jaw, knocking me unconscious. I woke up, to Simon, leaning over me, holding onto my bloodied T-shirt, saying, "If you tell Mum and Dad, there will be trouble." The next job we did was window cleaning in Lewisham on the outskirts of London. At the very first house and first windows, in the pouring rain, I slipped off the ladder from the second floor and landed in a rose bush. The street was full of identical, faceless, soulless houses, depressing as hell, but we had managed to secure more than fifteen jobs that day, through smooth talk and good looks. We were on to a winner and could return home to Swaziland, rich as buggery. Well, rich for a week or two. My fall was witnessed by many, and although I was punctured and possibly broken, I was keen to carry on. I think the street was in shock because suddenly no one else wanted their windows cleaned, after witnessing my tumble. Everyone had worried brows and looked at me pityingly, as I limped down the road, bloodied. Nod of shame and, 'No thanks'. End of that career.

10. When I was at the University of Edinburgh (not cleaning the windows, no funny comments, I was doing a degree), I decided to teach my friends 'Colditz'. It is a game where one person has a torch and has to guard a tree. Everyone disappears in the dark, and you have to touch the tree without getting shot (shone upon), and named. If you get shot, you are the resurrected guard. Simple enough, children's game. I realise how politically incorrect the name of the game is now, but I was six. Not at University obviously, the first time I played 'Colditz'. Being from Africa I decided to leopard-crawl the entire perimeter of the park, scale a gutter, jump across some buildings, onto a flat squash club roof and then jump into the tree that Martin was guarding. A top SAS plan. I made it, but when I jumped from the roof, the tree suddenly moved

further away, and I landed half on the pavement and half on the road and broke my leg. Queue ambulance noises and burly Scottish Ambulance women.

11. Back up a bit. Remembered another. I went home when I was sixteen, wiped my feet on the outside mat. It slipped away from me and I fell forward, chipping a piece of my elbow off, on the worst decorative scandal of all time; pebble dash wall finish. One of the ugliest and most abrasive exterior finishes imaginable and a danger to accident prone teenager's. That little piece of triangular bone is still travelling around my forearm. My parents never found out about that one. I have never removed the bone and sometimes it stabs me. If I jump randomly in the air, when I am talking to you, this is the reason.

12. I have had malaria in Mozambique, Peru, Ghana and Brazil. I had a relapse in the UK while working for a tree surgeon. He didn't believe that I had malaria in Tunbridge Wells, which I fully understand. I love malaria. It is mind-expanding and physically challenging.

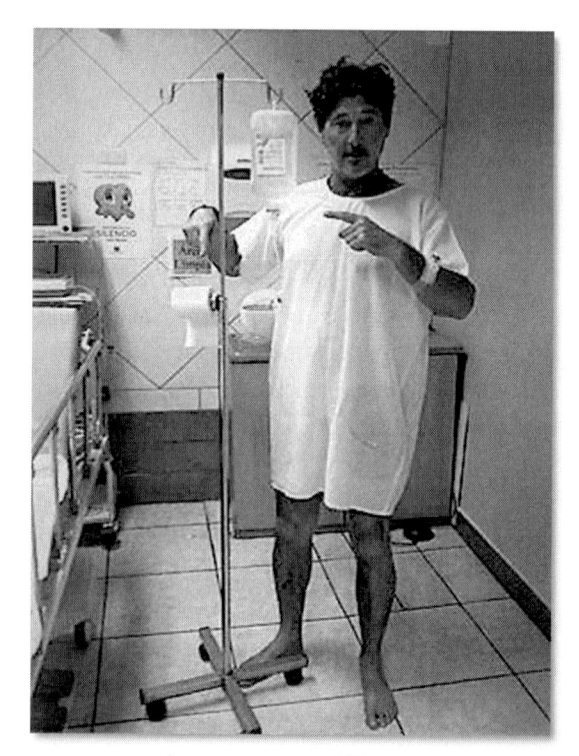

Serious malaria problem, but still nice legs in a dress

13. I was leaning on the banister of the upstairs, in our house, in Kent, UK, talking to Cathy and our daughters, Jesamine and Feaya, who were in the bedroom. I was about to impart some philosophical pearls of wisdom, to my favourite three girls in the world, and was not fully spatially aware. I missed leaning on the banister accurately enough and fell down fifteen stairs. (We counted them, after the event.) It was total Del Boy from 'Only Fools and Horses'. An ambulance was duly called and the children had another opportunity to make siren noises again, and laugh at me. I broke my collar bone and wrist. However, it is not all bad news. Despite the long fall, and the multiple breaks, the girls said I didn't make a sound. One has to be smooth and a bit Jason Statham sometimes, in front of your children. Keith Richards coconut accident, step aside.

14. During my circumnavigation of Africa I was in an arid area of Northern Kenya, totally alone. I was lying under my motorcycle, trying to tighten two bash plate bolts. A monkey ran past, at warp speed, screamed, and totally spooked me. I jumped up and caught the edge of my ear on the sharp plate edge. My ear split open and made Evander Holyfield's bite mark look like a false alarm. I cleaned it, put a wedge of toilet paper on it, and a bit of duct tape. I kept that on for a few days. My ear started to swell. I could hear. It didn't want to heal, but did eventually, after much persuasion, a bit of snipping and lots of yellow Savlon antiseptic. I drank a bit of Savlon too, to be sure. If you don't know Savlon and Zambuk, your adventure first aid kit is sorely lacking. Now I have a knobbly rugby player's ear, which divides in two at the top. Who cares. I can still hear. Maybe better than before.

15. As you know now I broke ribs in Bolivia. I spotted a beautiful, rusted Cadillac in the middle of the desert and decided I had to photograph it. I was successful, but when I went to jump over the fence, I turned into a person of zero co-ordination. I jumped, tripped over the barbed wire fence, that was no higher than your average ant, and fell. The camera on my chest decided to attack me as I landed and I ended up with broken ribs. Let's move on. I can surely improve.

16. I was attacked by armed bandits and shot off my motorcycle in Kenya and broke my ribs again and lost my nerve, for a good few years. That is worth more than one sentence, but not now.

17. Just when I was having a quiet patch, Him up above decided to give me Chicken Pox, at 39. I had pustules in every imaginable area of my body, including in my mouth and every visible part of my body. But there were even pustules in places the sun does not shine often. It was the most itchy experience that anyone could possibly imagine. If you care about your looks then don't scratch because you will end up with livid sores and unsightly scars and you will look like the Mexican actor, Luis Guzman, unless you are a female, then you will look like Luisa Guzman.

18. I got a job with Saga Rose Cruise Ships, at 32, and promptly fell down a flight of stairs. I might have semi-jumped, through total boredom, and desperation, to be away from the most self-centred, materialistic, fake people I have ever had the displeasure to meet. I didn't get along with anyone, except the Philipino staff who were fantastic.

On the way into Sydney Harbour during a storm, don't laugh, I was being harassed by the gays on board, and the Philippine Mafia, for being too friendly with the Philippine girls, which wasn't remotely true. They kept chatting to me. I remained civil, end of story. It was all too much work politics for me. I was from southern Africa. We don't bitch about our co-workers all day long. There are more important things.

I was pondering my dislike of cruising, and as I was scaling some stairs to the ballroom to deliver some silk sashes, for winners of the salsa dance competition, God help me. The whole cruise ship suddenly lurched, Titanic-like, and I was thrown forward down the stairs. I broke my leg. Badly. Best thing I ever did. Saga were very decent and flew me from Sydney to the UK to the best doctors. Thanks for that Saga, but people, listen to me, don't go on a cruise. It is full of backstabbing people trying to claw their way up the social ladder. And that is only the crabs on the hull. The crew are busy throwing each other overboard, as there are many rival gangs. The food is grim, service rubbish, atmosphere crap, people fake and lots of outbreaks of gastro enteritis. Everyone dresses up on a Friday and Saturday night in absurd penguin suits and ballgowns to go and meet the captain, unless they are suffering from gastro enteritis. Then they sit on the loo. What the hell for? Do people in airplanes queue up to meet the captain? Yes, I guess. It was the most pretentious baloney I have ever seen, as 70-year-old women flirted with the Captain and officers, in front of their husbands. Cruising is the most plastic that anyone can ever be. And the most claustrophobic village you can ever imagine. Apart from that it is superb.

19. After abandoning my children for a life on the sea, which lasted two Med cruises, two Canary Island cruises and a couple of world cruises, I had seen enough. Two years of my life wasted, in my opinion. I don't travel in groups. I don't take orders, so I was doomed.

It was so wonderful to see my girls again and on the second morning back I decided to bond with them and impress them with my long dormant skateboarding skills. We were living in a semi-detached, quiet, cul de sac road in a village in Kent, with a population of 200 on a busy month. I went down a hill, after twenty years of skateboard retirement, hit some unnecessarily placed Dad blockade. It was block paving; the skate board hit a raised brick and stopped. I continued, and decided to tuck my arm behind my back. First bit of action in that street since… I was last here.

There were lots of other men at Accident and Emergency that Sunday, doing Dad things, that ended in injury. Bit of football, tree climbing, first back flip or pull up in thirty years. That kind of thing. I noticed that there were not many wives there and the ones that had turned up were sighing and raising their eyes skyward, wondering when their husbands were going to grow up. Or die.

Most were on their mobile phones, scowling at it. But for me. Result. After an X-ray it was ascertained that I was fine and had no reason to complain. My arm was broken in three places and I had torn muscles. I can overcome.

20. I was stung by a hornet on the main island of Mahe in the Seychelles, where I spent four years teaching at the Polytechnic School of Art and Design (SAD for short). I was riding my motorcycle to pick up a girlfriend whose bike tyre had exploded, because she was too fat. I didn't look too James Bond either, as I was riding a 50cc monkey bike. A black hornet, with a vicious hanging sting, flew into my helmet and nailed me on the cheek. I tried to turn the other cheek, but the damage was done. I knew I was allergic, but didn't realise how much. I swelled

up like a loon, sorry, balloon and had to be flown by helicopter to the US Tracking Station for an adrenaline injection. My throat swells up within twenty minutes and blocks my airways.

21. It happened again in France, when I was stung by two mating bees (well, it wouldn't be one would it), who decided to fly into a hole in my well-worn boot, mid-intercourse. They injected me well; I injected myself badly with ephedrine, but made it to the UK. I had to wear a flip flop for 1,600 kilometres of riding, as I couldn't get my bike boot on because of the swelling. My integrity and coolness were not intact. I got a lot of odd stares on the Channel Tunnel train with my full bike gear and one fluorescent green flip flop with tropical flower on it.

22. We turned up at a campsite in Southern Chile at the beautiful town of Chile Chico. The campsite was a bit rundown. That was not a problem, but the fact that the whole site was set in an apple orchard should have rung some alarm bells. Wasps love apples. Wasps love me. I was feeding a wasp some steak at our wobbly wooden table and was fascinated. I had no idea that wasps loved steak. We ended up chatting and making friends. I made the error of stroking him, to cement our barbecue friendship. Sadly, he wasn't ready for that step in our relationship and he decided to sting me. One can't blame him as he was having a sip of my Coke at the same time as me. The result was a huge swollen lip, face and throat. (See out of focus photo, the only evidence we have of my Bart Simpson impression).

There was a vet in our group, and as I swelled, my head threatening to take off in the breeze, they were discussing if her dog and cat anti histamine medication would work on me. Meanwhile, I popped to the tent and lay there with laboured breathing. By some sixth sense Cathy checked on me, panicked, and our Chilean friends kicked into gear. They dragged me out of the tent by my feet, and unceremoniously dumped me in the back of a truck. I stopped breathing in the back of the pick-up, fifteen seconds before we entered the hospital gates. I was revived with massive adrenaline and a drip. I was not charged a penny by the Clinic. I live to die another day. Thank you so much Cathy, Christian and Eduardo and family. I owe you all my life.

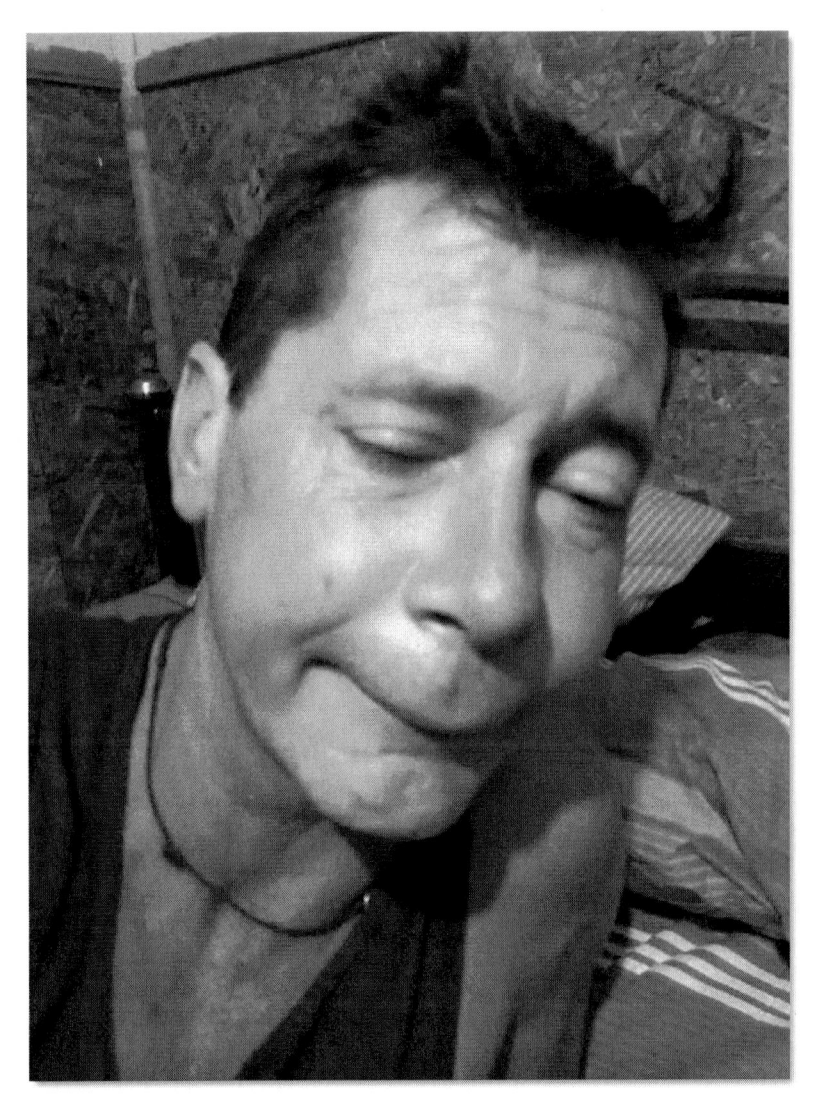

Apologies for out-of-focus selfie. Only evidence of anaphylactic effects on second day

23. I was nailed by bullet ants, which are supposed to be the worst pain you can imagine. I didn't like it.

24. If you want to argue that Fire Ants are worse, I have been there, done that. Bullet Ants are worse. How annoying am I. Bet you want me to get stung by something, or have an accident. OK. Let's continue.

25. Salar de Uyuni Salt flats crash and Tupiza tumble discussed already.

26. I thought this motorbike lark was getting dangerous, so for a very brief period of time I retired. I decided to do some English teaching, some manual labour and some decorating in the UK. An incompetent, weed smoker dropped a ladder on my head in the pouring rain. Unconscious, end of that job. As far as the English teaching job was concerned, Jemima turned up with her mother. After ten minutes of interrogation about my life history, I told them both to be gone. Evidently more politely. There were children present.

27. I went grape picking in the pouring rain (what again, rain in England) and freezing cold (what again, cold in England) with Cathy. It was 6.30am, dark, and everyone there looked like they wanted to kill themselves. After five minutes I wanted to kill myself too. I had to have a word.

"Cathy, we need to go, this is not for me. I have cut off the top of my finger with the secateurs."

I did not do it on purpose. I am not that desperate to get out of a job. Also, I am not Sir Ranulph Fiennes. And to this day, I have no fingerprint on that finger.

28. Snake, scorpion and spider bites. I cannot tell you how many times those have occurred. I went to an International College in Swaziland with the wonderful name Waterford Kamhlaba United World College of Southern Africa. Kamhlaba means 'Little World' and it certainly was. There were 300 students but an amazing 70 nationalities. It was a wonderful school.

Waterford School was opened on a mountainside at the edge of Mbabane in 1963, after founding Headmaster Michael Stern spent six years teaching in South Africa, first at an all black school, St Peter's, that was closed in 1956, then at St Martin's on the same site, where he was the founding headmaster. Under the apartheid regime, Michael Stern came to South Africa to teach in 1955, after responding to an article written by Father Trevor Huddleston called 'And the church sleeps on; But he became increasingly dissatisfied and frustrated with the pervasive environment of racial intolerance. In 1961 after several years of St Martin's work camps in the then British protectorate of Swaziland, and after it was clear that Michael could not teach and live his ideals in South Africa, he committed himself to the ideal of a multiracial school in Swaziland. Waterford was established and expressed opposition to the South African apartheid regime and its laws of racial segregation.

Michael Stern was not alone in his efforts to make Waterford School a reality. His colleagues Gordon Milne, Deon Glover and Jim and Jean Richardson left St Martin's to join him in Swaziland. Gifts of service and skill were also made, the most famous being architect and parent Amancio Pancho Guedes, who offered to design the school for free, and Stanley Kaplan, a consultant engineer whose combined efforts allowed the physical structures of campus to be built despite little funding.

Not only did a school need to be built, but the funders of WK wanted all students who qualified academically to be able to attend, regardless of their ability to pay, making funds for bursaries necessary.

The school opened with little fanfare on 3 February, 1963. The first students were sixteen boys. The boys consisted of seven white, six black, two coloured and one Indian student. The school was extremely successful. Despite this, many local and international observers deemed this diversity as 'sick' and 'unnatural'. Can you believe it. To those who supported racially segregated education and society, Waterford School was a threat. I am proud I went there. During the early days, this animosity was displayed through slashed car tyres, beatings, increased tension with surrounding schools, and taunting of white students at Waterford. Over the next couple of years, the school grew exponentially and with it support for its ethos and mission. In 1967, King Sobhuza II, the Ngwenyama of Swaziland, granted Waterford the name, Kamhlaba, meaning, Little World.

He said, "Wherever you are in the world, the world does not distinguish who you are. You live in whatever your color, whatever your religion, whatever your race. This is the meaning of Kamhlaba."

During the same time of Waterford founding, another movement in education was beginning in the UK. The United World College Movement. At a time when the Cold War was at its height, the aim of the UWC movement was to bring together young people from different nations to act as champions of peace through an education based on shared learning, collaboration and understanding. In 1981 the two movements came together when Waterford joined the UWC movement.

Waterford played a significant role in the struggle for racial equality in southern Africa, educating the children of Nelson Mandela, Walter Sisulu, Desmond Tutu, Nobel prize winning novelist Nadine Gordimer, the first president of Botswana, Sir Seretse Khama and the revolutionary leaders of Mozambique, Samora Michel and Eduardo Mondlane. In the post-apartheid era, Waterford has sustained its early vision to educate exceptional students regardless of race, religion, financial background or level of naughtiness. The school continues to nurture Africa's future political, business and civic leaders. Waterford has proven that young people can look and work beyond the barriers set by government and politicians; they can create a peaceful, welcoming environment that doesn't judge an individual on their individual characteristics. I feel extremely proud that I went to two of these incredible colleges. I was conscientious, and I realised I was at an incredible school, but it didn't mean I wasn't a handful.

Back to an African boy's basic instincts. Every breaktime at Waterford School, I would head to the nearby mountains and turn over every rock I possibly could, during the half-hour break. I almost always found a snake, spider, scorpion or some other fascinating insect and popped him in my pocket. Back in the class, it would be: "Spencer Conway, take that snake outside and free him and come and see me after class."

I admit to being quite disruptive if I could see that the teacher was not interested in teaching, or if I felt I had more knowledge than them, my respect diminished, and I admit that I became a bit of a brat. This was not the case with Mrs. Earnshaw, my history teacher. She was brilliant and I thought that I had behaved. Evidently not well enough.

When my brother's daughter, Ysabella, went to the same school, fifteen years later, on the first day of school Mrs. Pat Earnshaw was taking the register. She suddenly halted, stared at the list, looked up slowly and said, "Ysabella Conway, as in related to Spencer Conway."

"Yes, that's my uncle," Ysa answered.

Proudly, I hope.

"Right, sit at the front," was Mrs. Earnshaw's response.

Quite a few times I was taken to hospital from school with various stings and unidentified bites. I was hyper as hell. It was five kilometres from my house to Waterford Kamhlaba school. The school was perched on a mountain top with a steep curved road up to it. We had a school bus that chugged its way up, bellowing black smoke and moving at less than walking speeds. This was not for me. I used to run to school and run home. Sometimes I would run back in the late afternoon for football or athletics practice. Nothing better than being alone and running through Africa. And I found snakes, and lizards and sloe worms and tortoises and on... Loved it, but my school was not a zoo, so my additions were not welcome.

29. When I was leaving my house in the UK, to circumnavigate Africa, I didn't even make it out of my garage. I was loaded up with two panniers, an army sausage bag, the kitchen sink and a positive attitude. Austin Vince, the famous adventurer, came down to Kent to see me off with hs similarly famous other half, Lois Pryce. Austin saw my bike loaded up, put his hands on his hips, leant back and said, "You will learn, the whole house on the bike is no good".

He was right.

Mr. 'Fully in Control of his Bike'...

I flicked the kickstand up in the garage, caught it on a piece of rolled carpet, fell and tore a muscle in my groin. Begin as you mean to go on. Don't worry. When I finally left to Dover, the weather was so bad that the 100 bikes that turned up to see me off mysteriously disappeared into the mist within twenty miles of leaving Biddenden. At least they turned up to see me off. I wanted to give up one mile further. Totally grateful for the support and totally grateful I did not give up. 'Circumnavigation of Kent' does not really have the same ring to it as 'solo circumnavigation of the whole of Africa'. Would have been easier though.

Roll on the present. As I come to the end of this list, the bad luck has not subsided. More than a year ago I injured my nether regions in a ridiculous accident. It led to more than 2,000 comments about my meat and two veg on the internet. But no photographic evidence. My jewels nearly went viral. What a strange and wonderful world. I have never been one for toilet humour. It's just not me. But I will have to stoop on this occasion. Humour wise, and physically.

After riding through all twenty countries of South and Central America, I decided to injure myself, properly, in the Mexican beach town of Zicatela. After 100,000 kilometres, and many minor prangs, I rode up a flight of steps, to my room. Not a problem, it is something I have been doing since I was in nappies, to impress the girls.

On this occasion, it was the love of my life, Cathy, and three bikini-clad, oiled-up women, who were watching my manoeuvres. None of them, or their silicone, or Dental Floss bikinis, had any effect on my macho ego or concentration, I can promise. But… for some reason my stunt work was not up to par, and after successfully navigating the first eleven steps, I forgot the golden rule. Brick walls stop motorbikes. I planted my wheel against the wall, very expertly, flew forward, at a rapid rate, I might add, and unwisely used my 'meat and two veg' as a brake. It was the unforgiving twenty-three litre petrol tank that stopped me flying over the handlebars.

Roll on a year and I have ignored the whole issue, So, what happened? I woke up and my testicle was doing an impressive impression of a basketball. I could only stand up in a banana pose, curved over double in pain. It was time to act. I rode, very gingerly to the Hospital Angel del Mar (HAM, for short, which doesn't instill confidence). Luckily, it was only a couple of painful kilometres. I felt like I was sitting on an angry cushion.

The hospital was under renovation, full of builders with moustaches, fluorescent jackets and orange hard hats. They were demolishing a wall, so there was dust everywhere, a bit like a dry ice effect. It was like a scene from a Village People video, except there were patients in wheelchairs, waiting in the corridor, disappearing in clouds of dust. So much for the Covid masks, actually, thank God for them.

I went through the Covid routine of disinfecting my hands, putting on my mask, and passing through a bouncy castle type, inflatable tunnel, where they spray you to within an inch of your life, with something toxic. Then your temperature is taken and your hands sprayed with disinfectant gel. Annoyingly, they put enough gel on your hand to moisturise a baby elephant, so I ended up rubbing it all up my arms, on my face, my shorts and on other patients. Not the last bit, evidently, because psychiatrists would rapidly arrive, or security. I passed through the gauntlet, and myself and my testicle came out the other side, booked in, traumatised, but disinfected to the nth degree. Once in Reception, I didn't have to wait long, possibly because of my theatrical moaning and posture. A vertically challenged doctor approached me. Once inside his office, the diagnosis from Mexican Doctor Ronnie Corbett, was rapid, and shocking.

"You have a strangled testicle and possibly some other internal injuries."

All I had to hear was 'strangled testicles' and the room went white, and the ceiling started spinning, not that I am soft, or anything.

"We will have to remove it, chop it off. It is too late to save the testicle. But the other one is happy."

I heard him say this, in my befuddled brain, but what he actually said was; which is similar, when you are panicking, "You will have to come back tomorrow for a scan and to see the specialist, to see how we can proceed."

'See how we can proceed.' Jesus Christ, that sounds worrisome. I slept like a baby, not. Now, many of you have been bored and frustrated during lockdown, but at least you weren't in a foreign country, with a strangled testicle. Well, some of you might have been, but it seems unlikely. I know, none of you women readers have had this experience.

The next day I returned to the Hospital Angel del Mar, full of trepidation, and sweating more than the builders. My panic was intensified because I happened to mention my predicament on social media. I had more than 2,000 comments. I think it struck a chord with the men ('struck', not a good choice of words, or chord), and gave women a giggle. So, thank you, to everyone, worldwide, of all religions, and colours, who prayed for the safety of my left jewel.

It was saved. Blood flow was not compromised long enough. Strangely enough, the specialist was one and the same GP, Dr. Mexican Ronnie Corbett. At least he didn't don a disguise like the Egyptian border guard, who put on a hat and glasses, and pretended to be a totally different official.

I have no idea how Dr. Mexican Ronnie Corbett became a urologist overnight. Maybe he was pouring over a copy of the famous medical journal, 'All you need to know about strangled and distraught testicles', by Paul Oike. Actually, he was a star. As Dr. Mexican Ronnie Corbett was only five foot, on a tall day, and I am six foot four; the initial standing examination was quite embarrassing. The doctor's head was already at the correct height for a close examination of my angry orb. Once I had disrobed, of course. Ah, the humiliation. I believe that his optician was blind, and the prescription for the Doctor's black-rimmed glasses, were a guess. His eyes looked huge, like a shocked owl, but it was clear that he couldn't see anything. He leant in exceedingly close, and my trust began to falter. I began to worry that he was one of those psychos who wandered into random hospitals, stole a white jacket and stethoscope from a coat hanger and wandered confidently down a corridor, in search of a victim. One of those psychopaths who want to lick unsuspecting, Adventure Motorcyclists testicles.

My panic was unfounded. All he did was grab the sore veg, unceremoniously, and not that gently, and pulled it to the right.

"Did that hurt Senor James?"

I think my Olympic qualifying jump, answered his question. I hit the roof and uttered words that I wouldn't even want a six-year-old Manchester youth to hear. It seemed to help him with his diagnosis. Dr Mexican Ronnie Corbett, calmly announced, not in these words exactly, "You have a lacerated, twisted, traumatised, highly inflamed and very unhappy testicle."

"Not strangled at all then, such an exaggeration," I added, hopefully. "Will I be able to do wheelies, once it is fixed?" I enquired.

"No, Definitely not," he replied.

"I am not surprised, I couldn't do wheelies before this problem." He didn't laugh at my joke.

"The problem is, Mr. Spencer, is that you left this injury for more than eleven months."

"Tell me about it."

After plonking his podgy self behind his desk, shuffling a few papers, clicking a few pens, tapping a few keys on his '80s computer, and generally doing doctory things, he turned to me and said,

"No problem, si, big problem. No, no problem, just complicado Senor James," he said tapping his keyboard with a flourish.

"Get on with it. How long do I have to live?"

"Now, you have kidney infection, kidney stones, bladder infection, ureter infection, a squashed urethra… and a buggered bollock".

OK. Not the last two words, but you get the gist. So I was put on antibiotics and surgery loomed. It is important to stay positive. With all my accidents and mishaps and poor decision-making, success is basically stumbling from failure to failure, with no loss of enthusiasm. Defeat is not a bitter pill unless you swallow it. Success is getting what you want, happiness is wanting what you get. Sorry, bit philosophical;

back to injuries. Having ignored the need for surgery I did not have to wait long for the next episode.

A week after my diagnosis, I was cleaning our room and once again decided to wrestle with some Fire Ants. Women and stinging insects are magnetically attracted to me. I have no idea why. (Just joking.) Now I carry three epipens, ephedrine injections, everywhere, but prefer to save them for more remote areas, such as the Amazon Basin, or Patagonia-type terrain, where homo sapiens and injections are few and far between.

I rushed down to the HAM Hospital once more, and was seen by Dr. Ronnie Corbett's wife. She did not possess any ephedrine, or any adrenaline at all, so I made do with Phenadryl, Cortizone, anti histamine, two Ibuprofen, and a can of Modelo Especial Lager. It really was not a successful remedy. I had to put up with swollen sausage fingers that threatened to split, and an angry rash that covered my entire body.

I looked like the photo definition of chicken pox, which I have had too by the way. I must confess that the pain was nothing compared to bullet ants. But don't underestimate Fire Ants, they are toughies.

There are more than two hundred species, the most dangerous being the Red, Tropical and Ginger Fire Ants. Not only are they vicious as hell, they also have superb survival skills. The motto these Ants live by must be one of my favourites: 'Being defeated is a temporary condition. Giving up is what makes it permanent."

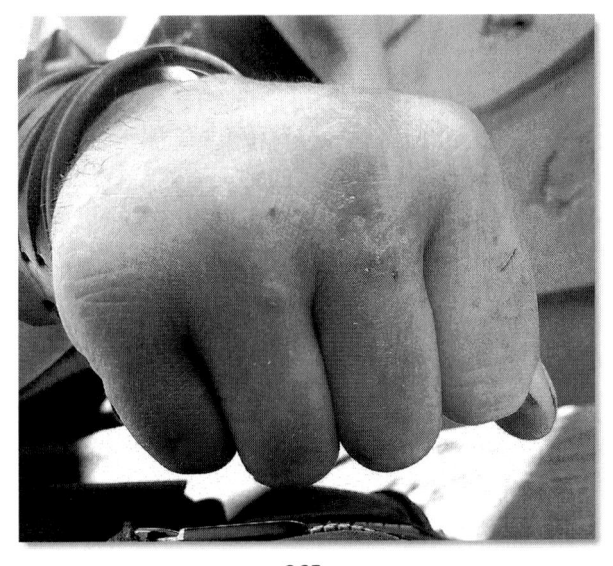

I am sitting in the Mexican coastal town of Puerto Escondido where we have been based for over a year since September 2020. So apologies for those of you that are sharp as hell geographically, and realise that Mexico is not in South America. I know that this book is supposed to be about South America, but it fits in with the present story, and I am a massive fan of tangents. Tangents are part of traveling too.

Not travelling has not diminished my bad luck though. A lot has happened. Puerto is not a boring place. We chose it when we realised that Covid 19 was going to close the world. We were planning to get to Panama to try and cross the Darien Gap. When this became an impossibility, we needed a place nearby and cheap. We liked Puerto because although it is touristy it caters to a more eclectic clientele, mostly surfers, extreme sportsmen, backpackers and Mexican families. More our scene.

The area around Puerto Escondido had been inhabited by indigenous people for centuries, but no towns of any size were established during the pre-Hispanic or colonial eras. The bay was known as Bahia de la Escondido (Bay of the Hidden) due to a local legend. A fierce pirate, Andre's Drake, brother of Sir Francis Drake, anchored his ship in the bay, when the area was uninhabited, to rest for a few days, unmolested by authorities. Some weeks before, he and his crew had kidnapped a young Mixtec woman from the village of Santa Maria Huatulco and taken her prisoner, onboard. While in the bay, the woman escaped from the cabin she was being held in, and being a strong swimmer, she jumped overboard. She was gone, and hid in the thick jungle beyond the beach. Since then, pirates and fishermen all refer to this woman as 'La Escondida', the hidden one. Every time the ship returned to these waters, the captain sent out a search party of most of his crew, to no avail. Hence, the name Bahia de la Escondido stuck.

For most of the 20th century it was a small fishing village that intermittently was used to ship coffee and there was no real town until 1930, when its activity as a port was more firmly established. Roll on to today and it is still a small fishing and now, lunatic surfer village. Puerto Escondido became famous for surfing competitions, held at Zicatela Beach, one of the most dangerous surfing spots in the world, and where our cabin of six months was located. The competitions attract entrants from the tops of the tops, worldwide. Nicknamed the 'Mexican Pipeline', due to the similar shape and power of the Banzai Pipeline in

Hawaii, the wave that breaks on Zicatela Beach draws an international crowd of surfers, body boarders and their incredibly beautiful, fit and tanned entourage. But don't be fooled. These people are not here just to party. They are hear primarily to face nature, and what a force of nature it is. Ron Cassidy, 2007, and Noel Robinson, 2011, were just two of the more than twenty names I read, on a memorial plaque, of surfers that have died on Zicatela waves. I am a very strong swimmer, and it is the closest I have ever come to drowning. It is a beautiful sport to watch and luckily our cabin had a view of the thundering waves and amazing athletes. But the sea is unforgiving and, just last week, a highly experienced Spanish surfer, Oscar Serra, lost his life in the heavy surf of Puerto Escondido. Surfing is not the only dangerous thing here.

Crocodiles are also a real threat. Another piece of news that made it worldwide, was a crocodile attack here just a few weeks ago. We had reporters from all over the world invading Puerto and I was even interviewed by a German news channel about my experience of crocodiles and my opinion of the attack that was less than sympathetic. No idea if it made it onto TV.

You would all be forgiven for thinking that Mexico consists solely of windswept deserts, rickety wooden towns, men with Sombreros, snoozing under the shade of a cactus tree; when they are not busy kicking an obstinate mule, along a dusty path, in the boiling sun, sipping Tequila (the Mexican, not the mule). A lopsided cart, on a lopsided mountain road, carrying a group of women in huge colourful dresses, to a local wedding, held on a football pitch. A group of men in white cowboy hats, sharing shots from a communal bottle on the pavement. A tiny woman, of three hundred, minimum, selling stale cakes from a wheelbarrow. I am delighted to tell you that this disgraceful stereotyping does exist. There are Mexican areas, exactly like this, in the dry north and all down the beautiful, desert, Baja peninsula.

But Mexico also has lush tropical jungle, and soaring, rugged mountains, with bubbling springs and plunging waterfalls. This is where the magical animals and insects of Mexico are found. We were lucky enough to be in Mexico's fifth largest state, Oaxaca, but *numero uno* for animal species. Massive tarantulas, boa constrictors, scorpions, spiders, monkeys, iguanas, parrots, hummingbirds in thousands of fluorescent colours, parrots, toucans, grackles, mockingbirds, stunning emerald spiny lizards, peeping frogs and salamanders. Don't forget Coral snakes, rattle snakes, giant toads, coatis and raccoons. Then we get to the big boys. Cougars, jaguars and crocodiles. When humans and these lot meet, it is often not in our favour during the encounter, and it is never in their favour afterwards. They get hunted down.

In a vibrant hostel, five minutes from our room here, in Puerto Escondido, Georgia Laurie, now sits, freshly discharged from our local hospital, which I know well, tapping on her phone, surrounded by backpackers, trying to make sense of the last few days. It is certainly the stuff of nightmares. She and twin sister, Melissa, from Berkshire in southern England, decided with a few friends to join a riverboat tour of the nearby Manialtepec Lagoon. Cathy and I have ridden there often. It is a hauntingly beautiful place and even boasts bioluminescent plankton, that light the lagoon up blue, at night. Truly spectacular. However, the shallows of the lagoon are full of crocodiles and are a favourite hatching area.

"I actually said to the guide, 'this looks like a place crocodiles would make their home'," Georgia said, with a wry smile. The bandage wrapped tightly around her wrist is evidence that she was right.

The guide, apparently a German national who was not registed with the tourism authority and has since fled, insisted that it was safe to swim. As the group enjoyed a dip in the cool of the afternoon (not a midnight swim, as originally reported), Melissa was suddenly tugged underwater. In what one local conservationist told me, it was most likely a female crocodile, defending her hatchlings. The animal went for Melissa on three separate occasions, puncturing her stomach and her leg, ever more deeply. Yet, rather than watch on helplessly, Georgia dived back into the water and started punching the crocodile over and over, with her sister in its jaws.

"It was fight or flight, and you have to fight for the people you love," Georgia said, in a quote that would be repeated the world over. One of the friends, Ani, scrambled onto the mangrove roots and called for help. A nearby boat heard the cries and headed towards the commotion. "I pushed through the undergrowth using my oar," said Lalo Escamilla, a boatman, who waded out to help the twins. Soon after the incident, Lalo took Cathy and I to the site of the attack. I for one would never swim where he showed us. It is too, glaringly, high risk.

Once on board, it was clear that Melissa's injuries were life-threatening. As well as lacerations and deep cuts, the twenty-seven-year-old had water in her lungs and also broken wrists. She would later develop sepsis from her ruptured intestine.

Such was the adrenaline pumping around Georgia's body, she didn't realise that she was also seriously injured until they reached the hospital. "It wasn't until the nurse opened my fist to clean my hand that I realised that it had been slashed almost through."

Understandably, all her focus had been on her sister Melissa, who by then had been placed in a medically induced coma. Making the call to her parents, at 4am, UK time, as Melissa's condition deteriorated, was one of the worst moments.

News coverage of the attack, June 2021

Thankfully, Melissa emerged from the coma. She must overcome her physical injuries and both women will need time to deal with the emotional and mental fallout of what they went through. The 'hero twin sister' label will always be there, and deservedly so. I hope both recover as fully as possible. Not the best Mexican tourist story.

After discussing surfing deaths and crocodile attacks, I am aware that respect is needed. It is very difficult to top those stories. Let's cheer things up a bit. I suggest that just a couple of scales down from that is a tarantula attack in your shorts, a bank robbery, an earthquake and Covid. Not that it's a competition towards death, but hear me out.

A couple of weeks after my unfortunate testicle-gate accident, I was totally awake at three in the morning, staring at the ceiling, as wide-eyed as an owl. I have the unfortunate affliction of insomnia and sleep on average, three to four hours a night maximum. The other six hours or so, I spend worrying about my life and my wife and my strife. Zicatela beach was in lockdown and normally I lie there in silence, frying in my own sweat and looking at Cathy jealously, snoring away. On this Sunday night I heard the most incredible, tearing of metal and revving of engines. I jumped up, ran out of the room, down a corridor, down 48 steps to the seafront road. As I arrived barefoot, and turned the corner, a battered Ram pickup pulled off with an ATM bank machine in the back. I ran the block to the corner, where the ATM station was usually located. The only one in this part of town. The front glass door was smashed and the ATM machine was gone. All that was left was a forlorn Santander sign, hanging at a 45 degree angle, and an orange crowbar on the glass strewn floor. I picked it up and took a quick selfie, whilst grinning at the empty hole in the wall behind me. When I got to the room and excitedly told Cathy the story, she pointed out a glaringly obvious error in my behaviour. Don't go to the scene of a crime just after it happened, don't put your fingerprints on the robbery weapon, and don't take selfies at the scene of the crime. Cathy got me to delete the photos. I thought it was a bit paranoid and over the top, but accepted the criticism. Cathy added, as an afterthought, which counts, in the caring and loving stakes:

"What were you doing running down there anyway? You could have been shot."

I wasn't, and I wasn't arrested, and I saved a photo of me with the crowbar. Sorry, Cathy.

The next seismic event, literally, was about two weeks later. I was owl staring at the ceiling once again, when the room started shaking. It was strong enough for Cathy, who can sleep through a cyclone and a tsunami, to wake up and say, "What was that?"

Well, this was an earthquake, and a real one. As she spoke, the whole building just moved a few inches over, towards the sea. There is no other way of describing it. It was a three-storey, albeit rickety, building, leaning over.

I jumped up and screamed, "Come on baby, run. Let's go, now!"

I grabbed her hand and we ran out of the room, down the corridor and down to the beach. Everyone was there, which was weird, in the middle of the night. But then, the word spread. If a tsunami was going to follow the earthquake, we were all in the wrong place. We had to get to higher ground. With that, everyone scrambled up the mountainside. There were four more earthquakes, and no casualties. The concrete steps up to our room did not make it. Fifteen of them fell, twisting the rebar that was supposed to hold them firm. Mad times.

So we have had a surfer death, a crocodile attack, earthquakes, bank robberies and other odd occurrences I might get to, but the Tarantula pants episode leaves me cold. I am very good with all creepy crawlies, and in fact hunt them out, but there are certain limits.

Be careful. There were fatalities here

Recently I had to change the front sprocket on my Tenere, as the teeth were worn, and the chain was slipping. I had a pair of fake Nike shorts on and a pair of fake Havaianas flip flops, and little else. I lay in the dirt under the bike, at 7am, the sand pleasantly cool on my skin. The bike was shaded by a huge palm tree and its abundance of coconuts. Life was good. I changed the sprocket like a real expert and headed in for a shower. We share our budget pit with numerous sizes and colours of scorpion, who are constantly waving their stings at us, menacingly. There are snakes regularly in our shower and cockroaches and geckoes have free rein. Leave a grain of sugar on the counter and a colony of monster ants will be intimidating you out of the kitchen. We always wear flip flops here, something we didn't even do in Africa. The mosquitoes, flying ants and one million moth species are a wonderful addition. I headed into the shower and felt into the only pocket of my Nike shorts, on the righthand side. My immediate thought was that there was a tissue in there, or a donut, but when I reached in, there was nothing. It was on the inside of my shorts and was moving. I had been nailed by a scorpion in Swaziland when I was eleven, and had never forgotten. It was like twenty cigarette burns on your fingertips. That's what I thought was in my shorts. I couldn't face another one.

I jumped backwards into the bedroom, flying in the air and managed to rip my shorts totally in half. It was better executed and much quicker than The Incredible Hulk. I threw my shorts against the furthest wall and hopped around the room, like the floor was lava, looking for the killer scorpion. Something had bitten my bum and was here. My shorts hit the wall with a thud and the biggest, hairiest tarantula I have ever seen fell to the ground. My shorts were too small for him, he was wearing Dr Marten's boots, and a serious attitude. He had a full head of hair and was an angry orange and brown.

Cathy totally flipped and eloquently observed, "Jesus Christ, that's massive," whilst backing out of the room, in Karate protective pose.

The tarantula scowled at Cathy, and maybe growled too, but that could have been my imagination. Don't get me wrong, I am a hard man, and can cope with any animals or insects, but when a hairy tarantula surprises you in your shorts, uninvited, that's another ball game. I must confess that I had many 'tarantula crawling in my mouth' dreams after that. Actually found it later outside and bagged a hairy tarantula photo!!!

After all these episodes in Puerto Escondido, it was a relief when we were commissioned to do an article for the world-renowned *Adventure Bike Rider Magazine*. It would get us out of our killer animal accommodation and into… well… the jungle. What could go wrong.

The idea was to do three spectacular routes from the south coast of Mexico through Oaxaca state. One was a tarred road to the east that had hundreds of hairpins. The second skirted the coast and beautiful beaches, before turning north, through the mountains to Oaxaca City. The third started at sea level and snaked through the mountainous rugged jungle, until at 2000 metres it broke into high altitude pine forest. This was the toughest road, the dirt road, washed away by mountain rivers, full of jagged, fist-sized rocks and rainwater carved ravines, cutting into the road. This was no car, no truck country, only us. This was rock fall and landslide area, cougar and jaguar territory, soaring kestrels and eagle land, rock rabbits and snakes, potholes and sink holes. This was the type of landscape we loved to ride in and would be the core of the article.

It didn't go well, you will be surprised to hear. On the first night we got to a mountain cabin and I immediately got bitten by a spider. I tried to ignore it, because the indigenous guy we befriended, Carlos, told us about a boy who had been attacked and killed by a jaguar. Although I was swelling up, I wanted to follow up on this story. Mexico was so safe. Not.

A young boy called Gabriel Trovolama, 12, went out into the fields to check crops when he was attacked by a cougar and died of internal bleeding. The residents of the area in Guadeloupe Siete Cerros, in the Canada region of Oaxaca, said there had been numerous fatal attacks against livestock and one adult, who managed to escape, had been badly maimed for life. They attribute all the attacks to one animal. Oaxaca is home to five of the six wild cat species; jaguars, cougars, ocelots, lynxes and jaguarundi all inhabit the mountain state. I found out from Carlos before we left (a necessity because of my rapidly expanding hand), that a farmer had recently killed a jaguar, thought to be the culprit. This was later proved not to be the guilty animal at all. Carlos sent me a grainy shot of the rotting corpse of a stunning male adult jaguar. Sad, when animals and humans clash. Never works out well.

We headed back to Puerto as I was suffering from the insect attack and was injected with epinephrine (adrenaline) at the local hospital. The swelling went down within an hour. When I talk about swelling when discussing my stings, this is only one of the symptoms of anaphylactic shock. Other common symptoms, all of which I suffer, are hives (raised, itchy bumps on the skin), flushing (extreme redness of face and skin), swollen lips, runny nose, swelling of the mucous membrane on the surface of the eyes and angioedema (swelling under the skin). This is one of my worst symptoms. My swelling is so extreme that a South African doctor who treated me once, stated that my skin was in danger of splitting, so extreme was my body's reaction. Even worse, in 20% of cases, of which I am a proven member, the tongue and throat swell up, the skin can turn blue (cyanosis), from lack of oxygen, and death can occur. Luckily, I pulled through again, but it was apparent to me, that each time I was stung it got worse. Anaphylaxis can be caused by the body's response to almost any foreign substance. In children and young adults, food is the most common trigger, even when the food is eaten for the first time. In the Western world, the most common causes are eating or touching peanuts, wheat, tree nuts, shellfish, milk and eggs. In the Middle East, sesame is the most common trigger and in Asia, rice and chickpeas often cause anaphylaxis. As I child I had no allergies to any foods and my severe anaphylactic response to venom from insect stings and bites only started in my thirties. This could be what ends my career as an adventure motorcyclist, or could even end my life. But it was time to try to film again in the mountains. Never give up.

On our next trip we stumbled across a very weird place, that Cathy and I will forever call, 'Mushroom Town, spot a clown'. San Jose del Pacifico is a mountain town, at 2500 metres, in central Oaxaca, that has the dubious honour of being the only place where magic mushrooms are legal. After travelling on rough, local tracks, through poor traditional Indian villages, mud and corrugated iron shacks clinging to the mountainside, litter and skeletal dogs peppering the rutted, muddy, single high street, that snakes through the village, we eventually joined an asphalt road. The road improved, the litter disappeared and even the road signs were smarter. Brightly painted wooden carvings of mushrooms, some as big as a man, started to crop up on the verge, on all the steep bends. Neat little huts, with palm leaf roofing, sold thousands and thousands of wooden mushrooms, ranging from a centimetre tall to over six foot. All were painted in psychedelic colours. The vendors also sold fresh jars of mountain honey, local coffee, infused with cinnamon, Ciel bottled water, soft drinks, crisps and sweets as psychedelic in colour as the carvings. Similarly brightly coloured shawls, woolly hats and gloves and ponchos were hanging on branch trellises, stretching along the roadside. As we got closer to the town, these stalls all joined into one huge chain of touristy hell. We started to pass minivans of pale-faced, acnied, greasy, long-haired tourists, and saw some signs in English. Our gut reaction was to turn around and get back to non-tourist, adventure Mexico, but we were intrigued by the appeal of San Jose del Pacifico.

The obvious appeal were the mushrooms, so what's it all about. Psilocybin mushrooms, commonly known as 'magic mushrooms', or shrooms, are a group of fungi that contain psilocybin, which turns into the hallucinogenic psilocin upon ingestion. This hallucinogenic species has a history of use among the native people of Mesoamerica for religious communion, divination and healing, from pre-Columbian times to the present day. Mushroom stones and motifs have been found in Guatemala. A statuette dating from c.200 CE, depicting the mushroom, Psilocybe Mexican was found in the west Mexican state of Colima, in a shaft and chamber tomb. A Psilocybe species known to the Aztecs as teonanacatl (literally 'divine mushroom'; agglutinative form of teotl (God, sacred), and nanacatl (mushroom in Nahuatl), was reportedly served at the coronation of the Aztec ruler, Moctezuma, in 1502. Aztecs and Mazatecs referred to psilocybin mushrooms as genius mushrooms, divinatory, or wondrous mushrooms, when translated into English.

After the Spanish conquest, Catholic missionaries campaigned against the cultural tradition of the Aztecs as idolators, and the use of hallucinogenic plants and mushrooms, together with pre-Christian traditions, was quickly suppressed. The Spanish believed the mushrooms allowed the Aztecs and others to communicate with demons. The irony was not lost on me, that 300 plus years after colonialism banned mushrooms, now the modern Aztecs were bringing in busloads of tourists to partake in them. So the traditional shamans were not allowed mushrooms for their age-old ceremonies, but German lesbians, with hairy armpits and matted hair were allowed to consume mushrooms to the point of gluttony and madness. Funny world.

The first mention of hallucinogenic mushrooms in European medicinal literature was in the London Medical and Physical Journal in 1799. A man served Psilocybe semilanceata mushrooms he had picked on a walk through London's Green Park to his family for breakfast. The results were alarming. The doctor who treated them later described how the youngest child was "attacked with fits of immoderate laughter, nor could the threats of his father or mother refrain him'. How wonderfully English! A child rebelling by laughing, after being drugged by his father, and then getting reprimanded for it.

In 1955, Valentina Pavlovna Wasson and R Gordon Wasson became the first known Europeans to actively participate in an indigenous mushroom ceremony. They published an article in *Life* magazine. Inspired by their work Timothy Leary travelled to Mexico, to experience psilocybin mushrooms himself. When he returned to Harvard University, where he was lecturing, he and Richard Alpert started the Harvard Psilocybin Project, promoting psychological and religious study of psilocybin and other psychedelic drugs. They conducted research with psilocybin on prisoners and later to graduate divinity students, but this inevitably caused controversy. Leary and Alpert were dismissed from their jobs in 1963 and they turned their attention toward promoting the psychedelic experience to the nascent hippie counterculture.

The popularisation of psychedelics by Leary and others, led to the use of magic mushrooms throughout the world. By the early 1970s, many psilocybin mushroom species were 'promoted' from temperate North America, Europe and Asia and were widely collected. Books describing methods of cultivation were also published and the wide availability of mushrooms has made them one of the most widely used of the psychedelic drugs. In present times psilocybin use has been reported widely among groups from Central Mexico to Oaxaca, including groups of Nahua, Mixtecs, Mixe, Zapotecs and others. This was exactly the area we were in, and the indigenous groups we were meeting. Mexico has the highest number of magic mushroom types, with more than 53 recorded, compared to 22 types in Canada and the USA, 16 in Europe, 15 in Asia and 4 types in Africa.

Armed with all this knowledge, we were interested to see this town. The interest lasted all of ten minutes. The centre of the mountain town was just a huge taxi rank full of soap dodgers and alternative people. To me, that's a code word for people who don't work and never grew up. That could be my own prejudice, but when I saw a sixty-five-year-old man, in round glasses, balding, with a long lank pony tail, communing with a speed bump, my patience was nearly gone. The icing on the cake was when we were offered the Peruvian drug, Ayahuasca, within ten minutes of arrival. We were already out of there. There was not much to report about the town. It consisted of a coffee shop, selling stale cakes and washing-up flavoured coffee. Unusual for an area famous for its mountain coffee. There were hundreds of cabanas and hostel rooms, stuffed to the hilt with tripping people.

Somehow, I couldn't grasp how people could spend hours in a minivan, on dangerous mountain roads, so that they could take drugs; magic mushrooms and Ayahuasca, neither of which were part of any of these tourists' cultures. This was drug tourism and I was too old for this shit. As far as I was concerned, this area was beautiful enough to 'trip' on, without drugs. We had no urge to commune with nature, or the Lord right now, so we made do with heading straight out the other side of the village and into our comfort zone; beautiful riding, local villages and not a tripping Gringo to be seen anywhere. Or a tacky mushroom-shaped house, or a tacky cup or statuette. The real world to me.

We breathed a sigh of relief, but annoyingly my sigh of relief was not as deep as Cathy's. There was something wrong with my breathing. I knew we were over 2500 metres and neither of us function very well over that feeble altitude. Oh well, we all react differently. It was time to get down to sea level again. The Tenere is also starved of oxygen when at altitude and runs like a geriatric train with asthma. We all needed more oxygen. We had two choices of route back to Puerto Escondido. A tar road with more than 400 twisties and mega trucks, trying to flatten motorcyclists on every corner, brakes screeching and smelling as they hurtled down the mountainside, killing everything in their path. That would take six hours of solid riding.

The other option was the one I wanted to do for the *Adventure Bike Rider* article, and Cathy was just as keen, as usual. It was a gruelling ten-hour, dirt road, river crossing, landslide, flash flood, desolate, corrugated, boulder strewn, slippery stone, no town, no petrol, no provisions, hell road. Perfect. Our dream. No people, beautiful scenery and photography, and the possibility of being eaten by a cougar or jaguar. What more could one ask for. After a quick test of my breathing capabilities; I had none, no change to my laboured breathing. It was decided to take the asphalt route and return for a third time to face the tough road, another day.

It was a good decision. We wound our way down the mountain, distancing ourselves with every kilometre from the drug tourists, who were the only traffic passing us in the opposite direction. Such was my desperation to get away, that I rode like a Dakar rider, and managed to boil the brake fluid, which led to a catastrophic failure of my rear brakes. In English, that meant, I nearly went off a cliff. By the way, if you have brake fade, and it was my first time in 40 years of riding, do not put cold water on the disc or the brakes. The change in temperature can cause cracking and damage. Wait twenty minutes, commune with nature and then ride so you don't need the brakes. Simple. The brakes improved, but my breathing worsened. This was strange. After seven hours of tiring hairpins and crampy legs, we finally saw the sea on the horizon. I was worse.

Time to visit my good friend, HAM - or Hospital Angel del Mar, to give it its full title. The village people builders had left and it was a truly smart experience. A camp night duty doctor did a few tests and said:

"You have Covid."

The next day I returned for the proper test, and yes, it was positive (This was in April 2021).

Keep positive (but not in a Covid sense). Failure is temporary, regret is forever. A minor hiccup in life's rich tapestry of accidents.

Enjoying nature: butterfly migration (Neotropical Giant Blue Morpho Didius) in Peru

Engulfed by a Giant Elephant Ear palm outside Cali, Colombia. There are two types of elephant ears: alocasias and colocasias (pictured). Colocasias display their leaves with tip of the heart pointing down, and prefer full sun and consistent moisture. Alocasias hold the tip of their leaves out or upward and prefer well-drained soil and a little shade

Tough times on the road: top left, ideal resting place; top right, need to clean boots; above, including the fuel and panniers, lifting 250 kilogrammes for the fifth time in a day is fun!...

...but a good meal is never far away. Baby Caiman (top), Long-eared desert rabbit stew or Tarantula soup anyone?

The bonus of circumnavigating continents: the ocean is never far away to cool down

All the gear, all the time (AGAT). Ride safe people

Chapter Nineteen
My Mother is Drifting Away… and it Hurts

I am the biggest fan of 'adventure motorcycling' that you will ever meet. We all know the cliches; 'Four wheels will move the body, two wheels will move the soul'; 'A bike on the road, is worth two in the garage'; 'Sometimes it takes a whole tank of fuel, on winding roads, before you can think straight'.

The reason that they are clichés, is because they remain true, throughout the generations. When someone says I am going for a ride to 'clear the cobwebs', we know exactly what they mean. Being clinically hyperactive, it takes a lot for me to quieten down my brain, and anything that requires 100% of my attention and focus I find liberating, and soothing, and that is the closest I have ever been to being totally happy and content. Idle is my enemy. The open road, the challenge, the technical difficulties, and the fresh air, are my therapy. There is nothing else in my life that gives me that feeling of freedom, and elation, feeling alive, and energised. It is the ability to free my mind, and focus solely on the here and now, that is so addictive. Enjoying the moment, as they say. I know that this is true for many of you. That is why we ride. 'We don't ride motorcycles to add days to our lives, but to add life to our days'. So true, whoever coined that one.

The other aspect of riding, that non-riders find difficult to grasp, is the danger element. Motorcycles are dangerous. Motorcycling is very unforgiving of inattention, ignorance, incompetence, stupidity, and lack of experience. Never twist your throttle with your ego. Never compete on the road. Compete with the road, and yourself. We all know this, but it is the danger element of bikes that bond us. Weird as we are. There is also the obvious point, that motorcycle culture is something that riders enjoy, no matter how different they are, in terms of religion, gender, language, race, skin color, or waist size. Even if they have a BMW GS. We accept everyone. Obese is not so good on a motorcycle though. Or serial killers.

When you combine the freedom of thought, and the danger element of motorcycling, it is a giddy mix. Not to put a dampener on things, it is a temporary escape, an opportunity to sort out your mind, and give you space doing it. It doesn't matter how far you ride, you will never escape your guilt, whether it is leaving family, mistakes you have made, wrong relationship decisions, wrong job decisions, you name it. I am no different. Motorcycling, without doubt, has given me the best years of my life. I wish I could just ride into the sunset, ramp off a pyramid, and shoot to the stars. Not that easy. I love some people deeply, as we all do. Motorcycling solves most of my hurt, but not all.

I think that most of you who know by now, or I hope you do, that I am a pretty positive person. But there is something I have been struggling with for the last three years. It is in no way unique, it is 'the cycle of life'. It doesn't make it any easier. My mother has had a suspected stroke and has dementia kicking in. It is my ultimate nightmare. My love for my mother knows no bounds. This is a very cruel way to lose a mother. I am sure everyone experiences it differently, and deals with it differently, but the same thread runs through all of it; total sadness.

No longer will I be able to have those conversations that I enjoyed so much, and took for granted that they would be forever. Selfishness crept in. I always wanted my parents to be proud of me, as does everyone, I am sure. I know my brother feels the same. When my first book on Africa was published, I was so excited for my parents to read it and give me their opinion. It was so important to me. I was nervous. My father rapidly responded and heaped praise on my writing, as a dad would. I was still super pleased. I asked if Mum had read it and the response was, "Not yet, she will get round to it."

That didn't sound like my Mum, who could do a thousand things at once.

"Yes, she has just started it."

But it became evident that my mother was not going to read my book. Because she could not. Her concentration levels had all but disappeared. Living my selfish life, rushing around on my motorbike, trying to break meaningless records, had once again made me blinkered to my dad's situation too. Also, he hid it well. Like many partners with a suffering spouse, they like to hide the severity of the situation. My father managed it in most emails and phone calls, to ease my worries.

I shouldn't have been surprised. My dad has always been, Mr. Smooth, and the glue that holds us all together. What an idiot I am, not to have seen it earlier.

"Your mother is sleeping."

"Mum's upstairs, we will call tomorrow."

But eventually, comments were popped in, "Your mother has put on weight. She has no motivation. I got her out for a short walk but she wanted to go home."

"Mum's memory is going a bit."

It is a slow drip of information, when you are thousands of kilometres away. Also, your brain doesn't want to accept the words. You want your mum to be, always there, always supportive, indestructible mum. It is easier to ignore the truth.

Wendy in 'Cats'

When we returned to England, after the circumnavigation of South and Central America and Mexico, it was a devastating blow to my heart, that I will never forget. My mother is a fantastic actress, artist, TV presenter, business woman and writer and much, much more. But the most important thing, that you can't explain in writing, is who she was when you met her. She was magnetic and dramatic, and positive and it always, always affected those around her.

At the very end of the '60s my mother was blonde, tanned and married to a super cool man, living in Kenya with two, blonde, bowl-cut haired, small children. Mum had huge hair, hippie dresses and outfits, but somehow presented herself, and pulled it off, like a chic *Vogue* cover. Mum was loud, but not overbearing, good-looking and very popular. She is quite simply a very nice person, with intense energy. So when I arrived at the door of my parents, I was emotionally punched. The next week was a massive adjustment. No longer were there discussions about travel, film, theatre, books, adventure; about people, about family, about life. Everything was condensed down to basics. The worst thing was Mum's eyes. She looked scared and bewildered, and said so. It showed in her eyes, the window to the soul. That spark, vitality and sharpness, that inspirational wit was disappearing. Now, it was the clichés, that we all hear about, but can never be prepared for, until it becomes personal. When it is the woman who brought you up from birth, nurtured you, taught you, kept you safe, and loved you unconditionally, despite your million faults and mistakes; that cannot get closer to a dagger in your heart.

When it finally dawns, that there is no past to relive. That you will never ever again have a deep, emotional and meaningful conversation with one of the biggest loves of your life, it is a part of you that is dying also. We are who we love.

When a lifetime of shared memories and growth, as a family, boils down to:

"Where are my glasses, have you seen my glasses? I am sure they were here."

"Would any one like a cup of tea," after having made five cups in the last twenty minutes.

This may sound funny and trivial to many, and totally recognisable behaviour to others; it is the beginning of a nightmare, for Mum and us. The worst thing was to see the frustration in Mum's eyes. Don't get me wrong. She seemed totally normal and chatty on the surface, but I could see the confusion in her eyes. Eventually everyone saw it. Then Mum saw it.

She knew what was happening, to some extent, and we tried to talk about it. She knew there was no going back, no miracle cure. She knows, and we know that she is drifting away. She even says to me, more frequently now:

"I am scared of dying Spen."

Drifting, is the only word I can use, because it somehow sounds gentle, and easier to write. But it is not drifting. It is a total wrench, a tearing of your heart, about the frailty of life, and the importance of love. Love for your family is pure. So, it hurts, so much, when it goes wrong. People from the dawn of time, have been saying:

"If only I had told her how much I loved her, how much I appreciated her."

That has got to be the most normal feeling anybody could possibly have. It shows love. Love is guilt too, you know. Tell the people you love, how much. I understand it if many of you, right now are probably reading this and going, "Jesus, this is a bit heavy. I thought it was a motorbike adventure book."

I agree. It is a motorbike adventure book, but sadly, real life gets in the way. This book goes back to humorous anecdotes in about five pages, if you want to make a coffee and skip this bit. But if you are someone who can relate to this read on.

The next thing that's taken away is my mum's independence. No more driving. Then the danger and safety element; burning meals, leaving candles alight, etc. making constant cups of tea, because it is something she can grasp, and it is welcoming and family-orientated. Mum had the rug of independence pulled from under her, so hit depression and panic attacks. So then you don't want to go to the shop, or even out, and the spiral begins. Physically and mentally, this is another blow. Then your motivation drops, then you start sleeping. It is the vicious truth of the brain dying. Terrifying.

I want my mum back. I want to discuss her life in Kenya, breakdowns in Amboseli Game Reserve, travelling across the world with two babies. Living in a hut in Machakos, Kenya, my dad building the first primary school there and my mum being the teacher. I want to talk about the best days of her life, what accomplishments she is most proud of. I want to know how she felt when they decided to move to Kenya when I was six months old, and Simon was two. I want to know who Mum considers her best friend to be, her favourite country, or singer, or worst experience. I know the answers to most of these, but I just want to ask them again. I want to get the same answers I am so used to, the favourite stories I have heard a million times. Everything I have done, I have done to make my parents proud. To have one of them disappear, slowly, is like a guiding light, a motivation, to be good and true, and strong, and most importantly, different; was fading.

When we had to leave to try and conquer the Darien Gap, I had to say goodbye to my mother and father. It was heart-wrenching. I waved goodbye, as Mum stood in the doorway of the beautiful Malt House, that she had turned into a work of art over the last twenty five years, but could sadly no longer cope with. I knew this was a real goodbye. A goodbye to the last shred of lucidity that Mum was hanging on to.

I knew already that her thoughts, and mind, were in a perpetual loop. It doesn't take a trained psychiatrist. When someone is disappearing in front of you, the look in their eye is not the one you have known so well, for fifty three years. The vacant, no, that is too harsh a word; the non-connected look is so heartbreaking to see in your own mother. I so desperately wanted to hold this small, frail, shadow of the huge character I had once known, and never let go. She made me, she's my blood and rock, and the biggest supporter you could ever dream of.

I have been crying for most of this chapter, because I am losing my mum, but so is Simon. My dad is slowly losing the love of his life for fifty seven years. His pain and worry must be indescribable, but if we can have Mum with us for the next ten years, no matter what state she is in, we are the privileged ones.

I am writing this in Mexico and I am 12,000 kilometres from my parents. I don't know why, but we left, against all my gut instincts. I had to act like the hard adventurer and head off again, to try and do something useful, no matter how misguided. When we left, I gave Mum and Dad a hug and a, "See you soon," tough man comment. Then we got in the car, waved goodbye and drove to the airport. That simple. I was breaking inside. I promised myself that I would conquer the Darien Gap within six months, and go back to England, to spend time with my mum. Covid put a halt to that. We are still sitting here, while talking to my parents on Messenger. Mum is now coaxed to the phone, but doesn't even really know where we are. She thinks we live down the road, and wonders why we don't visit. This is the cruelty of life, a person who was a 'starter' of things; ending up, a shell.

My mother started clubs, theatre groups, international arts and crafts events, and wrote plays for both European and African audiences.

She was responsible for the inception of Children's Television in the

Wendy the authoress

Seychelles, and was the main presenter. In Swaziland she was a presenter, and theatre actress, and received a MacMillan award for her play on the life of Sarah Bernhard. She also started a secretarial business called Expertype, which is still running in the capital, Mbabane, forty years later. On her return to UK she taught drama at Christ Church University, to overseas students. She started a school, a 'thinking woman's club' and had just finished a book of short stories, called *Mind the Raven*, when her dementia kicked in.

She even kick-started some people's careers as well as boosting so many others' confidence in themselves. She inspired people to do more. The only thing Mum didn't start was trouble, because she was a nice, moral, tough and loyal woman. And beautiful as can be.

The cruelest thing about this scenario is that the images I want in my head, of my memories, are of Mum dancing happily around a fire in the Highlands of Kenya, while Simon and I made a camp in the back seat of our car. I want to remember her pushing a VW Beetle out of the mud in a game reserve, or dancing across a stage, or presenting a children's TV programme, and seeing how the children sitting around her, were so enthralled and consumed, by attention and wonder at this powerhouse of artistic expression. I miss my mum's bohemian clothes and her deep emotions. Sadly, these are not the images I have in my head, and worse is to come. I see an old, disorientated, scared woman, none of those words could I ever have imagined using, in describing Mum. I made a mistake leaving her and want to go back as soon as possible.

The above was all written over six months ago. I never managed to get back to England. My absolute nightmare has happened. I received 'that' phone call. My mother has died from a massive brain clot. I am ruined. I cannot write about it now. It is too raw.

Chapter Twenty
The Jewel and the Clown

I do apologise for going on about Mexico and then my mother as neither are about South America, but I have found that when writing a book I cannot segregate it from real life. I cannot divide it and sanitise it. It takes two years to write a book and I don't want to banish all the thoughts and things that happened during the writing of this book, because they are part of the book. Having said that, back to South America.

The challenge of Venezuela started before we even got into the country. But it was a challenge well worth fighting for. We had been filled with negativity about our thirteenth, and final, country in our circumnavigation of South America. The news was plastered with comments about people eating dogs in the street, muggings, robberies, murders, scams, pickpockets, kidnappings and violence, all day, everyday, everywhere, and the total collapse of a state. There were government warnings (USA mainly), to not, under any circumstances, visit Venezuela, especially the mining towns where, apparently, they will cook you and eat you immediately. We are not the types to listen to the news, or even read it on the net. Of the one hundred and thirty five countries I have visited, I have done research into... none. That does not mean that I am ignorant of the countries I am about to visit. Not at all. I just don't like to follow the current news about any place. I like to approach a new country with a totally open mind. But such was the constant stream of negativity from family and friends during our months in Brazil, that Cathy decided she would not be coming with me into Venezuela. I was devastated, and I know she was.

We had clocked up an amazing 105,000 kilometres through 12 countries, and it was only Venezuela blocking our return to Colombia, where we started, some two years before. I wanted to be with her, and wanted her to complete the circumnavigation, but Cathy said, "If we both die, our children will have no parents. If you die, at least I am here for them." Sounded logical. Still depressing to enter the final country alone. But it wasn't to be.

After months of negativity, the scene at the Brazilian border with Venezuela changed Cathy's mind immediately. How superb.

We arrived late at night and managed to get a room, only two kilometres from the Santa Elena border. The whole town was a refugee camp, but not like the ones you imagine. The level of organisation was amazing. The roads were lined with makeshift tarpaulins, plastic sacks, gunny bags, all propped up with sticks and string and plastic bags, much like any refugee camp. Beds were made of cardboard boxes and rags. Diesel drums with the tops cut off, were on every street corner, fire and smoke billowing from them, creating a surreal, misty, acrid scene, as we drove through. Groups of young guys stretched their hands out to the flames, the chill of the late evening kicking in. Groups of children ran around, giggling, their mothers scolding them and trying to get them into tin baths that were lined up on the local football field. The bus station, directly opposite our room, had been spilt into two. On one side, it was just a huge clothes line, and on the other side was a cooking area, consisting of three large fires, circled with bricks. This was the women's social area, and all we could hear were whoops of laughter, as they stirred huge pots of steaming beans and rice.

On a metal street sign, with a fire underneath it, a grinning Venezuelan in a Chelsea shirt was cooking up huge strips of fat and bone. No idea where the meat went, as he only had scraps, but it smelt delicious, and looked appropriately greasy and tasty. Next to him, a woman was crushing fruit and adding it to 25 litre plastic drums of water and sugar. Food and drink for the whole camp seemed to be underway. We were so impressed. There was no arguing, no raising of voices, and although they didn't have houses, shops or amenities that any normal town would expect as a minimum, they had somehow delegated and divided all the jobs necessary to survive, and had produced a transient, but well run, street town. There was even a small bar on one street corner, with a generator, music distorted and blaring, but cheery and uplifting, like all Brazilian and Venezuelan music. There was a small overgrown park, with some rusty swings and slides. Four men were busy with machetes, cutting the grass back, under the light of one dim kerosene lamp, presumably for the children to have somewhere to play. Superb. There were a few tents scattered around, all hooked up to the electricity from overhead, a spaghetti junction of wires running between them. These were focal points for meetings. Dogs and cats ran around, scavenging what they could. There were no police or army, or officials to be seen, but the place was so serene. Remarkable really. We ended up spending the whole evening in the refugee camp and only made it to our room at 1.45 in the morning. It was a pivotal point for Cathy. We met Abraham and Carmen, a couple with two children, who we chatted to for hours.

"It is getting bad now. There is no work for anyone, and we are short of many products, but the worst is no food and no medicine," said Abraham.

"If our children get sick, what can we do?" Carmen added, pointing at the two young girls, playing with a chameleon, clinging to a stick.

"So, is it true that there are starving people, murdering each other for food, and dogs and cats being eaten in the street? Is it true that the rich were told on TV, that they must label their garbage, so that the poor can eat it?" I asked.

"I have not heard that, but it can happen," replied Abraham.

"It is getting worse, but you can visit, no problem. Venezuelan people are wonderful and will be happy to see you."

Cathy did two things I have never seen her do. One, she changed her mind, and decided to come to Venezuela. I was over the moon. Secondly, she offered Abraham and his family our tent. We never ever do things like that, but on this occasion I could not argue the point. They had small children and no shelter. It was made all the more worthwhile when Carmen took the inner lining of the tent, and gave it to her neighbours, who also had two small girls. Brilliant.

Don't get me wrong. This was not your typical, TV refugee camp, full of starving children, with distended bellies, scrabbling around in the dirt. That is on another level. But this was still a humanitarian crisis, with more than 4 million people willing to uproot and move to an uncertain future, in a foreign land. Nobody chooses to make themselves homeless and penniless, and traipse towards the unknown. So, why were people leaving Venezuela in droves? Venezuela has a population of 28 million, and in the past four years a staggering four million have left. Nicholas Maduro is the man to blame for the largest exodus in modern history.

Maduro (above) began his working life as a bus driver, but rose to become a trade union leader. He was appointed to a number of positions under President Hugo Chavez, and was (ironically, now that we have seen what he has done), described by the *Wall Street Journal* as 'the most capable administrator and politician in Chavez' inner circle'. After Chavez' death on 5th March 2013, Maduro assumed the presidency.

He has ruled Venezuela by decree since 2013, and has done an appalling job. Despite having the world's largest oil reserves, extreme shortages of many staple goods and plummeting living standards have led to protests, beginning in 2014, that escalated into daily marches nationwide, repression of dissent groups and a massive decline in Maduro's popularity. On this occasion, it was the *New York Times*, with a slightly different opinion: 'Maduro's administration is responsible for grossly mismanaging the economy and plunging it into a deep humanitarian crisis, whilst attempting to crush the opposition by jailing or exiling critics, and using lethal force against anti-government protests.'

Under Maduro's leadership, more than 10,000 people have been subject to extrajudicial killings, and this is a stab in the dark estimate. On 26th March 2020, the US Department of Justice indicted Maduro on charges of drug trafficking and narco terrorism, and the State Department offered a 15 million-dollar reward for information to bring Maduro to justice. It did not work, and what has it got to do with the

USA, anyway? Another subject there, sorry. So Maduro has kept a grip on power. Everything, except outright war, has been tried, to depose him. Even Maduro's nationality has been called in to doubt, in an attempt to oust him through non-violent means.

A group of prominent Venezuelans (probably not any more), asked the National Assembly to investigate whether Nicholas Maduro was Colombian, in an open letter. Maduro didn't help matters by refusing to show his birth certificate and changing his birthdate on three separate public occasions. He has lied so much, he doesn't even know when he was born. Remember Nicholas, if you never lie, you never have to remember anything. This ploy to oust him didn't work either. It gets sillier, and would be a hilarious story, if the backdrop was not so serious.

During a period when there were food shortages in the country and it was obvious it was getting worse, Maduro was criticised for gaining a lot of weight quickly, whilst his people were getting hungrier. Maduro timed his response perfectly, like a clichéd South American dictator. He was filmed, live, in front of the nation, before an important address, unaware that cameras were rolling, pulling two empanadas from under his desk, and wolfing them down. He started his address spluttering, mouth full, skin flushed, the look completed with moustache crumbs. Classic timing. He still wasn't ousted. For those of you from the UK, an empanada is like a Cornish pasty. Hogging two of those down, on live TV, in front of starving viewers, is not conducive to a long political career.

So, what next? A drone attack, of course. On 4th August 2018, at least two drones armed with explosives were detonated at a rally where Maduro was giving one of his two hundred hour-long speeches. Good enough reason to blow him up, apart from his human rights abuses. The explosions were miles away and didn't even ruffle the crumbs in Maduro's moustache. Not the kind of assassination attempt you would want to claim you had planned.

So we were entering Venezuela, Cathy on the recommendations of refugees who were fleeing. Not too bright really, but I understood her change of heart. The refugees were so positive about their country and people. It was only the president and the government and 'politics criminal' that they mentioned. It was absolutely beautiful.

So, in we went, through the South Eastern border with Brazil, at Pacaraima, leading into the town of Santa Elena de Uairen, the only border in Venezuela that was open. What an arrival it was. You are immediately riding in the fantasy land that is the 'Park Nacional Canaima', a 30,000 square kilometre area, known as the Gran Sabana. The Canaima National Park is the sixth largest in the world, the size of Belgium and is a well-deserved UNESCO World Heritage Site. Sixty five percent of the park is occupied by plateaus of rock called Tepuis, table top mountains, with vertical walls. These geological formations are between 1.5 and 2 billion years old, making them one of the oldest formations in the world. The most famous is Mt Roraima. Think of Table Mountain in Cape Town, South Africa, but on steroids.

The mountain really does loom over you, and follow you, wherever you go, much like Mona Lisa's eyes. To add to the wonder, there are waterfalls everywhere. The sheer cliffs of the plateau create wondrous drop offs, a perfect example being Angel Falls (pictured).

Angel Falls is the highest waterfall in the world at 979 metres. By comparison, the largest single drop on Niagara Falls is a mere 50 metres, making Angel Falls around sixteen times bigger. Angel Falls descends from a large tepui called Auyantepui, which in the language of the Pemon people means the 'House of the Devil'. It would seem reasonable to assume that the romantic name was somehow a continuation of this spiritual theme, but this is not the case. Although the indigenous people evidently knew of the waterfall's existence, the name only came into existence in the 20th century, when it was 'discovered' by American aviator, Jimmie Angel. He first flew over it in 1934 when looking for deposits of gold ore. Few people believed his story of discovering a 'mile high waterfall', just as they dismissed his earlier claims of discovering a river of gold, though both stories were true.

Jimmie Angel did manage to finance a further visit in 1937 and decided to land his Flamingo monoplane on the top of Auyantepui. Not a good plan. He landed the plane successfully, sort of, but unfortunately the wheels became bogged down in deep, wet mud, and the plane nosedived. It caused enough damage to be unfixable, but the passengers were in one piece. Just. The plane's occupants then had the arduous task of climbing down the Tepui, and reaching civilisation. This involved an eleven-day trek to the settlement of Kamaratu. The whole escape became a worldwide new story and Jimmie Angel became immortalised by having the waterfall named after him. His aircraft remained embedded in the mud on top of the Tepui, until 1970 when it was disassembled and removed. It has since been rebuilt and is on display in the Aviation Museum of Maracay.

The park is still remote, with only one road connecting towns, and a series of dirt tracks to the rest. Most transport within the park is done by light plane from the airstrip built by the Capuchin missions, or by foot, or canoe. Or in our case, by motorcycle. The park is home to the Pemon Indians, part of the Carib group. We glimpsed small settlements as we rode past, getting enthusiastic waves. Always a good thing. In such a beautiful environment, and with almost nothing around, except the odd Armadillo, green iguana or Roraima mouse, it was easy to forget the negativity that had surrounded our visit for the four weeks prior to entering. The first sign that all was not right came when we needed fuel. After a hundred kilometres of nothing, we came across a snaking line of traffic, waiting at the 'Estacion de Servicio Kamoiran', a two pump petrol station. They had no fuel and were not sure if it would arrive that day. We decided to head off on fumes, and see where we got to. This fuel situation would affect our whole journey, and I even witnessed a murder because of it. More of that later. The next hint that things were a bit off in Venezuela, was in the town of Las Claritas, the first town after the National Park solitude. We tried to get a cheap room and some cash, before heading off towards Ciudad Bolivar, the next morning. When you have been in a country, like Zimbabwe, or Venezuela, that is in total economic and social collapse, things you took for normal, become far from it. I mention Zimbabwe for a reason. We all know the stories, when Zimbabwe was in economic freefall, that people were pushing wheelbarrows of millions of Zimbabwean dollars, to supermarkets. One wheelbarrow of money might buy you a loaf of bread. We found out that Venezuela was no different. Not a single business would accept cards and there was no money at all in the three ATM machines. In fact, they were just shells of machines, long since vandalised. All we had were $20 notes. No one had enough money to change even $20 and the banks had also folded. Closed and forlorn-looking. Eventually, a fairly affluent guy of about sixty, in a powder-blue Ram truck, stopped and asked us if we needed help. I explained the money dilemma and he promised to return in forty minutes with enough Bolivares (the local currency) for $60. True to his word, he returned with a suitcase. Not any old suitcase. One of those massive, beige ones, with straps, from the '70s. You could fit your family inside it. But it was not full of people. It was full of money.

To give you some idea of the absurdity we faced, the highest denomination was the one million Bolivar note, which was worth about 20 cents. That value dropped daily. So for our $60, we received 14,909, 258.35 VEF (Bolivares). It was the first time in my life that I was a multi-millionaire, and I took a silly picture of our table covered in some of the wad of cash. It wasn't funny though, it was tragic. Furthermore, we only had a motorbike. If we changed $100, we would need to upgrade to a van. After a fitful night's sleep, atop wads of cash, we headed off towards the next town, the no-go, gold mining towns, more specifically, the aptly named El Dorado, or 'the golden one'.

A common theme when you are travelling is that you are always told by the locals, "We are lovely and friendly, and cuddly, but in the next town; they will kill you."

This was taken to the extreme in Venezuela, and if we weren't skinned and made into canoes within the next few hundred kilometres, then I would be surprised. Always carry a fork, so if the indigenous want to make a canoe out of you, just prick yourself a few times, and you will no longer be waterproof. We just smiled, thanked them for the prophesies of doom, and continued. We pushed on through the grasslands and misty mountains, the igneous bases on which they stand, estimated to be three billion years old. The rocks and mountains in the Gran Sabana area are closely related to those in Africa, and were formed when the two continents were joined.

The road snaked through the valleys between the tepui, waterfalls cascading everywhere, and as we headed closer to El Dorado, the grassy savannahs changed into large groves of Moriche Palm. Eventually we were riding through dense, green jungle, part of the 'moist forest' range of the Guayanan Highlands. It was stunning and no wonder this whole area was the inspiration for Sir Arthur Conan Doyle's book, *The Lost World*. Two kilometres outside El Dorado we spotted a very strange sight; a Swiss flag fluttering over a river. We took the little dirt road, baby caiman scattering off the sunny red soil and into the pools along the side of the road. We came to a thatched hut, pulled the bike up, popped a squashed Coke can under the foot rest, to stop it sinking in the soft ground, and dismounted. A chubby, round-faced guy of about thirty, with a scraggy Che beard, came out from the shadows of the hut, and approached us with a huge smile. This was Jeremiah, and he was running a small camp with three rooms and a little restaurant next to the Cuyuni River. It was a beautiful little place, with a lawn in the jungle and a small sandy beach in front of the restaurant, overlooking the sixty-metre-wide river. We immediately decided to stay for the night, because although basic, it was cheap and right down our alley; totally peaceful.

The camp was owned by his father, an ex-Swiss Army hard nut. (I asked him if he had a Swiss Army knife, he wasn't impressed.) Andreas only wore shorts, army boots and no shirt. He was about sixty, with a skinhead, mahogany brown body, and a scar from the centre of his stomach, at the waistline, all the way to his chest. When we first met him he came striding across the lawn from the Cuyuni River direction, with a twelve-foot Anaconda draped around his neck. Some impressive bush jewellery.

Andreas ran the camp and a bush mechanic workshop, while his wife pottered around, looking perpetually confused at where she had ended up. Jeremiah and his pretty, petite wife, Maria, lived in Caracas, the capital, where they were both 'studying and making baby'. They were down to visit their parents and to see if they could cope with jungle life next to the Cuyuni River. Jeremiah was having a constant battle with mosquitoes and the heat, and wasn't coping. (This nearly led to a tragedy, which I will come to.) His dad sauntered round like it was a spring day in the Alps, but I believe he was made of different mettle to his son. I suspected that Andreas, a Swiss man living a few kilometres from a dangerous gold mine, in Venezuela, had a few fingers in a few dangerous pies. My suspicions were backed up in two ways.

Firstly, Jeremiah told us that two years previously some people had come to the camp, and shot his father twice in the stomach. Andreas had survived and even drove to hospital, holding his stomach in. Hence, the livid surgery scar, that looked like a zip. Apparently it was because of a dispute he had back in Switzerland. We never found out why he was shot, but I am sure it wasn't for running an un-licenced florist shop. My hunch is that Andreas was an ex-mercenary. (If you weren't and you read this, Andreas, my apologies. Don't kill me, I have children.)

Secondly, I went with Andreas to El Dorado Town and he acted like he was the mayor of the bloody place. To fully understand this you need to know a bit about El Dorado. This was a town that his son, Jeremiah and daughter-in-law, Maria, refused to visit, along with most of the world.

El Dorado was founded in the 1890s and believe me, it has moved on a lot since then; about two years. It is the Wild West, or Wild East, to be geographically correct.

Gold mining was the reason for its existence, and still is. The town is totally insane. It consists of two main, muddy streets, the edges packed with stalls, fighting for space. The frames of the stalls were made out of roughly cut branches, the roofs fashioned from bits of corrugated iron, black plastic and blue tarpaulin strips, that looked suspiciously like United Nations tents. The vendors were colourfully dressed, and the fruit and vegetables similarly, but everyone was covered in a cloud of red dust from the waist up, and splashes of red mud from the waist down. Motorcycles and Tuk Tuks rushed around, avoiding each other in Valentino Rossi-type move. There were stalls selling mobile phone covers, chargers, out-of-date calendars, batteries, fish in plastic bags, upgraded fish in glass bowls, blowup swimming rings (what?), flip flops, vermin killer pellets that were bright green, broken watches, and women's stockings. There were bras that you could sleep in, ripped mosquito nets, SIM cards, Pawpaws, soft drinks, melted chocolate, wigs, and thousands of hair products. There was shampoo, moisturisers for Africa, umbrellas, Devilled Ham Spread, premium quality, in a dusty can, Rico Jam, and even Cock-flavoured soup mix. There was Gama fresh cement mix, a pudding, and even a washing powder called Vag Fresh. There was carne endiablada, Marichun Instant lunch noodles, plastic dinosaurs, pictures of Miley Cyrus, Madonna and Lay Gaga, and Michael Jackson's glove. All photos were signed by the stars. Don't forget safety helmets, goggles, knee protectors and gold. The last one is vital. Everybody has gold. Everybody is wearing enough gold to be rich in Europe. It is weird. There are groups of prostitutes on the corner, adorned with enough gold to buy a villa in Tuscany. Don't ask me how the world market works, but it is surreal as hell. These people are evidently dirt poor, but have more chains than 50 Cents, the rapper (or his equivalent rapper, '35 Pence' in the UK, according to current exchange rates).

There were also tables outside some of the houses, where teenagers are selling marijuana and cocaine, neatly laid out and weighed, into small plastic bags, the contents evident to all. All of the street teenagers had guns, tucked in their oversize, affected by TV style, pants. The only police presence in this town is at the petrol station, which is where I found myself with Andreas, the suspected mercenary. There are queues of taxis, and motorbikes, and trucks and Tuk Tuks and cars, and army Hummers. Andreas just breezes to the front, past thirty vehicles, removes the chain that is blocking the entrance to the petrol station, and ushers me in. The army do not bat any simultaneous eyebrows. They just greet him, seriously, but respectfully. Wow. He has some clout. Interesting indeed. Now, just when you thought El Dorado could not get any dodgier, they added a prison.

The Centro Penitenciario de Oriente El Dorado is overcrowded and has been described by the world's press as 'notorious' and 'not fit to exist in the 21st century'. In 2020 the press reported the completion of an 'upgrade' to the prison. That sounds a bit like giving someone a cushion on the electric chair. OK. I can exaggerate, but the prison is even mentioned in the book *Papillon*, the dodgy French man I discussed in depth in the chapter on French Guiana. Apparently he was imprisoned here, but as he has been in every prison in South America, I take it with a pinch of salt. I don't think *Papillon* would survive in this town. It's too tough. So, anyway, when the prisoners get released, with no money and no prospects where do they go? Straight into El Dorado. It's a vicious soup of illegals and gold mining and drugs, but somehow one of the most welcoming towns we went to.

The prostitutes were hugging Cathy, offering her more revealing dresses, kilos of gold for pennies, and steaming hot coffee, from an urn, set on an open fire. It was superb. Somehow, I lost my dipstick at the petrol station, and I am not talking about Cathy. A random gold miner offered me his. I said no but he insisted, and I have this dipstick in my bike right now. He just filled the opening to his oil reservoir with a rag. What a man. I still feel guilty enough to drive back there. A bit far though. My petrol wait was less than five minutes, thanks to 'maybe a mercenary', Swiss dude, and we were out of there.

Not before we met a girl with a mega infection from a snake bite. She had been bitten on the back of her calf, just below the knee joint. The wound was open, a hole as big as half a tennis ball, revealing a weeping, pus-filled wound, surrounded by a livid red infection. Her whole leg had swollen and had gone stiff. I suspected septicemia, which can be fatal. Andreas picked her up, and put her gently into the back of his clapped-out pickup, with one flat tyre and three bald ones, and we went back to the 'scene of the shooting' camp. I knew that Cathy had antibiotics, and disinfectant, and love for the afflicted.

Outskirts of El Dorado

She did get sorted out, as best as Cathy could, but if that girl can walk properly, I would be extremely surprised. We were to find out that this was one of the biggest problems that the Venezuelan people faced. They had no medicine in the hospitals, even down to basics, like paracetamol.

It was time for Cathy and me to head off towards the centre of Venezuela, to Ciudad Bolivar. Our experiences and the lunacy that we would face in the next few months would only increase exponentially. If I had known that, I would have turned round. No, I would not. I would repeat the whole experience again, straight after writing this page. We left Andreas, his Anaconda and scars, his silent wandering wife, his son; mosquito-scared Jeremiah, and his 'keen to bear children' wife, Maria, and El Dorado; the winner of Dodgy Town of the Year Award, with mixed feelings. Everyone had been wonderful and I felt guilt at wanting to leave. There was an edge to this place, and I knew that one wrong comment, things could go south.

We drove eighty kilometres out of El Dorado and drove straight into an armed roadblock. We had our first domestic argument in five years. It was more of a bike-travelling domestic, but Cathy was not happy with my behaviour. She hasn't spoken to me since. Sorry, that was a lie. No; wishful thinking. Joking, Cathy. We have been through hundreds of armed roadblocks over five years, and have never had a problem.

Always the same routine, always the same behaviour; pull up slowly, turn off the engine, take off your helmet, get off the bike, put on the biggest smile you can, and muster the most enthusiastic greeting. This normally works. But it was not going to be the case this time. I made a spilt decision that something was wrong. For some reason, these guys didn't fit the bill. They were too white, as in, hadn't been in the sun recently. They were too organised. They were all holding their guns correctly, pointing at the ground. I was used to roadblock personnel swinging their guns around their heads. They were also too clean. I am trying to think of reasons why I didn't stop. I just knew instantly that something was up. I am not a conspiracy theorist who believes in mercenaries etc., and I haven't watched too many films, but I had heard that small groups of American mercenaries were trying to destabilise Venezuela from within. Whichever way these guys were leaning, I did not feel good stopping, and had no time to warn Cathy. There were four of them, positioned equidistantly across the road.

When I was waved down, I slowed the engine, slowed my thoughts and realised I was going to do one thing; rocket past them, they were not your run-of-the-mill roadblock. I knew my instincts were right. I slowed right down, put them off guard, and then accelerated between two of them. I accelerated off, hoping it would not be a repeat of my Kenyan bandit attack. I felt they would have to make one serious decision if they were going to shoot the only 'tourists' in Venezuela for years. As we pulled away with no sounds of gunshots, and disappeared around a corner I felt super proud. I got a slap on the back of my helmet.

"What the hell are you doing? We could have been shot!"

"Sorry I didn't feel good about those guys," I replied.

"I am on the back of the bike, and if they shoot, I am the one who gets killed," Cathy replied, instantly.

I thought about this one deeply, and came up with one of the smoothest lines I could imagine. Clint Eastwood would have been proud. Clint Westwood too.

"Yes Cathy, but if they had shot at us, the bullet would have gone through you, and into me."

Cathy looked at me quizzically; if you could, in a helmet, behind someone. Now the Clintina Eastwood comment came out; Cathy just said, "Fair enough."

End of motorcycle domestic.

Apart from that brief disagreement, we travelled for at least three kilometres, before the next disagreement.

"Not true," says Cathy.

The next stop was Ciudad Bolivar, bang in the centre of Venezuela. When a country is on its knees, some images stick with you. Although El Dorado was chaos, it was functioning, and had products. Bolivar city centre was a ghost town. There was nobody around. There was a large shiny supermarket, about the size of a medium-town Tesco, in the UK. When we went in, there was nothing on the shelves but toilet rolls and tissues of various shapes, sizes and colours, but that was it. Rows and rows of toilet paper, for people without food, or money. Because of the collapse of the monetary system, everybody carries a white card. It is a credit card and pays for absolutely everything, from a chewing gum for 100,000, to a bottle of shampoo for 1,000,000. All salaries were paid into these white card accounts, the money lasting for a week of each month. When we came out of the supermarket; almost immediately, expressing our apologies to the forlorn-looking cashier (not strictly a cashier, if there is no cash in the country), a woman of about twenty with two small children, begged us for some food. There wasn't any. There were no shops, no stalls, no fruit sellers, no cars, no bikes, nothing. We couldn't have fed her if we wanted to. We eventually found a huge colonial-type building, with a beautiful inner courtyard, shaded by a two-storey mango tree. We managed to get a room, and began to unpack our panniers, to air everything out, when we heard a commotion outside. It was the only four other people in the city, two Russians and their girlfriends, who were in Venezuela on a fishing trip. So there were four other foreigners in Venezuela. They wanted our room, as they had booked it months earlier. We quickly agreed and were super friendly, but we got nothing in return, not even a stoic Russian nod. Oh well!

Off towards San Cristobal, the border town with Colombia. We were going to end up there for two months, in an attempt to cross the border. The most amazing thing for me, and I know it sounds silly, but from Ciudad Bolivar towards San Cristobal, we were going to be following the Orinoco River. That name was etched in my heart from my youth. Like Ouagadougou, Timbuktu and other iconic names, my geography teacher, Richard Eyeington, obviously Mr. Eyeington to me, had planted the seed of wonder in my head, the seed my parents had been watering diligently. Richard and Enid Eyeington, wonderful philanthropic, people lovers, who dedicated themselves to helping orphans in Africa, through their SOS Villages, were shot and killed by burglars in Zambia, while they were watching TV. God is a cruel judge sometimes. Rest in peace.

The route from Ciudad Bolivar to San Cristobal was… beautiful. The people were beautiful, inside and out, and super pleased to have foreigners visiting. When we started descending into San Cristobal, the world turned magical. The Valley of Flowers took us totally by surprise. Because we were running late, we arrived as the sun was setting, behind a lush green mountain. There were fields and fields of flowers, on steep mountains, all the way to the road, and as far as the eye could see. Strips of colour stretching across the hills and over them. There was every colour imaginable, and the mountainside looked like the most incredible patchwork quilt. But it gets better. Every field was underlit by electric light bulbs, each farmer buying bulbs of the same colour as the flowers, he, or she, was growing. It was a fairytale sight. Never to be forgotten.

There are many valleys going into San Cristobal, this is the eighth on the right. Hope you don't find it. Put valleys aside, let's talk mountains, of the human variety. We came into San Cristobal, the beautiful border town with Colombia, in the far west of Venezuela. We had crossed the whole country, and what a jewel of a country. We would spend two months here before we would succeed in crossing back into Colombia, the starting point of our epically exciting, and profoundly happy, circumnavigation of South America. There were many twists and turns to negotiate during our time in San Cristobal, and thank God for the man mountain. Within fifteen minutes of checking into a room, because camping was impossible in the city, we met a mountain of a man, a man that was to have a profound effect on myself and Cathy. A wonderful Yeti of a human called Stefano Lottici.

A quick thought here. I hope that you are all getting used to my writing style, and that it is not too annoying when I jump from one subject to another. Not only does it mirror the way I think but it also exactly mirrors the speed of change, and the randomness of events, when you are on a motorcycle. One minute you can be in a cosy room; fifty kilometres later, you could be in a riot. You could leave in the morning from a coastal town, sweltering in 35 degrees; two hours later you are battling at 3,000 metres in a -3 degree wind. Things move fast from scenario to scenario and this is the evident addiction of adventure riding and travelling in general. Adrenaline and decision-making come to the fore, and it is euphoric, and never boring.

Right; back to Stefano Lottici and the insanity that he lived in. Six-foot nine inches tall, one hundred and eighty kilogramme Stefano, was waiting next to my bike when I came out the next morning. He made the Tenere look like a Transformer toy, and made me feel small, which is extremely rare. On every long-distance journey there are people that stand out for their purity of character, their selflessness, and their pure enthusiasm for the country that they live in. Ashraf, the Felucca boat owner in Aswan, Egypt; Carl, the crazy Canadian, my best friend; and this man, Stefano. If you take Bud Spencer, make him better looking, put him in a laboratory, and double him in size, we are getting somewhere. Then add a more manicured beard, and full, red lips. The lips were a bit disconcerting as Stefano loved pouting and pretending to kiss me, whenever we were in public. It is a bit worrying when a man twice your size follows you around a restaurant, pouting, with lips that look lip-sticked, going,

"I love you, Spencer."

I needn't have worried, it was just his humour. He had a supermodel girlfriend; I couldn't hope to compete with her, even with my endless legs in high heels.

But I never got used to Stefano after a few Tequilas, coming towards me, like a giant Grouper; getting revenge on a fisherman that had hooked him. As usual, I jumped the gun. On our first meeting I walked up to Stefano, who was staring at the motorcycle and said, "Hey man. How you doing?"

He looked me straight in the eye; which is a great start for me. People who look down, or look at you sideways, are not to be trusted, believe me. It's called 'shifty', and the eyes are the windows to the soul. They will always give your true feelings, and indeed intentions, away. After speech patterns and giveaways, psychologists and forensic anthropologists, and general crime buffs, focus a great deal on eye, head and hand movements. Stefano passed all the tests.

"I am fine. I saw your motorbike, and wanted to meet someone with so many stickers, so many countries. I can't believe it. You have been all these places." He extended his hand, his fingers making Korkers' best sausages look malnourished. We shook hands and not in a floppy, modern way; I knew we would be friends. Because of this, out-of-the-blue meeting, we were about to be introduced to the elite of Venezuelan society. We were to go to banquets, meet cocaine dealers, with women friends in bikinis, on horses. We were to meet Cartel, the Government and the Uruguayan and Colombian National football teams. We were to enter Colombia illegally and comeback. We were about to make life-long friends. And we were going to interview a kidnap victim, one of the most harrowing tales Cathy and I had ever heard. Before all this madness unfolded, within fifteen minutes of meeting Stefano, we were in his suitably huge Dodge truck, on the hunt for petrol for the bike, chatting away, as if we had been friends forever.

Another symptom of a collapsing country is a shortage of diesel and petrol. Cathy and I had struggled to get petrol, all the way through Venezuela. Fuel stations were either shut down, empty of fuel, or had queues snaking down the road. We drove past one petrol queue that we measured. It was eighteen kilometres long. It is not unusual for people to queue for up to ten hours to get fuel. Venezuela has the largest deposits of crude oil reserves in the world, so how did this absurd situation arise? With Venezuela's refinery sector in disarray after years of mismanagement, the country has become increasingly dependent on imported fuel to generate electricity, and transport essential goods, including food, medicine and humanitarian supplies. None of these are getting through now. The international lifeline has been cut off by sanctions, introduced by the administration of former President Ronald Chump. (Not a spelling mistake.) Experts are warning that the humanitarian crisis and subsequent exodus of people will be one of the worst in history if President Joe Biden (the present incumbent), does not lift restrictions that are preventing the South American country from swapping its huge crude oil reserves for refined diesel fuel from abroad. No diesel shipments have arrived in Venezuela since October 2020. I am totally anti sanctions on any country. I am not a politician and I realise that regimes, like those in South Africa, were partly toppled by sanctions, but it is not the way to go. Who suffers when there is no fuel, no food, no medicine, because of sanctions? It is the everyday man. The government and bigwigs continue to have their banquets and discuss the country's plight, whilst the man and woman on the street is crippled by sanctions, daily life reduced to scrabbling for food. War and sanctions are a no. Stefano seemed to live by different rules, and it was the first time I realised he was a man of influence, power and extreme wealth. Helpful in any country, but especially so in a place crippled to the extent that this was. We had a difficult moral dilemma, hanging out with Stefano, in such a poor country, but I will come back to that.

We drove to the outskirts of San Cristobal, past an eight-storey construction underway, that Stefano pointed out was his family's new warehouse. Around a sweeping bend and into a valley, we could see a Total garage, a huge queue built up for several kilometres. Stefano drove past all the cars and pickups, lorries and trucks, on the wrong side of the road. The petrol station had huge, closed gates at both ends, guarded by the army. Vehicles were let in one at a time. Stefano drove straight up to the gate, nodded at the guard and the gate miraculously opened. At the pump, we skipped the cars that were already there. Very similar to my Swiss friend in El Dorado. The army stood around and allowed us a photo as Stefano filled a 25- litre drum, which was illegal anyway, slung it in the back, and we were off. Privilege indeed, but I wasn't complaining at this stage.

To the credit of employers and employees, the Venezuelans are given a day off work to get their fuel, and they really make the most of it. They set up barbecues on the back of their pickups, and the whole snaking row of vehicles becomes a long street party. That is actually too rosy a picture to paint. On another occasion, a month later, we saw a frustrated customer refused entry at 10pm, after queuing for fourteen hours. The gate was closed on him, just as his car was about to come in. He freaked out, started banging on the gate, and shouting at the army. He reached behind his back, and was immediately shot in the head, by what looked to me like a fifteen-year-old woman soldier. We did not stick around to find out if he was armed. It was grim. To make the situation even worse, he was literally shot for something that is free.

In the madness that is the Venezuelan economy, you may have to wait patiently for fourteen hours, but if you do get fuel, in a car, it is basically free. Petrol is two cents a litre. For motorcyclists like myself, it is actually free. To fill my tank of 23 litres, it costs 46 cents, so they just don't bother charging motorcyclists. Insane! But it sounds petty and bad taste discussing things that are free when people are losing their lives over this free commodity. And it is bad taste.

Stefano did not shy away from life. In his perfectly ironed jeans and chequered shirt, neatly trimmed, jet black beard, Elvis quiff and Ray-Ban shades, he looked a bit like a future dictator himself, but he didn't have it in him. Soft as hell. Stefano was very proud of his country but did not hold back his punches when showing us the controversial side.

Stefano introduced us to two people we would never forget; Pablo Putin, the Cartel drug dealer, and Luis, the FARC rebel kidnap victim. Two people at opposite ends of the spectrum, but both part of the rich/poor, and out-of-control tapestry that is Venezuela. Before Pablo and Luis come on the scene, let me introduce you to my spare parts smuggler. By an act of fate, good or bad, we were thrown in with the rich and privileged of a collapsing country, but also the desperate. I am not going to ponder on the morals of this scenario too much. I am just reporting what happened. The judgement is yours to ponder.

Chapter Twenty One
The One-Legged Tyre Smuggler

Venezuela is in a deep, deep crisis and there is no other way of putting it. President Maduro is a bastard, who has bled his country dry, like all classical despots. He spends most of his time on television, covered in medals, justifying his policies, a sure sign of a megalomaniac. Some of his speeches are seven hours long. I always like to stay politically neutral in my first paragraph.

My love for Venezuela has no bounds. I have spent the last ten years trying to find my new Swaziland, where I was raised. I can't help it. When people say that there is no place like home, it is one hundred percent true. My parents are from England, I am from Swaziland, that simple. They brought me up in Kenya and Swaziland. No going back on that blueprint. You cannot shake off the smell of your country, the food you were brought up on, the sounds in the morning, the climate, your memories of walking to school, your nerves on the first day of school, your first best friend, your first sports day win, the dirt roads, your first insect sting, your first crash on your bicycle on a dirt road, the smell of a piece of meat on a braai, being in the back of your dad's red sports car on corrugated, dusty roads, watching your father running in marathons, going on an outing to South Africa to watch the FA Cup, because Swaziland had no TV. This was a real dad/son moment, well it was for me. I didn't spend a great deal of time with my dad. He was either working hard or running. I guess that was his escape, his thinking time. Much like me on the motorbike, but I took the lazy, petrol-powered option.

Watching your brother heading down a valley with his motorbike and friends, and being jealous; the dogs, the insects, my new kitten getting eaten by the neighbour's Great Dane, doing my homework in my sweltering bedroom, listening to my Scottish neighbour Douglas, murdering a Clarinet, long corridors in our house, electricity men on motorbikes, snoring, drunk friends of my parents, laughter, half a grapefruit; with brown sugar on it, my dad's Shreddies Malted Cereal, scrambled eggs, swimming, sport, beautiful views that never stop inspiring, my mum's tapestries, and art and theatre, and her vitality and creativity for life itself, BBC World Service on the radio at breakfast (loved it, so posh and exotic), running eight kilometres to my school, because I liked it, waterfalls, valleys, mangy, rescued pets, purple medicine on our grazes, sleepovers, prisoners in black and white striped outfits clearing the roads, thunder and lightning, floods, my first Castle Lager, my first kiss, my first driving lesson, seeing my first dead person, most of all, just everything. You don't realise that where you were brought up, soaks into your very soul.

The number of times I said to Cathy, "How beautiful is this, reminds me of Swaziland".

I must have really annoyed her. I went through thirty four African countries, looking for my new Swaziland, my new home, where I would feel comfortable, and felt I belonged. I only found it in one: Swaziland. I went through a further twenty countries in South and Central America, to no avail. Venezuela was the last country we went to before returning to Colombia, where the circumnavigation had begun, nearly two years earlier.

I have never been in a country so warped, so messed up and so wonderful in my life. It is a paradise of incredible people and dreamlike landscapes, locked in a political hell. They are not lazy people, they are not workshy, dole scroungers. They are just normal people, who want to work and bring up their children, but cannot, because of politics. Absurd.

I judge my depth of feeling for a country with a silly little theory. Would I be willing to fight for that country if there was a foreign invasion? Yes, to Swaziland, yes to England, and super close to a yes for Venezuela. That's how much I love this country and the people who live in it. I know that Cathy feels exactly the same. I try not to get attached to any person, city, landscape etc, but had no choice in the matter. I haven't even told you about the Grand Sabana National Park, the first place you come to when you enter from Brazil.

There is a flat, enormous mountain, Mt. Roraima, set in a beautiful savannah landscape, that makes Table Mountain look like a mozzie bite.

Mt. Roraima

There is the Valley of Flowers, worth mentioning again, the mountainside and its thousands of different coloured flowers, lit up at night, in a spectacular show of colour. The winding mountain road through the centre is a dream in a country of potential nightmares. It makes Holland look destitute of tulips. Venezuela, which means little Venice, is heavenly and horrific in equal measure. Let me tell you about the border situation when we were leaving, without being too dramatic. What happened to us when we were there, I will have to come back to. You will see why.

The Tariba border post between Venezuela at San Cristobal and the town of Cucuta in Colombia is impossible to describe. (I love that cliché by writers, because then they immediately try to describe it.) As I will. As in many border towns, the frontier is divided by a river, the River Torbes, which features prominently in my story, unfortunately. There is a bridge joining the two countries. Which helps.

When we arrived there, no vehicles had been allowed through for three years, so us getting the motorbike through was as likely as me writing a good chapter. Not allowing vehicles through has not stopped a staggering 20,000 people crossing the border bridge by foot, every single day. They carry everything they own, some of the men hidden under a mountain of goods, folded over double, the wife and bedraggled children following. It is continuous. If you took a drone shot, it would look like a column of ants crossing a branch, or the Tour de France peloton and crowd, without bikes, or food, or money. It was intense.

A 2020 poll, by Consultares 21, estimated that up to seven million Venezuelans have fled the country. This is known as the Bolivarian Diaspora, the largest recorded refugee crisis in South American history. That's saying something, but it has been building. It refers to the emigration of millions during the presidency of Chavez, and now Maduro. The revolution by these two was to establish a cultural and political equality for all. Rubbish. It culminated in this refugee crisis, as serious as Syria and Cuba.

The government has denied any migratory crisis, stating that the United Nations and others are attempting to justify foreign intervention in Venezuela. Believe me, people, when I say that I spent three weeks trying to get my motorbike through the border and I saw the reality. The queue was incessant and permanent, every time I went there.

Cucuta Crossing

It was a total exodus. Not in the same desperate way as starving African children, as I mentioned at the border camp. There are no distended bellies, or flies around noses, or ribs showing. That is not the point. They were heading to countries that were alien to them, with all the prejudices that the label, refugee, entails. No one uproots their whole family, from the country they know and love, to head to an unknown destination, on a whim. It is desperation, not conning. So, no starving children yet, but it is coming. Seven million people will disappear into the ether of other countries' systems, and will forever be poor. What caused this massive exodus of people from this amazing nation, the jewel in the South American crown, until recently?

Simple! Corruption, social issues, political repression and bullying, economic mismanagement, censorship, unemployment, hyperinflation, shortages of food and essentials, international debt, human rights violations, as in Police and Army brutality, and more. Basically, a totally corrupt government, running their county for personal gain. Shocking. Never heard of that before. Except with every government on earth. I witnessed families splitting up, crying hysterically, not knowing when they would be reunited. No political system should do this to their people. I feel pathetic, going straight back to my irrelevant problems, but it was evident after numerous meetings with Venezuelan officials that we were not getting into Colombia on our motorcycle. This was disastrous news. But not in the big scheme of things, you spoilt Spencer, you. It actually meant that we would have to do the world's longest detour, no argument from any of you, please. Back through the whole of Venezuela, across the entire Amazon jungle, from east to west and then into Peru and Ecuador and finally, Colombia. A mere 12,000 kilometre detour. It became a reality.

After weeks of discussion with Generals, lopsided with medals, we failed. The detour was on. On a callous level, we had our own situation to deal with, and I am too old to save the children, let alone the world. We had a back tyre that was balder than Telly Savalas, as hairless as a snooker ball, and more slippery than a trout in Vaseline. If we were to break the world detour record, we definitely needed a tyre. Definitely. Or we would die, in a tragic slippery fate. Options. Not a lot. I had one option. Cross the bridge by foot, buy a tyre in Colombia and return. The biggest obstacle was that no new products were allowed in Venezuela, without forklift-sized amounts of paperwork, import tax payments that Elon Musk couldn't afford, and references from eighteen members of your direct family, and two from extended family, and your pet ferret.

I had a cunning plan, Baldrick. I smoothly and surreptitiously caught a taxi into Cucuta, on the Colombian side and bought a tyre. It was an original Micheloon Sirac, the famous French brand, with spelling mistakes; evidently one hundred percent genuine parts. They wanted $180. I nearly died on the spot. Enough to buy a sixteen-bedroom house in Venezuela, with six Miss Worlds looking after you. Oh well, what choice did I have. At least it was a genuine French tyre.

On the return journey, I jumped out of the taxi three hundred metres from the border control, around a bend (not me; the geographical location), out of view. I removed the red and white price tag, and various guarantee stickers from the tyre. I rolled the tyre in a muddy puddle, and then rolled it along the road, in the dust. I even rubbed it on a rock to give it some wear. That did nothing. It would have taken about three weeks to look worn. Anyway. Job done. I had cunningly disguised a tyre as secondhand, one that I had picked up in Cucuta, from a long-lost friend. I walked across the bridge towards customs, with zero confidence. I over-compensated for my nervousness with nonchalance and ended up walking, tyre slung over my shoulder, like John Travolta in 'Saturday Night Fever'. The Colombian customs were the first to deal with and had set up a check point in the centre of the bridge. I was alone, apart from the other 15,000 on the bridge. I would have been anonymous, but unfortunately, I was a head height taller than any refugee. They clocked me, and my original Michelson Sirac tyre from miles away. Time for some African bravado.

"Hello, can I pass please. Here are my papers. I picked up this old, very old tyre. It has been used many times, by numerous people. I could never afford a new tyre, so I got this tyre from an old friend. He is not as old as the tyre though."

The customs officer's answer was in Colombian Spanish, but translated roughly as, "That is a brand-new tyre over your shoulder, Mr. … Travolta. You bought it at the Moto tyre centre, near the Cucuta Mall from my good friend, Andre. Then you rolled it in a puddle, around the corner, so we couldn't see you. Then you rubbed it on a rock, to make it look worn."

Neither of those comments happened, but I got busted. I turned around with my tyre and went back to Colombia. Time for 'Cunning Plan 2', never give up. Especially for that price.

Luckily, my guardian angel turned up, hopping, I grant you; no wings to be seen, but he was my particular, tyre-saving, guardian angel. Andres Leonardo Jose Luis. I have seen this before. Once again he just picked the four most popular names in Venezuela, and used them when necessary.

"Andres Leonardo Jose Luis, alternative customs agent," he said, but added, "Just call me Rafael."

So, what is the point of the other four names? It transpired that; let's call him ALJLR, for short, could help me, with the complicated issue of importing my tyre into Venezuela.

"I can deliver this tyre in forty minutes, to Venezuela," he said confidently, his thin, high-cheekboned face breaking into a grin, revealing irregular, yellow teeth.

He had a sparkle in his blue eyes that I trusted.

"How are you going to manage that?" I asked.

"No problem, I take tyre."

I forgot to mention that my long-named friend only had one leg, but the title of the Chapter gave a hint. The other leg was replaced by what looked suspiciously like a broom handle, connected to a piece of rounded car tyre that was bound to his stump. Maybe he needed a spare tyre, and saw me as easy pickings. He could definitely go off road with that leg, with my tyre. Everything was strapped together with... a biker's dream, duct tape.

I didn't want to make a big thing about his one leggedness, what with political correctness. I don't want to make anybody feel awkward. We are equal, even if you have one leg. Well, obviously not in the final of the Olympics 100 metres, but you get my point. The fact that Rafael had one leg was not his defining feature. He had decent ears.

Anyway, Peg-Leg's plan was to pop the tyre over his neck, hop down to the jungle, hop through the river, hop through the sugar cane, and hop out the other side, victorious. Who was I to argue? He never used the word hop during our discussions, I added that. It didn't sound like a very balanced plan to me (joke). Long John Silver smelt some gold, and would probably be hopping mad if I refused his offer. It is difficult times. Try standing in his shoe.

To cut a long leg, sorry; story short, I accepted, and my hopping smuggler was successful. After about forty five minutes, as predicted, he popped out the other side, singing, 'Lean on me'. No, he didn't, but he did give the customs and the militia the thumbs up. I suspect he was in cahoots with them, but I didn't care. Top man, and we could now contemplate the twelve-thousand-kilometre detour through the Amazon. So glad we couldn't get through. Everything happens for a reason.

Top: Police helping migrants across the Torbes River on the Venezuela/ Colombia border. Bottom: border settlement

Chapter Twenty Two
Pablo Putin: the Cartel Cocaine Dealer

It was evident that Cathy and I were not going to make it through the San Cristobal/Cucuta border, and not for lack of trying on Stefano's part. The problem was that no private vehicles had been allowed over the border for three years. We even went to the main army base and spoke to Generals of note. At the entrance, the guard chatted with Stefano, while the car was searched with mirrors on sticks, for bombs. We were shown into an impressive colonial building, with high ceiling arches, and long airy whitewashed corridors. The waiting room had thirty foot high ceilings, and a huge ornate crystal chandelier hanging over a massive mahogany table, which had a quill and inkwell on it. Obviously hadn't been used since the Revolution of 1885. A beautiful red, woven carpet, the size of most people's houses, covered the cool marble floor.

The icing on the cake, and the feature that sent a shiver down my spine, were the portrait photographs. There were hundreds of photos of Generals and government leaders of all types, bedecked in enough medals and regalia, to make it difficult to walk. At least forty photos had a large red cross over the faces. I don't need to tell you that these were people who had fallen out of favour, and probably gone on a religious Sabbatical, indefinitely. It was like being in a weak 'dictator'-type film, starring Chuck Norris, or Jean Claude van Damme, set in… well, South America. It was too weird in real life, and when we met the General, who also had 5,000 medals, I couldn't help wondering if he walked past those portraits every day, starts sweating and wonders when he will be the next red cross.

The General was super helpful, spoke to the 'head' of immigration, and organised us, and the bike, exit from Venezuela. Sadly we were never to get entry clearance from Colombia. Cathy was never, ever searched, no matter where we went, including the President's office. Old school etiquette, but not so good if Cathy was a Maduro-hating suicide bomber. Despite all of Stefano's high-falluting friends, it was obvious after three weeks, that they were not going to change the law just for us. The Tenere was not going to get through.

A biker without a bike… is a person. Don't want to be one of those quite yet. We were about to do a 12,000-kilometre detour, the world's longest that I have heard of, through the Amazon jungle, rather than give up the bike, or the dream. But not before Stefano fed us until I looked like Pavarotti, showed us his business ventures, introduced us to his family and generally bent over backwards to give us the most incredible time. We went to waterfalls, walked across mountains into Colombia; illegally rode our bikes, drove around the neon green hills, listening to reggaeton. We sat under bridges, on beer crates and plastic chairs, discussing life. We frequented a cartel bakery; all the customers were men over 120 years old, all bent over conspiratorially, discussing life in hushed tones. It is also where I changed dollars, in the back room, amongst the flour-covered bakers. Totally legitimate croissant business, making millions of dollars. Stefano even nicked my bike, got the front wheel rim straightened without me knowing, and rode it back, triumphantly. I was surprised the bike hadn't collapsed in two, but was super touched by the thought.

One morning Giant Kid turned up, very enthusiastic and even more suave than normal. (To explain; Giant Kid is what we ended up calling Stefano, or GK, for short. He looked about eleven, with a beard.)

"I want to take you to visit a friend of mine in the mountains. Well, he is not really a friend, but it will be very interesting for your programmes."

Sounded a bit dodgy, a bit ominous, but why not. Stefano was looking particularly smart, with shining brown leather shoes, brown trousers and a blue and white chequered shirt. His Elvis hair had many products on it, and he glistened in the sunlight. He glistened with products that are as foreign to me as Mars. His 'Eau de Colon', I think that is the technical term, wafted around the air, in thick clouds, as he gestured animatedly, his eyes sparkling with dodginess, as usual.

We jumped into his truck which, although huge, still looked like a Dinky toy when GK (Giant Kid) got in. He took up the whole cab, the gears disappearing beneath his leg, which was touching mine, on the passenger seat. I became more and more squashed up against the passenger window, because GK had a habit of hugging me whilst he was driving, and pouting crimsonly in my direction. It was disconcerting, made all the more so by the fact that he was swerving all over the road, giggling, as he tried to kiss my forehead. Cathy was in hysterics, because she knows how 'manly' I was and not really into hugging, and open affection. The problem is that Giant Kid knew this, and thrived on making me feel uncomfortable, hugging me and kissing me at inappropriate moments. Not much one could do; fighting off an amorous grizzly bear comes to mind. We careered our way out of San Cristobal, Giant Kid keeping us amused with his hugeness and vitality, as he acted as tour guide and historian. Stefano's verve for life was made all the more remarkable by the fact that two months before our arrival he had dealt with a devastating tragedy.

Twenty-seven-year-old, fresh-faced Stefano is part of an Italian/Venezuelan family, who are as close as only a… well, as only an Italian/Venezuelan family can be. Mama Stefano worshipped the ground her three sons walked on, and they similarly heaped praise and love on their mother. Papa Stefano was the stalwart, work hard, look after your family at all costs, type. The family ran the biggest construction company in San Cristobal and one of the biggest in Venezuela, and it was still growing, during this crisis. The family all worked together, very hard and spent every weekend together, struggling to act normally, in a collapsing and increasingly dangerous country. His family had dealt with kidnap attempts and shootings. And worse. Seven weeks and three days before we arrived, Stefano's nineteen-year-old brother had keeled over in front of the family, and died from a catastrophic brain hemorrhage, gone from this world within ten minutes. There was no warning, no history of illness, and Stefano and his brother had been inseparable.

Although Stefano was a beacon of light, energy and positivity, I had occasionally glimpsed a different man over the past few weeks. I had caught him, very briefly, looking pensive and sad and, on one occasion, I found him crying. I asked if he was OK, and he brushed it aside, with a laugh. When Stefano finally confided in me, we both broke down, and he gave me a photo of his brother and the funeral poem, to carry around the world. My respect for this soft man-mountain was magnified exponentially. To lose a parent is devastating, and I know, because I lost my mum less than a year ago, and I am in no way over it. In fact, it gets more difficult. No one told me that when your mother dies, or someone who had a massive influence on you, millions of memories flood by, constantly, making you realise where you come from, and regretting your coldness. It doesn't get better. For me it gets worse. I won't lie. I miss my mum more now than the day she died. I will never be the same. You learn to live with it, but I will never accept that my mother is gone, she is here in every decision I make. If I could grab my mum right now, and give her the biggest hug ever, and tell her how amazing she was, I would give up everything. I miss her so much. But I need to be level-headed. I am not the only one with pain.

To lose a child, or brother and sister, is a different tragedy. Grief can split up families. Hurt digs deep and sometimes the emotional reactions become divisive and ruin families. Not in Stefano's case. They were all suffering, but they were together, and the tenderness and affection between them was humbling. The way Cathy and I were taken in, at such a heart-breaking time, was amazing. Stefano was suffering from the loss of his brother, and all he wanted to do was show us how much he loved his country. The country where his brother had just died. We loved Venezuela and Giant Kid, without the tragedy. We took everything in our stride, knowing Stefano was trying to give us the best TV programme, but hurting inside. I think that us arriving was a welcome focus for Stefano, but I could have been wrong. He might just be going through the motions. Whatever it was, I hope we helped.

We wound our way higher up into the mountains. Our next introduction, to another kind of Venezuelan life, was memorable, but not pleasant. San Cristobal, the capital city of Táchira District sits at the base of the northern Andes Mountains, at 818 metres, in a beautiful sun-kissed valley. We headed out on a steep, asphalt mountain road, with a dodgy precipice on our left. Luckily, Giant Kid was kissing and pouting less, and concentrating more on his driving. San Cristobal diminished into a little Lego town far below us, and the temperature dropped. The tar road turned into dirt and we bounced our way over rocks and ruts.

Over the next mountain and a tar road once again in the valley. There was a large double gated entrance, with a guard tower made of stone, wood and cement on the lefthand side. Two men stood on a platform, holding bottles of Regional Pilsen, machine guns hanging loosely from their shoulders. They gave us a cursory glance, saw Stefano, one of them whistled, and they were back to their conversation. A boy of about ten ran up to a button on the wall and the gates opened. On the righthand side was a perfect lawn, and a stunning Hacienda, overlooking San Cristobal. There were arches and Corinthian columns, and concrete lions, their eyes crudely touched up with colour by a local artist. Before I tell you what confronted us on the lawn, I must tell you that the man I am about to introduce was not called Pablo Putin. I decided to use a false name, and not pin his location on Google maps, because I want to live for a bit longer, and so does my family.

Pablo is obvious, named after Pablo Emilio Escobar Gavira, a Colombian drug lord and narco terrorist, who was the founder of the Medellin Cartel. Escobar died on 2nd November 1993, gunned down from a roof by United States Special Forces. During his lifetime Escobar amassed the absurdly huge estimate of $5 billion. Not millions; billions, and that doesn't include half his earnings. He was a bit averse to declaring earnings to the tax office, as you can imagine. To put it in perspective, in his heyday, Escobar was making more money than twenty countries combined. He even offered to pay off the National Debt of Colombia if they made him President. It was obviously couched less in the way of a bribe, but not much. Surprisingly, the offer was refused.

So back to our B Rate Escobar. The Putin bit comes from what we saw next. On the pristine, scissor-cut lawn, we were met by a man who to all intents and purposes, was the Venezuelan Vladimir. He was about sixty, short, portly and balding, but had obviously done a few workouts in his youth, and was evidently still proud of his physique He was dressed in camouflage military trousers, combat boots and was shirtless, sporting a thick gold chain, that probably weighed the same as Stefano.

Absurdly, the similarities to the Russian leader did not end there. I am sure you are aware of the famous photo of Vladimir Putin, shirtless, on a horse. This Pablo Putin (we never learnt his name, and I am glad), did one better. He was flanked by two women on horseback, both displaying pneumatic breasts, their modesty covered in bikinis that were evidently fashioned from dental floss. The dental floss bikinis were in the national colours of Venezuela. It was like walking onto the set of a dodgy porno shoot.

Pablo beckoned us over with a flourish and a bow. On closer inspection, Pablo was closer to 200 years old, but had gone down the drug dealer, botox and filler route. He looked pretty grotesque, as nothing on his face moved, so when he smiled it was more like a painful grimace. His face was expressionless and smooth, which looked even odder as his neck looked like crocodile skin. It was not an image I warmed to, but the welcome was warm. We were offered ice cold beers in frosted glasses and an array of snacks. The ladies hung on every word Pablo said, and giggled inanely, no matter what the subject.

"I killed Pancho and chopped off his thumbs, and put them up his bum."

Cue hysterical laughter, and much spilling of champagne.

"You are so clever, and strong, and tall, and funny, and handsome, and not really that bald," or whatever they uttered, to keep Pablo happy, and themselves alive. Pablo had the clichéd sidekick, who was tall, stick thin and wiry, dressed in black shoes, black trousers, a black shirt, and a black heart. He called himself Franco, Pablo called him Piedra. I called him evil. Franco looked like he had killed a few hundred people, and enjoyed torturing a lot more than that. He had long, greasy, black hair stuck to his cheeks, and cold, deep-set, charcoal eyes. They were the absolute opposite of Stefano's puppy-dog warm eyes; they were expressionless and dead. Although Franco was smiling and friendly on the surface, he always seemed distracted. Probably deciding whether to pull out our fingernails or toenails first. I did not feel comfortable around him at all, and to this day Cathy says she has never met anyone so scary and soulless.

Apart from the clichéd drug dealer image, with his clichéd prostitutes on horseback, his clichéd over the top villa, and his clichéd bodyguard, what else does every aspiring drug dealer need? A zoo of course.

Once again, this is the fault of the original Pablo Escobar. The 'Handbook of Drug Dealing' was written by Pablo Escobar and copied by thousands of wannabee drug barons throughout Latin America. Pablo Escobar is the perfect example of someone having too much money to know what to do with it. Pablo Escobar rented hundreds of properties, only to fill every room, from floor to ceiling with money. He even buried millions of dollars using JCB diggers. Millions was lost or rotted. He did try to spend some of it.

Hacienda Napoles was the luxurious estate built by Escobar in Puerto Triunfo, 1,500 kilometres east of Medellin. The estate covered thirty square kilometres. It included a Spanish colonial house, a sculpture park, and a complete zoo, with animals from all the world's continents. This included antelope, elephants, exotic birds and mammals in their thousands, giraffes, hippos, ostriches, horses and ponies. The ranch also boasted a massive collection of antique luxury cars and motorcycles, a private airport, a bullring, and a Kart racing track. Mounted atop the Hacienda's entrance gate is a Piper PA 18 Super Cub airplane, which transported Escobar's first shipment of cocaine to the United States. Other original features included dinosaur statues built with real bones, along with animal statues that children can climb and play on. Escobar had fifty decommissioned military vehicles, circling a huge hand sculpture.

After Escobar's death, ownership of the property eventually passed to the Colombian government. The Hacienda still has bison, rare goats and zebras wandering around. In a surreal twist of fate, Escobar hippos have escaped and become feral, living in at least four lakes in the area and spreading into neighbouring rivers. Contact between hippos and local fishermen have led to calls for the local hippo population to be culled. By 2020 there were at least thirty animals roaming wild, and forty plus hippos living in the grounds of the Hacienda; the most famous, a moody female called Vanessa.

Our Pablo did not have anything on the same scale, but he did have a zoo. Cathy had remained almost silent for the whole visit, and I knew she was feeling extremely uncomfortable. We are both totally against zoos. Why do we have the right to lock up animals in small concrete cages, so our children can gawp at them through bars, at the weekend? It is totally wrong, and when you see this sick, depressed animal pacing their cages, for years on end, you know it is wrong. They have not committed any crime. We have no right.

I knew the zoo tour would push Cathy over the edge, but we tried to stay polite. Pablo Putin had pythons in tiny cages, a token branch thrown in, for them to crawl along, for their whole lives. He had rows and rows of small prison cells made of brick, up to waist height, and chicken wire on top. He had capybaras, anteaters, green iguanas, a Harpy eagle, golden lion Tamarin monkeys, Anacondas, Jesus lizards, a sloth, raccoons and on... It was grim.

There was no plant material to be seen, the animals were wading in their own excrement, breathing it, sleeping on it. There was no escape from your own toilet, as in nature. For a millionaire drug dealer, he could have built huge enclosures, resembling jungles, but no such effort had been made. Cathy was grim, silent and bright red.

A capybara in the wild

The absolute limit was a beautiful, fully grown jaguar, a magnificent, elegant, majestic beast, in a tiny cage. No exercise, no stimulation, no movement. Prison, for one of the most hyperactive animals on the planet. The jaguar was lying listlessly in the corner. The smell was intense, and made me gag, but Pablo Putin and his killer friend seemed oblivious. Putin picked up a piece of reinforcing bar, and poked the poor creature in the ribs, to provoke a roar. He eventually gave out a roar of frustration, but you could see he had given up on life.

Putin looked round at us, grinning, for appreciation. "Very strong, very powerful animal."

Cathy walked away and burst into tears. I was also desperate to get away, but even more desperate to free all the animals, so that they could eat Pablo Putin for dinner and his dastardly sidekick for pudding. Bad people, bad place. But our escape was not on yet. I could see that Stefano's enthusiastic mood had died too, and that he also wanted to leave. Unfortunately, Stefano had mentioned earlier that he used to ride horses. One of Pablo Putin's sidekicks then turned up with a pony; no, a midget pony. Stefano had no need to climb on, he could just walk onto the pony from behind. I was worried that the pony's legs would splay out like in a cartoon, but miraculously that didn't happen. Stefano evidently had the same thoughts, as he sort of ran along the ground, with the pony running underneath him. Imagine a child pushing along a wooden horse, with wheels. It was a bit like that.

I was in hysterics, especially when the pony headed down a hill. Stefano lost his nerve and he started screaming in a high pitched voice, a nine-year-old girl would have been proud of. I was crying and the stony-faced look of the Cartel crowd, made it even funnier. Stefano survived the ride and we made our departures, politely, but quickly, though not before Stefano picked up the horse, and gave it a hug. What an experience.

We left a bit shell-shocked and Stefano dropped us off, promising not to introduce us to any more harrowing scenes. He was not true to his word. After rushing around for another ten days, trying to get our bike through to Colombia, and failing, Stefano turned up at our room one morning.

"I have good news, two bits good news. First we are VIP guests at the international football match between Uruguay and Venezuela. Second, I have organised interview with FARC rebel kidnap victim." And so it came to pass that we watched our first live football match, and it was superb. The stadium was full and the drumming was skin-tingling. Everyone had come to see Luis Suarez, the Uruguayan footballer, who likes biting opponents. Suarez, who played in the premiership in the UK, went all Mike Tyson, and had decided to bite the ear of Italian defender Giorgio Chellini. Consequently, the Estadio Polideportivo De Pueblo Nuevo was filled to capacity, with 38,755 people. I could never fathom this country. The economy collapsing, people eating out of rubbish bags etc., but many could afford football tickets.

We even witnessed the world's quickest riot. After the game a group of five boys, about eleven years old, started throwing stones at the Uruguayan fans outside the stadium. A very overweight, bored policeman, shuffled over, fired a tear gas canister, and everybody went home. It was an amazing day, that ended up with us having dinner with the teams and coaches. Stefano knew everyone of influence and if he couldn't get us to Colombia, no one could.

So we prepared ourselves for the 12,000 kilometre detour, back through Venezuela, through the Brazilian Amazon, into Peru, Ecuador, and finally, back to Bogota. Bogota was only 400 kilometres away, but needs must.

Before we headed off, we were introduced to Luis, the victim of a FARC kidnapping. Kidnapping is big business in Venezuela. Traditional kidnappings are when someone is taken, the family is called, negotiations are made. This is the worst type of kidnapping, the victims sometimes held for months, even years. This is the type of kidnapping Luis endured.

More popular is express kidnapping, where they take you in your car to ATMs and extract money from your accounts. They go to stores, they buy expensive watches, etc. with your credit card, and after an eight-hour ordeal they take your car, but leave you. Ironically, these kidnappings have become less popular because so many ATM machines are out of service. There is also virtual kidnapping, where your phone service is cut off, and during those hours when you are not available, the kidnappers pretend they have snatched you and demand a ransom from your family.

Like many businesses, kidnapping also takes advantage of telemarketing. Done from prisons. Inmates make calls to countless people on a list, saying. "We know who you are, we know the names of your children." Some people will pay, rather than risk kidnap. Stefano was a prime target also, because of his wealth and position. We interviewed him about it, but his family vetoed the footage. Fair enough.

Luis wanted to tell his story, maybe for cathartic reasons. He was five foot five, 40 years old, short neat brown hair, with perfectly ironed jeans and a light blue chequered shirt and cowboy boots. But the description is irrelevant. It was the look in his eyes and his body language that spoke volumes.

I had met people with post-traumatic stress disorder, and even have personal experience after my bandit attack in Kenya. Luis had all the signs. He had a haunted, distracted look, as though he was just going through the motions. He had that 'glance around constantly' look that you see only in films. He also chewed tobacco, constantly spitting on the lawn, as we spoke. It was more like a mental 'tic' than a pastime.

Here was a profoundly sad and broken man. He had kissed his wife and daughter goodbye, gone to work, and didn't come back for nine months. Luis owned a petrol station in the centre of San Cristobal. Last March he was getting out of his car at the gate, when he was pulled out, bundled into the rear seat, and was joined by three kidnappers, with pistols. Their stolen car was left at the scene, and they drove off, covering Luis's head with what he later found out was a motorcycle helmet bag, and pushed him into the footwell.

This was the beginning of eight months and twenty two days of mental and physical torture, that resulted in the shell of the man who Cathy and I interviewed.

They drove for forty minutes in total silence, and then swopped vehicles. This was where the FARC rebels took over, at the edge of the jungle, from the local kidnappers. They bounced along a road for a short while, before the classic 'trek up the mountain, to remote villages'. This went on for three days, with multiple swaps of personnel, before Luis was placed in a hut, where he would stay for a month, with no contact or demands.

"People say they relax and become resigned to their fate. It is not true. It is horror from beginning to end. All you want to do is escape, and be free. The physical pain is nothing, compared to the waiting, the not knowing. Knowing that you may never see family again. That is the control that kidnappers have and what breaks victims. Keeping silent and denying the victim information for months," said Luis.

The next step was of course, asking for money. It was two months until Luis spoke to his father.

"This was when I cried and cried."

The ransom money negotiations had started, but dragged on for seven more months. One day, as Luis was wrapped in his blanket, hugging a cat that had befriended him, to keep warm, the kidnappers came in and said the ransom had been paid, and they were leaving in one hour. That was it. They did everything in reverse, Luis still blindfolded.

They reached a main road, and Luis was rapidly duct-taped to a telegraph pole. Within ten minutes, he had been picked up by a passing trucker, and taken to hospital. Luis may have survived his kidnapping, but he never escaped from the memory of his ordeal. His trust for humans had gone. We thanked him for the interview, hugged him a lot, and headed back to our room with Giant Kid, to pack for our grand detour.

Venezuela is incredibly complex, and I really haven't told you all. It is exciting, dramatic, strange, divided, unpredictable, and impossible to work out. I am fully aware that in meeting Stefano, we were amongst the elite. But I will not reject someone because they are rich, just as I will not reject someone who is poor.

An experience is an experience. What cannot be denied is that Venezuela is a beautiful country, with beautiful people.

Chapter Twenty Three
The Golden Aztec King

The observant amongst you may have noticed that I omitted Paraguay, Uruguay and Suriname from my stories. There were also only cursory pieces on Brazil and Ecuador. This is despite the fact that Brazil is as large as all the other South American countries combined, and took us four months to cross. Similarly, we were in Ecuador for more than six months. The simple reason for this is that too much happened in those countries, and I cannot pay justice to my lunatic decisions during that time in a piece of writing, this short. All of that is in my next book. This book was never meant to be a sequential travelogue. I just wanted to give you a taste of the weird and wonderful things that happen to you as an adventure motorcyclist, but I realise when I look back at all my chapter titles, it is disaster after disaster. I am supposed to be inspiring people to travel, not scaring the living daylights out of them. I have two retorts to that.

Firstly, I am atypical. If the success of an adventure motorcycle trip, or any adventure, is based on a smooth, well-planned, well-executed, error-free journey, then I have accumulated a lifetime of failure. I am extremely unlucky, as you know from another cheery chapter in this book. And it runs in the family. I have broken most of the bones in my body. As well as accident-prone, I am also allergic to anything with eyes, expressions, wings or feet. Added to this, I am no good at directions, and get lost in my own head, and kitchen. These factors make me the perfect candidate to be rejected outright by the Adventure Motorcycling Academy (if there were one).

On top of that, I readily admit that I do not have a GPS, I survive on paper maps that are out of date, so I get lost a great deal, and consequently, end up in some questionable locations. I also search out edgy and dangerous areas. Don't ask me why, I am not sure myself. But I am sure that very few of you will visit the Barrio of No Return, or travel the Ghost Road, or go off track in the Salar de Uyuni, or hang out with Chucky and his Triceratops, or visit Venezuela during a near Civil War; or many of the debatable decisions I have made. Because you are sensible. Lead me not into temptation, I can find the way myself.

Ignore the muggings, we pushed it to the edge; ignore the malaria and bullet ants, and spiders and snakes, and Favelas, and guns, and cocaine dealers. So, please, forget everything you have read in this book, and definitely don't read it again. Or recommend it to anyone who wants to step out of their comfort zone. Get out there and enjoy this magical world, whenever you get the chance. Yes, travelling and exploring is edgy, but it is also life-affirming, and adrenaline-producing. That's probably the answer. I am looking for more adrenaline. It is very important to our wellbeing. The world is beautiful, and so are the unpredictable people and places in it.

We tend to live in the opposite way, searching out safety and predictability. We can get lost in the haze of our lives, dulled by routine and our duty. Duties that we must never shirk. But if you are unhappy with your life, you need to change it. Even if it is little things. The last thing I want to sound like, is that I am lecturing. I have made thousands of mistakes, and I am in no position to stand on any wobbly pedestal. If I could live my life again, would I? Yes. But we can't do that. It would be too simple to go back, and erase all the errors. But sometimes you do find yourself in a situation that is not right for you, a life you feel alien to, but somehow slipped into, like a sticky peat bog. I have been through it. I nearly got stuck, forever.

After studying for a degree in Social Anthropology at the University of Edinburgh, my brain just switched off, and I became rudderless. I had no idea what to do. I took a Teaching English as a Foreign Language course (TEFL), so that I could go to the Seychelles, and teach at the polytechnic, which I did. I taught for four years at the School of Art and Design, on the main island of Mahe. It is very difficult to motivate students who are going to be either fishermen or work in the hospitality industry, but I enjoyed it and my students achieved good results. Although teaching is a wonderful and rewarding job, I always knew it was not for me. I yearned to be out and about, in the world, not stuck in a shirt and tie, in 30 degrees, in a classroom. I needed animals, dirt, nature, and a physical and mental challenge. But, because of a failed relationship, some bad decisions, and a broken rudder; after my stint in the Seychelles, I ended up in England, 'just for a few months', which ended up being twenty years. (How many times have you heard that.)

I taught English at Skinners, a grammar school, in Tunbridge Wells in the summer. I dug up most of the roads in the UK, and laid pipes in the winter. I laid concrete, and patios and built fences. I then became a fully unqualified tree surgeon, swinging around in iced-up trees, for ten years. I was working with a hippie, called Graham, also known as 'Mountain Goat'. He was called that more because of his shaggy appearance; long electrocuted hair, impressive beard, and leaf-decorated, green woollen hat, than for his climbing skills.

One of my favourite lines was when Graham asked a petrol station owner what he thought of Graham's new woolly Christmas jersey: "Well son, if it was good enough for your great grandfather, it's good enough for you."

Graham's lack of fashion sense was only matched by his lack of health and safety sense. There was none. We used rotten, many times repaired, wooden ladders, bent aluminum ladders, frayed climbing ropes and harnesses, twisted carabiners, and generally shoddy equipment, that might have been good enough for his great grandfather, but they weren't good enough for us. The chainsaws were blunt and they broke down twice a day.

We were often lucky to get to the sites at all, as we got stopped in Graham's truck on numerous occasions. It didn't help that the truck looked like it had its last MOT before the First World War, and Graham looked like he could have escaped from some institution, as he never blinked, and his eyes were round, instead of the normal human shape. It made him look perpetually dodgy.

I escaped, relatively unscathed, from ten years of absurd risks, sliding around on three and four-storey roofs, covered in snow, no safety ropes, and frozen, unusable, sausage fingers. Whilst on the ground, steadying very dodgy ladders, on many occasions, branches, roof tiles, gutters and various debris, rocketed down towards me, with no warning, missing my bare, unsafety helmet-covered head by millmetres.

Once, I looked up, to see the top ladder extension, heading towards me, like a huge arrow. I dived out of the way, and the ladder embedded in the old lady's lawn. I was very lucky to walk away from Graham's employ, unlike a few of his other workers, well, half of Kent, who are suing Graham's twig-filled beard for broken legs, and heads, missing fingers, and other gruesome chainsaw mishaps. On I went, with the grim jobs.

I have cleaned out Hellman's mayonnaise factories, where I was lowered through a hatch, in full climbing gear. I used a shovel and ice pick, to chip off twenty-foot icebergs of grease and rot, from hundred foot high vats. The job had to be done at night, when the factory was not running and it was pitch black inside the hell vat anyway. On the first night, they forgot to provide me with a miner's helmet lamp, so I made do with my ninety-nine pence, camping head torch. I may as well have strapped a candle to my forehead. That first ten-hour shift was the worst. Like everything, you get used to it very quickly. I had breathing apparatus, but the smell was still indescribable, and when I got home, I was refused entry, and threatened with divorce, unless I threw away all my clothes. I cleaned out fourteen of those vats, over a period of a month. I smelt like rotten eggs for three more.

I have picked thousands of apples (Latvian, Estonian, Lithuanian and Polish workers, and me), in farms around the south of England, and have picked peaches in France (Tunisians, Moroccans, and me), falling off ladders many times. In France, I was so broke for the first week that all I ate were the peaches. I ended up with Toulouse Revenge, sprinting to the toilet, three times a day. I returned to England, and planted 1,050 saplings along a new motorway verge in Bexhill, East Sussex. I fixed gutters. I mowed lawns and did gardening.

I slaughtered three thousand turkeys one Christmas, for a deranged, nudist Kent farmer. His slaughter man didn't turn up, due to extreme intoxication from local 'scrumpy' cider. Electrocuting and slitting turkey's throats, while standing in a foot of congealed blood and feathers, is not the best. I have picked frozen broccoli and asparagus, in the middle of winter, until my fingers fell off. I have assembled picture frames in a freezing warehouse, and slid a tractor round a field, moving barrels of pears. I worked as a barman, I delivered beer kegs to hundreds of pubs around the south-east of England. I have sold double glazing, door to door, in the evenings, when everyone, rightly, wants to shoot you for disturbing their dinners. I sold fake Australian paintings door to door. I had things thrown at me, and not just verbal abuse. I even worked as a bouncer. The only job I enjoyed thoroughly was doing up two houses with my mum and dad, for resale. I learnt a great deal. I suspect that my father paid me handsomely, and made about £20 profit, £10 on each house, without telling me. It was good times, working with my dad. Learnt a lot about him. All good.

It was not the country I was in. It was not so much the jobs I was doing, it was more my frame of mind, and that of the people around me, that broke me. Work will never break me. I like very hard work. The worse my jobs became, the more I read about adventure, and travel, and explorers. It ate me up, but at the same time I revelled in the grimness of some jobs, working twelve-to-fourteen-hour illegal shifts. It was some sort of self flagellation; that I deserved crap jobs because of my bad life choices. At the same time, the people around me seemed depressed, grey corpses. There was no ambition or interest in the wider world. Interest had disappeared from their characters completely. I felt sad. I knew there was more. Everything, to them was about work, shagging, gossip, *The Sun* newspaper, what's for dinner, and television realityshows. Nothing is more alienating than being somewhere, full of people, whether in a work van, or a canteen, and realising, perhaps, mid-conversation, time and time again, that what they talk about belongs to a totally different plain of existence than the one in which you exist. I have realised that people are very open-minded about new things, as long as they are exactly like the old ones.

But there is nothing wrong with not fitting in. Believe me; I am the 'non fitting in' world expert.

But it is a sign; a warning light to change. You cannot change what you are, only what you do. That is exactly what I did. It took one particularly gruesome job that I stuck with for six years, to finally flip my starter switch. I worked in domestic drain cleaning, and on landfill sites, tapping off the methane gas for a company called Soiltech. Lovely.

I was working on a job in Lewisham, in south London, on a blocked drain, when I got a message from God, about how 'shit' my life was; literally, excuse the language. On a rainy, cold, grey day, in August 2009, I finally cracked. I was in a white van, with a guy called Pete Cloud (appropriate; the grey type, not the silver lining type), heading from Maidstone in Kent to Lewisham. This involves the M25 motorway, a road that makes grown men cry. It is always blocked, every day of the year; snails casually overtake the queues of cars. After four hours of being stationary, and Pete listing the merits of every striker in the Premiership football league, followed by another list of his 300 favourite meals, I was ready to kill myself. It got worse.

We arrived at an Indian restaurant, with a peeling façade that was 'The Bengal Tiger', in the pouring rain. According to the owner,

Aniruddha (grandson of Lord Krishna), the drains to the customer toilets had backed up, all the way to the road. After much digging, and retching, we ascertained that the problem was the junction, that went directly into the restaurant. It was cracked, and needed replacing; as poo, poo paper, and other nasties, kept snagging on the cracked section, and clogging up the run. Time for rodding, jet blasting and repair; dancing in the rain. We warned the staff not to use the toilet for the next two hours, and I jumped into the man hole (full of the joys of freezing), that connected all the runs to the street. It was very slippery and wet, and smelly. Pete was whittering on about some soap opera, that involved a pub fight scene (surprise, surprise). I had blocked his voice out an hour ago, now it was just a drone in the background.

I started rodding the blocked toilet run, turned to Pete for a new rod to screw to the existing poles, to extend it, when some bastard pooper decided to relieve himself and flush, despite our clear instructions. As I turned round, mouth open, to ask for the next rod, the flushing hit me in my face; faeces included in the package. That was it. I flipped out. I ripped off my clothes, rushed into the restaurant, past a surprised looking grandson of Krishnan, covered in excrement and soggy paper, and ran into the bathroom. I cleaned myself up as best, retching like a cat with a fur ball, even peeling some spoiled toilet paper out of my ear, and walked out, without saying a word. I told Pete to get me home. Now. I never went back to Soiltech, and never saw Pete again.

The very night of the poo-splattering incident, I decided that I was going to circumnavigate Africa, solo and unsupported, on a motorcycle, no matter what. And I did. I am not saying that we all have to make such extreme changes, but I had to. I am not saying that any of us want to leave our family and our children, for a year and rough it on pennies, circumnavigating Africa. That was my dream. Not to leave my children; to circumnavigate Africa. I also realise that few of us are in the position, financially or emotionally, to do that. I went a bit extreme.

But with every decision we make, whether you want to be an artist, change job, do a sky dive, volunteer for a charity, climb Kilimanjaro, see the Northern Lights, ride a horse on a beach, lose weight, give up smoking, move town, drop toxic friends, show more love for your family, leave a drainage company, or just join the gym. It doesn't matter.

It doesn't matter. It is all relative. In any given moment, we have two options; to step forward into growth, or step back to safety. When you realise that change is inevitable in life (a lot of it out of your control), but growth is optional; you are onto something.

Everything depends on attitude. Many of us think that holding on makes us strong, but sometimes it is letting go, moving on, and trying the new, that is strength. If you do not change direction, you might end up where you are going. Change may be painful, and difficult, but nothing is as painful as staying stuck somewhere you don't belong. The problem is that we get moulded from birth, and before realising it, we have become a shadow of our former selves, through no fault of any individual. And we all get moulded differently. We all have different experiences, different character strengths, different weaknesses and silly hang-ups and different ways of dealing with the stresses of life. It is society that expects certain norms, and rightly so. We don't want chaos. But what if you don't fit into those norms. That plan does not cater for you. You wither away slowly. That is when you have to fight to be different. Don't worry, I am not an anarchist, anti-government hippie. Quite the opposite. Let me try and explain with a quick story.

In 1620, in a small, very typical, remote, mountain village in Mexico, they had one extraordinary feature in the central square. There was a twelve-foot, solid gold statue of the Aztec King Moctezuma (also known as Montezuma), the ninth Aztec Emperor of Mexico, famous for his dramatic confrontation with the Spanish conquistador, Hernan Cortes. No other gold statues of Moctezuma existed. Nobody in the village knew who had made the statue, or where it came from. It had been there forever.

One day, a panicking, exhausted mountain athlete (guard and messenger), sprinted into the village, warning of a marauding army, that was sweeping through the land, looting anything of value, to pay for further expansion and conquest. The statue had monetary value to the villagers, but it had emotional and religious significance that was beyond gold. They held a village meeting, and decided that before they evacuated the area, and went into hiding in some nearby caves, they would cover the statue with a concrete-type substance and soil, to hide its true vitality and beauty. Both Mayans and Aztecs had developed a technique that used thin, mortared block walls, filled with 'cast in place' concrete, using a coarse limestone aggregate. The villagers quickly, and expertly,

Mask of Moctezuma, the King of the Aztecs

'walled' up the statue with concrete, and dulled it even further, with mud and dust, and twigs, and then they vanished into the hills. Sure enough, the marauding army took over the village, but only saw an ugly, grey, extremely badly made concrete statue of the Aztec King Moctezuma, unworthy of plunder. They moved on. After a month hiding in caves, the villagers returned, to find their houses burnt to the ground, but the statue unharmed. Worried about returning tribes, it was decided to leave the statue covered in concrete, and relocate to a safer mountaintop retreat, higher into the Andes. The village was abandoned.

Hundreds of years passed until the statue became a myth, that many scoffed at. One day a young Aztec initiate was wandering the mountains, pondering his life, when he spotted what looked like a concrete pillar. As he got closer, he realized it was an image of King Moctezuma, and fell to his knees, at the statue's feet, to pray. At the conclusion of his prayers, he looked up, and at that moment a weathered piece of concrete broke off the statue, and landed in the soil, rolled down, and settled against his knee. He peered into the hole that the loosened concrete piece had revealed, and to his astonishment he saw a shimmering 'gold-like' metal. He rushed back to the elders of his village, to tell them of his find. They saw it as a sign, as the village they inhabited was windswept and barren, and they were struggling to survive. They gathered mallets, and ten of the village's strongest men set off with the boy, to see the statue. Sure enough, it was there. They chipped away at the statue, and broke all the concrete off in less than a week, revealing the original, beautiful, solid gold, Aztec king. Within three months, a new prosperous and happy village had been built, watched over by the brilliant, solid gold King Moctezuma.

Why do I tell that story? Because the statue is me, and could be you. We are all full of potential and shining with enthusiasm for life, when we are born. We are pure and unadulterated by experience. We are an empty page, ready to be written on, or more importantly, torn up. We are all born with an open heart but at some point, as we are growing up, things happen in our life, and we begin to shut down slightly, and lose our sheen. It could be rejection at school, at work, rejection by a love, a friend, family or all. It could be not fitting in, wanting approval, needing encouragement but not getting it, judgment by other, comparisons and criticism from those around you.

We are told what to wear, what we need to buy, to fit in with the Jones family. It could be about your look, your race, your clothes, your gender, where you live, how to behave as a boy, as a girl, how to behave as a black man, your views, your aspirations, your life choices. It could be others, but it could just as easily be your own bad decisions. The time to blame is never. If you are not happy with an aspect of your life, the time to change is now. The pessimist complains about the wind; the optimist expects it to change; the realistic adjusts the sails. If you do not change, or at least try to change what you do not like, you will become that dull, lifeless, concrete statue. Break out, and try to be that golden statue again; for the rest of your life.

A lot of you will be saying, 'well, it costs money', easy for you to say. I totally understand that, and can't even imagine being a homeless man in Angola, or a shoe shiner in the slums of Rio, for example, just as I can't imagine being a billionaire on Wall Street.

That's why when somebody sighs, and says,
"Life is hard,"
I am always tempted to reply,
"Compared to what?"

I am not negating the cards we were dealt, and not denying that some people will never pull themselves out of the cycle of poverty. I am saying that we have to make the best version of ourselves, with the cards that we are dealt. I cannot apologise for everybody's situation, and I can't change the distribution of wealth and happiness. If I could, I would. But I can be nice to the people I meet, and try to inspire them to make even small changes. Facing fear, and taking risks is a big part of this process. The person you will definitely spend the rest of your life with, is you, so take the risk. Look to the future too, because that's where you are going to spend the rest of your life.

I took a risk, borrowed some money, left my family, and circumnavigated Africa alone, living on a budget that you would not even believe, if I told you. I left Cathy and the children for a year. It could have backfired. I was lucky that Travel Channel bought my series, and it allowed me to travel some more. But don't get me wrong. I am poorer than a burgled church mouse, and still owe a lot of money. But without making that decision, the last twelve year of my life would not have been magical. They would have been drudgery.

If I got hit by the proverbial Tata truck tomorrow, at least I could honestly say that I made the right decision. I have tried to live life hard and full on, with urgency. I am constantly aware that life is not a rehearsal. Again, I am not arrogant enough to assume that we can all just jump on a motorbike and ride round the world, or even afford to buy a motorbike. Or even want to do that, at all. I just want to give one person the strength to change their lot. If I do that, what could be better. We all have commitments, but we can fulfill them better if we are content within ourselves.

As a realist, telling the world's ugliest woman that she will win the Miss World competition, or a one-legged man that he will beat Usain Bolt's 100 metres record is not acceptable. It is cruel. But telling everybody to question their lot, to question their position, their limitations, that have been designated by others, is good. Do not let other people categorise you. Only you can do that. Your life is yours and yours alone. The choice of concrete or gold is in your hands. We all have our limits, but we can all stretch them. That is why I have lived a lot of my life through quotes, whether from Winston Spencer Churchill, Sir Ranulph Fiennes, Charles Darwin, Bob Marley, Muhammed Ali, and various explorers, or scholars of note. Quotes have always inspired me, pushed me, and given me a focus. So much so that I have three tattooed on my body, and I am not even a fan of tattoos:

'The only impossible journey, is the one you never begin.'

'Chase your dreams or forever regret.'

'Fear is temporary, regret is forever.'

The reason I chose those tattoos and those words is because they are both universal and timeless. They will never not be true. They are a visual template, a list, reminding me how to live my life. Fear stops many of us from pushing to our potential. I believe in every human's potential. If you think you are too small to make a difference, try sleeping with a mosquito. The key is to never, ever give up. I never will. The road to success is always under construction.

I am only human too. I do sometimes wonder if I will ever succeed in my goal of circumnavigating every continent and crossing the Darien Gap. And does it really matter? I have my crises of confidence, like everybody, but I try to banish the negative thoughts from my mind.

Having said that, I am getting older quickly though. When I was a boy, the Dead Sea was only critical. It is scary how quickly time goes by, exponentially, the older one gets. I am running out of time so it is vital I persevere, move faster, and maintain a drive, to commit to what I have promised. This is an internal promise, to myself. I have never felt in competition with anybody on this earth. I am 54 (as I write in July 2021). It takes two to three years to write a book, and that is only after you have completed the journey. I don't know how many books I will write before I die, but I hope there is one written about every continent. It is like a countdown. So, with each book, I am praying that I live until it's finished. So much for banishing negative thoughts. Time to speed up.

Life on the road is the easy part, I was born for it. No panic attacks when I am on my motorcycle. Out of my comfort zone, is where I feel euphoric. Being unhinged definitely helps, when coping with the topsy turvy world of life on the road, and insanity doesn't just run in my family, it practically gallops. OK. Let's call it an eccentric upbringing.

My father deals with his hyperactivity by working extremely hard, lecturing away at university, inspiring the youth, writing, producing, and directing plays, and putting in more road miles than Forrest Gump, whilst beating every other runner in his age category, in every road and cross-country race for the last sixty two years. My Tenere would be embarrassed about Dad's mileage, in comparison. My father runs for England at the age of 81. Obviously in his age group, this is not some Sci-fi movie. My mother had boundless energy and made a Whirling Dervish look sedentary. Her artistic talent was a marvel, her brain complicated, and slightly tormented, at times. My brother, Simon, is a wonderfully gentle man, an extremely talented structural and mechanical engineer, guitarist, carpenter deluxe, and professional hermit. Simon was the one who fuelled my interest in motorcycles and weight training. As for me, I have more issues than *National Geographic*, but we won't go there. They will be overcome.

Even our family deaths, or close shaves, are not normal. My mother's Uncle Bert was run over and killed by a steam roller, as I mentioned in a previous chapter. Don't even ask me how, but it is 100% true. My grandmother who was in a wheelchair due to polio as a child, was almost eaten by a lion in Kenya. A lion wandered onto our verandah, and all the macho men ran into the house, leaving Nanny Doris to the mercy of the lion. Luckily, it gave her a few sniffs, and headed off. Evidently, not that hungry. We weren't too popular after that. I just presumed that the lion was scared of Nanny Doris, because she had gumption; a word I am proud to associate with most of my family members.

I remember vividly when Simon, aged about thirteen, was having a proper fist fight with our neighbor, in Swaziland, a Scottish fellow, Kenneth Black, a big guy. I also remember that the family's surname was a bit awkward, because every time one of us said,

"I am going to visit the Blacks", it sounded highly racist.

Anyway, Simon was in our garden, pummelling Kenneth into the aloes, and I ran into the house, in a panic, to call my grandmother, to break it up. Nanny Doris came out, as fast as she could, on her leg callipers, to break up the fight. I was relieved, until I heard,

"Come on you little Spitfire, Simon, come on."

I couldn't believe it. The only complaint that Nanny Doris had, after the fight, was that Simon had broken his thumb, because of 'bad hand positioning'. Apparently, "If you hold your thumb inside your palm, it will break your thumb, when you hit someone".

Quality Lady.

Simon didn't need fights with Scottish behemoths. He has had his fair share of accidents too. The most memorable was when he nearly got killed by a steak. Many years after the Kenneth tussle, Simon swallowed a piece of steak, choked and stopped breathing. Luckily, he was five minutes from the hospital. Apparently, people are keeling over, all over the world, from 'Steakhouse Syndrome', otherwise known as Esophageal food bolus obstruction. I had never heard of it, until I nearly lost my brother. On another more serious note, we have had family members locked up for acting less than sane. It is an issue, but luckily I am free at the moment, touch wood.

I have had my sanity professionally checked, just to let you know, and I have been given a diagnosis. We met a Zimbabwean psychiatrist in a brothel in Bogota, Colombia, two days after we had completed circumnavigating South America, and were busy preparing for our assault on Central America and Mexico. Dr. Kutenda Katiyo certainly wasn't your average psychiatrist. He was around sixty, and as tall as me, but with a lot more midriff. He was sporting a pinstripe suit, a purple tie and handkerchief, and mirror-clean black shoes that, at a glance, looked about size twenty. Doctor Katiyo's hair was more mad scientist than psychiatrist. Although psychiatrists have a reputation for being the maddest and most unhinged of our species. The Doctor's hair was fairly long, sticking straight up to the heavens, and not expertly brushed. It looked like an explosion in a mattress factory. He also had a grey streak, along the centre, so looked like an alert skunk. He reminded me of a cross between Morgan Freeman, Don King and King Sobhuza of Swaziland. He beckoned us over and ordered two bottles of Club Colombia lager and an orange juice for Cathy. He was also on the Ron Viejo de Caldas rum, but not being a spirits drinker, I politely declined. Kutenda, which means 'to thank' in Shona, was a superb chap. Appropriate name too.

The entrance to the brothel was actually a bar, where snacks and drinks were cheaper than in more reputable establishments. That's why we were there, and Kutenda pleaded the same reason. He explained that he was attending a conference of psychiatrists at the University

Hospital of Bogota, and had just finished his presentation. He was trying to raise some funds for student scholarships (not at the brothel evidently), to try and get more Zimbabweans trained as psychiatrists and mental health workers. Kutenda explained the situation:

"There are two main indigenous groups in Zimbabwe: the Shona in the north, and Ndebele in the south; neither tribe takes depression and mental health issues seriously. Depression is referred to as 'thinking too much', in the Shona language, which, although partially correct, in my opinion, trivialises the disorder. Few people with mental health disorders in low and middle income countries, receive treatment, in part because mental disorders are still highly stigmatised, and do not enjoy priority and resources commensurate with the burden on Zimbabwean society. Zimbabwe now has 17 registered psychiatrists with 13 practicing in-country, for a population of 15 million people. There are 0·1 doctors and 1·3 nurses per 1,000 general population. Thus, the approach any psychiatrist takes for a patient must be a holistic one that involves taking care of physical health, psychological and emotional health, and social and spiritual health, all on a background of a large workload. The shortage of psychiatrists means that most wear multiple hats during the day. For example, I am employed by the Government (University), but also need time to do research as well as working in my private practice that starts at 4pm and can finish as late as 11."

Wow. Although I knew he was quoting from his recently finished lecture, Kutenda's English was perfect, better than mine. I told him about my experiences around Africa, where in Seychelles, all the mental health patients are released on Christmas Day, and chaos ensues, and about my circumnavigation of Africa, where every village throughout the continent has a resident naked person with mental health issues, sprinting around.

I told him about the work I did in hospitals in Swaziland, when I was a student, and the children's hospitals I visited in Angola and Cameroon, for Save the Children.

Kutenda and I hit it off, but I could see that Cathy was getting tired, so I was going to make excuses, when Cathy said, "I am going to head back to the room and sort out my panniers. You stay."

'Sort out her panniers.' Ha ha. Cathy wasn't at all addicted to travel. When Cathy left, that was it. My verbal floodgates opened. (Not because Cathy doesn't listen to me, or beats me, or something sinister like that.) It was just a build up of emotions and trying to process some experiences. It was time to bore a psychiatrist. Poor fellow, just trying to have a quiet drink, after being a psychiatrist all day.

I proceeded to tell Kutenda about the circumnavigations: the solo Africa trip, where I got attacked by bandits, contracted malaria, broke loads of bones, and loved every minute. I told him about the South America trip, about the Salar, about the mugging in the Barrio of No Return, about Chucky and his gang, about kidnappings and shootings in Venezuela, about the wonder of the Amazon and the Ghost Road, the incredible winds in Patagonia, and the superb people and wildlife. The funny bits: about the Love Motels, Franco off the cliff, the naked border guard in Peru, my naked Polish cameraman during the Dakar and how I thrived on it, all of it.

I told him about panic or anxiety attacks, that hit me at any time, making it impossible to breathe, and how I only manage to sleep a maximum of three hours a night, and that I am extremely hyperactive. But I have never had a panic attack on a motorcycle. I mentioned my sense of not belonging anywhere, the feeling of being in a bubble. I explained about my fanatical and erratic behavior and about my aim to be the first person to circumnavigate every continent. I told him about my obsessions to cross the Darien Gap and my dream to race the Dakar Rally, which was slipping away, because of my age, and lack of race experience. I told him how I can't stand failure, or criticism, but I am getting better at accepting it. I told him how Cathy was incredibly courageous during the South America trip, but I worried that she did not share my dreams. I said that I was worried permanently that I was being selfish, chasing my goals, to the detriment of my family. I explained how I had become introvert and a loner, when everyone expects a world traveller to be an extrovert. Giving presentations at shows had become difficult. I said how I only felt comfortable on the motorcycle and that crowds and subways and… I went on and on.

Kutenda listened quietly, and intently, like a well trained psychiatrist, and after I had settled down, after a long pause, he reached down to his briefcase and pulled out a pen. He picked up a napkin and smoothed it out and then folded it double, in front of him, on the table. He then proceeded to draw a large circle, with a smaller circle inside it. He then joined the circles, with equidistant lines, radiating from the smaller circle. He missed a few out.

"This is a wheel," he said.

Oh, clever. Imagery that the patient can relate too.

"You are this wheel, Spencer. As you can see, there are a few spokes missing from this wheel, but you will continue rolling on, and you will succeed in your mission."

Excellent. Glad I didn't pay him for that consultation and diagnosis. But on a positive note, all I have is a few spokes missing. I thought I was insane. Nothing like an expert diagnosis on a brothel napkin. He had more.

"Remember I said that I have to wear many different hats, in my job. Well, we all do; and in life. You have to wear the son hat, the father hat, the brother hat, the husband hat, the adventurer hat, the caring hat, the listening hat, the strong hat, the imaginary worry hat, and more. If you try to wear all your hats at the same time, they become heavy, and push you down. Learn to swop hats, and focus on one at a time. Then all your hats will become your favourite.

Just when I thought this analogy could not involve any more hats, Kutenda reached into his bag, and pulled out a set of keys, with a tassle. The tassle was a tiny leather cowboy hat. He proceeded to unfasten it from the ring. He held it up for me to see. In black, badly stencilled letters, it had 'Perseverance' on the brow. He spun it round, and on the back, it said 'Pride'.

"Mr. Conway, I want you to have this hat. You cannot wear it, because your head is too big (we both laughed), but you can carry it wherever you travel."

"It will remind you to breathe, to think, to focus, and to persevere, with pride."

So, the upshot of this meeting was that I have been designated as sane, to continue my mission. What a relief. I feel like I cannot live without my motorcycle, and moving constantly, and pushing myself to the limit. I have always thought, rather cynically, that meditation is 'thinking deeply about things, that really, you should be doing'. I am a 'doer' and not a planner. Mainly because of my hyperactivity, I have little choice. The reason that inspirational quotes are such, is because they capture thoughts that many of us relate to, and the following quote you will have heard, if you are a biker:

'In a car, you are watching a film, but on a motorbike, you are in a film.'

I don't want to be a member of the audience, a spectator in life. I want to play my lead role and I want to do it to the best of my ability. That is a why, since finishing this book, Cathy the Nel and I have managed to circumnavigate Central America, through Panama, Costa Rica, Nicaragua, Honduras, El Salvador, Belize, Guatemala and Mexico, before Covid 19 closed us all down. I have written it all down. You might be happy about that, or not. I really hope you have enjoyed this book, and if you didn't, please keep it a bit quiet. I pray that I don't get reviews, like the following. I will not name the books or the authors, because I am nice like that:

"Once you put one of his books down, you simply can't pick it up again."

"As a writer, he has mastered everything except language, and how to tell a story."

"This is not a book to be tossed aside lightly. It should be thrown with great force."

"Clumsy, ingrammatical, repetitive and repetitive." [sic],

"One of the most underrated books of the last ten years; and here's why…"

"I don't like depressing writing. If I want to be depressed I will just think, not read." (Kind of agree.)

"Your book is both good, and original. Unfortunately, the parts that are original, are not good, and the parts that are good, are not original."

Sometimes the critics get a little bit rough and even masterpieces are not spared. Here's a critic commenting on *Wuthering Heights*,

"How a human being could have attempted such a book as the present, without committing suicide before he had finished a dozen chapters, is a mystery. It is a compound of vulgar depravity, and unnatural horror."

"A mere ulcer, a sore from head to foot; a poor devil so completely flayed that there is not a square inch of healthy carcass; an overgrown pimple, sore to the touch. "

A bit harsh, I would say. Lastly:

"Reading this book makes me realise; what doesn't kill me, makes me stronger."

But if you don't feel the same way as the people above, join me in the next book where we get kidnapped in Panama, involved in a bank robbery. Not quite *Wuthering Heights*. There are wonderful rides, volcanoes and mountains, rivers and valleys, broken bones, anaphylactic shocks, and more crocodile attacks. And we move to Mexico permanently, ready for the Darien, or the next continental circumnavigation, whichever is feasible first. As always, wherever I go, Cathy will be there. I am very lucky. Cathy also wants us to walk the 'River of Doubt' in Brazil; the cheery person that she is. Life is a river of doubt, so bring it all on. Whatever happens, I will carry a photo of my mum, Wendy; my dad, Michael; and a photo of my two girls; Feaya and Jesamine. Much less important, and less personal, but still makes me smile; I now have a mini Zimbabwean psychiatrist's hat to get around the world too. Never give up. Peace, love and respect to all of you. Always.

Be the best you can. Bye for now.

12th May 2022, 2.26pm
Zicatela, Puerto Escondido, Mexico

Signing off. Sad it's over.

If opportunity doesn't knock, you might have to build a door

Until next time

I'LL LOOK BACK AND SMILE BECAUSE IT WAS LIFE AND I DECIDED TO LIVE IT.

Acknowledgements

I would like to acknowledge the following people for their support, help and contribution to my life, adventures and books.

Firstly to my dad, Michael, for editing my books, running my website, supporting me in every madcap idea, and for being the best father.

To my girlfriend, Cathy, for putting up with my circumnavigation of Africa, and then joining me for the South and Central America circumnavigation. One brave biker and camerawoman. I love you.

To daughters, Feaya and Jesamine. Love you both very much.

Greetings and love to my brother, Simon, and his daughter, Ysa.

Respect always to my best friend, Carl Routhier.

John Lacey, friend, web and book designer.

Anna Foster for her expertise in copy editing and compiling the book.

Biddenden Village and Parish Magazine.

I have to thank the following businesses and organisations:

John Lagerway at KLIM, formerly of Lindstrands, for more than twelve years of friendship and sponsorship;

Craig Carey Clinch and Barbara Alam of Motorcycle Outreach, for whom Cathy and I are Ambassadors;

Paddy Tyson and the team at Overland Event and Magazine;

Jim and Elizabeth Martin at *Adventure Bike Rider* Magazine and Festival;

Metal Mule Panniers;

Grinders boots;

Harley Davidson boots;

John Small at Cool Covers;

BBC News and Radio.

To everyone I have met on the road, and all my mad adventure motorcyclist friends.

The Japanese-Speaking Curtain Maker

Reviews

THE JAPANESE SPEAKING CURTAIN MAKER
SPENCER JAMES CONWAY
2019
ISBN 978-0-9956290-3-5

The Japanese Speaking Curtain Maker? What the hell does this title have to do with riding a motorcycle around Africa and becoming the first person to do so?

Strange title, you could argue that Spencer Conway is a strange bloke. In his unique way Spencer tells a tale of becoming the first person to circumnavigate Africa by motorcycle.

With wit and good humour Spencer rides the outer rim of the African continent exploring, the many and varied peoples, cultures and environments while also discovering a lot more about himself and other travellers than many would care to admit.

The Japanese Speaking Curtain Maker at times will have you laughing out loud, cheering in support and perhaps even shedding a tear or two. Spencer is a masterful storyteller who knows how to keep a reader engaged from start to finish despite the at times appalling bad jokes and puns (no, we didn't really say that Spencer).

Chance meetings with local leads to some lovely moments and demonstrate that no matter what you hear about a country or region you yourself must decide; exploration is the best way to discover. Spencer does so and we the reader are much richer for the experience.

Shot at by bandits in Kenya, partying with Nigerian celebrity and even a beer stash hidden in the forest, Spencer takes us on a fast-paced adventure yet slows down enough to experience the real Africa and its people.

The Japanese Speaking Curtain Maker is a book in two parts. The first, the ride down through the east to the south west. The second, the north west. It's the second that feels a little rushed, perhaps as subconsciously Spencer feels that this area has drained him enough to want out yet as Spencer returns to the UK, he realises that 'normal' isn't for him.

In The Japanese Speaking Curtain Maker Spencer has crafted what is perhaps the outstanding travel biography of 2019, it's well worth a read ... and we wonder, did they ever find a Japanese Speaking Curtain maker?

John Allsop, *Motogusto Magazine*

'I was alarmed and saddened by some of your adventurous mishaps and I felt for you. If anyone could navigate all of that with grace and determination it is you.'

Sam Manicom

It's not a title you might expect for a book about a circumnavigation of the African continent, but you quickly establish that Spencer Conway is anything but ordinary. Leaving Kent in a rain-storm, this petrified unconfident rider soon blossoms, and following a slightly hair-raising blast across Tunisia behind a compulsory guide and his alcoholic driver, has fully settled into his stride by Egypt.

Much of the story telling centres around the human experiences he has and one particular interaction, with Ashraf a boatman from Aswan, illustrates perfectly how he manages to reach into the lives of those he meets. I won't spoil it, or the myriad other tales, from Nigerian millionaires to Kenyan bandits, drunken soldiers, forests full of beer, malaria in Ghana or crossing borders that haven't been traversed for years, but I will say that what's interesting is the way that sometimes the stories are complete tangents. They can be recalled almost as vignettes, taking you away completely from the linear course of the journey, but done in a way that you barely notice, until you abruptly return to the main narrative.

The whole text is certainly high octane and you could never say Spencer is the luckiest of men, but he does make decisions many of us may not. And that of course is what creates the story. There's mud and guns and breakdowns and aggro and laughter; the whole nine yards.

This is certainly not a book that will bore you, and if you are considering Christmas presents for riders you know, you could do a lot worse. But if you are trying to justify to a loved one why it would be safe and sensible for you to head off for 6 months and discover the world from the back of a bike, I suggest you choose carefully where and when you read it!'

Paddy Tyson, *Overland Magazine*

I first read Spencer Conway's book about circumnavigating Africa on his Yamaha XT 660 back when it was first released in 2019. I loved it then for many reasons! I've just read it again and at a slower pace, I found plenty more reasons to like it, a lot! The man has a way with words! That means his descriptions of people, place and situation draw you straight into the story. I love the snippets of history that he weaves in too. At times you'll have a complete buzz from the sensation of standing next to him as he observes. At others you'll wish he bloomin' well wasn't such a good writer!

This is a story of courage, instincts, beauty, the rewards of taking risks, but also the price that can be paid. It's inspirational and I think that anyone planning a journey through Africa should read this first.

I've put it straight back on my 'Must read again' shelf.

Ian Harper

I really thought your Under the visor interview was brilliant. I learned a lot about you as a person and the stories only whet my appetite to learn more. You came over as a genuine, amazing adventurer and, yes, pretty normal...... as far as super-heroes go! You could also write a book about your "Robin", Batman...... "The Camera Woman and the Crazyman"..... All the very best of luck to you both for the next phase of the adventure, looking forward to catching up sometime in 2020!

Guy Terpin

DVD available at *www.dukevideo.com*

Mind The Raven
Wendy Daphne Conway

Part proceeds to Medecins Sans Frontieres.

It is the path that one seeks, not the destination. The destination is always the same, but each of us traces a different path that leads us to it.

Thought makes us what we are but the Mind determines.

Without Mind we are Lost.

Author Wendy Daphne Conway published 'Mind the Raven' in 2020, receiving critical praise for the varied content and literary style of the ten stories. The collection is set in various geographical locations, during several historical periods. The tone ranges from the humorous to the sad, covering a wide range of subjects. Dramatic incidents and the macabre draw the reader into the narrative, through insightful observation of human foibles and actions.

Available from *www.youbyyou.co.uk*

Books by Sam Manicom

From Para to Dakar
Joey Evans

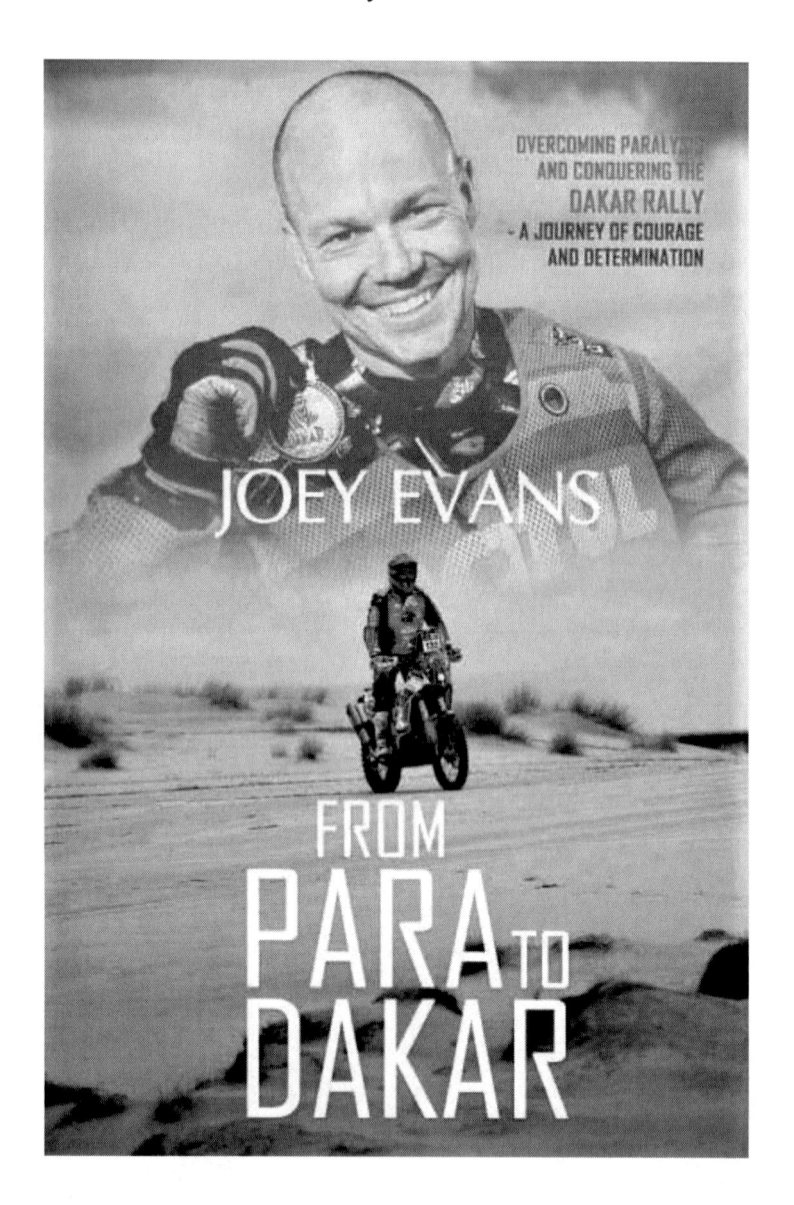

Many bikers suffer from stress, so please do not think you are alone. Contact: Mental Health Motobike

WHEN LIFE GETS TOUGH, WE ARE HERE TO LISTEN, TO SUPPORT, TO RIDE.

MENTAL HEALTH MOTORBIKE

www.mhmotorbike.com

Mental Health Motorbike is a free mental health support charity for the biker community in the UK

We exist to:

Promote the wellbeing benefits of motorcycling
Provide a network of support for bikers, by bikers
Improve wellbeing within the motorcycling community

@mhmotorbike
info@mhmotorbike.com
Registered charity number 1196406

Laguna is tops for all things bikers require. Excellent service and super-organised. Polite and accommodating

LAGUNA MOTORCYCLES

For the best in motorcycle gear go to
KLIM

If you need help to freight your bike to global destinations, contact Moto Freight

This is the podcast for you for up-to-date news and views on all things biking

The Orginal ADV Moto Podcast Since 2014

THE VOICE OF MOTO TRAVEL
ADVENTURE RIDER RADIO

RAW

Download Anywhere Podcasts Are Found

"Simply the best motorcycle podcast." Muzakmon

"Your podcast is outstanding, informative and fun." J Lesser

"I anxiously wait for the next shows appearance in the podcast lists." B Bridges

"Best show ever." G Smith

"Topics that come up are so pertinent" "You inspired me." G Guenther

"Great show." R Steiger

"The quality and quantity of information you all share is astounding." M Gebhard

"So inspiring and interesting." J Gillihan

"What you're doing for travelling bikers is fantastic." D Lilwall

"Always interesting and the stories inspiring." D Tsotsos

"Jim is hands down one of the best interviewers out there. " Mattylife

"The show is fresh and interesting every week" ITAdminUSMA

World's Most Downloaded Show of It's Kind